PRO[illegible]

The screen flick[illegible] dis-
playing an ima[illegible]y. Not just any man, Jer[illegible] Houser, his biology teacher. [illegible]mply lying there—he'd been nai[illegible] ground with spikes through his hands [illegible]t. He'd been cut open from chin to crotch, and his body cavity had been hollowed out. The man's organs were lying nearby, lined up against a wall in a neat row, and carefully labeled with index cards. Heart, lungs, stomach, liver, kidneys, spleen.

"Your other self does good work, eh, Jerome?" Freddy asked. "Very neat and precise. He has all the makings of a first-class surgeon—or serial killer."

In the same series

DREAMSPAWN
Christa Faust

SUFFER THE CHILDREN
David Bishop

More New Line novels from Black Flame

BLADE: TRINITY
Natasha Rhodes

CELLULAR
Pat Cadigan

FINAL DESTINATION
Dead Reckoning
Natasha Rhodes

Destination Zero
David McIntee

End of the Line
Rebecca Levene

Dead Man's Hand
Steven A Roman

FREDDY vs JASON
Stephen Hand

FRIDAY THE 13TH
Church of the Divine Psychopath
Scott Phillips

Hell Lake
Paul Woods

JASON X
Jason X
Pat Cadigan

The Experiment
Pat Cadigan

Planet of the Beast
Nancy Kilpatrick

THE TEXAS CHAINSAW MASSACRE
Stephen Hand

THE TWILIGHT ZONE
Memphis • The Pool Guy
Jay Russell

Upgrade • Sensuous Cindy
Pat Cadigan

Into the Light • Sunrise
Paul A Woods

Chosen • The Placebo Effect
KC Winters

Burned • One Night at Mercy
Christa Faust

NIGHTMARE ON ELM STREET™

PROTÉGÉ

BY

TIM WAGGONER

Based on characters from the motion picture A Nightmare on Elm Street created by Wes Craven

BLACK FLAME

To Dr Creep, host of Shock Theater, with thanks for so many fright-filled hours of fun.

A Black Flame Publication
www.blackflame.com
blackflame@games-workshop.co.uk

First published in 2005 by BL Publishing, Games Workshop Ltd., Willow Road, Nottingham NG7 2WS, UK.

Distributed in the US by Simon & Schuster, 1230 Avenue of the Americas, New York, NY 10020, USA.

10 9 8 7 6 5 4 3 2 1

ISBN 13: 978 1 84416 255 0
ISBN 10: 1 84416 255 9

A CIP record for this book is available from the British Library.

Printed in the UK by Bookmarque, Surrey, UK.

ONE

Joanna struggled to keep her eyes open as she drove her Jeep down the road. It was after one in the morning and she was exhausted from working a double shift at the Burrito Bungalow. It didn't help that she was seven and a half months pregnant either. She was tired all the time—and irritable and achy in places she hadn't known could ache.

She would have quit her job long ago, let alone avoided working double shifts, but she needed the money. She was due to graduate from high school in a few weeks and her baby would be born soon after. Her boyfriend, Don, was still trying to decide if he was ready to get married, and though her parents were going to let her continue to live at home and her twin sister Bekka promised to help take care of the baby, Joanna was determined not to be a burden on any of them. And so she worked double shifts, came home late and banked her pitiful excuse for a paycheck.

She yawned as she drove through downtown Springwood. The streets were slick from an earlier rain and they gleamed in the fluorescent glow of streetlights. The light made her eyes water and she squinted, tears of exhaustion running down her cheeks. She yawned again. God, she couldn't wait to get home, get into bed and get off her swollen feet.

Her eyes closed, just for a second, then they snapped open as she realized she'd almost nodded off.

"Stay awake, dummy!" she chided herself. "The last thing you need to do is fall asleep behind the wheel... Especially with a baby in—"

Joanna saw a flash of red in her headlights. She slammed on the brakes, but it was too late. She saw a Firebird framed by her windshield, seemingly motionless in the middle of the intersection, as if she were looking at a still picture instead of a vehicle that had run a red light doing at least fifty.

She'd never been in an automobile accident before, had never been seriously injured—never been hurt at all but for the usual assortment of childhood scrapes, cuts and bruises. But it looked like her luck was about to run out. There was no way she could avoid a collision. Omigod... What about the baby?

A strange calm came over her then, and she felt like nothing more than a detached observer, a passenger on a deadly amusement park ride, unable to do more than hold on and watch as the front of her Jeep rammed into the Firebird's rear quarter panel. She felt, more than heard, the awful sound of crumpling metal, followed by the scream of tires desperately trying to maintain their grip on asphalt. The world became a dizzying swirl as her Jeep began to spin, but then the front end of the Firebird swung around from the impact and smashed into the front of her vehicle. She experienced a sharp jolt, and her seatbelt snapped taut as the Jeep began to spin in the opposite direction.

She was still calm, though she thought maybe in shock was a more appropriate description, and she wondered why the airbag hadn't deployed yet. Maybe the system had been damaged by the initial impact. Or maybe her Jeep was just a piece of junk. She placed a hand on her stomach. Sorry, Junior. Guess I shouldn't have bought a used car.

The Jeep's driver's side rear wheel lifted off the ground, and for an instant Joanna thought the vehicle was going to tip over, but then the tire came back down with a jarring thump, and the Jeep finished out its spin on all four wheels.

At first, Joanna didn't realize it was over. She was so dizzy that it felt like the Jeep was still spinning. It was the silence that provided the first clue. No crumpling metal, no protesting tires—nothing but the soft *tic-tic-tic* of overheated engines starting to cool.

A cold wave of delayed terror along with concern for her unborn child rushed through her, and she looked down at her chest, arms, hands, stomach, legs, expecting to see spurting blood and jagged pieces of broken bone protruding from torn flesh. But she saw no blood, felt no pain. Maybe she was just numb from shock, but she didn't appear to be injured. She laughed in relief and patted her belly.

"Looks like we got lucky, kiddo."

But her relief was short-lived. She heard a low, wet moan, as if someone was trying to speak underwater. Or through a throat full of blood.

Oh God… The other driver!

She pressed the catch to release her seatbelt, and then reached for the door handle. She half expected the driver's side door to be jammed, but it opened easily, and she climbed out of the Jeep. At first her legs buckled under her weight, and she thought she was going to fall, but she managed to remain standing, if barely. She reached out and grabbed hold of the Jeep's door to steady herself as she examined the Firebird, or rather what was left of it.

It looked more like a giant wad of paper than a car, as if it had gone through a compactor instead of being involved in a simple traffic accident. The metal was bent and twisted, folded and compressed. Fluids leaked onto the asphalt—oil, water, gasoline—running together, merging into a single widening pool. And there was another substance in the mixture: thick, viscous, a red so dark it was almost black.

Sweet Jesus! No one could survive a wreck like that!

And then she heard a moan again, softer this time, trailing off into a series of wet choking coughs. Without thinking, Joanna stumbled forward, not knowing what she could do to help, only knowing that she had to try. She started toward the wreckage of the Firebird, shoes splashing in the foul liquid spreading across the street.

She reached the driver's side of the Firebird and stopped. The window was down, and she could see that the man inside (at least, she thought it was a man) was horribly scarred, his face a patchwork of leathery hide and exposed raw muscle, with hints of white bone visible. His bloodshot eyes were wide and staring, and the steering wheel had punched through his chest, soaking his green and red striped sweater with blood and pulpy bits of lung tissue. The dashboard had been driven in so far that she couldn't see the lower half of his body, and she feared that he might not have a lower half anymore. Lying neatly atop the dashboard, as if it had been placed there and ridden out the accident without being disturbed, was a brown fedora.

Cold nausea twisted her gut, and she stood frozen in numb terror. She recognized this man, this… thing. She'd heard numerous stories about him growing up, stories told on playgrounds in frightened whispers by children with red, sleep-deprived eyes.

Freddy Krueger turned his head toward her and grinned, displaying yellowed teeth flecked with blood.

"Well? Are you just gonna stand there all night or are you going to help me outta here?" Freddy's voice was rough, gravelly, his words laced with equal measures of mockery and hatred. "I gotta take a leak something fierce!"

A fissure burst open on his forehead, and a stream of blood jetted forth through the open window and splattered onto Joanna's cheek. Freddy roared dark laughter, but there was no humor in the sound. It was cold, nasty and utterly inhuman.

The blood was boiling and Joanna hissed in pain as it seared her flesh. She slapped at her face, trying to wipe the foul substance off as she stepped away from the wreckage and the awful cackling thing trapped within.

"Thanks for nothing, bitch!" Freddy growled. He raised his right hand, and Joanna saw that he wore a glove with long, sharp metal blades attached to the fingers.

"Good thing I got the claws of life!" He slashed at his own throat, the knives parting scarred flesh and bone as if they were no more substantial than paper. His left hand rose up and caught hold of the severed head before it could fall, and then, with a single heave, threw the head through the windshield.

Glass exploded outward, and Joanna turned her head to protect her eyes, though shards still pierced the side of her face and neck. When she turned back, she saw the head resting on the hood of the Firebird like some grisly ornament.

Freddy looked at her and winked. "If I were you, I'd start running now. Or in your case, waddling."

The Firebird began to restore itself to its original shape, metal popping, creaking and groaning as it lengthened, straightened and smoothed. The engine roared to life, sounding like a massive caged beast eager to be free to hunt. Four metal lances sprang forth from the Firebird's front bumper—shiny, sharp and curved, just like the blades on that glove.

Joanna decided to take Freddy's advice. She turned and ran as best she could with a belly the size of an overripe watermelon. She headed down the street, feet slapping wet pavement, heart pounding against her ribs so hard she thought they might break. Behind her she heard tires squeal on wet asphalt as the Firebird came after her.

Adrenalin coursed through her like an electric shock, and she ran faster, her feet virtually flying over the ground. But she knew that no matter how fast she ran, there was no way she could hope to escape the demonic Firebird and the cackling fiend whose head adorned the hood. But she had to try—for the baby's sake.

Get off the damn street before you end up shish kebabbed on those spikes! Like she needed to tell herself.

She darted right, sliding and nearly losing her balance in the process. But she managed to stay on her feet, and she ran toward the sidewalk. She intended to make for an alley, maybe run inside an open business. It didn't matter, just as long as it was someplace the Firebird couldn't go.

"Nice move, Joanna!" Freddy called out, his mocking voice somehow clearly audible over the engine's rumble. "But you know the old saying: 'You can run, but you can't hide'!" Freddy broke out in cruel laughter that seemed to come from everywhere and nowhere all at once.

She started running toward the sidewalk, hoping that she could escape Freddy by going into an alley too narrow for his nightmarish vehicle to follow. But just as Joanna was about to set foot on the sidewalk, the buildings around her became hazy, indistinct, as if she were viewing them through the rippling distortion of heat-waves. And then they were gone: the buildings, the sidewalk...

She quickly turned and saw that everything was gone. There were no buildings, no sidewalks, no trees, no cars—all that remained was the road, which seemed to stretch forever in all directions.

Freddy's mocking words echoed in her mind.

You can run, but you can't hide!

She understood what he meant: there really was nowhere, not anymore.

Joanna heard the Firebird's engine roar grow louder, and she turned just in time to see the car with its bumper spikes and grisly, cackling hood ornament bearing down on her. There was a sudden *whooooosh* and the car was wreathed in orange-red flame.

"It really is a Firebird now!" Freddy said. His laughter was the sound of knife blades being dragged across steel.

Joanna screamed as the hellish vehicle came at her. Instinct took hold, and she leaped to the right just as the blazing car would've struck her. Time seemed to slow down as the car passed, and Joanna saw Freddy's head turn to wink at her. Worse yet, she saw his headless body sitting behind the steering wheel. It lifted a knife-gloved hand from the wheel and gave her a jaunty wave. And then, like a film returning to normal speed, time sped up again. The edge of the front bumper clipped her left foot while she was in the air. The impact spun her around, and she felt a hot blast of air as the car surged past.

The baby! If she landed on her belly…

But she came down on her side, her right elbow slamming against the asphalt. Sharp pain shot through her arm from fingertips to shoulder, and she lay in agony on the wet street, cold rainwater soaking through her blouse and jeans. Her breathing came in rapid gasps, and she concentrated on ignoring the pain in her ankle and elbow. She wondered if they were broken, prayed that they weren't. For if they were, there was no way she'd be able to escape the demon car. No way she'd be able to save little Junior.

The blazing Firebird hit the brakes and spun around on the wet pavement, tires seeming to scream rather than squeal on the asphalt. The car came to a stop a dozen yards away, spikes pointed at Joanna once more. And now that she was half lying, half sitting on the ground, the spikes were level with her face.

Freddy cackled again. "Tag, Joanna! You're it!"

The Firebird's engine revved several times, the car lurching and shaking, a wild animal eager to be let loose for the kill. With every rev of the engine, the unholy halo of fire surrounding the car flared brighter.

"Sorry to do this to you, Joanna," Freddy said. "Aw, who am I kidding? I love doing this to you! And do you know why I chose you, Mommy? As much fun as I've had playing with you, I'm much more interested in the little bun you've got cooking in your oven. I had a child of my own, once, but she was taken from me. So I thought, if I can't have one myself, why not adopt?"

The spikes jutting forth from the Firebird's bumper began to change. They became clear, as if the metal was transforming into plastic or glass. The tips became leaner, thinner, longer, until they resembled large needles. The spikes had mutated into giant hypodermics, and as Joanna watched, pitch-black liquid began bubbling up inside, filling them with viscous ebon foulness.

"Now this might sting a bit!" Freddy laughed, and the car jumped forward, the rear tires spinning as they struggled to get traction on the slippery road.

For an instant, Joanna was tempted to remain still and let the hell car finish her off. She was in so much pain, and she was exhausted from running for her life. She didn't know if she had the strength to get to her feet, let alone start running again. But she looked at Freddy as the Firebird approached and the dark glee in his eyes filled her with anger. Joanna would rather be damned than let this bastard have her baby! She reached down deep inside herself for whatever hidden reserves of strength she possessed, gritted her teeth in anticipation of the pain to come, and then stood.

It was even worse than she'd expected, and she had to bite her tongue to keep from screaming. She took a lurching step forward, and her injured ankle threatened to buckle, but it held, so she figured it must not be broken. She increased her speed, half running, half hopping away from the Firebird across the endless open road.

The Firebird picked up speed, baleful flames trailing behind the vehicle as if it were a fiendish comet shot straight out of Satan's sulfurous bunghole. The car's engine roar grew louder until Joanna felt its vibrations ripple through the marrow in her bones. The heat of its flames became more intense, and she could feel the skin on the back of her neck blister, smell the rank stink of burning hair.

She turned, hoping to sidestep the Firebird and escape those deadly needles and the black ichor glistening on their tips. But exhaustion—both physical and emotional—had finally caught up with her. The Firebird's brakes engaged just as one of the needles plunged into the side of Joanna's swollen belly, and she screamed in agony. Time slowed down once more; she could do nothing as the hypo's plunger pushed forward, injecting its darkness deep into her.

Then time returned to normal, and the impact of the striking car flung her off the needle, and she flew though the air almost a dozen feet before landing painfully on slick asphalt. The Firebird sat motionless now, engine revving, flames flickering.

"It's been fun," Freddy said, "but you know what they say: 'All good things must come to an agonizing, blood splattered end'. But don't worry about your little boy—I'll make sure to take good care of him once you're gone!"

The Firebird started forward, Freddy cackling uproariously, and Joanna screamed as death came for her.

Her eyes flew open, and Joanna realized she was behind the wheel of her Jeep once more. She must have fallen asleep for a couple seconds, must have dreamt. The Firebird, Freddy Krueger, the awful injection of darkness—none of it had been real. She grinned in relief... until she saw that her Jeep was heading straight for a light pole.

She heard Freddy's final words echo in her mind:

Don't worry about your little boy—I'll make sure to take good care of him once you're gone!

Joanna screamed one last time, but she didn't scream for long.

Darkness: warm, secure, loving. This was his world, the only one he'd ever known, the only one he ever wanted to know. He had no concept of pain, no concept of fear. This was a good place, and he was safe here. He was connected on the most primal level to something greater than himself, something that sheltered him, fed him, even breathed for him. He felt an intense closeness to this wonderful something that one day in the future he would be able to express through a single word—love.

As he floated blissfully in the gentle darkness of his world, his tiny developing mind moved in and out of a state akin to what he would someday experience as the phenomenon called dreaming. And in this state, he became aware of something new entering his world, something long, thin, and with a sharp tip that came slowly toward him. And as it approached, for the very first time in his short existence, he knew fear. He tried to pull away, moving tiny arms, kicking tiny legs, but there was nowhere to go.

Terrified, he could only float helplessly as the tip of the long thing penetrated the fleshy coil that protruded from his small taut belly and connected him to the wonderful something that provided for his every need. Only the wonderful something had failed, hadn't it? Failed to keep the long thin thing out, failed to keep it from sticking into the belly coil, failed to keep the darkness—darkness of an entirely different sort than that which surrounded and swaddled him—from being injected into the belly coil.

Though he had no concept of color yet, somehow he knew the flesh of the coil turned something called black. He sensed the black move through the coil toward him, slowly, bit by bit. If he could've reached the coil and if he'd had the strength, he would've tried to tear it free before the black could get inside him, but it was too late. An alien sensation called "cold" began to spread through his small body, and he heard a horrible sound that seemed at once to come from within and outside his world—cruel, delighted laughter.

He'd thought he knew all about darkness, but his real education was just beginning.

TWO

Jerome stood on the sidewalk, shrouded in darkness as he gazed at the two-storey house. In the light of day, he knew it would be white, with a black roof and black shutters, but, in the dark, illuminated by the scant glow offered by a quarter moon, the house was an ominous gray shape looming against the night sky. Instead of a lush green, the neatly trimmed lawn was a mass in inky darkness, and the trees—one oak, one elm—rose upward from the yard like a pair of sinister sentries.

The porch light was on, a splash of yellow illuminating the black front door, but otherwise there were no other lights—at least none that were visible, Jerome corrected himself. It was entirely possible that the occupants had the shades down and curtains drawn, concealing the fact that they were still up, despite the lateness of the hour.

Orchard Street was located in the midst of a quiet suburban neighborhood in the town of Springwood, Ohio. The houses here looked like replicas of each other, with only slight variations in color and design to mark them as different. The lawns were well kept, professionally landscaped and lit by the cozy warm glow of porch lights. Luckily for Jerome, there were no streetlights here; the residents of this part of Springwood didn't want to spoil the night-time look of their neighborhood with the harsh garishness of fluorescent lights. Besides, this was a safe, pleasant, upper middle-class neighborhood. There was no need for streetlights here.

Jerome smiled. Snobbery always won out over practicality, at least when money was involved. So much the better for him. He'd had his ride drop him off a block away so as not to risk awakening the residents in the white-by-day, gray-by-night house. He needed absolute silence if he was going to pull this off.

He left the sidewalk and started walking across the yard toward the house, moving from one shadow to the next, just one more piece of darkness stealing through the night. It was early April, and the night held a lingering hint of winter's chill. Jerome wished he'd worn something heavier than his brown jacket, and he was grateful that there wasn't any wind to make him feel even colder. He put thoughts of the cold out of his mind then. If all went according to plan, he'd be inside within a few minutes, and he could warm up then.

The Starkeys didn't have a dog, so he didn't have to worry about a family pet sensing him and alerting its owners that someone was attempting to sneak into their house. Even so, he moved carefully and quietly, watching where he placed each step. The last thing he wanted to do was knock over a birdbath or trip over a length of hose left on the lawn. He stayed well clear of the porch light's glow, just in case anyone inside might happen to look out, and also because he knew better than to try going in the front. That's exactly what they'd be expecting. He made his way around the side of the house and into the backyard. It was completely dark here. No light in the windows, and the back porch light was off. Perfect.

Jerome walked up to the back porch, but instead of ascending the steps, he stepped into the flowerbed next to them, crouched down, and felt around until his hands came in contact with a small rock. At least it looked like a rock. But the surface was too smooth, and it gave a bit beneath the pressure of his hand. Jerome turned the "rock" over and ran his fingers across the strangely flat surface of its underside until he found a catch. He depressed it with his thumb and a small section of the rock sprang open. He reached inside with a thumb and forefinger and withdrew a metal key. He replaced the rock—which in truth was a camouflaged plastic key holder—in the flowerbed, then stepped up onto the back porch.

He opened the storm door slowly so it wouldn't creak, then carefully inserted the key into the deadbolt lock. He turned it until the deadbolt *clicked* open, then removed the key and inserted it into the lock on the doorknob. Another turn, another click, and the back door was unlocked. He withdrew the key, tucked it into his pants' pocket, then slowly turned the knob and opened the door the merest of cracks. He paused for a moment, listening, straining to hear any sounds that might be coming from inside—approaching footsteps, a voice speaking in hushed tones as the person spoke to an emergency operator on the phone—but he heard nothing, and the kitchen remained dark.

So far, so good.

He eased the door open far enough to allow him to slip through, then closed it behind him and took a moment to re-lock it. It wouldn't do to have someone discover the back door unlocked; they'd know for certain that he'd gotten in. Then he turned away from the door and started across the tiled kitchen floor, stepping lightly so that his footfalls made no sound. He'd done it! He was in! All he had to do was get upstairs without waking anyone and—

A sudden glare of light stabbed his eyes, and he raised his hands to shield them.

"Do you know what time it is?"

Jerome blinked furiously, trying to force his eyes to adjust to the light. He slowly lowered his hands.

"I don't know. One?"

"Try two forty-five."

Jerome's vision had almost completely adjusted by now, and he glanced at the digital clock on the microwave. The readout read 2:42am, but he knew better than to quibble with his stepmother.

He shrugged. "I guess I lost track of time."

His stepmom crossed her arms over her chest, cocked her head to the side and narrowed her eyes. It was a posture she assumed whenever she was angry with Jerome. He'd seen it a lot over the years.

"Is that all you have to say for yourself?"

Lynn Starkey was in her late thirties but looked ten years younger. She had short brown hair and a trim, petite figure that seemed almost swallowed by the blue terrycloth robe she wore. Her fuzzy slippers were also blue, but they were old and some of the fuzzy had worn off in several places. Jerome—at his dad's urging—had gotten her a new pair of slippers last Christmas, but she'd never worn them. As far as Jerome knew, she'd never even taken them out of the box.

She stood in the kitchen doorway next to the light switch, blocking the entrance as if she were some sort of guardian trying to prevent Jerome from coming any further into the house. Of all the women his father could've married after his mother died, he'd had to pick a light sleeper.

Jerome pretended to consider his stepmother's words for a moment. "Yeah, that is all I have to say. And by the way, you forgot to add 'young man', as in, 'Is that all you have to say for yourself, young man?'"

Lynn's cheeks turned a deep crimson. She was one of those people whose face always shows their emotions, no matter how much they might try to hide them, and one of the emotions Lynn often displayed, especially toward Jerome, was anger.

"Don't you smart off to me! Your father might put up with that kind of crap, but I won't!"

Sudden fury swept through Jerome, fast and hot as a surging wildfire devouring a field of dry grass. His hands clenched into fists at his sides, his jaw muscles tightened and his teeth ground together painfully. Jerome saw himself running forward, grabbing Lynn by the shoulders and shaking her as hard as he could. He imagined tightening his grip on Lynn's shoulders, feeling his fingertips digging into her flesh, grinding skin and muscle against the bone underneath. Lynn let out a soft gasp of pain as if she were a small frightened animal instead of a fully grown woman.

Jerome started to take a step forward, and when Lynn saw this, she flinched. She didn't move out of the doorway, though, but her eyes held a hint of fear—fear of him. The sight of that fear gratified Jerome. He envisioned himself letting go of her shoulder with his right hand and holding it before her face. No longer was it bare—it was covered by a worn brown leather glove with metal blades affixed to the fingers—blades that were razor sharp and covered with reddish brown flakes of dried blood.

"Scared, *Mom*?" His voice sounded harsher, more guttural than normal. "How about I give you something to really be afraid of?" Jerome pulled back his hand and brought it around in a vicious swipe aimed at his stepmother's face.

But at the last instant before the blades could slice into Lynn's flesh, Jerome jumped as if an electric current had suddenly passed through his body. Lynn, face intact and unmarked, raised her eyebrow.

"Are you all right?" she asked.

He was trembling, and he felt a line of sweat roll down his back, tracing the length of his spine. He glanced down at his hand, saw there was no glove, no knives. His anger drained away, leaving him feeling confused and shaken, as if he'd drunk too much caffeine on an empty stomach.

"Just tired." He was afraid that the guttural voice from his vision, imagining, whatever it was, would come out of his mouth. But his voice sounded completely normal, if a bit strained. "Sorry, Lynn." Jerome hadn't called her mom since he'd been nine. He wasn't sure what he was apologizing for, though. Coming home late, scaring her? Maybe both. "I was watching movies over at El's house and I fell asleep. El didn't know it, he didn't even take his eyes off the TV screen until the last movie was over. He woke me up after that, and when I saw what time it was, I had him bring me straight home."

Lynn narrowed her eyes again, as if she were trying to somehow see inside him and verify his story. It was true, though, every word, and evidently Lynn decided to believe him because her expression softened and she allowed her arms to drop to her sides.

"Why didn't you call? It is a school night."

Jerome shrugged again. He knew the gesture irritated Lynn, but he couldn't help himself. "It was so late, I figured everyone was asleep. I didn't want to wake anyone up and worry them. Especially the kids."

He hoped this would be enough to placate Lynn. The mention of his younger half-brother and half-sister—especially when he demonstrated concern for them—usually was. He was tired and, as Lynn had pointed out, he did have school tomorrow. All he wanted to do was get past her, go upstairs, flop onto his mattress and get as much sleep as he could before his alarm went off.

Lynn looked at him for another moment, as if trying to decide whether to press the matter of his lateness. Finally she said, "I appreciate that. Well... How about we discuss this further in the morning, okay?"

She gave Jerome a smile then, but it looked forced and awkward. He couldn't remember her ever giving him one that didn't.

Though the last thing he wanted was to discuss anything with her, he nodded, and as if the gesture was a signal Lynn had been waiting for, she turned to the side to make room for him to pass.

He walked across the kitchen, past his stepmother, then down the hall to the foyer. He hung up his jacket in the front closet, then headed for the stairs. Lynn was standing at the bottom, waiting to accompany him, as if she didn't trust him to make it up to his room on his own.

He felt an echo of the fury that had gripped him a few moments ago, and he fought to keep it from taking hold of him anew. All his life he'd had a bad temper, and he'd struggled to control it for as long as he could remember. For some reason, it seemed to have been getting worse the last couple of years. Maybe it was, as his father had suggested on more than one occasion, just one more in a series of adolescent growing pains. It was a pain, all right, Jerome thought. A pain in the ass. All his temper ever did was complicate his life and make things more difficult—not only for himself, but for the people around him.

He'd managed to keep from getting into a full-blown argument with Lynn in the kitchen, and he didn't want to start one up with her again, so he kept his mouth shut as he walked past her and started climbing the stairs. He heard her follow a moment later, steps creaking beneath her feet, palm sliding with a soft hiss along the wooden banister. He felt like a prisoner being escorted back to his cell by a suspicious and untrusting guard.

Jesus, does she really think I can't find the way to my bedroom on my own? What's she going to do when I get there, follow me inside and tuck me in?

Don't do it, he told himself. You'll only make things worse.

But before he could stop himself, the words came out of his mouth, almost as if someone else were saying them.

"Thanks for the escort, Mom, but I don't need you to hold my hand. I can make it the rest of the way on my own."

They'd reached the top of the stairs, and Jerome increased his pace, hoping to get away from Lynn before she could respond to his verbal taunt. But before he could take more than two steps, Lynn grabbed hold of his arm.

"I do not appreciate being spoken to that way, Jerome!" She kept her voice low so as to not awaken the rest of the family, and her words came out in a hiss that only served to make him angrier.

"There's a lot of things around here that I don't appreciate, but you don't hear my bitching about them, do you?"

Jerome didn't turn around, and he fought to keep from saying anything more, but his mouth, as it so often did, seemed to have a mind of its own. And, unfortunately, it didn't bother to whisper.

Before Lynn could reply, one of the bedroom doors opened, and Jerome's father stepped out into the hallway. "What's going on out here, you two?" He yawned the last few words and reached up to cover his mouth.

Don Starkey always slept in his underwear and nothing else. At thirty-six, he kept in shape well enough, though he leaned toward being almost too thin. Still, Jerome didn't like seeing his dad standing there in his underwear. Mostly because who wants to see their parents run around almost naked? But also because it reminded him that this was the way his dad slept with Lynn at his side. And the thought of the two of them lying in bed together, snuggling close, made him feel sick to his stomach.

Lynn answered before Jerome could explain himself.

"Your son decided to come home late… and he snuck in through the back instead of coming in the front."

Jerome glanced at his stepmother. They had different locks on the front and back doors, and Jerome, at Lynn's insistence, only had a key to the front door, especially to prevent him from doing what he did tonight. Lucky for him, he'd known where Lynn kept the spare back door key hidden.

Jerome repeated the excuse he'd given Lynn downstairs. "I didn't want to wake anyone up." The front door had a string of bells hanging from the inside knob—another one of Lynn's ideas—and they jingled loudly whenever the door was opened.

"Looks like you did anyway." Jerome's father scratched his sandy blond beard and stifled another yawn before turning to Lynn. "What time is it?"

"After three," she said.

"No way!" Jerome burst out. "It's fifteen till... Ten till at the most!" He was practically yelling by the time he finished, and a second bedroom door opened and a brown haired girl dressed in a Hello Kitty nightgown stuck her head into the hall.

"What's everyone talking about? Is it time to get up yet?" It was Mary, Jerome's six year-old half-sister.

Lynn gave Jerome a venomous look before finally letting go of his arm and going to Mary. Her expression softened as she put her hand on the girl's shoulder. "Everything's okay, sweetie. Let's go get you tucked back in." With a last look at her husband, Lynn ushered Mary back into her room and closed the door behind them.

Figuring that this was as good a time as any to make his escape, Jerome started for his bedroom.

"Hold up, Jay." Jay—or "J"—was his father's nickname for Jerome, and Jerome despised it. Still, he did as his father asked and stopped.

"You know you have a curfew, especially when it's a school night."

Jerome wanted to say that he was quite aware of his eleven o'clock curfew, thank you very much. But he was over seventeen, less than a year away from being a legal adult, and was therefore too old to have a curfew of any sort, let alone one so ridiculously early as eleven.

But his dad was speaking in his reasonable we're-both-two-adults-here voice, and he only used that tone when Jerome was in big trouble, so Jerome kept his mouth shut.

"And this is the second time this has happened in the last couple weeks," his dad continued.

Jerome kept on keeping his mouth shut.

"Last time you got a warning. This time... Well, I'm afraid I have no choice but to ground you."

Jerome couldn't believe what he was hearing. "Ground me? I haven't been grounded since I was in junior high!"

"Maybe you should've," his dad said. "Maybe I've been too easy on you."

Don Starkey was a supervisor in the IT department of an insurance company. Jerome thought that because he was a boss at work, his father sometimes acted like too much of a boss at home.

"But I've got to work tomorrow!" Jerome protested.

"Try to keep it down," his father half spoke, half whispered. "You've already woken your sister. Do you want to wake your brother, too?"

Half-sister, Jerome wanted to say. Half-brother.

"Of course you can still go to school and work," his dad said. "But that's it for the next week." Jerome started to open his mouth, but before he could speak, his father added, "And if you give me any lip about it, it'll be two weeks."

Jerome closed his mouth with an audible click. He clenched his teeth so tight that they began to ache at the roots, and he felt his temperature begin to rise as if he were afflicted by a sudden fever. He experienced an almost overwhelming urge to shout, to yell, to scream, to open his mouth wide and give voice to the anger that surged inside him, to release it in one violent, deafening burst and let it shake the house from foundation to rafters.

The fingers on Jerome's right hand twitched, and he imagined he heard the raspy sound of metal sliding against metal. He saw himself stepping toward his father, raising his clawed hand and...

But he denied the vision, blocked it from his consciousness. This was his dad, the only real parent he'd ever had since Jerome's mother had died shortly after his birth. He loved his father and didn't even want to think about doing anything to harm him, so he merely nodded acceptance of his punishment.

His dad smiled. "Good enough. Now why don't you get on into bed? Morning's not too far away, and we both have to get up early."

"Yeah, okay," Jerome mumbled. "Night." He turned and headed down the hall toward his room, which was the last on the left, right next to Don and Lynn's, unfortunately. He wanted to get inside and shut the door before Lynn came out of Mary's room and started on him again.

He reached his room, went inside and shut the door behind him before flipping the light switch. Unlike a lot of teenage boys—his buddy, El, being a prime example—Jerome's room wasn't very messy. His bed wasn't made, and a shirt and a pair of socks lay on the floor in front of his closet where they'd almost, but not quite, made it into the clothes hamper inside. But otherwise his room was virtually immaculate, floor bare, the tops of both his desk and dresser clean, bookshelves neat and organized, walls bare of pictures or posters. There was a reason his room looked like this, and it wasn't because he was a neat freak. He did his best to spend as little time at home as possible, and because of this he didn't have the opportunity to turn it into a typical male pigsty.

The sole decoration in the room was the Native American dreamcatcher hanging on the wall over the head of his bed. And he only kept it up because his Aunt Bekka had given it to him when he was just a baby. Over the years, she'd periodically made him promise never to take it down. He loved his aunt and didn't want to break his promise to her, but there was more to it than that. Rebecca Larkin was his birth mother's identical twin sister. So even though he knew it was childish, he couldn't help feeling that a promise to her was like a promise to the mother he'd never known. Thus, the dreamcatcher remained up, even though Jerome didn't particularly like it.

Looking at it, he could almost hear his aunt's voice as she'd explained to him for the first time how the dreamcatcher worked.

Native Americans belived that dreamcatchers could stop bad dreams—catch them in their weave like a spider traps a fly. There's a small hole in the middle, though. That's to let good dreams through. So as long as you keep this over your bed, you won't have any bad dreams, Jerome. Not one. You'll be protected from nightmares—and from the things that cause them.

Still struggling to control his anger over being grounded like he was a little kid, Jerome walked over to his bed, sat down and started to take off his shoes. He removed the first and let it drop to the floor, but as he pulled off the second, he was suddenly gripped by a fresh surge of anger. He turned and without thinking hurled his tennis shoe at the wall. It slammed into his dreamcatcher, there was a crack, and the collection of wood, string, and feathers fell onto his pillow. The shoe hit the bed, bounced off, then landed on the floor.

Jerome just sat and stared at the dislodged dreamcatcher, unable to believe what he'd done. He heard three muffled thumps on the wall, followed by his father's voice.

"Keep it down in there, Jay!"

Jerome didn't respond and his father said nothing more. Jerome waited several minutes to give his father—and Lynn, who'd presumably returned to their room—a chance to settle down. Then he scooted toward the dreamcatcher and gingerly picked it up. He examined it and was relieved to see that the damage wasn't too serious. The dreamcatcher had been constructed from circular bands of thin wood, and these were broken in several places. As a result, a couple of the strings that criss-crossed in the middle like a spider's web had come loose, but it was nothing that a little Scotch tape couldn't fix, at least cosmetically. Aunt Bekka would undoubtedly notice the damage even after he repaired it, but she didn't visit very often, mostly because she knew she wasn't welcome in Lynn's house. Jerome didn't like that, but at least he wouldn't have to worry about Bekka being upset at what he'd foolishly allowed his temper to make him do.

He stood and carried the broken dreamcatcher over to his dresser. He gently placed it on top, careful not to cause any more damage to it. He'd fix it and put it back up tomorrow or the day after. All he wanted to do now was turn out the light, crawl into bed and get this night behind him as quickly as possible. But as he started toward the light switch, he once more heard Bekka's words whisper in his mind.

"So as long as you keep this over your bed, you won't have any bad dreams, Jerome. Not one. You'll be protected from nightmares and from the things that cause them."

He couldn't remember a night when he hadn't slept beneath the protection of his dreamcatcher, but he supposed there was a first time for everything. Good thing he wasn't superstitious. But even if the dreamcatcher did keep bad dreams away—if only because his subconscious believed it would—he could go one night without it. And if he did have a nightmare or two, so what? He could take it.

Besides, how bad could a few nightmares be, anyhow?

He turned off the light and headed for bed.

THREE

"Are you asleep?" Lynn whispered.

For a moment, she didn't think Don was going to answer, but then he whispered back. "What do you think?"

She snuggled closer and put her arms around him. He held her and she nestled her head in the crook between his neck and shoulder. "Do you think I overreacted tonight?"

Don didn't respond right away, but she knew he was thinking and didn't press him. Their bedroom was dark, the curtains drawn tight to prevent even a smidgen of moonlight from entering. Lynn could never get to sleep if there was any light at all in a room, and she often wore a black mask over her eyes when she went to bed. But there was something about the darkness in the room that seemed ominous tonight, as if instead of merely the absence of light, the darkness was a solid, tangible thing surrounding their bed, filling the room from floor to ceiling. Despite being under both a sheet and comforter—and the proximity of her husband's warm body—Lynn shivered and wished that the curtains were open. She could use a little light right now.

"Don't worry about it," Don said at last. He reached up and began stroking Lynn's hair. Normally, she enjoyed it when he did that; would have closed her eyes and revelled in the sensation, but closing her eyes would have only intensified the darkness just then, so she kept them open.

"Jay's just pushing the limits to see what he can get away with," Don continued. "All teenagers are like that. I know I was when I was his age."

"You know he doesn't like it when you call him Jay. It makes him feel like a little kid. Besides, he's almost eighteen, Don. At his age, you were already a father. His father."

She felt Don's body tense. He was always uncomfortable discussing Jerome's early childhood.

"I was eighteen when he was *born*," Don pointed out, "but it took another couple years to convince Joanna's parents—and the courts—to give me full custody. I was twenty-one when Jerome finally came to live with me."

And twenty-four when you married me, she mentally added. Jerome had been nine then, ten when his brother Brian was born and twelve when Mary came along. Sometimes Lynn felt that if she'd just met Don sooner, had come into Jerome's life when he was younger... But she hadn't, and there was no use wishing otherwise.

"My point is that Jerome's birth—regardless of when you finally got custody—forced you to grow up in a hurry," Lynn said.

"So?"

"So sometimes I think you go too easy on Jerome, maybe because you're trying to keep him from growing up as fast as you had to. Don't get me wrong," she quickly added before he could respond, "I think you did a great job with Jerome. You were and still are a wonderful father to him, just as you've been to Brian and Mary. But I worry that in order to balance out your lenience with Jerome, I sometimes go too far and end up playing the bad guy." She sighed. "I'm sure he thinks I'm the ultimate Wicked Stepmother, and I don't want to be, Don. I really don't."

She felt as if she might start crying, but she fought to hold back the tears. She wanted to have a real conversation about this, not have Don say "There, there" as he attempted to soothe her.

"But..." She trailed off, uncertain how to proceed.

"But what?" There was an edge to Don's voice, as if he wasn't sure he really wanted to hear her answer.

"It's that temper of his." Lynn continued in a rush so she could get all her words out before Don could interrupt. "I swear I don't know where he gets it from. No one on your side of the family is like that, and neither are Joanna's parents. Rebecca might be... eccentric, but having trouble dealing with anger isn't one of her problems."

Though it wasn't always easy, both Don and Lynn were committed to maintaining as cordial a relationship as possible with Jerome's maternal relatives, for the boy's sake.

"When we were talking in the kitchen—before we came upstairs—there was a moment when he gave me this look." Lynn shuddered in her husband's arms. "I thought he was going to... to attack me. Just for a second, but... I was scared."

Don didn't say anything for a while, and Lynn feared that she'd upset him, but then he took in a deep breath and let it out in a long sigh.

"The same thing happened after you took Mary back to bed. He glared at me, and for a moment, I actually thought he was going to reach out and grab me. But you know... teenagers, they get upset sometimes. It's so frustrating. You're almost an adult but not quite."

"I remember, Don. Everyone goes through that stage as they grow up, but not everyone is so... so full of anger as Jerome. And it's not as if his temper suddenly appeared once he hit his teens. He had it long before that. Remember Kirby?"

Kirby was a pet gerbil that Jerome had when Lynn married Don. Less than six months after they'd started their new life as a family, Lynn discovered she was pregnant. Don was overjoyed, but when they broke the news to Jerome, he didn't react. Didn't do anything, didn't say anything for the longest time. Then, without a word, he slowly turned and walked upstairs to his bedroom. Don hadn't been overly concerned. "The boy'll be okay. He just needs a little time to get used to the idea, that's all." But Lynn hadn't been so sure, so she went upstairs to check on Jerome.

She found him in his room, holding Kirby. Kirby the Gerby, as Jerome sometimes called him. Jerome's face was a mask of anger, and he was squeezing Kirby as hard as he could. Kirby's moist black eyes bulged out of his head as if the pressure might make them pop out of their sockets any second. Lynn rushed into the room, intending to rescue the little animal, but before she reached Jerome, she heard the awful sound of tiny bones snapping and Kirby let out a last whine as he died. Showing no emotion whatsoever then, Jerome stared at the dead gerbil for a few moments before opening his hand and letting the misshapen lump of lifeless fur fall to the carpet. Afterward, Jerome displayed no regret for what he'd done to Kirby. It was almost as if he didn't remember squeezing the poor thing to death.

Don said nothing, so Lynn went on. "And what about when Brian was one and Jerome wanted me to bake chocolate chip cookies for him? When I told him that he'd have to wait until I put Brian down for a nap—"

"He bit your hand," Don finished. "I remember."

"Bit" was an understatement. Jerome had taken a good-sized hunk of flesh out of her hand, resulting in a 911 call, an ambulance ride to the emergency room and eighteen stitches. Her hand still ached when the temperature got cold enough, though she'd never told Don this.

"And there've been other incidents over the years," Lynn continued. "Maybe not as serious, but when taken altogether..."

"So what you trying to say? That Jerome is some kind of bad seed? That he was born evil?"

"Of course not." But she realized that maybe on some level that was precisely what she'd intended to say. "I guess I just want us all to be happy, Jerome included. I do love him, you know." And she did, but that didn't mean she wasn't also afraid of him.

Don held her tight and kissed the top of her head. "I know. I guess all we can do is our best for him and hope that's enough."

Lynn knew that Don was trying to end the conversation, but she wasn't finished yet. She wanted to talk to him about the possibility of getting Jerome some kind of help—therapy, maybe, or some kind of anger management class. But she sensed that she'd pushed the issue as far as she could with him for one night. Maybe they could pick up the conversation again tomorrow.

They fell silent after that and before long Don's breathing deepened, and Lynn knew he was asleep. Too worried to sleep, she stared up into the darkness, feeling as if it were pressing down on her, or worse, staring back.

Jerome opened his eyes.

It was a bright sunny day, clear blue sky with hardly a cloud in sight. He stood in a field of lush green grass, a gentle warm breeze caressing his body. He looked down and saw that he was dressed in a blue T-shirt and black shorts, though he couldn't remember putting them on. He was wearing elbow pads and shin guards, too, as well as cleats, and he realized that he had a soccer uniform on. So far the field had been quiet, save for the soft whisper of the breeze and the singing of birds somewhere off in the distance. But as if the realization that he was dressed in a soccer uniform was some sort of signal, the air erupted with noise: spectators cheering encouragement, coaches shouting advice, players panting as they ran hard, their shoes thudding on the ground as they raced up and down the field in pursuit of a round white ball.

A group of young men around Jerome's age—half wearing blue shirts, half green—ran past him. One of the blue shirts lagged behind and looked at Jerome as if he were crazy.

"What's wrong with you, dude? Don't just stand there—play!"

Jerome didn't recognize the boy, but before he could ask how he'd gotten here (for he didn't have any memory of that, either) the boy ran off after the others. Spectators on the sidelines—parents and younger siblings, mostly—started to boo him, and more than a few shouted for him to get his ass in gear. Still unsure what was happening but not wishing to disappoint anyone, Jerome began jogging toward the mass of players, who were crowded together close to one of the goals, feet lashing out as each team tried to get and maintain control of the ball.

As Jerome drew close to the other players, he said, "Whose goal is this?" to no one in particular, and one of the boys—he couldn't see which one, or which team he was on—said, "Green, dumbass! Just look at the goalie!"

Right. He hadn't been thinking. He took a quick glance at his shirt to double-check his own team. Yep, he was blue. So when the ball came rolling toward him he knew what to do. He took control of it and started running toward the goal, boys from both teams close on his heels.

It had been a long time since he'd played soccer. He'd quit after junior high, at least, he thought he had. But far from being rusty, he moved with a speed and agility beyond any that he'd ever possessed before. It was as if everything there was to know about soccer—all the rules, all the moves—had been hardwired into his body, were part of his very DNA. He charged toward the green goal, the other players falling behind, unable to match his pace. He moved the ball from foot to foot with the ease of a master juggler tossing a trio of objects into the air and catching them one by one before once more launching them into the air. There was no way anyone was going to stop him from scoring, and sensing this, the spectators roared their approval.

The green goalie crouched down, knees bent, shifting his weight from side to side, ready to dive in either direction and block Jerome's shot. He looked nervous but prepared. It didn't matter, though. Jerome was well and truly in the zone, and no amount of preparation was going to help the goalie stop him. When Jerome was within ten feet of the green goal, he took aim and drew back his leg to kick. As he brought his foot forward, he looked down at the ball and truly saw it for the first time. Instead of being smooth, white and spherical, the object was pale pink with an irregular surface and long yellow silken strands protruding from its top. But that was because it wasn't a ball at all. It was the severed head of a teenage girl with blue eyes—eyes that blinked as she looked up at him—and long blonde hair. Though Jerome had only ever seen the girl in photographs, he instantly knew who she was: Joanna Larkin, his birth-mother.

He tried to pull his kick, but it was too late. His foot connected with the side of his mother's head with a sickening *thunk*. Joanna shrieked in pain as her head was launched into the air by her son's kick. Jerome watched in frozen horror as she soared through the air toward the goal, which instead of being made from interwoven white rope was now constructed from rusted barbed wire.

Jerome prayed the goalie would be able to block the shot and prevent his mother's head from hitting the barbed wire, but the goalie was covered with blood, drenched with it as if he'd been plunged into a vat of liquid gore. When he tried to move, Jerome could see that his face, neck, hands, arms and legs were covered with deep slash marks. The kind that a steel-clawed glove might make. The goalie managed to take only a single step before he literally fell to pieces, bloody chunks of meat and bone pattering onto the grass like some sort of grisly rain.

Without anything to stop its flight, Joanna Larkin's head flew into the goal net and hit the barbed wire backing. She screamed in agony as the barbs bit into her flesh and held her fast. Rivulets of blood ran from her wounds and trickled down onto the grass, adding to the crimson puddle created by the disassembled goalie. Jerome stood in silent shock, unable to believe what he'd just done. A roar erupted from the crowd, the cheers punctuated by shouts of "Score!" and "Goal!" and "Way to go, blue!"

How could those lunatics cheer him after the abominable act he'd just performed? His paralysis broke and he turned toward the spectators, intending to denounce their barbarism, but he stopped when he saw the transformation they'd undergone. They were different sizes—some fat, some thin, some tall, some short—and they wore different clothing, but suddenly they all had the same face: horribly burned, bald, with a hook nose and nub ears. Eyes that danced with madness and malice, and a mouth stretched wide in obscene delight.

Jerome turned to his fellow players to see if they'd noticed the spectators' metamorphoses, but like the green goalie, they were all covered with blood and mutilated by slash marks. They were giving him the same twisted grin as the spectators, and then one by one they began to fall apart until all that remained of both teams were piles of shredded skin, muscle and bone.

"Hell of a shot, kid! I couldn't have done better myself!"

Jerome turned toward the voice. One of the spectators had stepped onto the field and was coming toward him. He had the same burnt features as the others, but he was dressed in a red and green striped sweater, brown pants, brown work boots and an old-fashioned fedora rested at a jaunty angle atop his scarred head. But the apparition's most striking feature was the leather glove on his right hand, a glove with four blades attached, one for each finger—just like the one Jerome had imagined when he'd been angry with Lynn and his father.

As the burnt-faced man came striding toward Jerome, the grass where his feet touched turned black, shriveled and died. Jerome sensed a presence about the strange figure, an unseen aura of malignant darkness that seemed to crackle silently around the scarred man like some sort of foul, negative energy. Anti-energy, sheer, absolute and total nothingness. It was the ultimate realization, the apotheosis of all that was dark and wicked and selfish and cruel and just plain wrong in existence. It wasn't merely evil, for that concept was far too simplistic, too limited to adequately describe this creature. This thing was as far beyond evil as a human being was beyond an insect on the evolutionary tree.

Jerome sensed one thing more about the grinning, scar-faced, claw-gloved man. Somehow, he was familiar, as if Jerome had met him someplace before. More than that, it was almost as if Jerome had known him all his life, even though he was positive this was the first time he'd ever seen the man.

The man's smile faltered for an instant, and anger came into his bloodshot eyes, almost as if he knew what Jerome had been thinking. But then the anger passed as quickly as it had come, and Mr Scarface was all smiles again.

The man stopped when he reached Jerome and just stood for a moment, grinning as he looked the boy up and down.

"You've grown some since the last time I saw you, Jerome." The man reached out with his left hand—the one without the claw-glove—and lifted Jerome's shirt up over his flat belly. "Got rid of the umbilical cord too, I see. Smart move. It's not healthy for a young man like you to be tied down to just one woman." He let go of Jerome's shirt and chuckled; the sound was like bones rattling in a tin can.

"Who are you? What do you want?" Jerome surprised himself by finding his voice. He was terrified of this man and yet, at the same time, he wasn't. It was almost as if Jerome's personality had been split in two. One half of him was scared to death by this razor-fingered madman, but the other half was... intrigued. That half of Jerome was the part that recognized the scarred man, and it was curious to learn more about him.

"Call me 'Freddy'." The man winked, his burnt, gummy eyelids sticking for a moment before pulling open again. "Everyone else does. And as for what I want, that's simple. Just to say howdy. I've been trying to talk to you for years, but I was never able to get through to you. We had a bad case of telepathicus interruptus, you might say. Until you had that little tantrum in your room and threw your shoe at the wall, that is. Now you're receiving me loud and clear, Jerome."

Jerome frowned. He couldn't quite remember what Scarface—what Freddy—was talking about. It sounded familiar, but when he tried to recall the specific memory, he came up blank.

A shadow passed over the field, as if clouds suddenly blocked the sun. Jerome looked up and saw a mass of pitch-black clouds, all right, but they weren't merely blocking the sun; they were devouring it, tearing moist yellow chunks out of it with sharp ebon fangs, thick lemony liquid squirting into the air with every bite.

Jerome looked back down and saw that the ground beneath his feet was no longer covered with grass, but instead a thick layer of tiny brown-furred bodies with long, thin tails. The creatures were obviously dead, for thick, writhing maggots squirmed over their still forms.

Freddy chuckled. "Kirby the Gerby," he said.

The sky continued to grow darker as Freddy walked toward the barbed wire goal, crushing dead gerbils and live maggots beneath his boots as he went. When he reached the goal, he grabbed Joanna's head by the hair and yanked it free of the wire. Joanna cried out in pain, and Freddy held up his gloved hand and jammed her head down onto two of his glove-knives, and this time when she tried to cry out, black blood dribbled past her lips and over her chin.

Freddy walked back toward Jerome, crushing more gerbils and maggots along the way. When he reached Jerome he stopped and held Joanna's head up level with the boy's eyes. The head was still impossibly alive, its own eyes moving back and forth, mouth gaping open and closed as if she was a fish gasping for air.

"We'll talk again," Freddy said. "Tonight was just the kick off, a chance for the two of us to touch base, get to know one another a bit before the fun really gets started. But before you leave—"

He shoved Joanna's head toward Jerome's face, and his mother spoke, but the voice that came out of her blood-smeared mouth belonged to Freddy, as if he were performing some sort of depraved ventriloquist act.

"Give mommy a kiss goodbye…"

Before Jerome could react, Freddy thrust the head closer and Joanna's bloody lips pressed against his. The cloud creatures devoured the last bit of the sun then, and the world was plunged into total darkness. The last thing Jerome was aware of as consciousness left him was the sound of Freddy's maniacal laughter.

FOUR

Rebecca Larkin was still asleep when she sensed that something was wrong—very wrong—and she was out of bed and halfway to the door before she opened her eyes. She stopped then, confused and afraid. No, more than that; she was terrified. Something had pulled her out of her slumber, but what? An intruder in the house? Maybe she'd heard a noise—a thump or the sound of breaking glass—something that her subconscious mind had registered and then sounded an alarm to stir her consciousness to action. Or perhaps there was a fire and she'd been awakened by the smell of smoke.

She stood motionless and listened. All was silent. No shrieking smoke alarm, and no thumps or bumps. She inhaled through her nose, but she didn't smell any smoke. No fire then, and no intruder—probably. But while her terror had ebbed to the point where her fear was manageable, she was still afraid. She didn't know what was happening, but she believed in paying attention to feelings. The rational mind, for all its useful qualities, was more than capable of deluding itself, denying the obvious, rationalizing away anything that wasn't easily explainable. But the irrational mind was incapable of such self-deceit. It felt what it felt, and because of that was often a more accurate barometer of what was real and what wasn't.

Rebecca returned to her bed, knelt, and reached underneath. Her fingers found smooth wood, and she curled her hand around a baseball bat, drew it forth from the darkness, then stood once more. Not much protection, perhaps, but she refused to risk the karmic repercussions of owning a gun. The makeshift club would have to serve.

She walked quietly to the bedroom door and opened it slowly, so as to make as little sound as possible. She emerged into the hall and, sensing no immediate danger, started walking, gripping her bat tightly with both hands. She lived in a small two bedroom, one storey house, and it didn't take her long to check all the rooms and determine that no one had broken in and nothing was on fire. Reassured, but still feeling the lingering remnants of the fear that had woken her, Rebecca went to the kitchen. She'd turned the lights on when she'd made her first pass through, so she propped her bat against the counter next to the refrigerator and started the coffee maker. It was only 4:30 in the morning, but she knew she wasn't going to be able to get back to sleep tonight. Not now.

She was dressed only in a flimsy blue nightgown, so while the coffee brewed she returned to her bedroom and put on a robe. She wasn't cold, but for some reason it felt right to put the robe on. It was dark blue and covered with the symbols of the zodiac. Jerome had given it to her last Christmas as an affectionate gag gift. She ran her hand across her opposite forearm, feeling the robe's soft fabric.

Jerome.

Could this strange sense of wrongness she felt have something to do with her nephew? Maybe. She didn't believe in coincidences, and something had urged her to put this robe on.

Rebecca left the bedroom once more and returned to the kitchen. The coffee was still brewing, so she headed for the front room, which she thought of as the sitting room, for it was here that she met her clients. It was rather plain. The carpet was an unassuming beige, and the walls were painted to match. There was a table in the middle of the room with three chairs around it. The chairs were well padded, soft and comfortable, the sort of thing that anyone might have in their living room. A cloth covered the table and hung down almost to the floor, obscuring the legs, but there were no fancy designs on it, certainly nothing to compete with her robe. The tablecloth was white, and though that meant she had to wash it quite often to keep it from looking dingy, she didn't mind. She liked the way the white represented purity of spirit and clarity of thought. It helped her focus and concentrate, and therefore was vital to her work.

Her one concession to clients' preconceptions was a small crystal ball resting on a black wooden base in the center of the tabletop. It was nothing more than an ornamental touch and one that she didn't particularly like, but her clients expected it of her, so she put up with it. The sole remaining object in the room was a polished wood cabinet set against the wall. Rebecca went to it, opened a drawer and removed a deck of tarot cards. She crossed to the table, sat down, pushed the crystal ball aside to give her more room to work, then began shuffling the cards. She knew using the tarot was, like the crystal ball, a cliché, and she would've preferred to do without them in her work. When she'd first set up shop as a "spiritual consultant" years ago, she was determined not to reinforce people's stereotypes of psychics as amusing loons at best or exploitative charlatans at worst. But the fact of the matter was that the tarot worked for her. She didn't use the cards the way they were intended, though. For her, the cards worked as a kind of lens that allowed her to focus her awareness beyond the physical and open her mind to the realm of the ethereal.

As she began dealing out cards and placing them face up on the table, she chuckled. Realm of the ethereal. She could just imagine what Lynn would say to that! Jerome's stepmother already thought she was crazy, but if she ever heard Rebecca talking like some renfair fortuneteller...

She finished dealing out twelve cards in two rows of six, then set the rest of the deck down on the table. She never looked at the cards as she was dealing them because she wanted to view all twelve together for the first time, so she could more clearly see whatever pattern might lay in them. But when she examined the cards, she began to wonder if maybe she really was crazy. For instead of the magician, the fool, the king of cups, the knight of pentacles, the hanging man, the tower, and all the rest of the standard tarot symbols, each of the cards she'd dealt displayed the same image: Jerome's face.

There was no mistaking it was him. The image was so detailed as to be near photographic quality. As she examined the cards more closely, she saw that the images weren't exactly the same. The six cards on her right showed Jerome as a smiling young man, but the six on the left portrayed a Jerome that was alien to her. His brow was furrowed in a scowl, and his eyes were narrowed and mean. His lips were pressed together as if he were clenching his teeth. His features—eyes, nose, mouth, chin, cheekbones—were unmistakably her nephew's, but the young man glaring out at her from these six cards was most definitely not Jerome, not as she knew him, at any rate.

The terror that had gripped her upon awakening began to return and her hands started to tremble. She knew she was receiving a message of some sort, a warning that something awful was going to happen—perhaps already had happened—to Jerome. But she wasn't sure what it meant.

She reached toward the cards, intending to pick them up, return them to the deck and reshuffle them in the hope that a second reading might clarify the strange message. But before her hand could touch any of the cards, the air was torn suddenly by a slashing sound, and all twelve cards were sliced in two, though no cutting instrument was visible. As Rebecca watched, the cards were slashed again and again, each time accompanied by a metallic slicing sound, until they lay in tiny pieces on the white tablecloth.

For a moment afterward nothing happened, and Rebecca began to think that whatever supernatural manifestation had taken place here was over. But then with a *whooooosh* the twelve tiny piles of card pieces burst into flame. The fires burned fast, hot and bright, like magician's flash paper. Before Rebecca could react, the flames had burned themselves out, leaving behind only smoldering scorch marks on the tablecloth. The card fragments had been completely devoured by the flames, but something had been left behind. The scorch marks were in the shapes of letters, twelve of them, and they formed a message far clearer than the dual images of Jerome they'd replaced:

HE'S MINE, BITCH!

Then, as if from a great distance—or perhaps only in her own mind—Rebecca heard the sound of mocking laughter.

FIVE

"Man, you look like something the cat refused to drag in!"

Jerome was trying to open his locker—for the third time—but he couldn't remember his combination. Frustrated, he slammed his fist into the metal door hard enough to cause the buzz of conversation in the hall to cease and heads to turn in Jerome's direction.

"Hey, it was just a joke. No need to go into testosterone overdrive."

Jerome turned to Ellery Belasco, otherwise known as El, and gave his friend a faint smile. "Don't flatter yourself. That joke wasn't good enough to make me angry. The truth is, I didn't sleep too well last night."

Seeing the two friends talking calmly, the other students returned to their own business, and soon the din of conversation was faster and louder than before, as if the kids were determined to make up for the few precious moments of conversation they'd missed.

"I'd have thought you'd feel well rested today, considering you were zonked out on my couch last night," El said. "Though how someone could possibly sleep through all three *Evil Dead* movies is beyond me."

Jerome started fumbling with his combination again, but El pushed him aside and went to work on the lock himself. Within moments, El had the locker door open.

He stepped back and gestured to the open locker with a flourish. "Ta-daah!"

Jerome frowned. "How did you do that?"

"I'm afraid that a true magician never reveals his secrets," El said. "But if you really want to know, it's no big deal. I've seen you open your locker so many times I have your combination memorized."

El was shorter than Jerome and possessed a slighter build. He had curly black hair and a thin dusting of facial hair above his lip that could only be called a mustache in the most generous interpretation of the word. He was long-sighted, and the glasses he wore made his eyes appear larger than they really were, giving his face a vaguely owlish aspect that made him seem more serious and studious than he really was. He was always full of energy, so much so that at times he almost seemed to vibrate. It was a quality that irritated a lot of people, but not Jerome. El's almost manic energy had a way of defusing Jerome's temper, especially when El made one of his lousy jokes. Though El acted goofy, he always dressed well, and today he wore a maroon sweater over a white shirt, neatly pressed khaki pants and polished brown shoes. When anyone questioned him about the seeming contradiction in El's personality, he always joked that he subscribed to *GQ for Dorks.*

Now that his locker was open, thanks to El, Jerome hung up his jacket and stowed his backpack. He was more plainly dressed than El in a slightly wrinkled red polo shirt, jeans that could stand washing and old tennis shoes of indeterminate color. Jerome had never cared much about clothes, certainly not to the degree his friend did. He reached into his locker and took out the books for his first couple classes of the day—biology, advanced composition and world history.

"I don't know why you signed up for biology first period," El said. "Everyone knows you take biology last period so you don't smell of formaldehyde all day."

Jerome smiled as he closed his locker and gave the combination a spin. "Maybe some people like the smell of formaldehyde," he said.

"And maybe some people like slamming their hand in a car door over and over, but that doesn't mean it's a good idea." El's tone became more serious then. "So why'd you have trouble sleeping? You get in a fight with your mom again?"

"Stepmom," Jerome automatically corrected. "And yeah, I did. I swear that woman is the lightest sleeper that ever lived. She probably woke up the moment I stepped on the lawn and bent a blade of grass."

"Maybe," El allowed. "But did it ever occur to you that maybe she was waiting up for you because she was worried about you?"

Actually, it hadn't, but Jerome didn't want to admit that to his friend. El wasn't like the stereotypical teenager in that he had a good relationship with his parents. Though he and Jerome had been friends since second grade, and though El knew him better than anyone, with the possible exception of his father, Jerome wasn't sure El truly understood his problems at home. Still, Jerome appreciated his friend's support.

"I didn't have any trouble getting to sleep," Jerome said, "but once I did, I..." He what? He'd been about to say something, but he couldn't remember what. It was as if the memory was there, but it was blocked off somehow, sealed away where he couldn't get at it. Weird.

"You need to learn to relax, that's your problem," El said. "You're so intense all the time. You got to lighten up a little."

Jerome grinned. "That's what I got you for, pal."

"What about me? What do you have me for?"

Jerome and El turned to see a tall brown haired girl looking at them with an amused half-smile.

"As much as I love a good straight line," El said, "I wouldn't touch that one with the proverbial ten foot pole."

Jerome felt his cheeks burn and he knew he was blushing. Both El and Cheryl laughed, then Cheryl gently touched Jerome's cheek. "That's one of the things I love about you, you know. Your feelings are always so close to the surface."

Jerome thought about the rage he'd felt toward Lynn and his dad last night, and of the disturbing images of violence that had accompanied it. "Too close, sometimes."

"Nonsense," Cheryl said. "Too many people keep their emotions bottled up all the time. Not only can't you tell what they're feeling, half the time they don't know what they're feeling. I'm so glad you're not like that."

Jerome knew Cheryl was trying to be sweet, so he accepted her words with a smile, but he wondered what it would be like to be able to control his emotions—especially anger—more effectively. Cheryl might think it was unhealthy to bottle up emotions, but that was because she wanted to become a psychologist some day. Being able to bottle up feelings, at least sometimes, sounded pretty damn good to Jerome.

He gazed at Cheryl, and for perhaps the thousandth time, wondered how he'd ever gotten lucky enough to end up with someone like her for a girlfriend. She wore a dark blue sweatshirt that was a size too large for her trim figure, faded blue jeans and a pair of scuffed black boots. Her make-up was understated, so much so that if he hadn't been her boyfriend he'd have thought she didn't wear any at all. But then, she didn't need much. She had a natural beauty and too much make-up would've spoiled it. She wasn't gorgeous in an anorexic cover girl kind of way, but she had a glow about her, he supposed was the best way to put it. The kindness, the gentleness, the grace, the sheer goodness of her spirit seemed to shine forth from her, and that made her more beautiful in Jerome's eyes than any other woman he'd ever seen.

"Do me a solid," El said to Cheryl. "I was nagging our good friend Jerome about how he needs to relax more. You know he never listens to me, but if you nagged him..."

Cheryl laughed. "Sorry, El, but I'm not the nagging kind." She paused for a moment, then frowned as she examined Jerome's face more closely. "Still... Your eyes are bloodshot and you do have dark circles around them. Maybe you should try to relax more. The way you throw yourself into your school work and your job, it's almost like..."

"Like what?" Jerome asked.

Cheryl looked suddenly uncomfortable. "I don't know. Like you're desperate to keep yourself busy, as if you're afraid of what might happen if you don't."

Jerome wasn't sure what to say in response, but before he could think of something, a fourth voice joined in the conversation.

"Starkey doesn't need to relax. He just needs to get something that more closely resembles a life, that's all."

The three friends turned to see Pat Cottril standing in the center of the hallway, almost—but not quite—leering at them. Though Jerome hated to admit it, Pat Cottril was one of the most handsome guys in school, if not the most handsome. He was tall, muscular, with clear skin and even white teeth. His sandy brown hair was always perfect, as if he'd just stepped out of a salon, and though he had a tendency to dress down—today he was wearing a black Slipknot T-shirt and jeans with holes in both knees—his choice of wardrobe only served to accentuate his good looks by contrast. The only flaw marring his features was a puckered crescent of a scar above his left eyebrow. A scar he'd received in kindergarten, courtesy of Jerome.

Standing next to Pat on the right was Eddie Jackson and on the left was Brent Haney. Eddie was a wiry, weasel faced imitation of his lord and master, down to the rock concert T-shirt—his band of choice being Velvet Revolver—and torn jeans. Brent also resembled Cottril, but only if Pat had undergone a reverse liposuction procedure. Haney wore a plaid button shirt untucked, probably because with his gut, he couldn't keep the shirt-tail in. Cottril, Jackson and Haney; the Three Pus-keteers, as El called them, but never to their faces. El might act nutty much of the time, but he wasn't suicidal.

The sight of Cottril's smirk sent a burning jolt of fury surging through Jerome. As far as he could tell, he didn't visibly demonstrate his anger, but El stepped closer to him and Cheryl laid her hand on his arm, as if to soothe him and help keep his anger in check.

"Isn't it a little early for you to start busting my hump?" Jerome asked.

"It's never too early to offer a bit of constructive criticism," Cottril said. "If you didn't have such a loser job, then maybe you wouldn't have to work your ass off to earn your pitiful excuse for a paycheck. And if you didn't have to work so hard for slave wages, maybe you'd be able to find some chill out time for yourself. And for your girl. A fine woman like her needs attention, Starkey. Work too hard, neglect her too much, and she just might start looking around to see if she can find a better deal, know what I mean?"

Eddie and Brent grinned at their leader's display of wit.

Jerome ground his teeth and Cheryl took hold of his arm and held it tight, as if she were afraid he might lunge for Cottril. Jerome wanted to tell the son of a bitch that he worked so hard because he wanted to pay his own way through college as much as possible. So he saved as much money as he could from his job at Showtime Video and studied as hard as he could so that he might land a scholarship. Going to El's last night after work had been one of his rare attempts to relax, and what had happened? He had fallen asleep, gotten home late, gotten into an argument with Lynn and his dad, and ended up more stressed than ever. But he wasn't about to share that much of his personal life with an asshole like Pat Cottril.

"You wouldn't be talking trash about our jobs because my parents had the good sense to fire you by any chance?" El's folks owned Showtime Video, where both he and Jerome worked. Pat Cottril had worked there too, about seven months ago. He hadn't lasted long, partially because he couldn't get along with Jerome, but mostly because he couldn't get along with anyone—including customers.

"Not at all." Cottril smiled at El, but there was no humor in his eyes. "Getting fired from that shithole was the best thing that ever happened to me. If I were unlucky enough to still be working for your parents, Ellery, I'd never have gotten my job at the golf course, and then I wouldn't be raking in all the sweet dough-ray-me I make on tips."

"You're a caddy, Patrick," El said. "You lug other people's shit around. How glamorous."

"Who gives a damn about glamorous?" Cottril countered. "It's easy work, I'm outside getting some exercise and I make more money than you two losers combined." He turned away from Jerome and El to face Cheryl. "You ever want to go on a date with someone who has the cash to take you someplace better than a McDonald's dumpster, give me a call."

Cottril turned back to Jerome and gave him a smile that said, "I can take your girl from you anytime I want—and you know it."

Jerome's anger, which had been simmering just below the surface for the last several minutes, came to an abrupt and violent boil. He pulled free of Cheryl's grip and stepped toward Cottril and his two sycophants. Before any of the Three Pus-keteers could react, Jerome grabbed hold of Eddie Jackson's head with one hand and Brent Haney's with the other. He then slammed their heads against Pat Cottril's with all the strength that his anger gave him, which was quite considerable.

There was a sickening hollow sound, as of melons colliding. For a frozen instant, Jerome saw the Three Pus-keteers' eyes go wide, heard grunts of surprise and pain escape their lips. Then their heads exploded like three flesh colored piñatas, spraying the air with a grisly fountain of blood and meaty chunks of what—at least for these three idiots—passed for brains. Jerome felt gore gush onto his hands, splatter his face, soak his clothes, and as the three lifeless bodies slumped to the hallway floor, he threw back his head and laughed in dark delight.

"You still with us, Starkey? Or did your so-called brain suddenly slip a gear?"

Jerome's vision blurred, and he blinked several times. When he could see clearly again, he saw Cottril, Jackson and Haney standing right where they'd been, heads intact. Jerome glanced at Cheryl, saw she had a worried look on her face, and also saw that she still had hold of his arm. Frowning in confusion, he turned back to Cottril. Pat sneered and shook his head.

"You're a lost cause, Starkey. Absolutely pathetic." He looked at Cheryl and gave her a wink. "When—not if—you get tried of Captain Feeb here, give me a call."

"And just what would that number be?" Cheryl asked. "1-800-I'M-AN-ASSHOLE?"

El burst out laughing, but Eddie Jackson and Brent Haney looked puzzled, unsure how to react. They looked to Pat for a lead, and Cottril stared at Cheryl for a moment without expression before finally allowing his lips to stretch into a slow smile. "Good one, Garringer." He glanced at Jerome and El. "Later, dorks." Then he turned and headed off down the hallway, Jackson and Haney in tow, each at his side, but staying a half-step behind their leader. The other kids pretended not to notice them, but everyone made way to give them room to pass.

"I hate those guys," El said. "I really do."

In his mind, Jerome could still hear the hollow pop of exploding heads, could still see a geyser of gore rising into the air.

"Me too," he said.

Jerome went to his homeroom after the first bell. He was still seething from his encounter with Cottril, and he wished either Cheryl or El shared the same homeroom with him. But they didn't, so he sat at his desk, gripped the wooden surface of the table, and pressed his fingers down as hard as he could, until his knuckles turned white and his hands began to ache. He hoped that by doing this he might be able to bleed off a bit of his anger. But when the bell for first period rang, Jerome felt just as angry as before, maybe more so. Without glancing at any of the other students in the room, or at Mr Blakesly, his homeroom teacher, Jerome scooped up his books, jumped out of his chair and ran to the door. He hoped to see Cheryl or El, maybe exchange a couple of words with them as they all hurried to their first period classes. Even just the sight of one or both of their faces would help to lighten the anger roiling inside him. But he rarely saw either of them between homeroom and first period, and today was no exception.

The biology classroom was located on the bottom level of Springwood High School, and the hallway smelled of decades' worth of formaldehyde. To make matters worse, the entrance to the cafeteria was on that level too, and the smells of cooking food often drifted into the hall and mixed with the formaldehyde to form a stomach-churning miasma of stench. Some of the kids that Jerome passed nodded and smiled at him, and some even said, "Hi," but most ignored him as if he didn't exist. Springwood was a small enough community for most of the students to at least know each other by sight, but that didn't mean everyone was best buddies. But Jerome didn't take being snubbed personally. It wasn't uncommon for people to be inwardly focused, so wrapped up in their own problems that they were barely aware of the world around them—especially here in Springwood.

Jerome had lived in Springwood all his life, and on the surface it appeared to be a pleasant Midwestern town nestled amidst picturesque farmland, only a convenient short drive from larger metropolitan areas. Maybe the people who lived here weren't rich, but no one was in danger of starving any time soon. Springwood was a place people moved to, not away from. The motto might as well have been: "Springwood: Official Home of the Good Life".

And yet…

People often seemed preoccupied here. Worried, depressed, even afraid. Not all the time, though. It came in waves, like a bad flu season that rolled around every few years. People would become quiet and withdrawn, and many of them seemed as if they hadn't been sleeping well. Bloodshot eyes, the flesh around them dark and puffy.

Just like me, Jerome thought with a start of sudden realization.

Something else happened during these times when, as his dad said, a "pall"—whatever that was—fell over Springwood. Death came to town. There would be a rash of suicides or murders, sometimes both, and then, just as suddenly as it had come, it would end, like a bad storm that had finally blown over.

As Jerome walked into Mr Houser's classroom, he put aside such thoughts. It wasn't difficult. Anyone who'd lived in Springwood for any length of time got used to not thinking about certain things if they wanted to be able to function from one day to the next. So by the time Jerome took his assigned seat, laid his bio book on the desk and tucked his extra books in the wire basket attached to the bottom of his chair, he'd forgotten about his dark musings, but their emotional aftertaste lingered in his mind.

"All right, you can make the first incision. Try not to be squeamish, now. These animals are quite dead—all humanely euthanized."

Several of the students whooped, one said, "Yeah!" while a few others groaned in reluctance. Still, they all picked up their scalpels, bent over the dead frogs pinned to the cutting boards, and went to work with nervous giggles and muted "*Eeeews*." The biology lab was in the rear of the classroom, though "lab" was too grandiose a term. It consisted of two long tables with black formica tops and built-in drawers and cabinets for holding supplies. The students stood in pairs, two to a workstation, as they began their latest adventure in dissection. Except Jerome. There were an odd number of students in the class, so someone had to do without a lab partner, and Jerome—never the most sociable of people—was only too happy to volunteer to go it alone. Unfortunately, that meant Mr Houser checked on him more often than the others.

Before Jerome could touch the blade of his scalpel to the frog's rubbery white belly, Mr Houser was at his side.

"Don't cut too deeply, now. You'll damage the internal organs if you do. You just want to make enough of an opening in the skin so you can peel it back and pin it down."

Jerome bristled. He'd paid attention when Mr Houser had first instructed the class on how to proceed. And even if Jerome hadn't, he wasn't an idiot. He had more than enough common sense not to hack the frog to pieces with his first incision. But instead of saying this to Mr Houser, Jerome merely nodded and made a noncommittal *mmm-hmm* sound. He didn't look up from the frog, hoping that if he didn't make eye contact, Mr Houser would wander off and go pester someone else, leaving Jerome to get on with his work.

Mr Houser was a small thin man who seemed to almost get lost in his white lab coat. He had short black hair, a neatly trimmed black mustache and black framed glasses. His shirt was white, his pants, socks and shoes black. His salt and pepper color scheme was ruined by his ruddy brown complexion, however.

The teacher hovered at Jerome's elbow for a moment longer before finally saying, "I'll leave you to it, then," and moving on.

Jerome let out a grateful sigh. He hated anyone watching him while he worked, with the exception of Cheryl or El, and even they made him feel uncomfortably self-conscious at times. But this time he was alone. Time to play frog coroner. He placed the tip of his scalpel blade at a point just below the underside of the frog's mouth and pressed down until the tip dimpled the skin. He pressed a bit harder and the white flesh pulled away from the metal as if it were a laser. Now that his dissecting cherry had been popped, Jerome began to draw the scalpel toward him, cutting a line across the frog's abdomen.

That's when the frog's left rear foot twitched.

Jerome's hand froze in mid-cut. He remained motionless as he stared at the frog's leg, waiting to see if it would twitch again. Seconds ticked by, but the frog remained still.

Probably just a reflex, Jerome told himself. He must've hit a nerve or muscle or something, which in turn caused the leg to move. He resumed cutting.

The right front foot twitched this time.

Jerome felt a crawling sensation on the back of his neck, and he slowly pulled the scalpel away from the frog.

The amphibian started screaming. It wasn't the sort of sound an animal would make—it was a very human scream; loud, high-pitched, filled with pain and terror. The frog began thrashing on the cutting board, as if desperate to pull itself free and escape. Its screams continued, increasing in volume, the sound sending electric chills racing along Jerome's spine. He turned to look for Mr Houser, intending to call the teacher over to help him deal with the screaming frog. But Jerome saw that he wasn't the only student whose supposedly dead dissection subject had suddenly started showing signs of life. The frogs on all the cutting boards—many of which were in a more advanced state of dissection than his—were thrashing about, and all of them were shrieking in agony.

Though their frogs were all screaming and thrashing, none of Jerome's fellow student's seemed to notice. They kept right on cutting.

"You son of a bitch! You sliced me open!"

Jerome turned back toward the sound of the tiny voice. His frog had lifted its head and was glaring at him with moist, bulbous eyes.

"What did I ever do to you, buddy? One minute I'm minding my own business, hanging out at the edge of my pond, looking to score a few juicy flies for lunch, and the next thing I know, some obnoxious teenager with a scalpel is opening me up!" The frog's voice sounded perfectly human, except that its volume was lower, no doubt due to the size of the mouth, throat and lungs that produced it.

Jerome didn't know what to say, didn't know if he even could speak, to address this creature's accusations, so he just stood and stared.

"I'll get you, you damn butcher!" The frog tugged its right front leg free of the pins that held it down—ripping off several hunks of skin in the process—then reached down toward the incision Jerome had made.

"You wanna see my guts so bad, why don't you take a close-up look?" The frog jammed its small hand into the opening in its abdomen, withdrew a length of intestine, and hurled it at Jerome. The coiled loop flew through the air toward the boy, but since it was still attached to the frog, it drew taut and stopped well short of hitting Jerome. The intestine plopped back onto the frog's open gullet, and the amphibian began thrashing even more violently, as if furious that its throw hadn't reached its tormentor.

"Just you wait until I get loose! I'm gonna crawl right up your—"

Jerome flipped the scalpel around until he was holding it point downward. He gripped the handle tight and then slammed the blade down into the foul-mouthed frog. Once, twice, three times. He continued stabbing the amphibian with increasing ferocity until there was nothing left but shredded meat and splintered bone.

When Jerome finished, he stood for a moment, breathing heavily. And that's when he became aware of the silence. He looked up and saw that his classmates were all staring at him, some with wide eyed fear, others with amused smirks. But there was one person in the room who clearly was not amused.

Mr Houser came over to Jerome, his ruddy complexion darkened to beet red.

"Just what the hell was that all about, Mr Starkey?" the biology teacher demanded.

Jerome glanced at the other students' frogs. None of them were moving, and from the way they remained pinned down, it looked as if they'd never moved at all.

"I don't know," Jerome said truthfully.

"Really. Well, maybe you'll be able to figure it out in detention tonight." He nodded toward the drawn and quartered amphibian. "Throw that mess away and get a fresh frog. And this time, try not to go psycho on it, okay?"

A number of the students laughed as Mr Houser walked away. But Jerome wasn't laughing. Not at all.

SIX

"Look who decided to grace us with his presence this fine afternoon."

Jerome groaned inwardly as he walked into the room. Bad enough that he'd been assigned detention, but having to serve it with Pat Cottril was infinitely worse. At least Cottril's buddies weren't among the half dozen other kids—mostly males—in the room.

"Grab a seat, sit down and be quiet. Make any trouble and you'll be back here again tomorrow."

The man sitting at the desk, whose face was hidden by the copy of *USA Today* he was reading, was Mr Neilson, one of the math teachers. Despite his temper, Jerome hadn't been in detention since junior high, and he'd never had Mr Neilson as a teacher, but he knew the man by reputation. All the kids in Springwood High did.

Along with teaching, Neilson was also a wrestling coach, and had an appropriately belligerent attitude to go along with the job. This same attitude also made him a natural to oversee the malefactors sentenced to afternoon detention.

Jerome decided it was best to keep his mouth shut and do what the man said. Since there were plenty of open seats, he took one in the front near the door, as far away from Cottril—who sat in the back—as possible.

"What did you do to get tossed in here with the rest of us criminals, Starkey?" Cottril asked.

Jerome ignored him and sat down.

Mr Neilson lowered his paper and glared at Cottril. "What part of 'shut up' don't you understand?"

Cottril scowled, but he didn't respond. Mr Neilson scowled right back, and he was far more skilled at it. A moment later, Cottril broke eye contact and looked out the window. Smirking over his victory, Neilson raised his paper and returned to reading.

Cottril had hated Jerome for years, ever since they'd been five. They'd both been in the same kindergarten class, and even then the basic make up of their individual personalities was in place. Jerome tended to be quiet and keep to himself not because he was shy, but because he didn't want to risk getting angry at anyone. And Cottril... Even then he was an asshole, just a smaller one.

They were out on the playground one January day. It had snowed several inches the night before, but, as was normal for Ohio, the weather had suddenly shifted to the low forties. The snow was already starting to melt, but there was enough left to play in during recess, which was all the kids cared about.

Cottril was throwing snowballs at several other kids, mostly girls. He was alone; Eddie Jackson was in another class and Brent Haney wouldn't move to Springwood for a couple more years. Jerome, as usual, was minding his own business, rolling a snowball around to increase its size so that it might make a suitable foundation for a snowman, when something cold and wet smacked him on the back of his neck. The snowball splattered apart on impact, and some of it slid down beneath Jerome's shirt. A finger of ice traced the length of his spine, though the sensation of cold did nothing to keep Jerome cool. Temper flaring like a sudden wildfire, he whirled around to see who had thrown the snowball at him. He wasn't surprised to see Cottril standing several yards away, pointing at him and laughing.

Jerome had only a handful of years so far to learn how to control his temper—so though he knew he shouldn't, that it would only get him in trouble with his dad when he got home, his dad, who had just legally adopted Jerome, changing the boy's last name from Larkin to Starkey—he started walking toward Pat Cottril.

Pat didn't have any cronies to gloat to yet, but enough of the other children on the playground had turned to witness what was happening to give him a fairly good sized audience.

"What's the matter, kid? Some snow go down your pants?"

These were kindergartners. Anything to do with bathrooms, butts, or a combination of the two was considered the height of hilarity. A number of bystanders giggled at Cottril's display of wit. Encouraged by his audience's response, Cottril continued.

"I bet your butt's turning blue... or maybe your pee-pee is!"

More laughter, mixed with a few gasps from children who'd never imagined they'd ever hear anyone say that sort of thing out loud, let alone on school grounds.

Jerome didn't respond, didn't react. He just kept walking toward Cottril. Pat was starting to get nervous. His eyes shifted back and forth from Jerome to his audience, and if no one had been watching, perhaps Cottril would have turned and run from Jerome. But they were watching—especially the girls—and Cottril held his ground.

"I'm gonna call you 'Snowball Butt' from now on! What do you think about that?"

Jerome had closed to within a few feet of Cottril, and he started running. Cottril squealed as Jerome jumped on him and began pounding the shit out of him with his tiny five year-old fists. Jerome might not have possessed the muscle to do much damage yet, but what he lacked in strength, he more than made up for in fury. Blow after blow rained down on Cottril, striking him on the head, on the shoulders, the chest, the face. He had sobbed, tears gushed from the corners of his eyes and snot had run from his nostrils like they were twin faucets. He begged Jerome to stop, threatened to tell a teacher, called out for his mommy, as if she might somehow psychically detect her son was in trouble and come rushing to his aid.

To be fair, Cottril did attempt to block Jerome's blows, though mostly all he managed to do was get hit on the arm instead of the inner body. Cottril started flailing his arms wildly then, and by sheer luck he managed to connect a fist with Jerome's chin. As frightened as Cottril was, the blow had almost no power to it, but Jerome's tongue had been protruding from the corner of his mouth while he beat on Cottril, and thanks to the love tap on the chin, his teeth clacked together, biting into tongue. Blood spewed from the cut, running out of his mouth, dribbling over his lips and down his chin to splatter onto Cottril's coat. The injury hurt, but Jerome really didn't care about that. What he cared about was the look of smug triumph that Cottril gave him.

"I got you! I got you and made you bleed, you… you a-hole!"

The kids whose ears were sensitive to such language gasped again, while everyone else just laughed.

As blood continued to drip from Jerome's mouth and onto Cottril's coat, Pat started laughing and repeated in a sing-song voice, "I got you, I got you. Oh yes, I got you..."

Jerome's pain dwindled to an infinitesimal spark as his anger surged to new heights. He let out a cry of rage that held only the most rudimentary relationship to a human voice, and then he knelt down, sank his teeth into the skin above Cottril's left eyebrow, and bit down hard. As white hot agony blazed across Cottril's nerve-endings, he shrieked like a wounded animal and struggled to pull free of his attacker. But Jerome refused to let go, and he was still holding the skin from Cottril's forehead between his teeth when adult hands suddenly had hold of him, and adult voices—some gentle, some stern, all alarmed—urged him to open his mouth and let Cottril go. It took five minutes for the teachers, who'd been summoned by Cottril's screams, to get Jerome calmed down enough to let go of Pat's flesh without tearing any off. Cottril, wailing as if he thought he was going to die any second, was whisked off to the school nurse's office, while Jerome was hauled off to the principal's, there to await the arrival of his father, whom the principal had called at work.

Seventeen year-old Jerome believed that one of the reasons Cottril hated him (not that someone like him needed an excuse to hate) was because of the scar on his forehead that no amount of stitches or surgery had been able to entirely remove. But much more than that, Jerome had humiliated him in front of other kids—especially girls. This was an absolutely unforgivable crime as far as Cottril was concerned. And so they'd been enemies ever since, and while Jerome was usually able to avoid Cottril most of the time, Cottril made it a habit—no, more like his holy mission—to irritate Jerome as much as possible. Like this morning, and like now.

Jerome was glad to see Mr Neilson put Cottril in his place. It was the first positive thing that had happened to him since biology class—not counting lunch with Cheryl and El, that is, though neither of them had been able to do much to cheer him up, regardless of how hard they'd tried. He hadn't told them the truth about what had happened; not the whole truth, anyway. How could you explain to your girlfriend and your best friend that you'd had a hallucination and murdered what you thought had been a talking, intestine-throwing frog? Since neither of them were in the class, he'd told them he'd gotten into an argument with his lab partner (not that he had one), gotten pissed off, lost his temper and sliced up the frog. Given his difficulty managing anger, both Cheryl and El had no trouble accepting his story, only they were more worried about him than ever before. Cheryl had gone so far as to suggest he might consider going to see a counselor or something. But just because a guy got mad from time to time didn't mean he was crazy, right?

What about a guy who thinks dead frogs can talk, a voice inside his mind whispered?

Jerome decided to ignore that thought and get busy on some homework. He unzipped his backpack, took out his world history book, opened it and started reading about the construction of the Great Wall of China. It was interesting enough, but it wasn't long before his mind started to wander.

He didn't have to worry about dad or Lynn finding out about his detention. The school didn't send a note home when you were in high school, and he was scheduled to work at the video store this afternoon, so it wouldn't seem all that strange that he didn't come home immediately after school. He often hung out with El or Crystal before going to work, too. Speaking of his friends, El had gone to the store to smooth things over with his parents so Jerome wouldn't get in trouble for coming in late. And even though Jerome had told Cheryl to go on home so she wouldn't waste her time, she'd insisted on waiting for him outside the school.

"It's only forty-five minutes," she'd said, "plus it's a nice day outside. I'll sit under a tree and do some homework."

Despite urging her to go home, Jerome had been pleased that she'd chosen to wait, until it had occurred to him that perhaps she was waiting not so much out of a desire to be with him, but because she was worried about him, afraid his temper would flare up and get him into even more trouble. Not for the first time he wondered if Cheryl would be better off without him. Despite his best efforts to control his temper, it was becoming increasingly difficult as time went by. He hated the way his temper worried Cheryl. He'd never been angry with her before, nor with El, either. But just being around him and watching him struggle to control his anger seemed to bring her so much pain. And the last thing in the world that he wanted to do was hurt her, even unintentionally.

"If you really loved her, Starkey, you'd break up with her."

Jerome whirled around to face a grinning Cottril.

"What did you say?"

"You care for Cheryl, right? Maybe even love her, or at least think that you do. Then the best thing you can do for her is to break up with her and stay out of her life before you ruin it completely. If you really do love her, that is. Maybe you don't."

Jerome couldn't believe what he was hearing. He had no trouble believing that Cottril would say these things, but to say them here, now, with Mr Neilson present…

Jerome turned to glance at the teacher. Neilson still sat at his desk, paper held up in front of his face. He didn't say anything, didn't so much as move. It seemed as if he hadn't heard what Cottril had said, but that didn't seem possible. Even if Neilson were somehow so caught up in reading that he hadn't heard every word, Cottril had spoken in a normal tone of voice, he hadn't whispered, and Neilson had to at least be aware that Cottril had spoken.

Jerome glanced at his fellow inmates, but none of the other kids sentenced to detention gave any indication that they had heard Cottril either. They stared off into space, glanced out the window, sat with their heads down on their desktops, napping.

"But then again, maybe Cheryl's already wised up, eh, Starkey?"

Cottril stood and pulled his Slipknot T-shirt over his head. His chest was hairless, lean, ribs standing out as if he were a famine victim instead of a middle-class Ohio teenager. But what grabbed and held Jerome's attention was the large tattoo that covered Cottril's chest. It was a detailed rendering of Cheryl and Cottril himself—and they were kissing. Jerome could only stare in stunned amazement at the tattoo, while Cottril stood bare chested, grinning at him. As Jerome watched, the tattoo images of Cheryl and Cottril began to move, as if Cottril's chest were a flesh-screen playing a realistic cartoon. They continued kissing, making out with increasing passion and fervor. Lips, tongues, hands roamed over one another, and clothes began to come off. Soon both Cheryl and Cottril were naked and doing more than just kissing. A lot more.

And Jerome thought he could actually hear the two of them—heavy, lust filled breaths, tremulous sighs, pleasure-induced moans...

Cottril's grin widened further. "Does she make those kind of sounds when she's with you, Starkey? Bet she doesn't."

Jerome knew something was wrong here; there was no way this could be real. He'd never seen a tattoo of near photographic quality like this before, let alone one that actually moved. But despite this knowledge, he couldn't stop his anger from rising. His anger didn't care whether the image on Cottril's chest was real or not, didn't care how mere ink injected beneath the skin could possibly be alive and animated. All it cared about was making the image stop and making Cottril pay for showing it to him.

Jerome bolted out of his chair and ran toward Cottril, shoving empty desks and chairs out of his way as he went. The other students in detention were snapped out of whatever daze they'd been in and some stared at Jerome, some laughed and some scrambled to get the hell out of his way. Dimly, Jerome was aware of someone shouting his name; an adult, he thought, though he wasn't certain. But whoever it was and whatever they wanted would just have to wait until he'd dealt with Cottril.

As Jerome drew near his grinning nemesis, he suddenly became aware of two Cottrils—two distinct and different images, as if Jerome were seeing a different one with each eye and his brain was having trouble reconciling the separate pictures. In one image, Cottril was bare-chested and grinning as his tattoo avatar cavorted with

Jerome's girlfriend. But in the second image, Cottril was still sitting at his desk, shirt on, and looking at Jerome with wide, confused eyes that held more than a hint of fear. Just as Jerome reached Cottril, the rational part of his mind—which was reduced to a small quiet voice compared to the furious roaring of his anger—suggested that Jerome wait to sort out the separate images before he did anything rash. But it was too late.

Jerome's hands shot out and grabbed Cottril's neck. Cottril's throat made a wet clicking sound as Jerome tightened his grip and began to squeeze. Cottril grabbed Jerome's wrists and tried to tear his hands from his neck, but Jerome's strength was fueled by his rage, and Cottril couldn't so much as budge his hands. Cottril's face began to darken, and his eyes bulged out like those of a frog—a dead frog pinned down and ready for dissection. Cottril kicked and thrashed, trying to dislodge Jerome's grip, but without success. Jerome continued to squeeze harder…

He felt other hands on him, pulling at his shoulders, tugging at his arms, but he ignored the sensations. Cottril deserved nothing less than death for profaning Cheryl's image like that, and that's exactly what Jerome intended to give him. He squeezed even harder, and Cottril's already red face began to edge toward purple. Cottril was clawing at Jerome's hands now, nails digging into the flesh of Jerome's fingers, ripping out tiny chunks of skin and causing blood to well forth.

Jerome was distantly aware of the blood, and the pain that came along with it, but he ignored it. It didn't matter, nothing mattered, except Cottril's death.

He heard shouting, felt the hands gripping him begin to pull him backward. There were too many hands for Jerome to resist, and he felt his fingers begin to slip away from Cottril's throat. Jerome let out a cry of rage and frustration as his grip was finally broken and Cottril gasped for air. He saw Cottril's image—the seated Cottril, the one still wearing his shirt—recede as he was pulled backward, and he tried to break free of whoever had hold of him, but they were too many and they were too strong.

"I don't know… what the hell's… wrong with you, boy," the adult voice said between gulps of air, "but you'd better… calm the fuck down now!"

Jerome—still clawing the air as if he might get hold of Cottril's throat once more—recognized the voice as belonging to an adult male, but he couldn't quite place it. Was it his dad? No, the voice was too low, the tone too harsh. And then he remembered: Neilson—detention—and just like that, his anger had subsided. It didn't drain away, didn't fade. One second it was there, blazing as fiercely as ever, and the next it was just gone, as if it had never existed. He stopped struggling, and Neilson and the others, who he realized were other young men sentenced to detention like himself, were able to pull him out of the room and into the hallway.

Just before he was pulled through the door and into the hall, he looked back at Cottril, saw the jackass sitting at his desk and rubbing his throat with his bare hands. When Cottril saw Jerome looking at him, he mouthed the words, "You're dead!" before Jerome was pulled all the way out of the room and Cottril was lost to sight.

SEVEN

"Explain yourself."

The words were delivered with just the right mix of authority and concern, intended to show Jerome that while Assistant Principal LeClair didn't intend to put up with any nonsense, she still cared about Jerome as a person. Jerome knew she was just doing her job and that she didn't care about him in the slightest. Still, he found himself responding to her tone nevertheless.

"Cottril—I mean, Pat—came up to me and a couple of my friends before first bell this morning. He said some things, tossed a couple insults around, then left. He made me mad, but I figured he wasn't worth getting into trouble over, so I left him alone."

Ms LeClair's office was small, but there was more than enough room for the two of them—him in front of the desk, her behind it. The surface of her desk was bare (he thought of a bumper sticker he'd seen once: A clean desk is a sign of a SICK mind!), with the exception of her PC, phone and a single manila folder full of papers, and he knew he that he was looking at an almost mythic document: his permanent record. There were framed diplomas on the walls—bachelor's and master's degrees—but otherwise the office had little in the way of decorative touches. A potted fern sitting atop a gray filing cabinet, a wall calendar with images of Japanese wood-block art and a plaque mounted on the wall that, "With many thanks for ten years of exemplary service to the Springwood School District."

Jerome had never seen that plaque before, and he'd had no idea that Ms LeClair had been at the high school for that long. She looked too young to have worked anywhere for ten years. She was an attractive woman with long, perfectly styled brown hair, gold bracelets on her wrists and gold earrings in both ears. She wore a long-sleeved white blouse and a light gray skirt that came to the top of her knees. Black open-toed shoes completed her ensemble, allowing Jerome to see that while she wore no nail polish on her fingers, her toenails were painted cherry red. Every guy in school lusted after her—especially with that authoritative dominatrix thing she had going—but she had a reputation as a hard-ass, and few of them wanted to end up where Jerome was.

Ms LeClair eyed him skeptically. "So you decided to wait and get revenge in detention?"

"I didn't decide anything," Jerome said, doing his best to keep the frustration he felt out of his voice and not quite succeeding. "It just kind of... happened."

Ms LeClair regarded him silently for several moments, as if trying to determine whether he was mocking her. Finally, she said, "Tell me, Jerome, how can someone choking another human being just kind of happen?"

Jerome started to explain, but then he stopped himself. What would Ms LeClair think if he told her about his vision of Cottril with an animated tattoo? Or about his hallucination of the talking frog in biology class? She'd think he was going crazy. Hell, *he* thought he was going crazy! So he kept his mouth shut and stared down at the floor.

"If you don't have an explanation for your attack on Pat Cottril, maybe you can tell me about biology class today. Mr Houser said you mutilated a frog you were supposed to be dissecting... Just cut it to pieces. And quite violently, I might add."

Jerome said the first thing that came to his mind. "It was a joke, you know?"

"A joke?" she repeated, as if it were the lamest explanation she'd ever heard during her ten years of exemplary service at Springwood High.

Jerome shrugged—the teenager's all-purpose response to any adult question. "I admit it was stupid. I apologized to Mr Houser, and he let me work on another frog."

"I might be more inclined to accept your story, Jerome, if you hadn't demonstrated violent behavior toward Pat Cottril later in the day. From what Mr Neilson said, you might well have killed the boy if he and some of the other students in detention hadn't managed to pull you off of him. Mr Neilson was so disturbed by your violent actions that he was in favor of me calling the police. In fact, he didn't want me to meet with you alone."

Jerome couldn't believe what he was hearing. "You're making me sound like I'm some sort of criminal!"

"I don't think that, Jerome. Obviously, or I would have followed Mr Neilson's advice." She looked down at the folder on her desk, opened it, and began shuffling through the papers it held. "I had a chance to glance over your file while you were waiting to see me. You've had a number of anger-related incidents over the years. Including, I noted, one with Pat Cottril in kindergarten." She closed the folder and looked up at him once more. "To be honest, Jerome, one of the first things we suspect in an incident such as your attack on Pat Cottril today is drug use—especially since you demonstrated erratic behavior earlier in Mr Houser's class."

"I don't do drugs," Jerome said, and it was true. He had enough problems controlling his anger without using chemicals that might make it even harder for him to keep his emotions in check. "Call the school nurse. She can test me right now if you want."

"Thank you, but that won't be necessary." Ms LeClair paused, as if trying to determine the best way to proceed. "From time to time, Jerome, certain... disturbances occur here in Springwood. Outbreaks of violence that often involve young people and their, ah, dreams." She leaned forward, suddenly intense. "Tell me, Jerome, have you been having any... unusual dreams lately?"

Give Mommy a kiss goodbye...

"Not really. I don't remember my dreams much."

Ms LeClair looked at him a moment longer before finally nodding and sitting back in her chair. For some reason, she seemed strangely relieved. "In that case, from the pattern I saw in your file, I suspect that you might have a problem of a different sort. There are certain conditions—sometimes psychological, sometimes biochemical, often a combination—in which a person experiences sudden unexplained flare-ups of anger and violent behavior. I believe there's a chance you may be suffering from one of these conditions, Jerome. Have you ever spoken to anyone—your parents, a doctor, a clergy man—about your anger?"

Jerome's instinct was to tell Ms LeClair that she was off base, that he didn't have any problem with anger. He'd spent his whole life trying to hide his anger—along with the shame it caused—from adults. But he took a deep breath and let it out in a long sigh. Maybe it was time that he stopped fighting. Or at least, stopped fighting alone.

"Just my friends," Jerome said in a quiet voice.

"I should suspend you for your attack on Pat Cottril," Ms LeClair said. "But if you're willing to go talk to a doctor at Westin Hills about these angry feelings you experience, I won't. To be honest, I'm more interested in getting you the help that you need instead of punishing you. What do you think?"

Though he wasn't sure why, Jerome shuddered at Ms LeClair's mention of Westin Hills Psychiatric Hospital. It was a mental health and drug rehabilitation center on the outskirts of town, no different than hundreds of others throughout the country. Sure, there were stories about it, rumors that it hadn't always been a modern hospital. Supposedly at one point in the past it had been closer to a medieval asylum for the insane, a place where the most dangerous madmen were locked away—and even then, atrocities too horrible to talk about were committed behind its walls.

Every town has a "bad place", somewhere that is reputed to be intrinsically evil, where awful events once occurred and the spirits of the vengeful dead are purported to linger. But Jerome knew all that stuff was a crock of shit. Sure, bad things did happen sometimes, but that was life. The junk about evil spirits people made up out of ignorance and sheer small-town boredom. Westin Hills was a hospital, and that's all it was. Nothing whatsoever to be afraid of. Besides, Ms LeClair's offer might well be the opportunity he'd been hoping for—a chance for him finally to get a handle on his emotions and start living a normal life.

"Okay," he said.

Ms LeClair smiled. "Good. I'll have to talk to your parents about it and get their permission, though."

"I understand." Jerome was surprised at the feeling of relief that washed over him. It was as if a tension that he'd carried for so long he wasn't even aware of it was finally beginning to drain away.

"All right, then. I'll call tonight after—" But Ms LeClair's phone rang before she could finish her sentence. "Excuse me." She picked up the receiver. "Yes? Well, can't it wait, Patty? I'm talking with a student and..." She sighed. "Very well, I'll be right out." She hung up the phone and looked at Jerome. "It seems the office secretary is having problems with her e-mail program and needs my help. It'll only take a moment, so if you don't mind waiting..."

"Go ahead."

"Thank you. I won't be more than a minute or two, and then we can finish up our discussion and you can be on your way."

She gave him a smile, one so genuine that it made him believe he'd been wrong about her. She wasn't just doing her job; she really did care. Then she came out from behind her desk, walked past him and out of the office, closing the door behind her.

Alone for the moment, Jerome slumped back in his chair as a sensation of weariness came over him. He'd been through a lot today, and he felt emotionally drained. When he got out of here, he'd have to see if he could go home and sneak in a nap before having to go in to work at the video store. He hoped El's parents would understand, especially once he told them the reason he was late and that he was finally going to get some help.

He sighed and closed his eyes, intending only to rest them for a moment until Ms LeClair returned. But they'd only been closed a few seconds when the office door burst open. Jerome turned toward the sudden noise and saw a pair of burly men in white uniforms heading toward him. Before he could rise from his chair, they each took hold of one of his arms with vice-like grips and held him down.

"What the hell are you doing? Let me go!"

Jerome struggled, but no matter how hard he tried, he couldn't break free from his two captors.

"You might as well not fight it, Jerome," the one holding onto his right arm said.

"It'll be a lot easier on you if you relax," the man's partner said, but then quickly added, "not!"

There was something oddly familiar about their voices. He looked at the men, first one, then the other. When they'd come at him they'd had normal—if nondescript—faces. But now both looked exactly the same: bald, flame-scarred skin, grinning yellow teeth and wide bloodshot eyes that danced with equal measures of madness and malice. Each of the hideous men had a nametag on his uniform, and both read the same: WESTIN HILLS PSYCHIATRIC HOSPITAL, F KRUEGER.

It was the man from his dream last night, Freddy, times two.

"You're not real," Jerome said. "Neither of you! I just fell asleep while waiting for Ms LeClair to get back, that's all. She'll come into the office—her real office—any minute now, and I'll wake up and you'll be gone!"

Both of the Freddys cackled.

"You wish!" said the one on the right.

"For you, it doesn't matter," the second one said. "Asleep or awake."

"We're always there!" they finished together.

At that moment, Ms LeClair came walking back into her office, exactly as Jerome had predicted.

"Ah, good. I see you have the situation well in hand."

"He's putting up a fight," Freddy One said.

"But it's nothing we can't handle," Freddy Two added.

"Good, good. But I think the procedure will go more smoothly if we restrain him a bit more… *securely*, don't you?"

Ms LeClair gestured, and Jerome hissed in pain. He looked down to see that his arms—from wrist to elbow—were now bound to the chair with loops of silvery razor wire. The wire cut into his flesh and thick drops of blood began to patter to the floor. Now that the razor wire was in place, the two Freddys let go of him, though they remained standing right next to his chair.

"I wouldn't struggle too much," Ms LeClair said. "You don't want to slice your hands off, and we certainly don't want them damaged. We have plans for those hands of yours, Jerome, and we'd hate to see them go to waste." She smiled. "As much fun as that might be."

Ms LeClair raised her left hand, and Jerome saw she was wearing a brown glove with metal claws attached. She slashed her face with the finger knives, her skin parted like tissue paper, and her features fell away to reveal yet another grinning Freddy beneath. The pieces of Ms LeClair's discarded face, hair included, evaporated like mist when they hit the floor.

"I'd say 'surprise,'" Freddy Three said, "but I bet you aren't, are you?"

The other two Freddys chuckled at this. Freddy Three still wore Ms LeClair's blouse and skirt, but instead of making him look ridiculous, the outfit somehow made him seem even more sinister than before. He stepped up to Jerome and touched the tip of the blade attached to his index finger to the soft underside of Jerome's jaw. The moment the metal came in contact with Jerome's skin, he drew in a hissing breath of air. The metal was damn cold, and the frigid temperature penetrated Jerome's bones and radiated cold throughout his body.

Freddy leaned closer, allowing Jerome to get a whiff of the foul odor wafting from his open mouth. Inhaling Freddy's breath was like dunking your nose in raw sewage in which large chunks of rotting animal flesh had been marinating for several weeks. His nasal passages and throat felt suddenly thick and coated with the stench of Freddy's rancid breath.

"Got a news flash for you, Jerome. You've been a pet project of mine for the last seventeen years. I haven't been able to keep up with you the way I would've liked during that time, thanks to the dreamcatcher your bitch of an aunt gave you, but now that you and I have been reunited, you can bet I'm going to make up for lost time."

Freddy pulled his finger-blade away from Jerome's chin, turned it downward, then hooked the tip over the collar of his shirt until it touched the first button. He put a bit of pressure on it, and the button popped off. Freddy repeated this procedure until every button had been sliced away and Jerome's shirt hung open to reveal his scrawny white chest beneath. When that was done, Freddy nodded to his other two selves, and they each put a hand on Jerome's shoulders to steady him.

"Tell me something, Jerome. Ever hear of a little guy named Pinnochio?"

Despite the pain of his wounds and his growing fear, Jerome answered. "I saw the cartoon when I was a kid."

Freddy leaned forward and practically shouted his reply. "I don't mean the cutesy wutesy Disney version! I'm talking about the real deal, the actual story that started it all!"

Jerome shook his head.

"Then permit me to smarten you up, kid. The story begins and goes along pretty much the same as the wimp-ass version you're used to—without all the sickly sweet songs, of course. A lonely woodcarver makes a marionette and wishes it could be a living boy to keep him company. The puppet, which he of course names Pinnochio, comes to life and decides to go off and seek his fortune. A cricket warns old woodenhead against going, tells him that he'll be breaking Gepetto's heart if he leaves. Pinocchio considers the cricket's advice for a moment before crushing the obnoxious little bug beneath one of his wooden feet and heading off into the big wide world to have himself a little fun."

"That's awful!" Jerome said.

Freddy Three shrugged. "That's fairy tales for you. They can be awfully 'Grimm' sometimes. Your situation is similar, Jerome. I'm Gepetto and you're my puppet. But before I can pull your strings, I need to squash a nasty little thing you've picked up over the years I was forced to neglect you."

"What's that?" Jerome said.

Freddy grinned. "A conscience." He jammed his knife-glove into Jerome's bare abdomen, and the boy screamed as he felt the icy blades pierce skin and muscle before sinking deep into his soft parts. Jerome tried to pull away from the blades buried in his gut, but the razor wire around his forearms held him fast to the chair, as did the other two Freddys standing behind him. Jerome continued to scream as Freddy explored his insides, stirring his knives around as if he were looking for something. The pain was intolerable and just as Jerome thought he was going to pass out, Freddy shouted, "Gotcha!" and yanked his finger-claws out of Jerome's gut in a spray of blood and chunks of shredded intestine. Jerome felt something slipping out of him, heard something soft and wet hit the floor with a moist smack, and he realized with horror that he'd been disemboweled.

Freddy held up his claw-glove and through blurry, tear-stained eyes, Jerome saw that a tiny squirming insect was speared on the tip of the index finger-claw. It was a cricket.

With a flick of his claw, Freddy popped the cricket into his mouth and crunched it between his crooked, yellow teeth.

"Not bad," Freddy said as he chewed thoughtfully. "Could use a little salt, though."

Freddy laughed then, his voice a cross between fingernails raking a chalkboard and bones caught in a meat grinder. The sound cut through Jerome more effectively than Freddy's claws ever could—and it cut far deeper, too. Deeper than meat and organs, deeper than bone or marrow. It cut into Jerome's very soul.

Fury beyond anything he'd ever known erupted in Jerome, wild, crazed power as if every cell in his being was suddenly aflame. Gone were the pain of his injuries, the horror of being mutilated, the fear that he was going to die. All that remained was Freddy, that damn laughter of his, and the overwhelming need to snuff it out once and for all...

Jerome yanked at the razor wire restraints that bound him to the chair. The razors stripped the outer flesh from his arms as Jerome pulled them free. Both arms were raw, bloody messes from the elbow down, but Jerome didn't care; all he cared about was getting his blood-slick hands on Freddy.

The other two Freddys—the ones dressed as hospital orderlies—tried to stop him, but he shrugged them off with ease, as if they possessed no more strength than a pair of sickly toddlers. Jerome ran behind Ms LeClair's desk, opened the middle drawer and found what he was looking for: scissors. He wrapped his fingers around the handle, and when one of the white-coat Freddys came at him, he stabbed the son of a bitch in the throat. Blood sprayed from the wound as if the fluid in the orderly's circulatory system was under high pressure, and his coat wasn't so white anymore. As the first orderly slumped to the office floor, the second came at Jerome, with the same results. As the two Freddy doppelgängers lay bleeding to death on the floor, Jerome turned to the last Freddy, scissors gripped tight, blood dripping from their tips.

Far from being upset at seeing his two other selves taken out by a scissors wielding punk, the remaining Freddy seemed to find it hilarious. He roared with laughter, his mouth seeming to stretch wider… wider… Far wider than a human mouth could, and still it stretched further, until Jerome could no longer see those bloodshot eyes full of madness and bloodlust, could no longer see the scarred and cracked skin, the witch-hook nose, the crooked yellow teeth, until all that remained was the darkness that swirled inside the impossibly huge mouth. That and the mocking laughter echoing throughout all existence.

Jerome threw himself toward the darkness, knowing that Freddy was in there somewhere. All he had to do was slash out with his scissors—

"Jerome, honey?"

He knew that voice; knew it as well as he did his own, if not better. He experienced a dizzying moment of vertigo, as if the entire world tilted to the side for a moment before slowly righting itself.

He blinked. The darkness was gone, and he was looking into Cheryl's face. The pain of his wounds had vanished as well, and when he glanced down at his hands, he saw that they were whole and unmarked, save for where Cottril had scratched him earlier. And one of those hands—his left, strangely enough, as he was right-handed—was still holding the scissors.

"What are you doing here?" He asked, the question coming out harsher than he'd intended it. If he hadn't come out of his dream or hallucination or whatever it had been in time.

Cheryl eyed the scissors in his hand and frowned, but she answered his question. "Detention was over, but you didn't come out with the other kids, so I came inside and checked the office. Ms LeClair's out there helping the secretary with her computer, and she told me you were in here and that it was okay if I came in to see you."

Jerome had the sense that Cheryl wasn't telling him the whole story. Most likely Cottril had told her what had happened after he was released from detention, but Cheryl didn't want to risk upsetting him further by mentioning Cottril's name.

Cheryl nodded toward the scissors still clutched in his left hand. "What are you doing with those?"

"Nothing. Just messing around." He placed the scissors down on Ms LeClair's desk, then turned back to Cheryl. Before she could challenge his lame excuse, he said, "I'm so glad it was you that came in."

Cheryl's frown deepened. "Why?"

He couldn't tell her the real reason: that he was terrified of what he might have done if Ms LeClair had been the one to walk through the doorway while he was in the grip of the delusion.

He forced a smile. "Because I'm always glad to see you."

Cheryl looked at him skeptically for a moment before smiling and reaching out to take his hand.

"Charmer," she said.

Yeah, that's me, Jerome thought as he remembered how he'd stabbed the two white-coated Freddys in the throat, and how he'd intended to do the same to the third one. I'm a real sweetheart.

EIGHT

After his catnap in Ms LeClair's office—and its disturbing results—Jerome didn't feel like going home and sleeping anymore. He decided he might as well head on over to the video store and work. If nothing else, keeping busy might take his mind off of the strange things that had been happening to him lately.

Despite the fact that he was seventeen and had a job, Jerome didn't have a car. Neither did Cheryl and for the same reason. Cars were expensive, and they wanted to save as much money as they could for college. So they had to walk from the high school to downtown Springwood, where Showtime Video was located. Jerome really didn't mind. It was a nice day, and he had Cheryl at his side, holding his hand as they walked. He knew it wasn't over, if only because Ms LeClair was going to phone his parents tonight. Jerome couldn't predict how his dad and Lynn would react to the news of what he'd done today, let alone that he wanted to see a doctor at Westin Hills. But he'd worry about that when it happened.

After several minutes of breathing in the spring air and walking in companionable silence with the girl he loved, Jerome began to relax, and if he didn't entirely forget about weird dreams featuring cackling, scar-faced madmen with claw-knives, at least he stopped dwelling on them. Cheryl started telling him about her gym class that afternoon, and how Olivia Drake—perhaps the largest-breasted girl in Springwood High—hadn't worn a bra to class. Several of the boys had been so distracted by Olivia's outfit (or lack thereof) during archery practice that they missed the target entirely, their arrows soaring into the parking lot and scratching the paint on the Accord owned by Ms Dickey, the gym teacher.

Jerome didn't care about Olivia Drake and her breasts, nor did he care about Ms Dickey's paint job. Nevertheless, he hung on Cheryl's every word as if it were the most fascinating story ever told in human history, nodding, smiling and laughing in all the right places. What was so great about the story was how absolutely normal it was. And a dose of normality was exactly what Jerome needed right now, so he drank in Cheryl's words with the eagerness of a thirsty desert traveler fortunate enough to stumble across an oasis.

By the time Cheryl had gotten around to describing the particular shade of crimson Ms Dickey's face had turned as she yelled at the two idiots whose wayward arrows struck her car, Jerome was laughing so hard that tears streamed down his cheeks. But his laughter quickly died away as they drew near Showtime Video and he saw who was standing on the sidewalk in front of the store. It was his aunt Rebecca.

Cheryl was the first to say anything about her. "Isn't that—"

Jerome cut her off. "Yeah. But I have no idea what she's doing here." Jerome loved aunt Bekka and got along well with her. Ordinarily he'd be happily surprised to see her here, but after what he'd been through today, anything out of the ordinary immediately took on sinister overtones to him. He was tempted to turn around and leave before she could see them, but Bekka smiled and waved, and he knew it was too late to retreat. Forcing a smile, he headed over to Bekka, still holding tight—perhaps a little too tight—to Cheryl's hand.

Rebecca Larkin was his mother's twin sister, and every time Jerome saw her, he knew that he gazed upon an image of what his mother would look like today if she hadn't died in that car crash seventeen years ago. A date that, because he was delivered only moments before Joanna died, was also his birthday.

Rebecca was a pretty woman in her early thirties, blonde, petite and thin. She liked to wear her hair loose, and regardless of the weather, it always looked windblown. She wore little make-up, though she preferred odd colors of eye shadow such as pastel greens and purples. She wore a southwestern-style poncho with a stylized design of an eagle on the front. In addition, she wore blue jeans, striped socks and brown leather sandals. Large hoop earrings dangled from the lobes of her ears, so large and heavy that they actually stretched the lobes, making them look like elongated blobs of Silly Putty.

Rebecca came running up to Jerome and Cheryl, still smiling, but there was worry in her eyes. His aunt was usually such a cheerful person that Jerome was immediately concerned. His first thought was that something bad had happened, so bad that Bekka had come to Showtime Video to tell him in person instead of phoning. Had something happened to his dad? Or to Lynn and the kids? He surprised himself when he realized he was just as afraid of anything happening to his stepmother and half-siblings as he was anything happening to his dad.

Bekka stopped before she reached them, a look of alarm on her face. "Jerome, I'm so sorry—I didn't mean to frighten you. Everyone's fine."

Cheryl frowned in confusion and turned to Jerome. Relieved, Jerome gave his girlfriend a smile. "She's psychic, remember?"

Though he said it with a flippant tone, Jerome wasn't making fun of his aunt. He wasn't sure he truly believed that Bekka could read minds or predict the future, despite what her clients might think, but he had no doubt she could intuit others' feelings.

He turned back to his aunt. "So, if there's no big emergency or family tragedy, why the visit?"

Bekka didn't reply. Instead she gently took Jerome's hands by the wrists and lifted them up so she could look at them.

"Where did you get these scratches?" Her tone was wary, almost as if she was afraid to hear his answer.

Jerome knew he couldn't lie to Bekka. She'd immediately sense any dishonesty on his part, so he hoped to get away with a half-truth. "I got them in a fight with another guy at school. No big deal."

Bekka glanced at Cheryl as if seeking confirmation—or denial—of Jerome's story. Cheryl couldn't meet Bekka's intense gaze, though, and she looked down at the sidewalk.

"Hmpfh," Bekka pronounced skeptically, but she released Jerome's arms.

Funny, but he just realized that Cheryl hadn't said anything about the scratches on his hands. Maybe she just hadn't noticed.

Of course she had noticed. She just didn't give a damn.

The thought came in his own voice, but it didn't feel like one of his. For a moment he was frightened that Freddy had somehow gotten into his head, but then he remembered. Freddy wasn't real. Still, the thought, along with the vague feelings of smoldering anger it stirred—anger toward Cheryl—was disturbing.

"Make sure you wash those scratches good," Bekka said. "You don't want them to get infected. There are all sorts of nasty things that can get into a person and start growing if you aren't careful." There was something about the way she stressed these last words that made it clear she meant more than she was saying, but whatever message she was trying to send, Jerome wasn't getting it.

But that was Bekka. She often spoke in subtle, indirect ways—too much so for Jerome. Usually, he was forced to ask several follow-up questions to get her to clarify what she meant, but after everything he'd been through, he didn't have the energy or patience.

"Don't worry, Bekka. I'll take care of them," Jerome said. "I don't want to be rude, but I'm already late for work. Maybe we could talk later?"

"I'm sorry to bother you, Jerome. I know you're busy."

From someone else, this statement might've been designed to elicit guilt, but not Rebecca. For all her tendencies toward indirect communication, she wasn't one to try to guilt people. Nevertheless, Jerome did feel guilty.

"It's not that, Bekka, but I really should—"

"This'll only take a moment, I promise." She hurried on before Jerome could reply. "Something happened late last night, something that caused me to wake up terrified. Did anything out of the ordinary happen to you last night?"

"Not really. I got home late and Lynn and Dad weren't too happy about it. Otherwise..." He trailed off. He remembered anger and frustration surging through him after arguing with Lynn and his dad, remembered getting ready for bed, taking off his shoes, being so mad that he hurled one of them at the wall.

He remembered it striking the dreamcatcher Bekka had given him when he was still an infant; remembered the dreamcatcher falling onto his bed, broken.

"I, uh... accidentally broke my dreamcatcher before I went to sleep. That's about it." He smiled. "It's a bummer, but I don't think it qualifies as an emergency, do you?"

Bekka's face paled. "You have no idea," she whispered.

Jerome was surprised by the intensity of her reaction. "I'm really sorry, but it's not broken too bad. A little glue and tape and it should be almost like new."

"I don't know if I can fix it or not," Bekka said, almost as if she were talking to herself. "I'll need to do some research, see what I can find out..." She trailed off and thought for a moment, pursing her lips as she concentrated.

Jerome nodded. He supposed there wasn't much he could do; Aunt Bekka was like a force of nature sometimes. Unpredictable, unfathomable and unstoppable.

Bekka nodded once then, as if she'd reached a decision. "I'll come over tonight and take a look at your dreamcatcher, see what I can do with it. All right?"

It wasn't all right. Lynn didn't get along with Bekka, and considering that Ms LeClair had promised to call his folks about his trouble in school today, Jerome wasn't certain that he wanted Bekka around either. He'd have a hard enough time dealing with Lynn and his father as it was, without Bekka getting involved.

"I don't know if that's such a—"

"What did you dream about last night, Jerome?" Bekka asked.

The question caught him off guard. Bekka knew damn well that he didn't dream, or at least didn't remember his dreams. So what had made her ask "what"—not "if"—he'd dreamed?

Because your dreamcatcher was broken, idiot, his thought voice supplied. Without it, you didn't have any protection.

Protection against what? Jerome wondered, but his thought voice remained silent. If it had any more answers, it didn't feel like sharing them, it seemed.

"Did you dream about a man?" Bekka asked. "A man with a burned face and knives attached to his glove?"

A cold pain lanced through Jerome's gut, right where Freddy's finger claws had penetrated during his dream in Ms LeClair's office.

"I'm sorry, Bekka. I've got to go." He turned and gave Cheryl a quick kiss. "I'll call you later, okay?"

Cheryl looked startled by his abrupt goodbye, but she nodded and said, "Sure."

Jerome then turned back to his aunt, gave her a quick peck on the cheek, said, "See you soon," then hurried into the video store. For a moment, he was afraid that Bekka might follow him inside, but she didn't. Through the front window, he saw her exchange a few words with Cheryl, and then the two women went their separate ways down the sidewalk.

I wonder what they were talking about, Jerome thought.

Me too, said the voice inside his head.

He's back, Bekka thought as she hurried down the sidewalk, leather sandals slapping on concrete.

No, that wasn't right, because he'd never truly left, had he?

Freddy fucking Krueger, the demonic child-killer that had haunted the dreams of Springwood's residents for decades—and the son of a bitch that had murdered her sister.

Rebecca and Joanna were not only born identical twins, they'd been conjoined. Not by much, just a thin flap of skin that linked their hands, easily cut by the doctor that delivered them. But Bekka had always thought that bit of skin was an indication of how close they were destined to become. For as they grew up, it became apparent—to the girls if no one else—that they shared a psychic link so strong that what one felt too, the other felt; what one knew, the other knew too. But from the very beginning they had different reactions to their "special bond", as Bekka liked to think of it. Where Bekka saw it as something wondrous and beautiful, Joanna found it an annoyance at best and a gross invasion of privacy at worst. As children, Bekka had always wanted to be near her sister—play with her, eat with her, sleep in the same bed with her. But Joanna, though she loved Bekka very much, preferred to be on her own as much as possible. While Bekka reveled in the intimacy of their bond, it was just too intense for Joanna, and Bekka did her best to understand and not be hurt by her sister's need for separateness.

By the time their teenage years rolled around, their bond had "grown quiet", as Bekka thought of it, and they were no closer than any other siblings. They each had their own group of friends and their own concerns. Joanna began dating Don Starkey and worked hard to save money for college. Bekka found school restraining—she wanted to be free to live, to travel, to see, hear, taste and touch everything that the world had to offer. So she threw herself into her school work, studied hard, and graduated high school a year early. She left Springwood almost the very moment she had her diploma in her hand.

She'd started seeing someone by then, a singer-guitarist named Lionel, who worked as a wandering minstrel in renaissance fairs. Bekka hooked up with him and began working as a renfair fortune-teller. For the next several months, she and Lionel traveled from fair to fair, town to town, all across the country, going wherever they could find work and wherever their fancy took them.

Come April, they found themselves in a tiny New Mexico town called Chloride. Bekka had chosen it because of the name, which she later learned had to do with the discovery of a vein of silver chloride that led to a silver rush a hundred years ago. By this time, Bekka was already planning to head back to Ohio so she could attend Joanna's high school graduation. Plus, Joanna's last letter had hinted that she might be pregnant. Bekka was thrilled at the prospect of being an aunt, and she was determined to remain in Springwood so she could help her sister through her pregnancy and then help her take care of the baby. Joanna would need the help if she still planned to go to college. Bekka hadn't gotten around to informing Lionel of her decision yet. In truth, she'd been putting it off because she was afraid he wouldn't go back to Ohio with her. Lionel wasn't exactly the type to put down roots.

One mid morning, while Lionel was still dozing in their motel room, Bekka—for some unaccountable reason feeling restless—decided to go out and explore the town of Chloride. According to the brochure she'd picked up in the hotel lobby, Chloride had once been a ghost town, but you couldn't tell it today. Wherever she went, everything seemed new. New houses, new business, new cars, new families. Except for the surrounding mountains and the hot dry air, Chloride reminded her an awful lot of Springwood. The thought depressed her for some reason, and she was thinking about returning to the hotel when she spotted a square two story building across the street. The upper half of the building was plain red brick, while the lower half was painted white, with a red door and red trim around the windows. At the top, painted in blue, were the words: Frontier Store.

Bekka smiled. Now this was more like it!

She hurried across the street, which given the building's appearance, should have been unpaved and dirty, but was in reality covered with blacktop like any other street. She walked up to the red door and pushed it open. A bell jingled, the sound muffled and flat for some reason. She stepped inside and before her eyes could adjust to the dim interior, her nose was hit with the smell. Mildew and strange spices; foodstuffs on the verge of going bad; traces of chemicals, which might or might not have been used to clean the place; old fur and sawdust, as if the art of the taxidermist was sold here. The mixture of scents wasn't unpleasant exactly, but there was something about it that disturbed Bekka, made her feel as if she stood not in some re-creation of a Wild West general store, but rather in an ancient mausoleum, a place of forgotten death and lost time.

As her eyes began to get used to the interior darkness, she saw that the floor was made of gray wooden planking while the walls were red brick. Shelves lined the walls, taller than Bekka and filled with all manner of objects. Home-made sweets, jars of chili peppers, turquoise jewelry, books, posters, key chains, bean bag animals, maps of the area and of New Mexico in general. Clothing hung on rods: shirts, ponchos, serapes, hats, beaded purses, all Southwestern themed, and many with the word Chlorine prominently displayed on them.

Bekka felt a wave of disappointment. It wasn't a true replica of an old-time general store. It was nothing but a tricked out gift shop, as cheesy and dull as any of the dozens she'd seen during her travels with Lionel. She was about to turn around and leave, when suddenly a man appeared behind the sales counter. He didn't walk into the room from somewhere else, and he hadn't risen from behind the counter. It was as if one minute he wasn't there and the next he was. Normally, Bekka might have chuckled at such a wild thought, but she didn't find it amusing just then.

There was nothing particularly sinister about the man. He was African-American, his skin dark and shiny as polished obsidian. His nose was broad, ears tiny, and either he was bald or shaved his scalp. His eyes seemed too small for his face and set too deep into the sockets, almost as if they were trying to hide in his skull. His skin was smooth and unwrinkled, but there nevertheless was a sense of age about him, a kind of hard-won dignity that made him seem far older than he appeared on the surface. Bekka guessed his age at anywhere between forty and eighty, but that was a close as she could come. He wore a short-sleeved white shirt and a black bolo tie with a silver cow skull clasp in the center.

"Looking for a gift?" The shopkeeper's voice was a rich baritone, and it filled the store as if it were a physical thing. Bekka could imagine the sound waves washing over her, vibrating through her.

"Yes," she said, though she wasn't sure why. It just felt like the right response.

"For anyone special?" Though the shopkeeper phrased this as a question, from his tone, it sounded as if he already knew the answer.

Bekka stepped up to the counter. "My sister. She's going to have a baby."

"A joyous occasion indeed." Despite his words, the man almost seemed to be offering her his condolences. "You sure you wouldn't rather get something for the child? It's a hard, dangerous world, and a little fellow needs to get off to a good start."

The man said "fellow" as if he knew Joanna's baby was male. But if Joanna herself knew the gender of her baby, she'd made no mention of it in her letter to Bekka. Maybe the shopkeeper was just sexist and referred to all unborn children as fellows. But that wasn't the sense Bekka had.

The shopkeeper looked at her for a long moment and time seemed to slow down, seconds stretching out like minutes. His sunken eyes seemed to move forward, as if the man were consciously focusing them on Bekka like some kind of camera lens. Though the man stared straight at her, she had the feeling that he was seeing something else, something far away.

Finally, like a rubber band snapping back into place, time resumed moving at its normal pace once again, and the shopkeeper's eyes were just as they had been when Bekka had first walked in.

"I've got just the thing. Wait here." Without pausing for Bekka to reply, the man came out from behind the counter and walked to the rear of the shop. He passed between two rows of shelves and was momentarily lost to Bekka's sight. When she couldn't see him any longer, she had the feeling that she was all alone, that the shopkeeper was no longer in the store. But she hadn't heard him leave through a back door, and he couldn't have simply vanished.

Could he?

There was one way to find out. All Bekka had to do was follow after him, head down the same aisle between shelves where he'd walked. If there was a back door, she'd find it. If not...

She didn't know what she'd do. She stood for a moment, trying to decide whether or not she truly wanted to know where the shopkeeper had gone. She'd finally decided to follow him, when suddenly she sensed the man's presence once more. A moment later, he came out from between the rows of shelves, but was carrying an object made of wooden hoops, string and feathers.

"It's a dreamcatcher," Bekka said.

"That it is." The shopkeeper returned to his post behind the counter and lay the dreamcatcher on top for Bekka to inspect.

She reached out for it, but at first couldn't bring herself to touch it. She could sense power in the object, so much that the air near it seemed to crackle with electrical discharge. Finally, she forced herself to touch the object, half expecting to get shocked. But she wasn't. The dreamcatcher felt like ordinary wood and feathers. The tingling feeling of power dissolved, and there was nothing that remained to distinguish the dreamcatcher from any other sold at gift shops and curio stands around the West.

"It would look quite nice hanging over a crib," the shopkeeper said. "And then later, when the boy's older, on the wall above his bed. It'll keep him safe because it'll keep him out."

Bekka could tell from the way the shopkeeper emphasized the second him that he wasn't referring to the baby twice.

"Keep who out?"

The shopkeeper didn't answer her question. Instead he said, "It's yours to take... if you promise to give it to the baby and make sure he sleeps under it every night. Don't worry if he misses a night here or there, though. The effect is cumulative and will linger for several days up to as much as a week or so when he's away from the dreamcatcher. As long as it's intact." He stressed this last bit in a way that made clear the warning was of vital importance.

Bekka gently lifted the dreamcatcher and held it up, imagining what it would look like dangling from the ceiling over a baby's crib.

"The boy's going to start out with a couple strikes against him," the shopkeeper said. "Not fair, but that's the way it is. That dreamcatcher will hopefully buy him enough time to grow up and become strong before..." The man trailed off, either having said his piece or reluctant to continue for whatever reason. Perhaps a bit of both.

"So are you going to take it?" he asked.

Bekka knew she should be seriously creeped out by what was happening, but she wasn't. In a strange way, it all felt right. "Yes. How much is it?"

The man shrugged. "If you insist on paying for it, five dollars will do."

The price seemed low, but Bekka didn't argue. She paid the man, and he tucked the bills into his shirt pocket without looking at them.

"One thing," the shopkeeper said. "This is one of a kind, and it's very fragile. Once it's been broken, it'll never be the same."

Bekka looked at the dreamcatcher. It didn't seem all that different than any other she'd ever seen, and from what she could tell, it appeared sturdy enough. It wasn't like the thing was made out of glass or anything. Still, she said, "I understand," and the shopkeeper seemed satisfied with her answer.

"In that case, I thank you for your business," the man said.

Bekka nodded and carried the dreamcatcher without a bag (the shopkeeper hadn't offered one and she hadn't asked) toward the door.

"Take good care of that boy," the shopkeeper called out after her. "He's going to need all the help he can get."

A chill slithered down Bekka's spine, and she turned around to ask the man what he meant by that. But when she did, she saw he was gone. She quickly left the shop and didn't look back.

Later that day, she returned to the Frontier Store with Lionel in tow. The place looked exactly the same, but it didn't feel the same, and the old woman manning the counter—who looked a little like Popeye the Sailor Man without any teeth—said that she'd been the only one working at the store all day, and that no black people worked there, male or female, though she thought the woman who worked weekends had a little mestizo in her.

Lionel teased Bekka after they left, said that maybe she'd taken one too many astral journeys for her own good. That's when Bekka told him of her intention to return to Ohio, and the next morning she started hitchhiking northeast—alone.

It took her almost five days to get back to Springwood; three days too late to attend her sister's funeral. Bekka had sensed Joanna's death during the trip while riding with a trucker based out of Memphis. She insisted he drop her off at the nearest

rest stop, and she'd spent the rest of the night in the women's restroom, alternately crying and throwing up. When she finally got back to town, the first thing she did was visit Joanna's grave. The second thing she did was go to the hospital to visit her new nephew.

Though little Jerome had been born five weeks early, he was doing fine. He had been kept in the hospital so he could get over a case of jaundice, and he was released the same day Bekka arrived. Bekka's parents decided to raise Jerome and it took a bit of persuasion on her part to convince them to allow her to put the dreamcatcher in Jerome's room—the same room that had been his mother's. Up to that point, Jerome had been having trouble sleeping through the night, but as soon as the dreamcatcher was up, he slept peacefully through the night and, with the exception of those times when he was sick or badly troubled, he had ever since.

In order to stay close to Jerome, Bekka remained in Springwood and set up shop as a "spiritual advisor". Over the years she'd developed and strengthened her abilities. She'd also learned—through treating clients plagued by nightmares—more about Freddy Krueger, what he'd been and more importantly, what he'd become after his death. Though she had no evidence of it, her feelings told her that the malevolent spirit of a once mortal child killer was in some way responsible for Joanna's death and for little Jerome's sleeping troubles. Bekka didn't know who that mysterious shopkeeper in New Mexico had been or how he had known Jerome would need a dreamcatcher, a real one, not some mere decoration. But she knew one thing: the man had warned her about damaging the dreamcatcher.

This is one of a kind, and it's very fragile. Once it's been broken, it'll never be the same.

As Bekka continued walking down the sidewalk, heading for the block where her business was located, she feared that whatever magic the dreamcatcher possessed had been lost when Jerome had accidentally broken it. And if that had happened, then Krueger could now get at Jerome. From what she'd sensed of Jerome's confused and upset state of mind when they'd spoken outside the video store, she was afraid he already had. That was the message the cards had relayed to her last night. Perhaps her own powers were responsible for the message, but then again, perhaps it had been sent by Freddy himself—to taunt her, to let her know that the creature responsible for her twin sister's death was going after her nephew, and there was nothing she could do about it.

Bekka was determined to protect Jerome, the only part of her sister that remained alive. The question was, what could she—could anyone—do against an evil as strong as Freddy Krueger?

It was a question she was still pondering when she reached her building and entered through the back door. She had a few hours until she intended to go over to Jerome's house. Best to get to work now. Bekka put the closed sign up in the front window and turned off the lights in the reception area. Then she went into the back room and started up the stairs to her living quarters/library. It was time to do some research.

Directly across the street from Showtime Video was a small coffee shop called, imaginatively enough, Sacred Grounds. Sitting at the table next to the front window were three teenage boys, one with a scar on his forehead. They watched with interest as Jerome and Cheryl arrived at the store only to be confronted by a nutty-looking woman, before Jerome entered the video store to do whatever he did there that passed for work.

"So what do we do now, Pat?" Brent Haney asked. "Follow Cheryl? Go into the video store and start hassling Starkey?"

The three of them were drinking coffee—not lattes, not cappuccinos, not espresso. Just coffee. Pat took a sip of his and shuddered at the bitter taste and even worse aftertaste. The truth of the matter was he didn't want to go into the store. El's parents weren't the type you could intimidate with attitude, and they didn't screw around. If you caused any trouble, they called the cops.

"We sit and finish our coffee," Cottril said. "Give Starkey a chance to get settled and start working. And then…"

"Then what?" Eddie Jackson asked eagerly.

Cottril unconsciously fingered the scar on his forehead. "Then we deliver a little payback right at the bastard's head."

Brent and Eddie laughed, but Cottril didn't. He kept looking through the window of the video store and tried to imagine what Jerome's cries of pain would sound like. Would he beg for mercy? Cottril hoped so. God, how he hoped so!

NINE

Jerome didn't know what El had said to his parents about his being late, but whatever it had been, it must've worked because neither El's mom or dad said anything to him when he came in other than, "Hi". Knowing he was getting off easy and grateful for it, Jerome went straight to work checking returned movies back into the computer system. The work was boring, but easy, and Jerome finished quickly. He then carried a stack of returned movies out onto the main floor and began returning them to their proper places on the display shelves so entertainment-starved patrons could snatch them up and start the whole cycle over again.

There were several video monitors located throughout the store, and at the moment they were all playing Mr Belasco's favorite film, *The*

Sound of Music. Sometimes Jerome couldn't believe that Mr Belasco and El were really related. El was in the back room—probably to escape having to listen to Julie Andrews sing—opening boxes of new movies that had been delivered by UPS earlier that afternoon and getting them ready to go on the shelves. Jerome would've loved to work in the back with El, but it was just about five, and the store got real busy once folks started getting off work. Jerome knew Mr and Mrs Belasco wouldn't like both him and El to be in the back for any length of time. But Jerome did manage to sneak into the back room to say a quick "Hi" to El.

"How was detention?" El asked as he sliced open a box of movies with an exacto knife.

"More eventful than I would've liked," Jerome admitted.

El raised a questioning eyebrow, but Jerome said, "I'll tell you about it later, I promise."

"I can't wait. Sounds like a real juicy story." Though El's words were flippant, his tone was one of concern. "You doing okay, though?"

Jerome didn't want to lie to his friend. "Like I said, we'll talk later." Then he went back out into the main part of the store and returned to work.

Showtime Video looked like any other movie and video game rental store. Movies were displayed on shelves arranged in sections by genre, and large poster cut-outs of various celebrities were plastered on the walls. The only individual touch was the small section devoted to employee recommendations. El was the only one who ever put any movies there, and he always chose the worst, most obscure cult films he could find, with titles like *Godzilla vs The Smogmonster, Bronx Warriors 2* and *Master of the Flying Guillotine*. No one ever rented the stupid films, except El, of course, and Jerome when he was dumb enough to let El talk him into viewing one of those stink bombs.

El's mom and dad were a study in opposites. She was tall, thin and pretty; while he was short, chubby and plain. Like El, his father was always well-dressed, usually in a crisp, clean white shirt, stylish tie, neatly pressed slacks and polished shoes. El's mom would come to work in a dirty T-shirt and ragged sweatpants if she could. She usually wore a simple blouse, jeans and tennis shoes. But despite their surface differences, Mr and Mrs Belasco shared similar easygoing personalities and a sharp sense of humor, much like their son.

Five o'clock rolled around and, as always, the evening rush started. People started coming into the store a few minutes after five, and they were busy until almost five-forty. When the last after-work customer was gone, Mr and Mrs Belasco left to eat dinner, and El came out of the back room and joined Jerome at the front counter. Now that he was finally alone with his friend, Jerome relaxed.

"I don't know how you did it, but thanks for smoothing things over for me with your folks."

El grinned. "No prob. How could they resist granting a favor to their beloved only child? Besides, I promised I wouldn't complain the next time we did inventory."

Considering how talkative El was, Jerome could see how such a promise would be a major enticement for his folks.

"Now that mother and father have left, I think we can safely dispose of Julie Andrews." El reached beneath the counter and pressed the stop button on the DVD player sitting on the center shelf. The monitors throughout the store suddenly displayed a silent blue screen, as if they were patiently waiting for whatever they would be asked to play next.

Mr and Mrs Belasco insisted that only "family-friendly" films be played in the store, so as not to offend any customers. But when they were gone, El played whatever he wanted.

"So what's this evening's selection?" Jerome asked.

El removed a DVD box from the shelf beneath the counter and held it up for Jerome's inspection.

"*Two Heads are Deadlier Than One?*"

"It's a classic!" El said.

"Classic piece of crap," Jerome said with a smile.

El laughed. "What's the difference?" He popped the disc into the player and the blue screens disappeared as the monitors began showing the film.

Jerome might have joked about the movie, but the truth was, it made him nervous. It didn't matter that it was likely going to be another cheap Italian gorefest with lousy special effects. All horror films made Jerome nervous. Part of it was the level of violence in those movies. It always seemed to spark Jerome's anger, and he'd find himself becoming more agitated and upset as the film went on. But there was something else. Sometimes Jerome had a different reaction to the more extreme violence in some horror movies. It got him excited, almost sexually so. He'd never admitted this to anyone, not even Cheryl or El, partially because he didn't understand it well enough to explain, but mostly because it deeply shamed him.

Hey, no need to get all girly about it. Like they say, it's only a movie, right?

Not for him, not always.

As the opening credits came up, with John Saxon fighting the flesh eating Vietcong, El turned to Jerome. "So, are you going to tell me what happened in detention or do you plan to leave me in suspense until I'm old enough to check into a nursing home?"

"It was no big deal at first, but then—"

The door opened, a bell tinkled, and a customer walked in. A woman in her mid-twenties, luckily without children in tow, so El didn't have to turn off the horror movie playing on the monitors.

"To be continued," Jerome whispered, and El nodded.

The woman wanted to fill out a membership application and get a rental card, so while El took care of her, Jerome decided to go around and straighten up the movies and games. People always picked up a film or video game, carried it around for a while and then, once they changed their minds about renting it, they put it down wherever they felt like it. It was a constant annoyance, especially when some idiot left a *Sorority Girls Gone Crazy* DVD in the kids' section.

Jerome did his best to ignore the movie El had put on, but considering there were video monitors mounted throughout the store, it wasn't easy. The film began with two small-time criminals fleeing from police after robbing a bank. Their getaway car was a battered old Ford, and there was no way that they were going to be able to outrun the cops. To make matters worse, their right front tire blew out, sending the car into a screaming spin on the highway. The driver tried to regain control of the vehicle, but to no avail. The Ford crashed through a guardrail and plummeted down the side of a cliff, bouncing several times before exploding in a ball of fire.

Jerome turned away from the monitors, battling a sudden attack of nausea. Because his mother had died as the result of a car wreck, he'd never been able to stomach watching similar accidents in movies or TV shows, and he couldn't bring himself to play any video games that had car crashes in them, no matter how ridiculous and cartoonish they might be.

Another few customers came in after El had finished setting the woman up with her membership. Jerome glanced toward the front of the store to see if El needed any help, but El shook his head, so Jerome continued straightening the shelves.

In the movie, the two criminals—mutilated and barely alive—were found by a mad doctor and taken to the isolated farm where he conducted bizarre experiments in organ and limb transplantation. The doctor was a thin old man with a wild tangle of white hair and an insane glint in his eyes. His assistant was a fat drooling moron clad only in a pair of blood-splattered overalls. In the scene currently playing, the two criminals were laid out side by side on two adjoining operating tables, and the doctor was gowned, masked and gloved, ready to perform surgery.

"Whatcha gonna do wif 'em, Doc?" the man Jerome thought of as the Drooler asked.

"They've both been critically injured," the mad doctor replied, voice muffled by his mask. "There's barely enough left of them to make one complete body—so that's exactly what I shall do! One body... with two heads!"

The doctor let out a cackling laugh, and the Drooler joined in.

Jerome just shook his head. How could El watch this crap, let alone love it as much as he did? That was one aspect of his friend's personality that Jerome doubted he'd ever understand.

He'd finished straightening the stock everywhere except for one section: Horror. Jerome usually left that section for El to deal with—and El was usually happy to do so—but he was still busy with customers. Jerome considered skipping this section, but it was one of the most popular, which meant it was also one of the messiest. He sighed, told himself to suck it up, and headed for the horror section.

On the monitors, the mad doctor and his moron of an assistant were in the midst of their delicate operation. As Jerome watched, the doctor cut the head off one criminal with a hacksaw and hurriedly attached it to the body of the second criminal, sewing the new head onto the juncture of the man's neck and shoulder. Jerome had taken enough science classes to know what a crock of shit this operation was. How did the doctor attach the new head onto the host body's spinal column? How did he connect it to the lungs and circulatory system? What about the neck muscles? What did he attach them to so the second head just didn't flop around on its new body? Jerome knew what El would say if he were privy to his thoughts.

Relax, it's just a movie. You're not supposed to think about it. Just enjoy it for what it is.

Jerome figured El's attitude was ultimately healthier than his own skepticism. After all, who had time to waste worrying about how stupid movies could be? But try as he might, Jerome just couldn't bring himself to follow his friend's example.

He turned away from the video monitor he was watching and entered the horror section. The entire store had a kind of musty smell, like a library or used bookstore. Jerome figured that was because the movies were rented out to so many different people, who handled them, had them in their cars, took them to their homes, ate snacks and even dinner while watching them. All the different smells the movies were exposed to clung to their boxes, if only a little, and when they were returned to the store and put back on the shelf, the new smells they brought mingled with all the others to create a miasma of funk. Jerome had smelled similar odors in health clubs and bowling alleys, and while he didn't find it particularly pleasant, it didn't bother him much.

Until he came to the horror section.

He didn't know if it was his imagination, but this section seemed to have a stronger smell than any of the others. It smelled of sweat and desperation, of fear and nervous tension, and of a sour-sweet musk that reminded Jerome of the scent that lingered in the air after sex. But worst of all was the sharp coppery tang that lay beneath every other smell: the rich, rank, stink of spilled blood.

If it was his imagination, certainly the covers of the movie containers didn't help. Vampires, werewolves, demons, mutants, freaks, serial killers—some masked, some not—wielding a variety of killing implements, victims recoiling in terror, sometimes with torn, bloodstained clothes or visible wounds on various parts of their flesh. A few of the more extreme images on the boxes showed neither killer nor victim, but rather severed body parts—a bloody hand, a single detached leg, a decapitated head—all of them drenched in crimson gore.

Jerome tried not to look at the covers of the movie boxes as he straightened the displays, but they were difficult to ignore. One box showed an image Jerome found especially disturbing: a bald, white-fleshed head of a woman with her eyes, nostrils and mouth sewed shut. Her lips were dry and cracked, and a thin line of blood trickled from the corner of her permanently closed mouth.

Horrible, Jerome thought with a shiver of disgust.

I don't know, said the voice in his head. I think she's kind of cute. Whoever sewed her up did a sloppy job, though. They should've done her ears, too.

As if the thought were some kind of trigger, the bald woman's head suddenly came to life. She turned toward to Jerome and struggled to open her eyes, muffled cries sounding behind her sewn lips as she tried to speak or perhaps scream.

Jerome backed away from the video box, knowing that he was just experiencing another hallucination, that the woman hadn't come to life, that she wasn't begging him to help her. But as he drew closer to the opposite set of shelves, he backed into something sharp that poked him painfully between the shoulder blades. He pulled away from it, then turned around to see what he'd bumped into.

From the cover of the box for *Hayride to Hell* protruded a scarecrow's hand made from pieces of thick coarse brown cloth haphazardly stitched together. The fabric was full of holes through which moldy yellow-gray straw stuck out. In its brown gloved hand, the scarecrow held a small hand scythe, its curved blade rusted in several places, but the tip was still sharp, to which the pain in his back and the rivulet trailing down his spine could attest.

Maybe this section didn't really need to be straightened anyway. Jerome started for the end of the aisle, but before he could reach it, dozens of hands shot forth from movie boxes. Clawed hands, furred hands, green scaled hands with black talons, hands wrapped in moldy Egyptian cerements, hands criss-crossed with scars and crude stitches, undead hands covered with grave mold, hands with only four fingers, three, two... Hands holding butcher knives, machetes, electric drills, saws, screwdrivers, dental probes, scalpels, hatchets, hooks, switchblades. They clawed, swiped, grabbed and reached for Jerome, and he danced wildly about, trying to avoid getting caught, cut, sliced or stabbed.

Panic rose in him as he desperately searched for an opening in the gauntlet of murderous hands that would permit him to escape. He knew he was acting crazy, that there were no hands, that they were all in his mind. All he had to do was deny this illusion, close his eyes and shut it out, then walk down the aisle until he was out of the horror section. Since the hands were nothing more than products of his own disturbed mind, nothing would happen to him as he walked past the shelves. And when he finally opened his eyes, he'd be safe and completely unharmed.

But if that were true, how come he could hear the hiss as weapons cleaved the air, feel the breeze stirred by their passage? How could the movie boxes jump and shudder on the shelves as the hands protruding from their surfaces struggled to get at him? He could hear the boxes rattling on the shelves, could feel their vibrations through the soles of his feet. What kind of hallucinations came with that sort of detail?

You think too damn much. Let me handle them.

As if of its own volition, Jerome's left hand shot out and grabbed the scythe-wielding scarecrow's wrist. He squeezed, feeling nothing but cloth and straw beneath his grip, and the scarecrow's gloved hand sprang open. The rusty scythe began to drop toward the floor, but Jerome's hand released the scarecrow's wrist and snatched the weapon out of the air with blinding speed. Jerome felt like little more than a passenger in his own body, a distant observer as his hand began swinging the scythe in vicious arcs at the other hands that groped, clawed and swiped at him. The scythe's blade might have been rusty, but its edge was razor sharp, and the metal bit into flesh, parting it as easily as paper. Blood—red, black, green and yellow—gushed from wounded hands. Ichor, hot and foul smelling, splattered Jerome's shirt, dappled his face and hands. He felt bile splash the back of his throat, and it took a supreme effort to keep from vomiting. Weapons dropped to the floor as hands withdrew into the boxes from which they'd come rather than risk further injury.

Well, what are you waiting for? Start walking!

Jerome obliged the voice in his head, and as his hand continued to wield the gore smeared scythe with a mind of its own, he began walking toward the end of the aisle. A half dozen steps later, he was past the homicidal hands, most of which had been wounded and retreated into their boxes. He was covered with varying shades of blood, but none of it was his, and that was all that mattered.

His left hand suddenly went limp, as if whatever force had been operating it finally relinquished control. The bloody scythe slipped out of Jerome's hand and fell to the carpeted floor with a dull thump.

"Don't tell me you got caught up in the movie despite yourself."

Jerome turned to see El standing there grinning at him. He looked down, saw his clothes were clean, saw no scythe on the floor. He glanced back at the horror section. The floor was free of blood and discarded weaponry, and all the movies were lined up in straight, neat rows.

He turned back to El, realizing as he did so that he was standing in front of a video monitor. On it, the mad doctor and his drooling assistant watched in anticipation as their patient—covered by a white sheet speckled with blood—sat up on the operating table. The sheet slipped down and scary music blared as the patient looked around with his two heads. The moronic assistant clapped his fleshy hands together while the mad doctor laughed in triumph.

"Yeah, I guess so," Jerome said, unable to think of any other reply.

El's grin widened. "I knew it! This stuff grows on you after a while, doesn't it?"

Jerome looked back over his shoulder at the empty horror section.

"Sure does," he whispered.

TEN

Jerome had planned to tell El everything—about his weird dream last night, which he recalled with almost perfect clarity, and the hallucinations he'd experienced today at school. But after this latest hallucination, he was so freaked out, so afraid he was going crazy, that all he did was give El a highly edited version of his time in detention, making it seem as if Cottril had provoked him into attacking.

"I hate to say it, but maybe LeClair calling your folks will be a good thing."

They were hanging out behind the front counter, the store empty save for the two of them. *Two Heads are Deadlier Than One* was still playing on the video monitors, the film lurching toward its predictably lurid climax. The two-headed monster had kidnapped a buxom hairdresser that one of the heads (Jerome couldn't keep them straight) had used to date. The monster, who was of course completely insane by that point, was taking the hairdresser back to the mad doctor's farm so that he could cut off her head and attach it to his creation, so it would become a three-headed monster.

"We've been friends forever," El said. "And as long as I've known you, you've had what the psychobabblers call anger management issues. Maybe LeClair will be able to get you some kind of help."

Jerome bristled at El's choice of words. It made him sound as if he needed to be locked up in a padded cell in Westin Hills, dressed in one of those funny white coats where the sleeves tied in the back. But Jerome knew his friend spoke solely out of concern, so he didn't say anything.

"Oh, man, I almost forgot!" El pressed a couple of buttons on the register and the cash drawer opened. "We're running low on small bills." He pulled out three twenties, then closed the drawer. "Do you mind watching the store while I go down to Diana's Pizza and see if she can break these twenties for us?"

The thought of remaining here after what he'd experienced in the horror section held little appeal for Jerome.

"I'd hate for you to miss the end of such a fine motion picture," Jerome said, nodding to the wall above the checkout counter. The two-headed monster had managed to get the hairdresser into the doctor's laboratory, and he/it/they were strapping her down to an operating table—careful to make sure that the straps were positioned in such a way as to prominently display her large breasts.

El glanced up at the monitor screen, and Jerome could sense him hesitating.

"I'll go," Jerome said. "I don't care if I miss the ending."

El mulled over Jerome's proposition for a moment. "I appreciate the offer, Jere, but I don't like feeling that I'm pawning my scut work off onto you. Just because my parents own the store doesn't make me your boss or anything."

"I know that." And he did. El never acted like he was important just because his parents ran the store. As far as he was concerned, he was just another employee like anyone else, and Jerome admired him for that attitude.

"All right, then." El handed the three twenties to Jerome. "If you hurry, you might get back just in time for the big surprise ending."

"Let me guess," Jerome said as he pocketed the money. "The hairdresser escapes and sews both the mad doctor's and the assistant's head onto the monster, making it the incredible four-headed creature."

El just stared at Jerome for a moment, then laughed. "Maybe you've been hanging out with me a little too much lately."

Jerome laughed then, too.

Pat Cottril was working on his third cup of coffee—along with a serious case of caffeine jitters—when he saw Jerome walk out of Showtime Video, turn left and head down the sidewalk. He took a last gulp of his coffee, set the styrofoam cup down on the table, then grinned at his two compatriots.

"Time to have ourselves a little fun," he said.

Jerome walked out of Diana's Pizza with a pocket full of ones and fives. The smells of baking pizza and subs inside had set his stomach to growling, and he was thinking about coming back to pick up dinner for El and himself after he took the money to the store. He was halfway to Showtime Video—and had decided on ordering either a personal size pizza with pepperoni and red onion or a ham and Swiss sub—when he walked in front of the entrance to the alley between Wertz's Hardware Store and Luxury Travel. He saw movement out of the corner of his eye, but before he could react, hands came out of the alley, grabbed hold of his arm, and pulled him into darkness.

Suddenly off balance, Jerome stumbled into the alley. He might well have fallen if whoever—or whatever—had yanked him in didn't still have hold of him. Someone grabbed his other arm and Jerome realized there were at least two of them, whoever they were. Jerome couldn't make out the faces of his attackers. The sun hadn't gone down all the way yet, but it was close enough to nightfall for the alley to be shrouded in gloom.

His two assailants shoved him hard against the alley's brick wall and held him there. A third form then detached itself from the darkness and started toward him. Cold fear twisted his gut as the dark silhouette came closer, and he waited to hear the sound of mocking laughter and the whisper of finger-knives sliding one against the other. But then the shadowy figure spoke, and Jerome knew this wasn't another hallucination. This was real.

"Hey, Starkey. How's it hanging?"

Cottril put his hands on Jerome's shoulders and slammed his knee into Jerome's crotch. Dull, heavy pain spread through his groin area, and Jerome drew in a hissing breath through his teeth. Nausea exploded in his stomach, and he fought to keep from throwing up. Not that he would mind shotgunning vomit all over Cottril, he just didn't think it would be in his best interests right now. He slumped forward and would've fallen if the other two—who had to be Brent Haney and Eddie Jackson—hadn't kept his shoulders pinned to the wall.

"I bet you think you're pretty tough, attacking me in detention like that." Cottril tried to sound tough himself, but Jerome could detect the fear in his voice, and it frightened Jerome more than the near certainty of further physical violence, because a truly scared man was capable of just about anything. "But you're not so tough now, not without a teacher around to protect you."

Cottril's right hand curled into a fist and he hit Jerome hard on the jaw. Jerome's head snapped back and smacked against the brick wall. Light flashed along his optic nerves, followed by darkness. He thought he'd lapsed into unconsciousness, but he could still hear his own ragged breathing, along with that of Cottril and his two flunkies. They panted with excitement, like a trio of hounds that had cornered their prey and were eager to start tearing into living meat.

Jerome's eyes were closed, his head lowered, chin resting on his chest. He struggled to raise his head and open his eyes, but pain erupted on the right side of his jaw, and his mouth filled with hot coppery blood. He tried to spit it out, but the best he could manage was to open his mouth and allow the blood to spill onto the ground by itself. He wondered if his jaw was broken. As bad as it hurt, he wouldn't be surprised.

He felt his anger rising inside, like the smoldering remains of an almost dead fire stoked with new fuel. He did his best to forget about Cottril, Jackson and Haney, to forget about the pain that throbbed in his jaw and the back of his skull. He focused the full power of his concentration on the flame that burned in the deepest core of his being and willed the fire of his anger and hate to grow...

Thanks, bro. I'll take it from here.

The darkness that came for Jerome then had nothing to do with whether or not his eyes were closed, and for a time he knew no more.

As sweet as this was, Cottril was almost disappointed. He'd expected Jerome to put up more of a fight. As it was, it looked like the wuss was just going to stand there and let the three of them stomp his ass. It was almost too easy.

Cottril wasn't the most literate young man in Springwood, and thus wasn't familiar with the admonition "Be careful what you wish for, you just might get it", but he was about to gain intimate firsthand knowledge of the concept.

Jerome's head snapped up, eyes open, mouth stretched into a grin. The blood from his split and rapidly swelling lip smeared his mouth and teeth, giving his smile an aspect of insane wildness. His arm muscles tightened, and then with a single motion, he brought them forward and down. Eddie Jackson and Brent Haney still had hold of Jerome's wrists, and the two lackeys were yanked off balance and slammed onto the alley floor. Free of their restraint, Jerome straightened and looked at Cottril with eyes that held nothing. No humor, no understanding, and certainly no pity. It was the same look Cottril had seen when Jerome had attacked him in kindergarten, and again when he'd tried to choke the life out of him in detention. This was what truly terrified Cottril, far more than Jerome's strength or his savage unpredictability: the dead look in his eyes, as if what lay behind them wasn't really human.

Jerome took a step toward him and Cottril turned and, quick as a rabbit, bolted out of the alley, leaving his two friends behind to deal with Jerome as best they could. For the Three Pusketeers, it most definitely was not one for all and all for one. More like, get out of my goddamned way, it's every man for him fucking self!

As he ran down the sidewalk, Cottril heard the sound of someone screaming back in the alley. But he didn't hear it for very long.

Eddie was already in the process of getting back up on his feet when he saw Pat run out of the alley, followed closely by a stumbling, staggering Brent. A distant part of his mind cried out in betrayal at seeing his friends abandon him, but his head hurt too much for him to worry about them right now. He wasn't sure, but he figured he must've conked his head on the ground when Jerome had thrown him and Brent down. Man, that dude was strong!

Eddie managed to stand, but he wasn't confident in his ability to remain that way. He was dizzy, and he was having trouble getting his eyes to focus. He wondered if he had a concussion. He hoped not. He hated going to the doctor.

Eddie started shuffling toward the alley's entrance, keeping one hand on the wall to steady himself. But he froze when he heard someone speak behind him.

"And just where do you think you're going, young man?"

Eddie's first thought was that it was his father, and his bowels turned to ice water. His old man was meaner than a rattlesnake with the clap, especially when he had a few beers in him. If he knew he'd held onto Jerome so Pat could wail on him, his dad would beat the shit out of Eddie for being a coward. If it had been Eddie himself doing the punching, his old man wouldn't mind so much.

He turned around, wobbling and almost falling over as he did so.

"Look, Dad, it was all Pat's idea..." He trailed off as his vision cleared and even in the alley's gloom, he could tell it was Jerome, not his father, that he spoke to.

"I have no trouble believing that," Jerome said, his voice eerily calm, almost toneless. "But it looks like Pat's made a run for it. Brent, too. That just leaves you and me, doesn't it?"

Jerome's mouth was smeared with blood, and for an instant, Eddie feared that he'd torn out Pat and Brent's throats with his teeth, or worse, maybe devoured them. But then he realized that was ridiculous, just a morbid imagining produced by his scrambled brains. Still, all that blood made Jerome look damn scary.

Eddie held up his hands in a placating gesture. "Look, I'm sorry about holding on to you so Pat could get in a couple free shots. I know it wasn't fair, but since you choked Pat in detention, you kind of had it coming, you know? So why don't we just call it even?"

Eddie knew that Pat would never allow anyone else to speak for him, and given the way Pat held a grudge, Eddie doubted he'd ever feel he was truly even with Jerome. But Eddie didn't have any problem lying, especially if doing so would keep Jerome from retaliating against him.

Jerome kept walking toward Eddie and didn't stop until they were almost nose to nose.

"I don't think so," Jerome said.

Eddie tried to run, but Jerome was too fast. He grabbed hold of Eddie's wrist, spun him around, and slammed him face first into the alley wall. Eddie shrieked in pain as his nose burst like an overripe tomato, gushing crimson all over the brickwork. Eddie staggered backward and raised his hands to his face, but all he found was a warm, wet depression where his nose had been.

"You sudubadish! You broke my fuhhin' node!"

"I'm sorry," Jerome said as he calmly advanced on Eddie. "I was trying to break your whole goddamned head."

Eddie screamed as Jerome grabbed a fistful of his hair and shoved him toward the wall. The last thing Eddie saw before his head was reduced to a bloody pulp of brain tissue and bone fragments was the gory smear where his nose had smashed against the wall only moments ago, rapidly coming toward him. It was funny, but the blood had formed a pattern that resembled a smiley face.

Life sure is weird sometimes, Eddie thought.

It wasn't a particularly insightful thought, but as it was his last, it would have to do.

The first thing Jerome was aware of as he returned to consciousness was the tinkling of the bell attached to the front door of Showtime Video. He paused as the glass door slowly closed behind him, troubled by the vague notion that something was wrong but having no idea what it might be. And then the pain hit him. His jaw throbbed, the back of his head hurt, and his testicles felt like swollen lumps of lead. He was taken off guard by the sudden sensations of pain, so much so that his knees went weak and he thought he was going to fall.

El still stood behind the checkout counter, gaze fixed on the video monitor where the words "THE END?" appeared in red letters designed to look like they were formed by dripping blood.

"Talk about lousy timing," El said after a quick glance in Jerome's direction to make sure he wasn't a customer. "The movie just ended. But if you want, I can reverse back to..." He stopped and turned toward Jerome, his eyes going wide. "My God, what happened to you? Were you mugged or something?"

At first Jerome wasn't sure what El was talking about, then he looked down and saw that his shirt was splattered with bloodstains, and—he reached up to touch them—they weren't dry yet. His hand came away bloody, far more so than the stains on the shirt could account for.

"I... don't know."

El hurried out from behind the counter just in time to catch Jerome before he fell.

"Christ, you look like something the cat dragged in, thought twice about, and then dragged back out!" He started half walking, half carrying Jerome toward the checkout station. "We need to call the life squad for you!"

"No, I'm not hurt that bad," Jerome said weakly, sounding like he was hurt that bad, if not worse. "I'll be okay once I've had a chance to get cleaned up and rest a little. Help me into the back, all right?"

El didn't look happy about it, but he nodded and did as his friend asked. There were a few chairs in the back and El helped Jerome sit on one. Jerome moaned as his butt came in contact with the chair, putting pressure on his abused testicles.

El looked at him with a worried expression. "I really think you should let me call the paramedics. You've obviously been in some kind of accident or fight. Your jaw's swollen and starting to bruise, you've got a busted lip—which I guess accounts for the blood all over you—and there's blood in your hair, too. I think you may have been hit on the head. Head injuries are nothing to screw around with, and it's not like you're such a genius that you can afford to lose any of your little gray cells."

Jerome attempted to smile at El's nervous joke, but it hurt too much so he gave it up. "If I was seriously injured, I'd not only let you call an ambulance, I'd insist on it. But I'm okay." He reached up to touch the back of his head and winced. "At least, I will be as soon as I've had a chance to shake off whatever happened to me."

"But that's my point!" El said, exasperated. "If you can't remember what happened, how can you be okay?"

Images and sensations flashed through Jerome's mind. Cottril's grinning face, Eddie Jackson spinning around, screaming once before falling suddenly, terribly silent.

"I'm sure it'll all come back to me in a minute. Once I've had chance to rest."

Before El could protest any further, the front bell tinkled in the outer part of the store. El looked suddenly unsure what to do, and Jerome said, "Go on and take care of whoever it is. I'll be fine back here."

El hesitated a moment longer before finally nodding. "All right, but I'll be back in just a minute, okay?"

"Sure, sure. Take your time."

El looked doubtful, but he turned and hurried out into the main part of the store, closing the door to the back room behind him. Jerome was glad El had listened to him. He really was all right, and besides, El's voice had been giving him a headache; he'd never realized just how loud his friend talked. All he wanted to do was sit here in silence, close his eyes for a few minutes, and rest.

ELEVEN

A gentle bobbing; up and down, up and down. Water lapped against the sides of a small boat. Sunshine warmed his face; breeze stirred his hair. He had hold of something in his hands, and even before he opened his eyes, he knew it was a fishing pole.

He opened his eyes, and sure enough, it was a fishing pole, but not a hi-tech one. He held an old-fashioned cane pole, the kind his dad had started him off using when he was still in preschool.

They're a little easier to learn how to fish with. And though his father hadn't added, for someone as little as you, Jerome had known what his dad meant. But he hadn't cared. He'd just been thrilled to be out on a real lake in a real boat with his dad. He'd been so glad grandma and grandpa had let him come.

Besides, who needs all that fancy equipment? It's a lot more fun to fish like this, right?

Jerome's dad had been using a cane pole, too, even though he had a much nicer one back in the van.

Right, Jerome had said.

It was a good memory, one of his best. Just sitting and fishing with his dad as their boat drifted in the lake. But he was alone, and without the slightest idea where he was or how he'd got here. He looked around, saw a distant shoreline, tall green trees, a heron standing close to the bank, scanning the shallow water in search of fish. He was sitting in a small outboard in the middle of what he'd used to call Big Fish Lake because his dad had once caught a huge catfish here. It had been so long since Jerome had been here that he couldn't recall the real name anymore.

"Emerald Lake," someone said. Someone with a raspy, guttural voice, as if his vocal cords were a mass of scar tissue. Someone who was sat in the boat facing Jerome.

Freddy wore his green and red striped sweater, but instead of his fedora he wore a brown fishing cap with a picture of a skeletal fish on the front. He was equipped for angling as well, only his pole wasn't made out of wood like Jerome's; it was fashioned from yellowish sections of bone fitted one to the other, each segment smaller and thinner than the last, until at the very tip was what Jerome guessed to be the end bone from a pinkie finger. A line of barbed wire stretched from the bony finger and down into the water.

Freddy winked at Jerome. "A smart fisherman knows to use good bait."

Jerome glanced down at Freddy's shoes and saw an open tackle box wedged between them. Inside were freshly severed tongues and moist eyeballs. His stomach lurched, but it had been so long since he'd eaten that nothing came up.

Freddy took in their surroundings and grimaced. "This place has a major case of the blands. Time for a Freddy-style makeover!"

Freddy did nothing special that Jerome could detect, but the leaves on the trees began to wither and die, falling off their branches with tiny shrill deathcries. The heron at the edge of the shore looked suddenly alarmed. It spread its wings and launched into the air, but not fast enough to avoid the maw full of teeth that rose up out of the water beneath it, clamped down on its long bird legs and dragged it down. All that was left was a small slick of blood and several loose feathers drifting on the water. The sky began to grow crimson, the reddish illumination making the water resemble blood. Jerome sniffed the air; it even smelled like blood, warm and rank.

"Much better," Freddy said, but then he frowned, the action causing the scarred skin of his brow to crack and clear serum to ooze forth. "But it's still missing something..."

Flames erupted from the water around them, as if the surface was covered with gasoline and someone had just tossed a lit match overboard.

"Perfect! Much more festive, don't you think?"

Jerome felt heat rolling off the burning lake, and sweat began beading on his skin. "Festive? Are you insane?"

"Since the day I was born," Freddy said with a feral grin. "Though I have to admit that I've gotten a tad worse since I died." He roared with laughter, the sound of his dark merriment echoing across the burning lake like thunder. "This is a celebration, Jerome! You've reached an important milestone, gone through a rite of passage, have come of age! You've killed!" Freddy's bloodshot eyes glittered. "Felt great, didn't it? Believe me, I know."

Sweat poured off Jerome, and he tried wiping it off his forehead with the back of his free hand—for he still had hold of his cane pole with the other—but all he succeeded in doing was smearing the moisture around. "What the hell are you talking about? I haven't killed anyone!"

"I'm talking about what you did in the alley when Cottril and those two little weasels that follow him around jumped you. Sure, a couple of the losers got away, but you took care of the third one, slammed his head against a brick wall and made his skull pop like a water balloon!"

Memories came slowly trickling back to Jerome then. He remembered going to Diana's Pizza for change, remembered being hauled into the alley by the Three Pus-kateers, being restrained by Eddie Jackson and Brent Haney while Cottril took a few cheap shots at him. And after that, Jerome didn't remember anything before returning to Showtime Video.

"I don't have any idea what you're talking about," Jerome said, though he couldn't escape the feeling that somehow he was lying, even if he didn't know it.

"Sure you do, Jerome, old pal. Or at least part of you does. A part that's been inside of you since you were born, a part that's been slowly growing all these years, and is just about ready to burst out of its shell big-time!"

Freddy leaned forward and his eyes blazed with reflected light from the fires that surrounded them.

"A part I put inside you, Jerome… Just before I killed your whore of a mother."

Before Jerome could react to Freddy's mad pronouncement, his bone pole jerked.

"I got a bite!"

Freddy turned toward the port side of the little boat and hauled back on his pole. Something rose forth from the fiery crimson water with a splash, and Freddy brought the object in closer to the boat. He gripped the barbed wire line with his ungloved hand, causing black blood to trickle from where the barbs punctured his scarred palm. He then held out his catch—which dripped red gore—for Jerome's inspection. The thing wriggling on the end of Freddy's line resembled a hideously deformed fetus. Its body was small, its limbs stunted, but its head was nearly full adult size, and it possessed features that Jerome knew all too well, for he saw them in the mirror every day. The creature had a length of barbed wire caught in its teeth—with, presumably some sort of hook attached—and was furiously gnawing at it, shredding its lips to bloody tatters.

"Recognize this cute little fellow?" Freddy asked.

The fetus thing struggled at the end of the barbed-wire line, but it didn't look as if it were suffering, despite the gobbets of blood and flesh falling from its ruined mouth. Its brow was furrowed, its face red, its eyes blazing with fury. The thing wasn't in pain, and it wasn't afraid. It was mad—mad as hell.

Jerome couldn't answer Freddy. All he could do was stare with revulsion at this distorted version of himself.

"This is you, Jerome. Part of you, anyway. I know what you're thinking: he's a shrimp with a melon-sized head. But that's only because you've kept him locked up inside you for so long that he hasn't had a chance to grow much. But that's all going to change now that I'm here to help him." Freddy gazed at the writhing, wriggling creature with an expression that was almost one of affection. "And you, too, Jerome. Thanks to your letting him out in the alley to get a little exercise, he's already had a growth spurt. Just look at the size of that noggin! But he's still too small to keep, so we have to cut him loose—for now." Freddy held fetus-Jerome over the burning water, then slashed out with his claw-knives. Steel blades cut through barbed wire as if it were thread, and the stunted creature with Jerome's face plunged back into the fiery lake, giving Jerome a last poisonous glare before disappearing beneath the surface.

Jerome stared in disbelief at the spot where the thing had dropped back in to the water. "What was that?"

"One of my children, Jerome. Just like you are."

Freddy tossed his bone-pole overboard, and as it sank, he spread his arms wide. The burning surface of the lake started to bubble and roil, as if its flames now blazed hot enough to bring the water to a boil. Wisps of steam rose from the lake as shapes broke the surface—hands, arms, heads, shoulders—dozens, no, hundreds of them, children and teenagers, boys and girls. They moaned, cried, shouted and screamed as the flames licked their flesh and the boiling water cooked them alive.

"These are my children, too," Freddy said. There was none of the usual mockery in his voice—only a sinister, dark love for these poor screaming, burning creatures. "Each one special to me in his or her own way." Freddy lowered his arms and looked at Jerome.

"But of all my sweet, beautiful children, you're one of the most special, Jerome. You and your..." Freddy smiled, "...brother."

Jerome knew that Freddy wasn't talking about his half-brother Brian. He was referring to the stunted, malformed thing he'd hauled out of the lake several moments ago.

"You see, they," he gestured toward the screaming, burning youths thrashing in the water, "are the children of my heart. But you and your brother are the children of my darkness. You're a smart kid, so by now you've probably figured out that I exist within the realm of dreams. It's a great place. After all, here I'm—"

Freddy vanished from the boat and his scarred face filled the entire sky.

"GOD!" he said in a voice of crashing thunder.

Jerome shrank away from the gigantic countenance, but then he blinked and Freddy was his normal size once more, sitting in the boat and facing him again.

"But as omnipotent as I am here—and as much as it chaps my ass to admit it—I'm limited when it comes to the trouble I can cause in the physical world. I keep trying, but something always happens to send me right back here. Usually some snot-nosed punk," he growled. "But do I give up? No way! Not Freddy Krueger, the Springwood Slasher! Stubborn old boogeyman that I am, I came up with a plan to establish a permanent presence in what you bone-bags so smugly refer to as the real world. And seventeen years ago, I put that plan into action."

A cold chill raced through Jerome, as if his entire blood supply had suddenly been replaced with freon.

Freddy leaned forward and slowly pulled scarred, cracked lips away from twisted, yellow teeth in a terrible parody of a smile. "You're that plan, Jerome. You… and your brother."

Freddy cackled and gripped the sides of the boat. He began swaying back and forth, rocking the outboard, slowly at first, but then with increasingly violent motions. His laughter grew louder, wilder, darker, and his eyes blazed with madness. Jerome tried to grab hold of the boat to steady himself, but the metal of the hull crumbled to rusty-red flakes beneath his hands. Freddy gave the boat a hard jerk to the right, and Jerome, unable to stop himself, slipped overboard and plunged into the flame-flecked lake. Every inch of Jerome's skin burned as if he'd been dunked in acid. The heat from the boiling water instantly penetrated his cells and began cooking him from the inside. His mouth was open as he went under, and he took a reflexive breath, sucking in double lungfuls of liquid fire. He tried to scream, but all that came out of his mouth was a shower of bubbles. His eyes began to poach in their sockets, and he squeezed his eyelids shut, but the thin layers of flesh were no protection against the water's heat.

Jerome thrashed his arms and legs in the desperate hope of reaching the surface and somehow climbing back into the boat. He didn't care about the flames burning on top of the water, didn't care that Freddy still waited for him in the boat. The super-hot lake water was boiling him alive, and he had to get out of it if he were to have any hope of surviving.

He felt himself rising upward—at least, he hoped it was upward; his eyes were closed and he was in so much pain that at the moment he wasn't the best judge of direction. But before he could reach the surface, he felt hands all over him, grabbing his clothes, clawing at his skin, snatching at his hair. At first he thought Freddy had leaped into the lake to come after him, but there were too many hands. And then he knew what was happening. Freddy's children, the ones that had been burning and screaming in the lake, had converged upon him, taken hold, and were attempting to prevent him from reaching the surface. Despite the maddening pain caused by his boiling flesh, Jerome fought his attackers—hit, kicked, gouged and bit—in an attempt to force them to let him go. But they held on fast, as if they no longer experienced any pain of their own.

Jerome's exertions soon grew weaker, his energy drained from the pain that seared his nerve-endings and from lack of oxygen to his brain. Freddy's children seemed to have no such needs—or at least, not to feel or care about their lack of. Jerome soon stopped thrashing and just lay in the boiling water, held under by the boys and girls that had preceded him into death, courtesy of Mr Freddy Krueger. And then a darkness much deeper and more final than the mere absence of sight came for him. And as it engulfed him, he thought he heard Freddy's mad cackle one last time, then he heard no more.

"Jerome? Honey, wake up!"

The voice seemed to come from far away within the darkness that surrounded him. No, not from within the darkness. From outside it.

He opened his eyes and saw a blurry image of someone kneeling next to him. His vision quickly focused, and he saw that it was Cheryl, gazing at him with an expression of concern. He looked around and saw that he was still in the back room of Showtime Video. He must've fallen asleep when El went back out front to take care of the customers.

He smiled weakly. "Hey, babe. What are you doing here?"

"I called her."

Jerome glanced past Cheryl and saw El standing just inside the open doorway. Probably so he could keep watch on his friend and the store at the same time.

"You wouldn't let me call the paramedics, so I figured Cheryl was the next best thing," El said, then frowned. "If nothing else, maybe she'll be able to talk some sense into you so you'll agree to go see a doctor."

"Since when have I—or anyone else—ever been able to talk sense into him?" Cheryl said. Her words were obviously intended to lighten the mood, but from the way her voice broke as she said them, it sounded as if she might start crying any moment.

Jerome reached out to comfort her and caught sight of his hand. The skin was smooth and unblemished, showing no signs of having been burnt. Yet he knew that the burning lake hadn't been a dream. Or at least, hadn't been *just* a dream. He put his hand on Cheryl's shoulder and gave it a loving squeeze.

"Don't worry. It looks a lot worse than it is."

"That's good." The tears began in earnest. "Because you look like shit."

She hugged him then and held him hard. He hugged her back with equal strength, and tried not to think of what Freddy had said in his dream.

You're that plan, Jerome.

You...

...and your brother.

"Jesus," Brent whispered. He sounded as if he were going to spew any second. Pat didn't blame him. He felt exactly the same way, but he wasn't about to admit to any weakness in front of his... Friend wasn't the right word. Pat didn't have friends. He had people that he liked or didn't, that did things for him or didn't. And from the look of Eddie, he wasn't going to do anything for Pat—or anyone else—ever again.

"Jesus God..." A liquid gagging sound burbled up from deep within Brent's throat, and he turned and vomited noisily onto the ground.

Pat was glad the dumbass hadn't thrown up on Eddie's corpse. If he had, that would've set him off for sure. As it was, just the hot smell of Brent's acidic stomach contents was enough to make his own gut start doing cartwheels.

Pat gazed upon the dead body of his... former associate... with as much clinical detachment as he could muster. He held a pencil-sized flashlight in his hand, and he played the thin beam of light back and forth over Eddie. He lay face down on the alley floor. Well, not quite, Pat thought. How could someone lie face down when he no longer had a face? Or even a fucking head? Eddie's neck ended in a ragged pulpy mass of flesh with a broken tip of spine sticking out. There was a smear of blood and brains on the wall at roughly eye level. Much of the gook had slid down the brickwork to splatter onto the ground near Eddie's neck stump, as if the contents of his head were slowly trying to ooze back into their former home. Skull fragments and teeth littered the ground around the body, all of them coated with varying amounts of blood. Several feet from Eddie lay a sodden black mass, and Pat's stomach lurched when he realized he was looking at Eddie's scalp.

"Who...? How...?" Brent's voice was raspy from vomiting, and his breath smelled like sour milk poured over rotten meat.

Vomit bubbled up into Pat's throat then, and he clamped his mouth shut and with a supreme act of will swallowed the shit back down. A moment later, when he was relatively confident he wasn't going to produce a technicolor yawn, he turned to Brent and elbowed him in the ribs.

"Don't stand so goddamned close—not until you've had a chance to gargle with an industrial-size drum of mouthwash!"

Brent rubbed his ribs and took a step back, but he didn't go far. "Jesus, Pat, look at him! What the fuck happened?"

From Brent's tone, it sounded as if he were close to hysteria. Pat didn't bother to tell him to try to keep calm. It was all he could do to keep himself from degenerating into a trembling, mewling, pants-pissing little boy.

"Jerome Starkey happened."

After Jerome had suddenly changed from wimp to pro streetfighter, Pat had fled the alley, not caring whether Eddie and Brent got away. But when Brent caught up to him a few blocks away—without Eddie—they'd both headed back in the direction of the alley, hoping they'd run into him along the way. Pat had hoped they'd also encounter Jerome again, so they could "give him the nastiest ass-beating in history". At least, that's what he told Brent. The truth was he didn't want anything more to do with Jerome tonight, and maybe not ever. But they hadn't run into Eddie, and when they reached the alley, Pat was secretly glad Jerome was gone. But he wasn't so glad anymore once he saw that Jerome had left them a present. One that was missing a head.

"Man," Brent said, exhaling yet another noxious cloud of puke-breath. "I knew Starkey was nuts, but I didn't think he'd ever do something like this!"

Pat reached up and massaged the scar on his forehead. "Can't say I'm surprised." He dropped his hand to his side and turned away from Eddie's mutilated corpse. "C'mon, let's get out of here."

As he flicked off his pencil light and tucked it into his back pocket, Brent looked at him with both surprise and disbelief. "But we can't just leave him! Not like this!" Brent gestured toward Eddie's corpse, but Pat refused to look at it again. He'd seen it enough already, enough to last him for eternity.

"We have to. There's no way we can explain to the cops what we were doing here. They might even blame us since we were waiting to jump Starkey. Hell, the son of a bitch might even claim he killed Eddie in self-defense, and the dumbshit cops might even believe him!"

"So what do we do?" Brent sounded like a lost little boy who desperately hoped that someone would show him the right direction to go.

"We haul ass out of here and call the cops from a pay phone. We leave them an anonymous tip about where to find Eddie, and then we hang up. They'll find Eddie and make sure he's taken care of." Pat wasn't exactly sure what would happen after that, but he did know one thing: Eddie's funeral was definitely going to be closed casket.

"So Starkey just gets away with killing Eddie?" Brent practically wailed these words.

Pat shook his head. "We'll take care of Starkey ourselves. That way we'll know for sure that justice has been done. Besides..." He forced a grin. "It'll be more fun that way."

TWELVE

"I'm not sure this is such a good idea."

Jerome sat in the front passenger seat of El's silver Eldorado while Cheryl drove. El had loaned them his car so Cheryl could drive him home. She'd helped clean him up in the rest room at Showtime Video, and while he still looked like a guy that had been in a fight, he no longer looked as if he were one step away from needing the services of an undertaker.

"Well, I do," Cheryl said. "It's going to be hard enough for you to explain what happened to your folks on your own." She gave him a quick glance. "Especially after what happened in detention between you and Pat Cottril this afternoon. I insist on being there when you talk to your dad and stepmom, for moral support if nothing else."

Jerome wanted to argue the point further, but he knew it was no use. Once Cheryl had made up her mind, there was no changing it. Especially if she believed she was doing the right thing. While part of him worried that her presence would only complicate the situation when he got home, he was also glad to have her support and was touched by her love and loyalty. Not for the first time, he wondered what he'd ever done to deserve someone as wonderful as Cheryl Garringer as his girlfriend. He figured it was most likely due to some cosmic screwup on the part of the universe, but whatever the reason, he was grateful that she was in his life.

They drove through one of Springwood's nicer residential neighborhoods, though not quite as nice as where Jerome lived. Full night had fallen and Cheryl had the Eldorado's headlights on. She slowed as they approached an intersection, and in the wash of the headlights' illumination, Jerome saw the street sign on the corner. They were at the intersection of Poplar and Elm.

Elm Street.

Jerome wasn't sure why, but he felt a cold prickling on the back of his neck upon seeing the sign.

Cheryl activated the left turn signal, but before she could perform the maneuver, Jerome said, "Why don't you keep going straight?"

He tried to keep the nervousness he felt out of his voice, but he knew he'd failed by the half puzzled, half suspicious look Cheryl gave him.

"But it's faster to go down Elm," she said. "Unless you want to postpone talking to your folks as long as possible. Then I'll be glad to take the slow way."

Jerome wasn't looking forward to talking with his dad and Lynn, but that wasn't the reason for his reluctance to take Elm Street. But since he couldn't express why he was reluctant, he said, "Nevermind. Elm's okay."

Cheryl looked at him for a moment longer, as if giving him a chance to explain. But he said nothing more, so she faced forward, pressed down on the gas, pulled into the intersection, and turned left. As soon as they began driving down Elm Street, a cold shivery feeling settled into the pit of Jerome's stomach and made itself comfortable there.

Halfway down the street, they came to it. The House.

Two stories, gray unpainted wood, roof full of holes and ready to collapse, planks nailed over the windows, front steps chipped and cracked. The yard was covered with dead brown weeds, and the few trees that still survived were stunted leafless mockeries of plant life.

Jerome didn't know anything about the house, beyond the fact that it was a Bad Place and everyone—especially kids—were supposed to stay away from it at all costs. Not only that, but people didn't even like to look at it as they went past. It was almost as if the citizens of Springwood were determined to make believe that the house didn't exist, like if they could just make believe hard enough, maybe it really would go away. But it never did. It was always there, sitting like some sort of stubborn growth that defied all attempts to have it removed.

Then they were past the house, and Jerome's unease began to subside, though it didn't disappear entirely.

They continued on in silence and several minutes later Cheryl pulled the Eldorado to a stop in front of Jerome's house. The lights were on, of course. He couldn't be lucky enough to find dad and Lynn had given up on waiting for him and gone out for the evening. And to make matters worse, there was a green Volkswagen Beetle parked in the driveway, with bumper stickers that proclaimed MIRACLES HAPPEN! and THINK GLOBALLY, ACT LOCALLY.

Jerome groaned. "Bekka's here, too. She said she was going to come over, but I forgot all about it. I hope she hasn't been here too long. The more time she and Lynn spend around each other, the more they end up fighting."

He was tempted to tell Cheryl to start the car up again and drive off, but he knew he couldn't avoid his family forever. Besides, after everything that had happened today, he was actually kind of looking forward to seeing them—even Lynn. He hated to admit it to himself, but he needed to be around them, to be around normalcy again. So what if he didn't always get along with his family? That didn't seem to matter so much anymore... Not since Freddy had gotten into his head.

So he and Cheryl got out of the car, and she took his hand as they crossed the walkway to the front door. He recalled trying to sneak in last night. It seemed as if that had happened weeks ago, instead of less than twenty-four hours.

At least this time I'm going in the front, he thought.

He pulled his house keys out of his pocket, unlocked the front door and stepped aside so Cheryl could enter first.

She gave him a smile and squeezed his hand. "Such a gentleman." Then she entered and Jerome followed.

He half expected Dad and Lynn to be standing in the foyer waiting for him, arms crossed, stern expressions on their faces. But no one was there. He closed the door and locked it, then paused and listened. Usually Brian and Mary were screaming like banshees as they fought over who got what toy or whose turn it was to play GameCube. But he heard nothing.

Cheryl cocked her head as she looked at him. "What's wrong?"

Jerome shook his head, not sure yet how to reply. He started slowly down the foyer, and Cheryl followed, frowning. He felt as if he should tell her to remain by the front door as he checked the house out, but he didn't want to look like a paranoid idiot. What was he afraid of, anyway? That Freddy Krueger—whatever the hell he was—had somehow escaped the realm of dreams and entered the real world? That the scar-faced lunatic had used that bladed glove of his to cut Jerome's entire family to shreds? That he would find bits and pieces of them scattered around the house—a finger here, an ear there—as if Freddy had set up some kind of obscene scavenger hunt?

As much as it chaps my ass to admit it, I'm limited when it comes to the trouble I can cause in the physical world.

But what if Freddy had been lying? What if everything he'd said had been a lie, all part of whatever sick mind game the bastard was playing? What if Freddy was in the house right now, standing over the eviscerated bodies of Jerome's family, his finger-knives dripping with thick strands of blood and body parts...

Fear surged in Jerome's chest and he broke into a run, leaving Cheryl behind. His shoes pounded on the hallway carpet as he moved deeper into the house.

"Dad?" he called. "Lynn?"

"Jerome, what's wrong?" Cheryl called after him, and he heard the sound of her running to catch up to him. He didn't slow down. He raced to the dining room, and when he got there he stopped so fast that he nearly lost his balance and fell.

His family sat at the dining table—dad, Lynn, Brian, Mary and Bekka. As usual, Lynn sat as far away from Bekka as she could. Brian sat next to Bekka, while Mary sat on her lap. Both of his step-siblings had chocolate smeared across the lower half of their faces.

"Hi, J'rome!" Mary said with a chocolaty grin. "Aunt Bekka brought cupcakes!"

On the table was an open plastic container that did indeed hold cupcakes, though not so many as it had when first opened. Each of the adults had one sitting on a small plate in front of them, along with cups of coffee and, in Bekka's case, herbal tea, though as yet they'd only nibbled at their desserts. From the chocolate on their faces and the crumbs on their plates, it was obvious that Mary and Brian had absolutely devastated their first cupcakes and were now hard at work on seconds. His stepsiblings were far too engrossed in their treats to take note of Jerome's condition, but the three adults weren't so distracted.

"My God, Jerome. What happened to you?" Lynn said, starting to rise from her chair. "Did you have an accident?"

Before he could say anything, Cheryl caught up to him and joined him in the entryway to the dining room. She put a hand on his shoulder as if she were afraid he might take off again if she didn't hold him in place.

"Hi, everyone," she said.

Lynn stopped in mid-rise, as if unsure whether she should stand up all the way or sit back down.

"Hello, dear." She looked to Don, then Bekka, then back to Don again. Jerome's father shrugged and Lynn decided to take her seat once again.

The only one who didn't look surprised by Jerome's appearance was Bekka. She did, however, look concerned, and for some reason sad.

"Why don't you two sit down?" Jerome's father said. "We'll get you something to drink and then we can talk about whatever's going on." When he was finished speaking, he gave Bekka a sideways glance. She nodded almost imperceptibly and Don relaxed. Lynn noticed Bekka's nod, though, and frowned, but she didn't comment on it.

Jerome was glad for Bekka's presence. Because she'd brought cupcakes, the kids were still here, and that meant dad and Lynn would be reluctant to start yelling at him right away. Plus, since Bekka was his mother's twin, Don tended to defer to her when it came to Jerome, almost as if she really were his mother. It was one of the numerous reasons that Lynn wasn't especially fond of Jerome's aunt, along with the way Brian and Mary called her "aunt" when she was no relation to them by either blood or marriage.

As if seizing an opportunity to get away from Bekka, Lynn said, "I'll get the drinks," and started to stand up again. "Coffee okay, Jerome?"

He nodded, then winced as the motion set his head to hurting again. "Regular, please." He had no intention of sleeping tonight—maybe ever again—if he could help it.

"Tea for me, if you don't mind," Cheryl said.

Lynn's answering smile seemed genuine enough. Jerome had the sense that she really liked Cheryl, which always came as a relief since she didn't like Bekka. Lynn finished getting up and left the dining room. There were only two chairs unoccupied—one of them by where Lynn had been sitting. Without waiting for Jerome to express a preference, Cheryl walked over to the seat next to Lynn's and sat down. It seemed his girlfriend intended to serve as a buffer between Jerome and his stepmother if need be. He smiled at her thoughtfulness, though it made his swollen lip crack open and start to bleed again. He rubbed at the cut with his fingers and wondered yet again how he'd ever gotten so lucky to have someone as great as her to care for him. Jerome walked over and took the last empty seat. Everyone was silent for several moments after that. At least, no one spoke. The kids were devouring their second cupcakes with such gusto that the dining room echoed with their chewing, smacking, slurping and gulping sounds.

Lynn soon returned with plates and saucers, then went back to the kitchen and brought out their coffee and tea. She set the drinks down on the saucers in front of Jerome and Cheryl, and said, "Help yourselves to one of Bekka's cupcakes," then sat down next to Don. She looked at Jerome expectantly, her expression calm enough, but her eyes quivered with worry and nervousness, and her right foot tapped rapidly against a chair leg—a sure sign she was upset.

Jerome took a deep breath and then started to talk. He gave them an edited version of events—no possessed frogs, no nightmares, and absolutely no Freddy Krueger. When he was finished, Lynn's face had become a shade or two paler, and his dad looked as if he wanted to both hug and throttle his son at the same time.

"We should take you to a doctor," Lynn said. "If you can't remember what happened in the alley when you were attacked, it might be because you've sustained a serious head injury!"

"El told me the same thing," Jerome said. "But I honestly feel fine." Maybe not so honestly, but he didn't feel like he was going to keel over dead any minute either. "It was dark in the alley and everything happened so fast. More than anything else, I think that's the main reason my memories of the attack are so fuzzy."

You lie like you were born to it. The interior voice sounded amused, and this time it was accompanied by a mental image of the fetus thing Freddy had pulled from the lake in Jerome's last dream. Was that who the voice belonged to? To that... that creature?

"That makes sense," Don said. "We'll just keep an eye on you and see how you do. If it looks like we need to take you to a hospital, we will. Sound good to you, Lynn? Bekka?"

Lynn didn't look too happy, but she didn't disagree with her husband. Bekka had remained silent the entire time Jerome had been telling his story. He'd had the feeling that she was perfectly aware that he was lying—or at least omitting certain details—but she'd done nothing other than sit quietly while he talked. But now that Don had put a direct question to her, she responded.

"Jerome's injuries—his physical ones, anyway—aren't so serious that he needs a doctor. As for his spiritual wounds..." she trailed off.

Jerome looked at Bekka hard, willing her to receive the thought message he was broadcasting.

Please, no weird stuff! Not now, not here! Just let me do my own thing, and I'll figure it all out before too long, I swear!

But if Bekka had received the mental message, she gave Jerome no sign of it.

"Please, Bekka," Lynn said. "You know how I feel about anything of an occult nature being discussed in my house." She glanced at Mary and Brian, their faces still dirty, bellies bulging from all the cupcakes and milk they'd ingested. "I don't want to expose the children to such things."

From the way she stressed that last word, it was clear that by things she really meant horseshit. Not that Mary and Brian were paying any attention; they both looked on the verge of falling asleep.

Don rose. "Tell you what, I'll go get the kids washed up and ready for bed, and once they're tucked in, I'll be back."

Lynn looked as if she wanted to protest being left with Bekka without Don there to referee, but she nodded. Don stood, went over to Bekka, and picked up a nearly unconscious Mary. Brian was equally tired, but he was older and bigger, and thus had to walk on his own. The kids mumbled good night to Bekka, kissed her on the cheek, then allowed their father to escort them to the bathroom for face washing and tooth brushing.

Brian held onto Don's hand as they left the living room. "Is Jerome going to be okay?" he asked sleepily.

"Of course he is," Don said, though Jerome could hear the doubt in his voice.

Once Brian and Mary were out of the dining room, Bekka resumed speaking.

"What I'm going to tell you might sound ridiculous at first, Jerome… Cheryl… but you need to believe me. Your lives may well depend on it."

Lynn gripped the edge of the table so hard, her knuckles turned white. "Don't do this, Bekka." There was anger in her voice, but also a tone of pleading. "You know how important it is that we don't say anything about… him."

Jerome felt as if Lynn's words had struck him a physical blow. She wasn't telling Bekka that she was nuts. She sounded like a co-conspirator urging a comrade to maintain secrecy.

That's exactly right, the voice in his head whispered. *They're in it together. All of them—Lynn, Bekka, your dad…*

In on what, Jerome thought?

In on the lie, came the answer.

"We have to tell them, Lynn," Bekka said. "It's the only way."

Lynn looked at Jerome's aunt for a long moment, and then she let go of the table edge and placed her hands in her lap. She released a sigh, then nodded.

"All right, go ahead."

Jerome wanted to interrupt, to ask Lynn and Bekka why they were suddenly talking, if not like friends, then at least like allies. But he feared that if he said anything Lynn might rescind her co-operation, and he and Cheryl might never get a chance to hear what Bekka had to say. Besides, he already knew, didn't he? They were in on it—both of them.

"Many years ago, a child killer stalked the streets of Springwood. He murdered dozens of children before he was caught. But instead of going to prison, he got off on a technicality. Outraged, the town's parents banded together to take justice into their own hands. They confronted the killer... and burned him alive."

"How awful!" Cheryl said.

Jerome took her hand and gave it a reassuring squeeze, but his gaze was focused on Lynn. She looked down at the table, as if she didn't want to meet Bekka's eyes. Or was afraid to.

At least she has the decency to look ashamed about lying to you all these years, whispered the voice in Jerome's head. *Lying and keeping secrets...*

Jerome felt the first stirrings of anger inside him, and he fought to ignore them, to stamp out their sparks and prevent them from becoming a raging fire.

"But the killer didn't die," Bekka continued. "At least, not as most people understand the concept of death. His body was destroyed, but his foul spirit somehow survived and found a new home in the realm of dreams. There, he became far more powerful than he'd ever been as a mortal killer, and he began to plot his revenge against the parents who had taken his life."

Though the dining room was warm, Jerome shivered as if a cold breeze suddenly wafted through it.

"Freddy Krueger," he whispered.

Lynn jumped at the sound of the killer's name, as if saying it might somehow be enough to summon him. But Bekka just nodded. "That's right. Freddy used his new dark powers to reach out to Springwood's surviving children—many of them now grown into teenagers—through their dreams. And the killing began again."

You see? Bekka knew about Freddy, too. And she never said a word about him to you your entire life.

The anger began to build again, and this time, Jerome didn't bother to try to control it.

Lynn looked up at Bekka, her expression defiant, though her voice trembled. "They stopped him, though."

"For a time," Bekka acknowledged. "But while Krueger was beaten, he wasn't destroyed. He retreated to the dream realm to lick his wounds and restore his strength. This cycle would be repeated a number of times. Months, sometimes years, would pass, and then the killing would start anew."

Bekka paused then, but Jerome couldn't speak. He wanted to deny what Bekka was saying, wanted to tell her she was full of shit, then get up and walk away and pretend that he'd never heard of Freddy Krueger. But he couldn't, not after everything that had happened to him in the last twenty-four hours. He understood then why Ms LeClair had asked him if he'd been having any strange dreams lately. She knew all about Freddy Krueger, too. It seemed like everyone knew—except him.

They're liars, the voice said. *Every one of them...*

"That old abandoned house on Elm? The real spooky one?" Jerome said. "That's his home, isn't it?"

"Yes," Bekka said. "And it's still the center of his power in the real world. Even people who aren't psychically aware can sense Krueger's evil when they're near it."

"If all this is true," Cheryl said, "then why haven't Jerome or I ever heard anything about this guy? Even if he was only a regular human killer, he'd be a local legend. Kids would pass his story down from one generation to the next. But I've never heard the name Freddy Krueger in my life."

"That's because after decades of losing their children to this monster, the adults of Springwood—many of whom had been children themselves during Freddy's earliest rampages—realized that the only way to defeat him was to cut off his access to his victims," Bekka said. "Various medications were tried to suppress the children's dreams, but while they worked for a time, drugs ultimately proved ineffective."

Lynn picked up the story from there. "So the adults reasoned that if they couldn't stop their kids from dreaming, maybe they could at least keep them from dreaming about Freddy. And if they didn't dream about him, if no one did, he wouldn't be able to get at the children, and maybe he'd even cease to exist altogether."

"Did it work?" Jerome asked. Maybe the adults had a reason for their lies and their secrets, he thought. His anger didn't recede, but it didn't get any worse—for the moment.

Cheryl shot him a look as if to say, "You're not really buying this stuff, are you?" But she didn't say anything.

Bekka and Lynn exchanged glances. "More or less," Bekka said. "The adults still know... Some of us, anyway, so Krueger's not completely forgotten, but we've worked very hard to make sure that no children or teens know about him. As a result, the killings have been fewer in number and more years pass between them. Krueger's like a disease. If you inoculate enough people against it, eventually the disease dies out because it can't find any new hosts. That's what we're hoping will happen with Krueger one day: that no one in Springwood will remember Freddy Krueger as anything other than a long-dead killer, and he'll become just another forgotten nightmare and vanish into the realm of dreams forever."

Bekka and Lynn fell silent after that. Cheryl looked at Jerome, then at the two women.

"So you're telling us you really believe this... this ghost story?" She fixed her gaze on Lynn. "Both of you?"

"Both of them what?"

Don Starkey came back into the dining room and took his seat next to Lynn. Jerome felt a renewed surge of anger upon seeing his father. His own dad, in on it with the rest of them.

"Got them both down," he said. "Hopefully the little monkeys will sleep through the night and have pleasant dreams."

"Or no dreams at all," Lynn amended.

Don's expression became grim. "You told them about Krueger." It wasn't a question.

"Yes, they did," Jerome said, struggling to keep from raising his voice. "But what I want to know is how you could've kept this knowledge from me my whole life."

Don frowned. "Didn't they tell you about the containment strategy?"

"We did," Lynn said, and Bekka nodded.

Jerome understood then why his father had taken Brian and Mary upstairs: to prevent them from hearing about Freddy and becoming "infected" by the knowledge of his existence.

"So what don't you understand?" Don asked. "We're just trying to protect you." He glanced at Cheryl. "All of you."

"I'm not talking about that," Jerome said, feeling his anger start to rise again. "I'm talking about how Freddy Krueger killed my mother."

THIRTEEN

Lynn gasped as if Jerome had slapped her, and Don's face went pale. Bekka's expression, however, showed only sadness and sympathy.

"But your mom died in a car accident," Cheryl said. She then added, "Didn't she?"

"It might have looked like an accident," Jerome said. "But it wasn't, not really."

They all turned to look at Don Starkey, and in a soft voice he said, "Freddy was the one who caused her to crash. At least, that's what we always figured."

By "we," Jerome knew his father meant himself and Bekka.

The liars... The secret-keepers...

"After Joanna died, I dreamed about Freddy," Bekka said. "He taunted me, told me how he'd chosen her... and why." She looked at Jerome, but then quickly glanced away. "I think he wanted to kill me, too, because he didn't want me interfering with his plans later on down the road. But I was psychically stronger than my sister, and more importantly, I was prepared for him. Despite his best efforts, Krueger was never able to kill me, and after a while, he gave up trying. I haven't dreamed about him in years."

There was something about the way Bekka said this last statement that made Jerome think that while it might technically be accurate, it wasn't the whole truth.

"Your dreams were probably just a coincidence," Cheryl said. "If people still talked about Freddy when you were younger, it only makes sense that you'd dream about him from time to time. Especially if you were trying to come to terms with such a traumatic event as the death of your twin sister."

Bekka smiled. "You'll make a wonderful psychologist someday, Cheryl. But I assure you my dreams were real."

"Please understand, Jay," Don said. "We couldn't tell you the truth about what happened to your mother—not if I wanted to keep the same thing from happening to you. Krueger took Joanna, but I'd be damned if I was going to let him take you as well."

Part of Jerome was touched by the fierce love in his father's voice, but another part, the part where his anger sprang from, couldn't believe what he was hearing.

"So you—all of you adults—decided for us. You decided it was safer to keep your children in the dark instead of warning us about Krueger, instead of teaching us how to protect ourselves."

Go, man, go! his inner voice urged. *Let 'em have it with both barrels!*

Don seemed suddenly unsure of himself. "I... *we* didn't think of it like that, Jay. We—"

Jerome slammed his fists down onto the table and spoke in a low, dangerous voice. "Don't... call... me... Jay!"

Don glanced at Lynn, then Bekka before saying, "Sure. Whatever you want."

Cheryl put a hand on Jerome's arm. "It's okay, honey. Calm down. They were just doing what they thought was best."

He looked at Cheryl's hand and experienced an urge to yank his arm away from her touch, but he didn't. She was the only thing helping keep his anger somewhat in check.

"What about what we think is best?" he countered. "We're adults now, or close enough. We should be able to make decisions about our own lives."

Cheryl didn't respond, and Don and Lynn exchanged regret-filled glances.

"You've encountered Freddy in your dreams," Bekka said. "Haven't you?"

Jerome didn't want to answer.

Why should you tell them anything after they concealed the truth from you for so long?

But Bekka kept looking at him, her eyes filled with love and concern. Eyes set in a face that was the image of what his mother would look like today if she'd still been alive. And he found he couldn't ignore her question.

"Yes. The first time was last night, after I… I accidentally broke my dreamcatcher. I've dreamed of him a few times since. Whenever I doze off, even if it's only for a couple minutes, he's there."

Cheryl opened her mouth as if she were going to say something, but then she closed it and gave his arm a reassuring squeeze. She might not believe in Freddy Krueger, but the message was clear: she believed in Jerome.

"Why didn't you say anything?" Lynn asked.

"What was I supposed to say? 'Hi, Dad, Lynn. Guess what? I dreamed about a scar-faced killer who's some kind of undead dream demon last night. Pretty weird, huh?'"

"Don't get smart, son," Don corrected, but there was little force behind the words, and Jerome realized—with both a thrill of excitement and a pang of guilt—that his father was afraid of him, afraid to make him any angrier. Afraid of what Jerome might do.

Jerome tried to soften his tone as he added, "Why would I say anything? I'd never heard of Freddy Krueger before."

"That dreamcatcher was… special," Bekka said. "It contained real power, enough to keep Freddy from entering your dreams."

Jerome remembered something Krueger had said in one of his dreams.

"I've been trying to talk to you for years, but I was never able to get through to you. We had a bad case of telepathicus interruptus, you might say. Until you had that little tantrum in your room and threw your shoe at the wall, that is. Now you're receiving me loud and clear, Jerome."

It seemed the dreamcatcher had been the real deal, and like an idiot, he'd gone and broken it.

"Over the last several hours since I saw you outside the video store, I searched through my library," Bekka said, "looking for some information, no matter how vague or obscure, that might allow me to repair your dreamcatcher so Freddy will once again be denied access to your dreams. I found a few things, and I'll give the repairs my best shot, but I'm not at all confident that I'm up to the task."

"So Freddy's still going to be able to waltz into my skull whenever he feels like it," Jerome said.

Bekka didn't reply. She didn't have to.

"There's something I don't understand," Cheryl said. "Why did Freddy kill Jerome's birth mother, and why is he coming after Jerome all these years later?"

"I'm not sure Krueger needs a reason," Bekka said. "He's not human anymore... if he ever really was to begin with. Causing pain and suffering amuses him, feeds him the same way food, air and drink sustain us. But if I had to guess, I believe he went after Joanna because she was pregnant. Once Krueger entered Joanna's mind, he had access to Jerome as well because he was still inside Joanna, still connected to her. I think Freddy... did something to Jerome while he was still in Joanna's womb. Something that marked him somehow. Changed him. Whatever Krueger tried to do seventeen years ago, he didn't accomplish his goal. But now that Jerome's no longer protected by the dreamcatcher, he's returned to finish the job."

A sudden look of understanding came over Lynn's face. "Do you think that might explain Jerome's problems with anger? That they're the result of whatever Freddy did—or is still trying to do—to him?"

Jerome imagined himself standing up, calmly walking over to stand beside Lynn, cupping the back of her head with the palm of his hand, and then slamming her forehead against the tabletop. Once, twice, three times, until the dining table was covered with blood, brains and bone and his stepmother's face was a crushed ruin.

Jerome gave his head a shake to clear it. He was still in his seat, and Lynn's face remained intact.

Bekka nodded. "I'd considered that, yes."

Listen to them talk about you as if you weren't even here, Jerome's inner voice said.

He felt his anger begin to build again.

"So Jay—Jerome's been, what?" Don said. "Infected by Freddy somehow?"

They're talking about you like there's something wrong with you, the voice said. *Like you were born wrong, like you're some kind of fucking freak!*

He saw himself grabbing his coffee mug, flinging the still hot contents into his dad's face, then reaching across the table to slam the mug hard against his temple. He imagined hearing the twin sounds of breaking porcelain and shattering skull as his father's eyes rolled white and he collapsed to the dining room floor.

Jerome's hand twitched in the direction of his mug, but he didn't take hold of it and did his best to shove the image out of his mind. Stay calm, he told himself. Dad's just worried about you, that's all.

Worried about what people are going to think of him, you mean. Worried that everyone will find out he fathered a sideshow attraction...

Jerome clenched his teeth and tried to ignore his inner voice, but the rage continued to swell inside him, and he knew there was nothing he could do to stop it. He had to get out of here now, before he did or said something he'd regret.

He turned to Cheryl. "Give me El's keys." His voice was harsh and raspy. It didn't sound like him at all.

Cheryl blinked in surprise. "What?"

"The keys," he repeated, almost growling the words this time. "Now."

Cheryl frowned but she reached into her jeans pocket, removed the keys and handed them to Jerome.

When they were in his palm, he curled his fingers around them and made a fist. The points of the keys dug painfully into his flesh, but he didn't care. In fact, he rather liked the sensation. He turned to go, but before he could, Bekka reached over and took hold of his wrist.

"Please, Jerome! Don't leave. It's important that you remain here with us... so we can help you!"

An image flashed through his mind. He saw himself yanking free of Bekka's grip, grabbing a fork off the dining table and ramming it into her left eye. He saw the eyeball pop like an overripe grape as the tines of the fork penetrated its surface, saw viscous goo mixed with blood pour down her cheek. He imagined shoving the fork deep into her brain and then twisting it around, as if he were trying to twirl a forkful of pasta.

Bekka gasped and pulled her hand from Jerome's wrist as if she'd been burned. She reached up to touch her left eye and seemed both surprised and relieved to find herself uninjured.

Jerome was overwhelmed by a sudden surge of guilt that, instead of blunting his anger, only seemed to intensify it. But the guilt vanished almost as soon as it had come. He remembered the dream he'd had in Ms LeClair's office, in which Freddy had told him the story of Pinnochio before jamming his finger-blades into Jerome's gut. He remembered Freddy withdrawing the blades, remembered seeing a cricket impaled on one of them. Remembered Freddy popping the insect into his mouth and eating it. What had Freddy said then? Something about Jerome's conscience getting in the way of his plan—a conscience Freddy had removed and devoured.

"I have to leave." Jerome turned and ran out of the dining room. He heard Lynn call out after him, heard Bekka say, "Let him go. He's leaving to protect us as much as anything else."

Then Jerome was down the hall, in the foyer, opening the front door, running across the lawn toward El's car. He got behind the wheel, inserted the key into the ignition, turned it and pressed the gas pedal to the floor before the engine caught. The silver Eldorado leaped forward with a screeching of tires. The back end of the vehicle fishtailed, and Jerome nearly lost control, but he eased off the gas and managed to straighten the car out. He then flipped on the headlights and roared down the street. He had no idea where he was going, but that didn't matter, just as long as it was away.

So focused was he on putting as much distance as possible between his family and his anger that he didn't notice a pair of headlights wink into existence in his rear-view mirror and begin to follow him.

"What did I tell you? What did I fucking tell you?"

Pat Cottril gripped the steering wheel of his 1976 Camaro so hard that it looked as if the knuckles might burst through the skin at any moment. In the passenger seat beside him, Brent Haney had both of his hands pressed against the dashboard to brace himself. A Godsmack CD was blasting out of the car's speakers, the bass so loud that Brent could feel the vibrations in his marrow. He would've worn his seatbelt, but Pat always said that belts were for "babies and pussies", so Brent never wore one when riding with Pat. But he wished he'd risked Pat's disdain and put one on this time. He had the feeling this chase was going to get real hairy real fast.

"Yeah, you told me, all right." Brent knew from long experience that Pat never asked rhetorical questions. He might not always want your opinion about something—all right, he never wanted your opinion—but he always wanted an answer, preferably one that praised him somehow.

After finding Eddie's body and calling in an anonymous tip to the cops, they'd parked Pat's Camaro down the street from Showtime Video and waited for Jerome to show himself. They were both surprised when Cheryl Garringer arrived and escorted Jerome out to El's piece-of-shit Eldorado, and equally surprised when Cheryl drove. As the Eldorado had pulled away from the curb, Pat hit the Camaro's ignition and followed.

"We'll just hang back for now," Pat had said, and though Brent didn't know the specifics of what his friend was thinking, his meaning was nonetheless clear. Pat might want revenge on Jerome, but he didn't intend to hurt Cheryl to get it. So they'd tailed the Eldorado to the Starkey residence, parked down the block, killed the engine, and watched Jerome and Cheryl go inside.

"Now we wait for Starkey to come back out," Pat said.

Brent wasn't sure what they were doing was smart. Sure, he was freaked out by Eddie's death and wanted his killer to pay, but he wasn't excited about the idea of he and Pat personally exacting vengeance—especially if they got caught. But more than that, he couldn't get the image of Eddie lying headless in the alley out of his mind. Jerome had killed Eddie with his bare hands—what might he do to the two of them if given a chance? But Brent wasn't about to voice his fears to Pat. It wouldn't do any good, and he certainly wasn't going to ask Pat to let him out of the car. Even if he did (which Brent doubted) he'd make sure Brent paid for his cowardice later—and paid big. Like it or not, Brent was along for the ride on this one, and there wasn't a damn thing he could do about it.

Brent had wanted to ask what they'd do if Cheryl accompanied Jerome once more when he left the house (a distinct possibility as far as Brent was concerned). But Pat wasn't exactly tolerant of questions. His usual reply to them was "If I want any shit out of you, I'll squeeze your head." So Brent had remained silent. But not long afterward, Pat's patience was rewarded when Jerome came running out of the front door, alone, and got into El's car, still alone, and drove off like he was desperate to qualify for a Nascar race.

Brent had wondered why Cheryl hadn't come with Jerome. Had they had a fight or something? But he didn't bother saying anything to Pat. He'd just say it didn't matter, just as long as Jerome was alone, and Brent figured that was true enough. So he stopped worrying about anything except being prepared to beat Jerome's head in—or worse—when they finally caught up with him.

Pat hung back several car lengths, which Brent thought was a smart move. Pat's Camaro could no doubt leave the Eldorado in the dust, but they didn't want Jerome to get wise that they were following him. They trailed Jerome for several blocks. He was moving fast, and not once did he use his turn signal or come to a full stop at an intersection. To Brent, it looked like Jerome was driving back and forth through various neighborhoods without any destination in mind, but after several minutes, Pat said, "He's heading out of town."

Brent glanced out the window and saw that the houses were now fewer and farther between, the yards larger and trees more numerous. They weren't quite in the country yet, but they were getting there.

"Do you think he's seen us and is trying to make a run for it?" Brent asked.

Pat didn't answer right away, and Brent figured he was going to tell him to shut up. But instead he said, "By now he's probably noticed that a car's behind him, but I don't think he's figured out it's us. It's too dark and we're too far behind for him to recognize my Camaro, so I think we're cool. Lucky for us the fucking murderer is heading for the country. Plenty of room to play there, and no witnesses to worry about."

Pat grinned and leaned forward like a wolf that's caught a strong whiff of its prey. He pressed down on the accelerator, and slowly the distance between the two cars began to narrow.

Wimp! Coward! Feeb!

Jerome tried to ignore the names his inner voice was calling him. He wasn't aware of it, but his lips formed the words as they swirled in his mind.

I can't believe you're running away!

"I'm not running," Jerome muttered. "I'm driving."

Har-de-fucking-har! So you're not just a loser, you're a funny loser!

"I'm not going to hurt my family—hurt Cheryl—like..."

Like what? Or maybe I should say, like who?

Jerome experienced a flash of memory, of slamming someone's head against a brick wall.

"Nevermind." He flipped on the radio and cranked the volume in an attempt to drawn out the voice. The gentle tones of Stone Temple Pilots's "Lady Picture Show" filled the Eldorado.

Like Eddie Jackson. Despite the music, the internal voice came in loud and clear as ever.

"No."

You're too much of a coward to face it, so you refuse to remember what we did. But in your gut you know what happened. We took Eddie out once and for all... Pulped his head like a rotten melon!

Jerome slammed his palm down on the steering wheel, making the car swerve a little, but not enough for him to lose control.

"No!" he shouted. But the voice was right. He could deny it at the top of his lungs until the day he died. But deep down he knew it was true: he'd killed Eddie Jackson. That was why, after driving around aimlessly for a while, he'd finally decided to get to his destination.

What are you talking about? The voice sounded suspicious, and also a little afraid.

"I... We are going to Westin Hills. I'm going to check myself in before anyone else gets hurt."

The voice was silent for several moments, and Jerome began to hope that it was going to leave him in peace, if only for a short while. But it turned out to be a vain hope, for the voice said, *You can't do that.*

"Watch me."

Jerome had reached the edge of town, and it would only take a few more minutes until he reached Westin Hills. He didn't know if the doctors there could help him, but if all they could do was lock him away so he'd no longer be a threat to anyone, that would be good enough. And whatever kind of plan Freddy Krueger had for him, it would be awfully hard to execute if Jerome was locked up in a padded cell, or wherever crazy fucks like him were put these days.

You've kept me trapped inside you all your life, Jerome. And every time I managed to get out of my cage, you put me right back in. But now that I finally have a chance to gain my freedom for good, I won't let you take it away from me!

Jerome started to reply, but before he could speak he noticed headlights in his rearview mirror. They'd been back there for a while, and he hadn't thought too much about them. But now their reflection was getting larger; whoever was behind him was coming up fast. Maybe whoever it was just wanted to pass. There were hardly ever any cops patrolling out in the country, and people—especially teenagers—often drove as fast as they wanted out here.

Jerome eased off the accelerator and the twin beams in his rearview mirror merged into a single glare of light. An instant later there was a loud crunching sound, and Jerome's head whipped forward.

"What the fuck?"

He tightened his grip on the steering wheel and glanced over his shoulder to look out the back window. All he could see behind him was the bright wash of headlights, and then another impact came, and Jerome's head snapped front again. His seatbelt tightened and held him back, and the steering wheel suddenly felt strange in his hands, too loose, and he wondered if the second impact had done something to the steering or one of the wheels. Nevertheless, he jammed his foot down on the gas. The crazy bastards were trying to run him off the road, and he wanted to get as far away from them as fast as he could.

The old Eldorado hesitated for a moment, but El took good care of his car, and the engine let out a deep roar as the vehicle surged forward. But it was too little, too late. The car behind him slammed into the Eldorado's bumper once more, and this time the rear end started to swerve to the right.

Jerome was gripped by pure terror. Ever since he'd first learned as a child how his mother had died, he'd been terrified of dying in a car accident. His fear was so bad that he almost hadn't taken the driver's ed, and after he passed the class, almost hadn't got his license. Even then, he still didn't like to drive all that much, and wasn't that upset that he didn't own a car of his own.

The swerve became worse and the Eldorado headed into a spin.

"Shit!"

Shit's right, and we're in it deep, bro. But I can get us out. All you have to do is let me drive for a while. What do you say?

The words passed through Jerome's mind with the speed of thought, and as the nose of the Eldorado began to swing around to face his attacker, Jerome knew the voice was right. It possessed a strength and savagery he did not, and it was his best chance for survival, just like in the alley.

"All right, damn you! Do it!"

Jerome felt a welling up of glee, and then the darkness took him and he knew nothing more.

FOURTEEN

As the Eldorado started to spin, Brent really wished he'd put on his seatbelt. He grabbed hold of the door handle to steady himself, and pressed both feet down hard against the floor. He had no idea how effective either of these actions would be should Pat's Camaro slam into the silver Eldorado, but they were all he could think to do, so he did them.

Pat whooped with delight, as if he were riding a particularly wild rollercoaster. He eased off the gas—much to Brent's relief—though he didn't hit the brakes. Illuminated by the Camaro's sole remaining headlight (the other had broken when Pat rammed the Eldorado for the second time) Jerome's car spun several times before sliding off the road and into a ditch. Pat slammed on the brakes then, and the Camaro's tires screamed as the car skidded to a stop. Silence hit Brent's ears like a physical force, and all he could do for a moment was sit while his heart fluttered in his chest like a tiny terrified bird.

"C'mon, asshole! Let's go see if we got him!" Pat turned off the car, though he didn't remove the keys from the ignition. He punched a button to turn off the Godsmack CD, then threw open the driver's side door, leaped out of the Camaro, and started running as soon as his feet touched the road.

Brent didn't want to get out of the car, didn't want to see if they'd "gotten" Jerome. It was one thing to make fun of a dork like Jerome Starkey. After all, the freak practically begged for it. But it was another thing to intentionally try to kill the guy. Brent knew Jerome had killed Eddie, and he thought that he'd shared Pat's outrage over Eddie's death along with his need to avenge it. But now that he was here—sitting in the middle of the road on the outskirts of town, heart pounding, listening to the ticking of the Camaro's engine as it began to cool—all he wanted to do was go home, crawl in bed, and pretend this day had never happened.

A fist pounded against the passenger window, making Brent jump. He turned to see Pat looking in at him, his face a mask of anger and impatience.

"I said come on!"

Pat's voice was slightly muffled by the window glass, but his message came though more than clear enough. Get your ass out of the car or else!

Brent knew there was no way he could avoid this, so he opened the car door and stepped out onto the road with weak, shaky legs. Pat, of course, was standing right there waiting for him.

"That's more like it!" He grabbed Brent's arm and started hauling him toward the spot where Jerome had run off the road.

At that moment as he was running to keep up with Pat—rubber soled shoes pounding on asphalt, fat gut joggling, night air sliding in and out of his lungs like quills of ice—Brent wondered for the very first time in his life just why the hell he hung out with Pat Cottril. He was surprised and more than a little saddened to realize that he really didn't have a good reason. Couldn't, in fact, remember the first time he'd become friends with Pat, if indeed "friends" was the right word for what they were to each other. It seemed like he'd always been one of Pat's sidekicks and always would be, as if he'd been born for no other purpose than to fulfill that role. He wondered if Eddie had felt the same way about being Pat's "friend", wondered if he'd had any regrets before he'd died. He figured there was at least one thing Eddie had regretted: not running fast enough to get away from Jerome Starkey.

And Pat was leading him right to Jerome, and there was nothing Brent could do about it.

The Eldorado had stalled out when it hit the ditch, but the car hadn't flipped over. Brent didn't know if that was because the spin had bled off some of the Eldorado's momentum or what, but aside from a few minor dents, the car looked to be in reasonably good shape. The Eldorado's headlights were still on, though they were shining upward at a slight angle. The engine ticked loudly, as if small pieces were spontaneously snapping off inside, and the air was filled with the rich stench of hot rubber. Pat still had his penlight, and as they drew closer to the Eldorado, he pulled it from his back pocket, turned it on, and aimed the beam at the driver's window. There was no sign of Jerome.

"Maybe the bastard's slumped over onto the seat or something," Pat muttered. Still gripping Brent's arm with his free hand, Pat stepped closer to the Eldorado, Brent accompanying him step by step.

When they were close enough, Pat leaned forward and peered through the window. Brent didn't take a closer look. Seeing Eddie dead in the alley that way, head pulped to a mess of blood, bone and brain jelly, had been enough gore to last him the rest of his life. But he needn't have bothered holding back.

Pat straightened and said, "He's not in there. The passenger door's cracked open. I figure he must've got out that way." He shone his light around, searching for some sign of Jerome, but there was none.

It was hard to tell in the dark, but Brent figured that Jerome had ditched his car in front of a property owned by a farmer. There was a chest high rusty wire fence on the other side of the ditch with weathered gray posts. On the other side was a grassy field dotted with weeds and patches of bare earth in numerous places. Brent was no country kid, but he figured that this was probably a field where some kind of animals ranged. Cows, maybe, or sheep. They'd probably been scared off when Jerome ditched the Eldorado and had retreated to the far side of the field.

This wasn't good. If animals ranged there, that meant a farmhouse was probably close by. Close enough, maybe, for someone to hear the accident and call the cops. Even then, Springwood's finest might be barrel-assing toward them, pedals pressed firmly to the metal.

"Pat... I think we should get out of here." He hated how small and frightened his voice sounded, but he couldn't help it.

Pat still had hold of his arm, and gave it a painful squeeze. "What the hell are you talking about? We got Starkey right where we want him!"

"Really? That's news to me."

Brent whirled around at the sound of Jerome's voice just in time to see the edge of a plastic ice-scraper coming toward his face. He tried to bring up his arm to block the blow, but he wasn't fast enough and one of the scraper's sharp tips caught him on the face just below his left eye. He shrieked with equal measures of pain and fear, and stumbled backward, hand reaching for his injury. Warm crimson splashed onto Brent's fingers, and he pressed his hand tight to his wound, a Midwestern little Dutch boy trying to plug a hole in a dike of flesh, but with far less successful results than the original. Blood gushed past his fingers, ran down his cheek and chin, dripped onto his neck and oozed beneath his shirt collar.

Grinning, Jerome stepped toward Brent and brought the ice-scraper back in a reverse slash aimed at his throat.

Brent's gaze locked onto Jerome's. And what Brent saw there—or rather, didn't see—chilled him to the core of his soul. Jerome's eyes were dull, blank, dead—they contained no hint of emotion, no sign of reason, nothing that Brent recognized as remotely human. They were less alive than an animal's eyes, for even the most primitive of animals displayed some sort of life, no matter how small or simplistic their brains might be. But Jerome's eyes might as well have been fashioned from plastic for all the life they held. They were doll's eyes, mannequin's eyes. The eyes of Death itself.

Brent knew he had only a split-second before the sharp tip of the ice-scraper bit into his throat and laid open his jugular. Reacting completely on instinct, Brent allowed his legs to go limp, and he started to slump toward the ground. As he fell, the ice-scraper nicked the top of his head, and he felt the plastic cut open the skin and scratch against the skull underneath. Fresh blood poured from this second wound, and a patch of his scalp flapped in the night air as he collapsed to the road surface. Without conscious thought, he curled into a fetal position to protect himself, squeezed his eyes shut, and lay still.

He heard Pat scream, "Goddamn motherfucker!" then he sensed Jerome step over his shivering prone form to confront Pat.

A wordless impulse hit Brent then: haul ass! Brent didn't waste time debating whether or not it was a good move, and he certainly didn't feel any guilt at the idea of abandoning Pat. After all, hadn't they both ran off and left Eddie when Jerome had fought back in the alley? It was every man for his fucking self, right?

Brent rose to his feet and started staggering toward the rusty wire fence, wiping blood out of his eyes as he went. Behind him, he heard the sounds of Pat and Jerome fighting, but he didn't turn back around to look, didn't so much as slow down as he leaped over the ditch and began climbing over the fence. Halfway over, he slipped and fell, hitting the ground hard enough to knock the wind out of himself. But he'd made it over the fence.

He climbed to his feet once more and started moving again, wheezing as he fought to draw air into his lungs. He had no idea where he was running to, and he didn't care—as long as it was away from Jerome Starkey.

Pat saw Brent get up and make for the fence, moving like a drunk with a severe inner-ear disorder. He wanted to shout after him, denounce the fat bastard for the fucking traitorous coward that he was. But Jerome was coming toward him, grinning like a maniac, eyes cold and dead as a shark about to sink teeth into its prey, and Pat no longer had any time to spare for thoughts of Brent's betrayal. He was too busy trying to stay alive.

Jerome stepped forward and slashed out with his ice scraper. Pat leaped backward, arms up, spine curved inward, and the scraper hissed through empty air. The scraper was a small handheld tool, with a plastic head and yellow rubber grip around the handle. If Pat hadn't already seen Jerome wield the scraper to deadly effect against Brent, he would've laughed at Jerome's choice of weapon. But now he respected the ice scraper as if it were a finely sharpened blade of high density steel. A wild thought occurred to him then.

It's not the size of the tool, but how you use it.

It sure as shit was true in Jerome's case. He'd cut Brent good with the fucking thing, but Pat didn't intend to give Jerome the chance to do the same to him. He turned and started running like a sonofabitch toward his Camaro. As his feet pounded on the asphalt, he imagined Jerome right behind him, ice scraper raised in preparation for his next strike. Pat imagined the feel of a sharp plastic point cutting into the back of his neck, parting flesh and muscle, exposing the stacked ridges of his neck bones. When he felt the ice scraper hit, he wondered if he'd piss himself. Would he end up dead like Eddie, a mutilated corpse with a urine stain on the front of his jeans?

He'd covered half the distance to the Camaro, but he didn't dare glance back to see how close Jerome was. Doing so would only slow him down, and it would be a hell of a good way to catch a pointed edge of the ice scraper in one of his eyes.

Damn it, life wasn't supposed to be like this!

Sure, Jerome was a freak, had been ever since kindergarten and probably from the day the bastard was born. But while he'd demonstrated the occasional flare-up of violent behavior, the episodes had never lasted long, and they'd never been as intense as this before. Pat—though he'd never admit this to another human being—was scared of Jerome, had been since the fucker had given him the wound that had become the scar on his forehead. That was why Pat always made sure someone else was around whenever he approached Jerome. Why he'd befriended Eddie and Brent in the first place, so he'd always have someone watching his back, just in case Jerome should snap again. Someone to make him feel safer when he taunted Jerome, and maybe even one day to help him kick Starkey's ass—assuming Pat would ever work up the courage.

Jerome's attack on him in detention, followed by Eddie's murder, had finally given Pat the courage to confront him at last, but courage—along with his surviving sidekick—hadn't been enough, not by a damn sight.

Three-quarters of the way to the Camaro, and Pat was glad he'd left the car door open and the keys in the ignition when he'd jumped out. He was going to have to get in quick, fire up the engine, and blaze the hell out of there before Jerome caught up to him and started to slice and dice Pat with his makeshift weapon.

Almost there.

He reached the Camaro and threw himself into the driver's seat. He grabbed the door handle with one hand and yanked it shut, while turning the key with the other. The Camaro's engine roared to life, and Pat locked his door, then the passenger's. Only then did he risk turning and looking through the back window to see where Jerome was. At first he saw nothing, and he feared that Jerome had somehow passed him, circled around the car, climbed in, and crawled into the backseat. Any second and Jerome would jump up and slash Pat's face with his ice-scraper.

But when Pat looked down into the backseat, he saw that it was empty.

Confused and frightened, he looked up and gazed through the back window once more. He spotted Jerome then, standing not far from the ditched Eldorado—exactly where he'd been standing when Pat had taken off running. Not only hadn't Jerome given chase, he hadn't moved so much as a single step. As fast as Pat had run, as scared as he'd been, Jerome hadn't been behind him at all.

Pat figured it was too dark out for Jerome to be able to see him inside the Camaro, especially with its tinted windows, but Pat nevertheless had the impression that Jerome was well aware that he was looking at him. Jerome sneered then, and Pat knew precisely what message the son of a bitch was sending.

You ran from me, ran like a scared little boy. Pathetic.

Pat slammed his palm onto the steering wheel in frustration. Jerome no longer needed to touch Pat to humiliate him, and the fact that Pat knew this just made it all the worse. He threw the Camaro into reverse and hit the gas. The car's rear end whipped around until the front was pointing directly at Jerome. He was now illuminated by the Camaro's single unbroken headlight, as if it were a mini spotlight trained on him. Jerome stood relaxed, ice scraper held at his side, still sneering. Pat gripped the steering wheel tight and pressed the gas pedal a couple times to rev the engine.

"I'm going to park on your face, spin my tires, and grind that goddamned smug expression right off," Pat whispered.

He threw the Camaro into drive.

Tires burned rubber as the car leaped forward, its engine roaring like a hungry animal eager to sate its bloodlust. The Camaro crossed the short distance to Jerome within seconds, but even in that short a time, Pat had managed to get the vehicle up to forty miles an hour. And just as the Camaro's front bumper was about to slam into Jerome's legs, he leaped to the side, and suddenly there was nothing between the Camaro and the Eldorado but air.

Pat didn't have time to put on the brakes. He didn't have time to cry out in fear and frustration. Didn't have time to do anything except close his eyes, grit his teeth, and hold on tight to the steering wheel as his car reached the edge of the road and its front wheels became briefly airborne. An instant later, Pat had good cause to regret his dislike of seatbelts when the front of the Camaro smashed into the side of the Eldorado, and Pat's forehead came in brief but violent contact with the windshield and everything went black.

Jerome rose to his feet and brushed dirt and gravel off his shirt and jeans. He regarded the twisted mass of crumpled metal that had, until only moments ago, been a pair of cars, but which now looked like a couple of gigantic and poorly designed accordions trying to make love.

Jerome climbed down into the ditch and walked over to what was left of the Camaro's driver's side window. The safety glass was spiderwebbed with cracks but still remained in the window frame. Jerome pounded it out with the ice-scraper, then peered inside to check on his good buddy Pat. His face was a mask of crimson, but he was moaning softly and stirring in his seat. Not dead, then. At least, not yet.

Jerome figured Pat wasn't going anywhere on his own steam for a while. He'd keep. Jerome decided to leave Pat and attend to other unfinished business. He walked around to the Eldorado's driver's side, opened the door, and popped the trunk. He then walked around to the rear of the car and looked inside. There, held in a pair of small brackets next to a spare tire mounted on the side of the trunk, was a tire iron. Jerome tucked the ice-scraper handle first into the back pocket of his jeans, then reached out and removed the tire iron from its berth. He hefted the metal object to get a feel for its weight, and then swished it back and forth several times to get a feel for wielding it.

It'll do, he decided.

He started walking toward the fence.

Brent ran through the dark. Above him the sky was dotted with cold bright stars, but they provided little illumination to see by. The moon was a thin sliver of a crescent, its light a pale yellow-green and no help to him either. He couldn't see the ground beneath his feet, could only feel it as he ran. It seemed like he was running across solid shadow, and he couldn't escape the feeling that during the next step he took—or the one after—his foot would come down and touch nothing, and he'd find himself falling forward into darkness, tumbling forever downward through an endless black void…

His pulse thundered in his ears, and every gasping breath he took felt like white-hot knives stabbing into his lungs. He was carrying a lot of extra weight, and he wondered if it was possible for a seventeen year-old to have a heart attack. Sweat poured off his body and mixed with the blood oozing from his scalp wound before running into his eyes, making them sting and obscuring his vision even further.

Brent was by no means religious. He'd attended Sunday school as a child at Christ United Methodist Church, but only because his grandmother had insisted on his going, and his mom and dad—who near as he could tell believed in nothing except cable TV and cheap wine that came in a box—hadn't bothered to protest. So Brent had suffered through boring lessons about Bible stories, none of which he remembered by Monday, dressed in itchy clothes that his grandmother got him every Christmas and birthday, and which he only wore to church, and then only because she made him.

So when his grandmother finally died, Brent no longer had to get up early on Sundays and suffer. On the way home from her graveside service, Brent had said his last prayer: Thank God I don't have to go to church no more! And that was the last thought he'd given to matters religious.

God, I'm really, really sorry for all the shitty things I've done in my life... that I let Pat and Eddie talk me into. I'm sorry we left Eddie's body lying in the alley, and I'm sorry that us picking on Jerome got him so mad in the first place. I'm sorry that I let Pat talk me into riding shotgun while we chased Jerome. Hell, I'm sorry for just about everything I ever did in my sorry excuse for a life. But please don't let me end up like Eddie, please keep Jerome from finding me! If I get out of this alive, I'll go straight to the police and tell them everything, I swear! And then I'll—

A shape loomed in front of him, black against black, outlined by the stars it didn't block.

Brent screamed and tried to veer around the shape but he was moving too fast and his feet slipped out from under him. He fell onto his side, and he felt a sharp fiery pain in his ribs, and he knew he'd cracked one or more, maybe even broken them. He raised his hands in a gesture of either warding or supplication. Perhaps a bit of both.

"Don't hurt me!" he sobbed. "Please, please don't hurt me!"

He waited for the dark shape to say something, but the sound it made then wasn't human vocalization. It was low, deep, resonant, and it sounded for all the world like...

The cow turned and started trotting away from Brent, lowing nervously as it sought to distance itself from the strange noisy interloper that had invaded its home.

Brent lay on his side and watched in disbelief as the animal hurried away. A cow! Jesus Christ, it was just a fucking cow! He began to laugh in relief.

But then Brent realized that a new shape was standing over him, this new silhouette was human, and it held something in its hand—something that looked uncomfortably like a tire iron.

"What's so funny?" Jerome asked.

Brent's laughter died, and a few seconds later, so did he.

The throbbing in his head was what finally brought Pat around. He just hurt too damn much to remain unconscious. And it wasn't just his head—his wrists hurt, too. He glanced down and, though his eyes were reluctant to focus, he saw he was sitting amidst broken shards of window glass and that somehow the seatbelt had become wrapped around his wrists during the accident. No, not wrapped, he realized as he saw that the seatbelt strap had been looped through the steering wheel. Someone had used the seatbelt to tie his wrists together.

Sudden panic hit him, and he turned to Brent and held out his bound wrists.

"Get me out of these..."

He trailed off when he saw that Brent no longer possessed anything remotely resembling a face. Someone had buckled a seatbelt around him the normal way—he sure hadn't done it himself—and it was the only thing keeping Brent's body from falling forward and smacking the bloody ruin where his face had been against the dash.

Pat tried to pull away from the corpse of his friend (the second that he'd seen today) but he was bound too tightly and could only move a few inches toward the door. The rest of his memories returned then: following Jerome in his Camaro, forcing him off the road then trying to run him down, seeing the sonofabitch jump aside at the last instant and then the Camaro slamming into the ditched Eldorado…

He must've passed out after the collision, and while he'd been unconscious—fuck—that's what he got for buying a classic car. He should've gotten a newer one with airbags.

Someone tapped on the driver's side door, startling Pat. He turned quickly, setting off a fresh wave of pain in his skull, and saw Jerome looking at him through the open area where the window glass had been.

"'Bout time you woke up. I thought you were going to be out all night."

Jerome's tone held a cold mockery that shrunk Pat's balls, but he forced himself to sound unafraid. "Untie me right now, you fucking freak, or I'll—"

"Do what? There's no teacher here to help you like in detention. You're all alone… unless you count the incredible faceless wonder over there." Jerome nodded toward Brent, but Pat didn't take his gaze off Jerome. He didn't want to look at Brent's crushed ruin of a face again.

"Cut the bullshit, Starkey. You're not going to kill me. If you wanted me dead, you'd have offed me while I was out of it." Pat hoped he sounded more confident of his reasoning than he felt.

"It would've been easier that way," Jerome admitted. "But a lot less fun." Jerome's smile widened, and for an instant Pat thought his teeth were yellow and crooked, thrusting forth from dry, scarred gums. But then his teeth looked normal again, though his smile remained just as unsettling. It was the kind of smile a predator gave to its prey right before taking the first bite of flesh.

"I didn't bother trying to conceal Eddie's murder. To be honest, it didn't even occur to me. But I figure I shouldn't be too hard on myself. After all, it was my first killing, and I'm sure I'll get better at it as I go. If you wouldn't mind, I'd appreciate it if you could give me some constructive feedback on my latest attempt."

Jerome pointed to the Eldorado, and although it was a bit of a strain for Pat to see at this angle, the rag sticking out of the car's open gas tank was clear enough.

"There's another cloth sticking out of your car's trunk," Jerome said. Then he held up his hand and showed Pat the disposable lighter he held.

All pretense of being a tough guy vanished when Pat understood what Jerome had in mind.

"Please, man, don't do it! I'll never bother you again, I swear! I'll leave El alone, too, and I won't so much as look in Cheryl's direction, let alone ever talk to her again!"

Jerome looked at Pat thoughtfully for a moment, as if considering his offer. Finally, he said, "Tempting, Pat, but I'm afraid it falls under the heading of 'too little, too late'." He flicked the lighter and a small yellow-orange flame was born.

Pat couldn't take his eyes off the tiny flickering flame.

"Please..." Tears began to roll down his cheeks, but he was completely unaware of crying them.

"As much as I enjoy hearing you beg, I'm afraid the answer is 'no'." Jerome grinned. "Time to flame on, Pat."

Jerome moved away from the window and started walking down the length of the Camaro toward the location of the gas tank opening.

"Damn you, Starkey!" Pat pulled and yanked and thrashed in his seat, but no matter how violent his attempts, he couldn't loosen the knots in the seat-belt that bound his wrists together and kept him tied to the Camaro's steering wheel. He then saw Jerome run to the Eldorado's gas tank and light the rag protruding from its fuel tank opening. As soon as the cloth caught fire, Jerome ran like hell away from the pair of wrecked cars.

"Starkeeeeeeey!" Pat yelled.

And then his universe became a maelstrom of noise and heat and pain that lasted far too long before finally being replaced by blessed numbing darkness.

Jerome—or rather the personality in control of his body—stood several dozen yards away, ears still ringing from the explosion of the two gas tanks, and watched the Camaro and Eldorado burn. The flames looked quite beautiful contrasted against the night sky. Jerome doubted he would ever see anything so lovely again. When the flames had finally burned down a bit, Jerome started to walk back toward the two cars. Or rather, what was left of them.

Only one last detail to attend to.

Though the heat was so intense that he felt the skin on his face start to burn, Jerome didn't hesitate. He extended his left hand and thrust it into the flames. The pain was excruciatingly delicious, but he didn't cry out. When he felt like he'd cooked the hand enough, he withdrew it from the fire and backed away from the cars. He sought out an appropriate spot in the ditch—not too close to the fire, but not so far away as to make it look unlikely that he was thrown there by the collision of the two vehicles. He then went to that spot, lay down, and waited for the first of the emergency vehicles to arrive, luxuriating in the agony of his burned hand to keep himself entertained while he waited.

FIFTEEN

Jerome sat slumped on the couch, bandaged left hand resting on a pillow, right hand holding the cable remote. He had his thumb firmly pressed on the channel up button, and the image on the TV screen changed every few seconds. It didn't matter what came on, though; it all sucked. TV was lame enough as it was, but daytime TV was the absolute pits. Nothing but soap operas, talk shows, kiddie cartoons, reruns of moldy old sitcoms and bland reporters yacking away on dull news programs.

When he'd been little, staying home sick from school had been a real treat—provided he wasn't too sick. It was only 2:30 in the afternoon, but he felt as if he'd been stuck at home for at least a week. It didn't help matters that he'd been awake since he'd returned to full awareness to find himself being treated by a paramedic at the scene of last night's accident. It looked like his hand wouldn't require surgery, but it still hurt like a motherfucker. But he refused to take the pain pills that the ER physician had prescribed for him. Drowsiness was one of the medication's side effects, and the last thing he wanted to do was sleep, not with Freddy Krueger waiting for him in the dream realm. In a way, he supposed he was grateful for the pain; it definitely helped keep him awake. That, and the entire pot of coffee he'd consumed since this morning. He had a second pot brewing in the kitchen.

Both his dad and Lynn had offered to stay home from work to take care of him, but though he would've appreciated the company—even Lynn's—he'd told them he'd be fine. He was seventeen, after all. He didn't need anyone to stay home and babysit him, as much as he might've wanted someone to. Both his father and stepmother had called several times to check on him, but though the calls made him feel a little less lonely, whatever cheering effect they had was temporary, gone almost as soon as he hung up. He wished Cheryl was here, but after sitting with him all night in the hospital, she'd been exhausted, and Jerome had insisted she go home and get some sleep. He thought about calling her, but he didn't want to wake her up. He could wait for her to call him, though it wouldn't be easy.

As he continued flipping through the channels, his mind wandered and he remembered being questioned by a police officer in the hospital.

"When did you first become aware that you were being followed by another car?"

"You already told me about the incident with Pat Cottril in detention. Can you think of any other reason he might have wanted to run you off the road?"

"That's a nasty burn. I suppose the car was already on fire when you came to, is that correct?"

"Were you aware that Eddie Jackson was killed earlier this evening near where you work?"

"To the best of your knowledge, did Pat Cottril or Brent Haney have some sort of disagreement with Eddie?"

Talking with the police had been awkward to say the least, considering that Jerome had only hazy, fragmentary memories of what his other self had done while in control of his—their—body. Jerome had understood one thing well enough: his alter ego had rigged the scene to look like nothing more than a simple car accident that only he had been fortunate enough to survive. Evidently the other Jerome had done an effective enough job of staging the scene, for the police had bought it and let Jerome go home.

El's mom and dad were less than thrilled that Jerome had totaled their son's car, but El himself wasn't angry.

The damn thing was a gas hog anyway, he'd told Jerome when he'd called from the hospital. "I'm just glad that you're okay. And I might be a cold-hearted son of a bitch for saying this, but I'm not exactly going to shed a tear for Pat or Brent, you know?"

As Jerome continued to watch the ever-changing kaleidoscope of images on the TV, he realized that he'd gotten away with murder—three of them, as a matter of fact. Intellectually, he knew he should feel remorse or regret. Something. But emotionally he didn't feel much of anything beyond a certain satisfaction that the Three Pus-kateers would never bother him, or anyone else, ever again. Besides, he hadn't killed them—his other self had.

Well, maybe. But he had willingly turned over control to his alter ego, had let the beast out of the cage to do his dirty work for him. Even if he hadn't been conscious and in control when Pat and the others had been killed, he still shared at least partial responsibility. So why didn't he give a damn?

He remembered Freddy cutting him open during the dream in Ms LeClair's office, remembered Krueger jamming his claw-knives into his gut and pulling forth a blood-covered cricket, as if he were some diabolical version of Little Jack Horner. In the dream, Freddy claimed to have removed Jerome's conscience. Was such a thing possible? Had the undead madman somehow performed a kind of psychic surgery on him?

The TV suddenly displayed the image of a bald man sitting behind a news desk, and Jerome lifted his thumb off the channel up button. Not because he was a big fan of news, but because the man's suit had green and red stripes, his tie was brown, and his skin was a wrinkled, puckered mass of scar tissue. He was looking at Freddy Krueger.

"Welcome to the afternoon newscast here on WDED, where we're all DEAD, all the time!" Freddy shuffled papers lying in front of him, the blades of his claw glove scratching the wooden surface of the desk and leaving long, thin gouges. "Today's top story: last night, local teen Jerome Starkey upped his overall body count to three. When asked how he felt about his achievement, Jerome had this to say."

The picture of Freddy sitting behind a news desk was replaced with one of Jerome. From the dark sky and the flashing red and blue light of nearby emergency vehicles, the footage had obviously been shot at the scene of last night's accident. And while local news crews had arrived shortly on the heels of police and rescue crews, Jerome had no memory of anyone shoving a camera in his face and asking him questions. Stranger yet, the Jerome on the TV looked younger than he did. That Jerome was ten, maybe twelve at the most.

"I had a lot of fun killing these three fuckers," young Jerome said in a voice too cold to belong to a child. "I'm looking forward to killing again. And again and again and..."

The picture switched back to Freddy.

"Looks like your inner child had a real growth spurt, huh, Jerome?"

Jerome looked around. The living room appeared the same as always. He pushed down on the couch cushion with his good hand. It felt real enough, but if Krueger was on the TV—and talking directly him, no less—then this couldn't be real. He must've fallen asleep on the couch without realizing it.

Wake up, he told himself. Wake up now!

Krueger's laughter was as brittle as the sound of snapping cartilage.

"Do you really think you're the first person to try waking yourself? Once you're in my world, it's not that easy to get out."

"What do you want?"

"Just to congratulate you, Jerome. You bagged a two-fer last night, and that's on top of doing Eddie in the alley earlier in the day. A grand total of three. Not bad at all for your first day as a homicidal maniac."

"I didn't kill anyone! He did!"

The TV picture blurred, and when it came back into focus, Freddy was dressed in his fedora and sweater once more. He stood in front of the burning wreckage of Pat's Camaro and El's Eldorado. Standing beside Krueger, his head reaching almost to the bastard's shoulder, was the other Jerome. He was dressed just as the real Jerome had been last night, though his clothes were sized to fit his smaller frame. His left hand wasn't bandaged, but it had obviously been burned. The skin was red and blistered, clear serum running from open fissures.

"By 'he' I assume you mean this charming young lad." Freddy put his hand on the younger

Jerome's shoulder and gave him an affectionate, almost fatherly look. "If you want to be technical about it, I suppose you're right. But before too much longer, there won't be two of you anymore. There'll just be one." Freddy patted young Jerome's shoulder. "This one."

The boy gazed up at the scar-faced lunatic with dark adoration.

"What the hell are you talking about?" Jerome demanded.

"During our little fishing trip I told you that I'd decided to create a son. What I didn't tell you was why. You've learned by now how the adults of Springwood have tried to make all of my children forget about me in order to weaken my power over them and ultimately isolate me in the Dreamscape and render me... harmless." Freddy looked as if he almost choked on this last word.

"Yeah," Jerome acknowledged. "So?"

"So if I have a son who can operate in the physical world for me, he can make sure that no one ever forgets the name Freddy Krueger. Not only will I stay strong, I'll be even more powerful, because thanks to Junior here, I'll be able to terrorize both the dream world and the physical world! We'll be an unstoppable team, father and son, wreaking havoc on two separate planes of existence!" Krueger roared with laughter, and the young Jerome joined him, his voice a close match to his father's.

"What makes you think I'll help you?" Jerome said. "Now that I know what your game is, I'll never let him have control of my body again!"

"That threat would've carried a lot more weight yesterday, when Junior was still just a squirming little fetus. But he's grown since then, grown strong enough to resist you. You won't be able to stop him from taking control of your body to kill again. And with each death, he'll grow increasingly stronger, until he's able to remain in control of your body… His body… Forever!"

Jerome felt a cold wave of fear ripple through him. If his other self assumed control of his body, what would happen to his original personality? What would happen to him?

"I'll stop you, Krueger. I don't know how, but I swear, I'll find a way!"

Young Jerome fixed his gaze on his older counterpart on the other side of the television screen.

"You can't stop me, bro, because I'm part of you. I'm going to replace you bit by bit, just like cancer cells replace healthy tissue, until there's nothing of the original Jerome Starkey left. And now that the process has begun, there isn't a damn thing you can do about it."

Young Jerome walked toward the TV screen until his nose was almost against the glass. He reached up and pressed his fingers to the other side of the screen and pushed. The screen bowed under the pressure of his hand and began to bulge outward.

"But maybe I won't wait," Young Jerome said, his voice louder, fuller, more real, as if he weren't inside the TV, but actually present in the room. "Maybe I'll just take over your body right now!"

He continued pushing against the other side of the screen, and it continued to bow outward, the spot where his fingers touched stretching and growing thin, as if the screen was made of rubber being stretched close to the breaking point.

Jerome knew he had to do something fast. Even though this was one of Freddy's nightmares, if his other self got out of the TV and attacked, it could all be over for him. He knew he couldn't simply will himself awake; he'd tried that earlier without any success. But there had to be another way…

The rubbery surface of the bulging TV screen had grown so thin that the tips of Young Jerome's fingers were starting to break through. There was a sudden tearing sound and a ragged tear opened along the vertical length of the screen. The substance of the screen resembled flesh more than glass now, and blood gushed from the tear and splattered onto the Starkeys' living room carpet. Like some hideous mockery of birth, Young Jerome withdrew his hand and thrust his head through the slit he'd created, smearing his face and hair with blood.

Jerome glanced at his bandaged hand, and he knew what he had to do. He raised it off the pillow and lifted it over his head. He leaned forward and brought his burned hand down fast and hard on the surface of the coffee table. The pain that exploded in his hand was excruciating, beyond anything he'd ever known, but it did the job. Jerome cried out in agony and opened his eyes.

He sat on the edge of the couch, his bandaged hand resting on the coffee table, the cloth wet with serum from burst blisters. The TV screen was smooth, flat and unbroken. No longer did it show Freddy and Jerome's other self. Instead, a nature documentary was playing, and some enthusiastic Australian in khaki shorts was waxing poetic about dung beetles. Jerome did his best to ignore the pain in his burned hand while he searched for the remote. He found it on the floor by his feet and decided he must've dropped it there when he'd fallen asleep. He reached down, picked it up, and turned off the TV just as the Australian naturalist was about to demonstrate how dung beetles had come by their charming appellation. Jerome then lay the remote down on the coffee table. He'd had enough TV to last him for a while. He leaned back on the couch and gritted his teeth while he waited for the pain in his hand to subside.

That had been a close one. He was going to have to do everything he could to keep from falling asleep. He might not be so lucky next time.

After several minutes, the pain had lessened to the point where Jerome could tolerate it. He started to rise off the couch—intending to go see if the new pot of coffee was finished brewing yet, and maybe change his bandage—when the phone rang. The hand held unit was on the coffee table where he'd left it after the last time his dad had called. Hoping it was Cheryl, he started to reach for it, but then stopped as a thought occurred to him. What if the dream wasn't over? What if he only thought he'd woken up? What if it was Freddy on the line, calling to taunt him further?

The phone continued to ring, and though Jerome knew it was probably his imagination, its electronic warbling sounded increasingly insistent. He hesitated for several moments, trying to decide what to do, hoping that while he debated whoever—or whatever—was calling would give up and disconnect.

But the phone kept ringing.

This was exactly what Krueger wanted, Jerome realized. To keep him off balance and doubting himself, doubting his own sanity. Well, Jerome wasn't going to play that game. He picked up the phone and thumbed the talk button.

"Hello?" He was both surprised and pleased at how steady his voice sounded. In your dog meat face, Krueger!

"Jerome, this is Aunt Bekka. How are you doing?"

Jerome relaxed and started walking toward the kitchen to check on the coffee. "I'm all right. My hand hurts, but I'm sure you didn't need your psychic powers to tell you that."

As he entered the kitchen, he smelled the rich scent of freshly brewed coffee and inhaled deeply. He loved the smell of coffee much more than he loved the taste, but he wasn't drinking the stuff for its flavor, not today.

Bekka chuckled at his joke, but it sounded strained, as if she didn't really mean it. "Everything else going okay? I ask because I just had a strong feeling that you… were in some sort of trouble."

Jerome got a clean mug from the cupboard, one with a picture of a kitten dangling from a tree branch by its front paws above the caption, "Hang in there, baby!" As he poured hot coffee into the mug, he considered lying to Bekka, but he doubted he could pull it off. Besides, if he'd never quite fully believed in Bekka's powers, after the last couple nights he'd experienced too much of the shadowy world that lay hidden behind what he'd always thought of as reality to ever automatically doubt anything again.

As he leaned against the kitchen counter and waited for his coffee to cool to the point where he could drink it, he told her everything—about what had happened in the alley, about the "accident" last night, and about the dream he'd just had. He was sketchy on some of the details since his personality hadn't been in control when the events in question occurred, but he was able to tell her enough.

After he was finished, Bekka didn't reply right away. Her silence made Jerome nervous, but he sensed it was best to give her a bit of time to think. He took advantage of the lull in the conversation to take a gulp of coffee. It was still too hot, and it burned his tongue and throat as he swallowed, but he didn't care. As long as it helped keep him awake.

He was afraid of what Bekka was going to say. Would she think him weak for not being able to resist Krueger? Worse, would she tell him that this "other self" crap was nonsense, that there was only one him, and that he alone was responsible for the deaths of the Three Puskateers?

When Bekka finally spoke once more, her voice was filled with sympathy. "I'm sorry, Jerome. You must feel awful about everything that's happened."

Jerome smiled with relief. He should've known his aunt would stand by him, no matter what.

Bekka went on. "If only I'd managed to repair your dreamcatcher last night..."

Bekka had succeeded in putting the pieces back together while Jerome had been out playing demolition derby with Pat and Brent. But—as she'd told him early this morning at the hospital—whatever power the object had once held was gone. She'd brought the dreamcatcher to show to him. Jerome hadn't been able to see any difference from the way it was before, but he'd thought he understood what Bekka had been talking about. The dreamcatcher had felt lifeless, fragile and brittle, as if it really was what it appeared to be: nothing more than a patched-together conglomeration of wood, leather straps, feathers and beads.

"You shouldn't blame yourself," Jerome said. "You had nothing to do with Krueger choosing me to 'adopt'."

"You're not only my nephew, you're my sister's only child. After Joanna died, I made a vow to her spirit that I would always protect you—and I failed."

Jerome was the one Krueger was stalking, the one whose body he wanted to steal and give to his evil little dream clone. But despite that, at the moment all Jerome was concerned about was comforting his aunt.

"You did the best you could, better than anyone else could have. You kept Krueger away from me for seventeen years. And if I hadn't been dumb enough to lose my temper and throw my shoe at the dreamcatcher, I might've been safe my whole life."

He could hear Bekka's smile in her voice as she replied. "It's sweet of you to try and make me feel better, but we need to take care of you right now. I took your dreamcatcher apart once I got home, and I've been playing around with the pieces. I've consulted various reference books I have, and I've surfed the Net and sent some emails to friends of mine in the psychic community and posted some questions on message boards. I'm not sure, but I think I've found a way to, if not exactly fix your dreamcatcher, then... recycle it."

After showing Jerome that her repair job had been a failure, Bekka had taken the dreamcatcher back home with her to continue working on it. At the time, she hadn't sounded very confident in her ability to find a solution, but it seemed she'd actually come up with something. The question was what.

Jerome frowned. "I don't understand."

"That's okay. You don't need to right now. I still have some work to do before I'm finished, but come over here around six, and I'll show you what I've got. Make sure to have someone else drive you. In your sleep-deprived state, you'd only end up getting into an accident."

"You mean another accident."

This time Bekka didn't even attempt to fake a chuckle at his joke. He supposed he couldn't blame her; it wasn't a very good one.

"All right, I'll see if dad will lend me his car, and I'll ask Cheryl to drive. But why do we have to go to your place? Couldn't you just bring whatever it is over here?"

"I could," Bekka conceded, "but Krueger's already established a strong psychic foothold at your house. The spiritual environment at my home is much stronger, the result of years of my working to build psychic shields against Krueger and other evil forces."

She paused then, and when she resumed speaking, she didn't sound quite as confident as she had a moment ago.

"My defenses are far from perfect, but right now they're all we have."

"Whatever you say, Bekka. I'll be there at six."

"Good. Now try to get some rest—but don't fall asleep."

Jerome finished the rest of his coffee in two swallows and refilled his mug.

"You can count on it."

SIXTEEN

Bekka put the hand held receiver down on her reading table. She'd pushed the crystal ball off to one side, and bits and pieces salvaged from Jerome's dreamcatcher lay spread out before her on the new tablecloth, a replacement for the one Krueger had burnt.

So the situation was even worse than she'd feared. Krueger wasn't simply trying to kill Jerome, as awful as that would be. He wanted to replace him with a creature of his own making. Jerome needed her help more than ever. She only hoped she'd prove up to the task.

She'd been at the hospital most of the night with Don, Lynn and the kids, first waiting to see how serious Jerome's injuries would turn out to be, and then worrying what charges, if any, the police might bring against him. It was only once

Bekka was certain Jerome was going to be all right, both medically and legally, that she returned home to continue working on his dreamcatcher. She'd meditated and researched, and she thought she finally had the answer, if she could find the courage to try it.

She'd want you to do it, Bekka told herself. You know she would.

Bekka sighed and nodded, though no one was there to see the gesture. Then she reached for a small piece of carved wood and began working. Despite her earlier misgivings, her hand moved with a surgeon's dexterity and confidence, and a half hour later she was finished. She had taken the pieces she'd saved from the dreamcatcher—pieces that still held a slight residue of mystic power—and fashioned them into a smaller version, about the size of a half dollar. She added a leather thong to the miniature dreamcatcher and tied it off to make a loop. Jerome's dreamcatcher, or at least what was left of it, had become a medallion.

She placed it gently, almost reverently, on the table, then put her hands palm down on either side of it. She then closed her eyes and focused her awareness on the medallion, or more accurately, on the energy that it contained. At first she felt nothing, and she feared that she'd failed, but just as she was about to withdraw her awareness and open her eyes, she sensed it. An echo, a whisper, the merest suggestion of the power the dreamcatcher had once contained. But it was there, and it was real. She was sure of it, she didn't know if it would be enough for what she had in mind, but since it was all she'd been able to salvage from the original dreamcatcher, it would have to do.

Bekka let her hands remain where they were and kept her eyes closed. Only, instead of training her awareness on the medallion, she refocused it, split it in two, and directed one half inward and the other half outward. She was searching for a doorway, a very special one that existed simultaneously at the core of every being's soul and farther away than the outermost star in the galactic perimeter. As she searched for this doorway, she continued to breathe slowly and evenly, her body relaxing a bit more with each exhalation. As tired as she was, it was tempting to allow herself to drift off to sleep, but Bekka was well experienced in meditation and trance techniques, and she knew how to keep both her mind and body relaxed without allowing them to succumb to the need for rest. Besides, falling asleep at this juncture could well prove suicidal considering who she was fighting against.

After a time she became less and less conscious of her physical self, and though she knew her body remained seated at the table, eyes closed, lungs breathing, heart pumping, she could no longer feel it. It was at this point that most inexperienced astral travelers panicked and returned to their bodies, but Bekka had done this a time or two before, and she pushed past the rising panic, the horrible feeling of being cut off from one's body and lost in the immaterial realms for all eternity. She toughed it out long enough for the fear to subside and when it was gone, she would've let out a sigh of relief if she'd still fully inhabited her physical form. Then she became completely free and unfettered, able to roam the astral plane at will.

It wasn't a realm of the physical senses, so there weren't any sights, sounds, taste, touches, or smells here. Instead there were feelings, impressions, seemingly random thoughts and emotions so intense that even the most pleasant of them burned the spirit like fire. Movement here was simply a matter of will. You decided where you wanted to go, concentrated on that place, and you were on your way.

She concentrated on the doorway she was searching for, and after several moments—not that time held any objective reality in this place—she felt a gentle pulling sensation toward one particular direction. She relaxed and allowed her spirit to be pulled toward it, and soon she sensed that she had reached her destination. She gave her spirit a moment to get used to this placeless place, and opened her eyes. Or rather, she imagined she did.

She was standing before a white door at the end of a long, narrow hallway. So long, in fact, that she couldn't see the other end of it, and she wondered if it even had another end. The hall was illuminated by hovering globes of soft light spaced at regular intervals near the ceiling. The globes were unattached to anything, and as Bekka watched, she thought she could see the globes bobbing so slowly that their motion was all but imperceptible. The gentle glow of the lights revealed that the ceiling, walls and floor of the hallway were just as white as the door. Even its hinges and knob appeared to have been fashioned from some manner of ivory colored ceramic.

Now that she was there, Bekka was suddenly gripped by a fear that had nothing to do with Freddy Krueger. She was afraid of what lay on the other side of that door. Afraid that if she opened it—which was exactly what she'd come here to do—she might be drawn inside and trapped forever. As a stalling tactic more than anything, she spent a few moments imagining herself a body. Not that she necessarily needed an avatar to operate on this plane, but since the door had manifested to her as a physical object, it only made sense that she adopt a physical semblance if she intended to open it.

Though she felt no different than she had upon first entering this realm, she "looked" down and saw that she indeed did have a body, and it was wearing the same blouse and jeans she'd had on back on the earthly plane. Seeing her clothing made her feel a bit more solid, though she still felt no physical sensation. She reached out a hand that she knew was just an abstract concept in a place constructed from concepts far more abstract, took hold of the white door's knob, turned it and slowly opened the door. As white as the hallway was, it was nothing compared to the light that poured through the open doorway.

It was like looking into the white-hot heart of a blazing star. And though the light didn't cause Bekka pain, exactly, its intensity threatened to overwhelm her, to force her back from the open doorway and avert her gaze from the flood of illumination. And once she did that, she knew her connection to the door would be severed and her spirit would be instantly yanked back to her true body like a stretched-tight rubber band that was suddenly released at one end. It took all of her mental and spiritual strength, all of the experience she'd gained during a lifetime of having her psychic abilities, but she did not turn away from its light.

Though the light did not diminish, it became easier to bear, and soon Bekka became aware of a figure coming toward her from the center of the light. It seemed to take the figure a long time to draw near, as if it had to cross a great distance to reach the open doorway. Bekka tensed as the figure came closer, prepared to find herself faced with one of Freddy Krueger's cruel tricks. But just before the figure reached the doorway, its features resolved into those of a young woman—a woman Bekka hadn't seen in seventeen years—and she relaxed.

"Hi, Sis," Joanna said with a sad smile. "I wish I could say that it's good to see you."

At first, Bekka couldn't reply; she was too overwhelmed with emotion upon being reunited with her lost twin. But the sisters had work to do, and

Bekka knew they couldn't afford to waste time chatting. There was no telling how much longer they'd have before Freddy became aware of what Bekka was up to and came to stop her.

"Then you know why I'm here."

Joanna nodded. "It's a long shot. It might not work, and it might even make things worse."

"I know," Bekka said. "But it may well turn out to be the only chance Jerome has."

At the mention of her son's name, Joanna's eyes filled with equal measures of love and sorrow.

"Of course. Then let's do it."

Joanna held out her hand palm up, and Bekka reached out and—though her own hand had been empty but a second before—gently placed the dreamcatcher medallion in her sister's grasp. Joanna looked down at the miniature hoop of wood, string and feathers for a moment, her expression unreadable. Then she cupped her other hand over the medallion and a soft glow began to pulse, its light visible through the spaces between her fingers. The rhythmic glow made Bekka think of a heartbeat, except Joanna had no more physical reality in this place than she had. A soul beat, then, the ebb and flow of power that made up the complex pattern of energies that resulted in consciousness.

After several moments, the glow became dimmer, its pulse weaker, until finally it extinguished altogether. Joanna looked into her sister's eyes once more, and Bekka was shocked to see that her twin appeared transparent and out of focus, as if she were having trouble maintaining the illusion of physical form. Or worse, that her spiritual energies had been severely depleted.

Joanna held the medallion out to Bekka, and the psychic reached to take it. The miniature dreamcatcher still seemed solid enough (in a metaphysical sense), but when Bekka's fingertips brushed her sister's, instead of touching them, Bekka's fingers passed through Joanna's, as if she held no more substance than mist.

"I've given all I can," Joanna said, her voice so soft that Bekka had to lip-read to make out her sister's words. "It's up to you now... and to Jerome. When you see him again, tell him... tell him..."

Joanna's features blurred and her lips were no longer visible. Her voice was little more than the merest hint of a whisper, too soft and faint for Bekka to understand. But that didn't matter. She knew what message her sister wanted to pass on to her child.

"I'll tell him, Joanna."

And, as if Bekka's words granted her spirit release, what little remained of Joanna's form collapsed into particles of light which were instantly absorbed by the sea of illumination on the other side of the open doorway.

Bekka stood alone, holding the medallion, grateful that she had no physical body in this place, else she would be bawling like a baby right. But she couldn't afford to linger there and wallow in emotion. She needed to get the medallion—and the power Joanna had infused in it—back home. With her free hand, she closed the white door, then turned to head back down the hallway the way she had come. But she'd only taken a single step when four razor-sharp claws thrust upward through the floor.

She was too late; Krueger had found her. The Dreamscape was located at a dimensional tangent to the astral plane, but she'd hoped Krueger wouldn't sense her presence here in time for him to find a passageway from one realm to the other. From appearances, it seemed that he hadn't been able to locate such a passage, so he was making one by brute force. Bekka couldn't comprehend the amount of sheer mystical power such a feat required, but if she had been frightened of Freddy Krueger before, she was absolutely terrified of the fiend now.

Freddy continued slashing the floor with his claws, sweeping them back and forth in broad, violent strokes. Bekka knew it would only take him seconds to cut his way through, so if she intended to act, she had to do so at once. She started running down the hall toward Krueger, and when she reached the spot where he was cutting his way into this dimension, she jumped over his claw-knives. They swiped at her feet, barely missing her. She landed on the other side and kept running, not bothering to take so much as an instant to revel in avoiding Krueger's strike. She still had a long way to go before she could start celebrating.

"Come back here, bitch, and I promise to make your death slightly less agonizing!" Krueger roared with dark laughter, but Bekka didn't turn around to look at him. She could well imagine that he'd cut himself a hole large enough to crawl through and was pulling himself up into the hallway.

Bekka tried not to think about Krueger, about what the monster would do to her if he caught her, about what would happen to Jerome if she failed to bring the medallion charged with Joanna's spiritual energy back to the physical world. Instead she concentrated on running, on putting one foot down, while raising the other, on fleeing down the hallway as fast as she could.

"C'mon, Bekka! Didn't your mommy ever tell you that you can't run away from your problems?"

From the corners of her eyes, Bekka saw movement on either side of her. She was so startled that she forgot to keep her gaze fixed forward, and she glanced to her right. She saw Krueger's gloved right hand, claws and all, right next to her face. She turned to her left and saw his other hand, uncovered, flesh a mass of wrinkled, discolored scar tissue.

"Gotcha!" Freddy shouted from what sounded like a long way behind her, and then his hands grabbed Bekka's shoulders. She screamed as the hands yanked her backward and momentum caused her feet to slide out from under her. If Krueger's hands hadn't been holding onto her, she surely would've fallen. But the hands held her upright, so tight it hurt, but she didn't fall. She hadn't been cut, either. Freddy had grabbed her in such a way as to make sure his claw-knives didn't harm her. At least, not yet.

Krueger's hands lifted her in their powerful grip and held her several feet above the floor. She thrashed, shook, kicked, but nothing she did would break his hold.

"I could say, 'tag, you're it'," Freddy said, for some reason still sounding far away. "But I'm not in the mood to stretch out our little game any longer than necessary!"

The way he stressed the words stretch and longer aroused Bekka's curiosity, and she glanced back over her shoulder.

Krueger was coming toward her down the hallway, walking at a slow, unhurried pace. His arms stretched forth from the sockets like gigantic red and green striped serpents, thick and boneless, extending all the way to her, at least fifty feet, maybe more.

"You heard of the long arm of the law?" Krueger said. "Well, I'm the long arm of the claw!" He turned Bekka around to face him, his arms withdrawing back into their sockets to take up the slack as he continued to walk toward her.

"You thought you were so damn clever reworking the dreamcatcher into a protective medallion, and then paying a visit to your dead mess of a sister to get her to power the fucking thing! But you're too late, Ms Psychic. My

Jerome's a big boy now, and he's getting bigger by the second. Soon he'll be strong enough to resist your pathetic little souvenir. 'My aunt traveled to the Land of the Dead, and all I got was this lousy medallion!'"

Krueger laughed once more, and the sound slammed into Bekka like a physical blow. This close, she saw Krueger as two overlapping images. One was his normal manifestation, the scar-faced boogeyman-clown in his Christmas-colored sweater, old-fashioned hat and homemade claws. But the other image—the deeper, truer image—was far worse. For beneath his manic exterior lay a darkness beyond anything that Bekka had ever conceived of. It wasn't simply evil, though it was that—Evil with a capital "E". And it wasn't just madness and bloodlust, rage and cruelty, though of course these were all present, and in great abundance. It was as if Krueger was a repository of every negative emotion that human beings were capable of feeling, every dark imagining and twisted thought, every blasphemous word and wicked deed.

As if he'd read her mind, Krueger said, "Dreams may be the mind's playground, but nightmares are its trash heap. All the rotten gunk stinking up people's psyches—their fears and hatreds, their loathing of themselves and others—it all gets purged in nightmares and left behind in the Dreamscape where it just sits and festers, waiting for some evil sonofabitch like me to come along and put it to use."

Freddy had already reached her—a few more feet and his arms would have returned to their normal length. Bekka didn't know what would happen then, but she was sure it wouldn't be good.

"That's why you can't beat me, Bekka. No one can. Because as long as people have bad dreams, I'll have an unlimited supply of power."

The dark energy that Krueger radiated was so strong that Bekka felt she might be swept away by it, her essence torn to shreds by his psychic maelstrom. She fought to hold on to her identity, to her sense of self, for it was the only weapon she had to fight with.

"Th-that may be true," she said in a shaky voice that became stronger as she went. "But it's not the whole truth. People purge their darkness because they want to get rid of it, to forget it. Just like they want to forget about you. And once they do, you no longer have any connection to their dreams, no way to get at them. And then all your power is meaningless. What's a killer without a victim? A nightmare without a dreamer? Nothing, that's what. That's your deep, dark secret, Freddy Krueger: beneath your demonic clown exterior, beneath even the accumulated darkness of all the nightmare energies you've managed to absorb, you're nothing. And you know it."

As she spoke, Krueger's face changed. His scorched flesh took on a crimson hue, and his ears tapered to points. His brow became more pronounced and furrowed into a deep scowl. His lips curled back in a feral snarl, his teeth no longer crooked and yellow, but instead ivory fangs that wouldn't have been out of place in a shark's mouth. His eyes withdrew into their sockets and became red pinpoints that blazed like fire.

"Let's cut to the chase, sister." Krueger's voice was deeper, little more than an animalistic growl without the slightest trace of humor, mocking or otherwise. "I've caught you, and I'm going to destroy your little mystic talisman, then I'm going to torture you until your soul screams throughout all existence for release. And there's not a goddamned thing you can do about it."

Paradoxically, because Krueger had revealed his true face to her, Bekka was no longer quite so frightened of him. The greatest fear was fear of the unknown, but she knew what Krueger was, and while that didn't make him any less dangerous, it made him something that could be fought.

Bekka smiled. "There's one thing I can do. When you first appeared I was so scared that I forgot where I was—and what I really am here. This isn't the physical world, and it's not the Dreamscape. You've wandered too far from your center of power, Krueger, and you can't hold me here, not if I don't wish to be held." Bekka closed her eyes and thought a single word.

Home.

She felt a sudden rush, as if the ground had opened up beneath her and she now plunged rapidly through empty space. She more sensed than heard Krueger shout, "Noooooo!" and then she opened her eyes.

Bekka was looking down at the top of her reading table, palms flat against the surface, the recycled dreamcatcher medallion resting between them. She wanted to shout in triumph over her escape from Krueger, but she couldn't afford to lose control, not yet. She had one more task to perform.

She turned her hands upward until each palm faced the medallion. She then concentrated on releasing the spiritual energy Joanna had given her and directing it into the medallion. Bekka had carried a simulacrum of the medallion on the astral plane, but it had only been a metaphorical construct designed to represent the true transfer that was now taking place. She felt the energy leaving her and infusing the medallion, bonding with the remnants of mystical power that lingered in the pieces Bekka had salvaged from the original dreamcatcher, and strengthening them. But it wasn't enough; Bekka had to contribute a significant portion of her own life force, and she felt her life energy draining from her body and entering the medallion.

Within moments, the transfer was complete, and Bekka slumped back in her chair, suddenly overwhelmed by a sense of weariness and loss. Having Joanna's energy inside her had been like having Joanna herself back, alive and vital, the psychic link they had shared as twins once more present and strong. Transferring the energy into the medallion created a void inside Bekka, one so painful it felt as if she'd lost her sister all over again. And it had also taken another toll on her.

Tears began to trickle down her newly wrinkled face, but she didn't try to fight them. They were tears of relief as much as loss. Everything was going to be all right now, just as soon as Jerome got here and put the medallion on. He'd be protected then, by the loving power of his own mother's spirit. He'd be safe at last.

She hoped.

Hands that now shook as if palsied resting in her lap, rheumy gaze fixed firmly on the dreamcatcher medallion, Bekka waited for Jerome and Cheryl to arrive.

Freddy Krueger stood upon the Dreamscape, its dark energies swirling and roiling around him in a constantly shifting riot of color and form. This chaos was the Dreamscape's natural state, and though Freddy took great delight in the deadly scenarios he created for his playmates from these energies, he much preferred this maelstrom of madness. It was his kind of place. But at the moment he was too busy seething with frustrated rage to enjoy the insanity that surrounded him.

The psychic bitch's words echoed in the diseased lump of rotten flesh that passed for Krueger's mind.

That's your deep, dark secret, Freddy Krueger: beneath your demonic clown exterior, beneath even the accumulated darkness of all the nightmare energies you've managed to absorb, you're nothing. And you know it.

"Thought you were pretty slick escaping me like that, didn't you, Bekka? And now you think you're safe out there in the physical world... Think I can't touch you there..."

He flexed the fingers in his claw-glove and the metal blades hissed against one another.

"But I've got a longer reach than you think, bitch, and it's getting longer all the time!"

Dark laughter bubbled forth from Krueger's throat and echoed throughout the length and breadth of the Dreamscape. All across the face of the earth, sleepers shivered beneath their blankets in fear, and when they awakened, they would remember only that they'd had a terrible nightmare and never again would they truly know a good night's rest.

SEVENTEEN

"Nice, huh?"

"Sure is. I've never driven a Lexus before."

"Well, don't get too used to it," Jerome said. "You saw how hard it was to get my dad to agree to let us borrow it. And this is a life or death situation."

Getting his dad to loan them the car had turned out to be more difficult than Jerome had anticipated. Jerome argued that Cheryl was going to drive, and they weren't going far, only to Bekka's to get something that might help him against Freddy. Don had been reluctant to let Jerome leave the house after what had happened last night, and Lynn had been less than thrilled to hear Bekka's name invoked in her house again. But in the end, they both gave in—as much for Cheryl as for him, he thought. Now they sat in the front of Don Starkey's prized Lexus, Cheryl behind the steering wheel and Jerome only a passenger. He was a bit jealous of Cheryl; his dad hardly ever let him drive the car. But in his condition—sleep deprived, hand burned, and the target of an undead lunatic—Jerome knew he wasn't in any shape to drive. Besides, he was nervous as hell. What if this trinket Bekka had whipped up didn't work?

He looked out the passenger side window, and when he realized what direction they were going, south instead of northwest, he felt the first stirrings of panic in his gut.

"Don't go this way!" he said. "This is..."

"What?" Cheryl asked.

Jerome felt ashamed for telling her this, but he'd never been able to keep any secrets from her. "This way will take us onto Elm... Past the old Krueger place. I'd... rather not see it right now."

"But it's the fastest, most direct route to your aunt's." Cheryl's voice sounded calm enough, but Jerome thought he detected a hint of exasperation in her tone. "If Bekka's come up with a way to help you, then every moment we delay only places you in more danger."

Jerome couldn't argue with her logic—and he knew she was only acting out of concern for him—but he couldn't escape the feeling that driving past Krueger's deserted house wasn't the smartest move. Maybe he was just being overly cautious. After all, it wasn't as if Krueger lived there anymore. He was dead, and his spirit inhabited the Dreamscape, not an old construction of rotting wood and crumbling stone. Besides, they were only going to be driving past, not going inside. Still, Bekka had said it was Krueger's center of power in the real world.

He mustered a smile. "All right, but don't expect me to look at the damn thing."

Cheryl smiled back. "Deal."

Less than a minute later, Cheryl slowed and hit the Lexus's turn signal as she came to an intersection. She stopped then turned onto Elm Street. Jerome might've closed his eyes if someone other than Cheryl had been driving. He knew she'd understand if he did, but though he realized it made him a macho jerk, he couldn't bring himself to show that kind of weakness to his girlfriend. Instead he kept his gaze fixed on the road ahead of them and avoided looking at the houses as they drove past.

The asphalt was a dull, weathered black, the line painted down the middle faded white. As he stared out the windshield, his eyelids began to grow heavy, and he struggled to keep them open. He pinched the small web of skin between his thumb and forefinger, bit the inside of his cheek nearly hard enough to draw blood. But these actions helped only for a few seconds at best, leaving him feeling even more weary than before.

Though he wasn't looking in the direction of Krueger's house, he nevertheless sensed when they were drawing close to it. It was like an invisible weight settled on his shoulders and the air in the interior of the Lexus suddenly became too thick and stale to breathe. The sensations became increasingly oppressive, until finally Jerome couldn't stand it anymore, and he turned to look. Krueger's house sat in the middle of its barren lawn like a spider squatting in the middle of its web. Jerome had the impression that the house had been waiting for him to pass by. He blinked several times, his eyelids suddenly heavy as stone, and he heard a single word whisper through his mind.

Sleep…

If it hadn't been for the reason behind this trip, Cheryl would've enjoyed driving Mr Starkey's Lexus a lot more. The car was only a couple years old and still in great condition. But she wasn't capable of appreciating the experience, wasn't capable of feeling anything beyond worry for Jerome. He might've died in last night's accident, might still die—just like his mother—if they couldn't find a way to stop Krueger, or at least keep him away from Jerome. She prayed that whatever Bekka had come up with would do the trick. She loved Jerome so much, and she couldn't bear for anything to happen to him.

Jerome's head lolled forward, his eyes closed.

Cheryl felt a jolt of fear. Omigod, was he asleep? "Jerome, are you all right? Jerome!"

She took her right hand off the steering wheel and started to reach for Jerome, intending to shake him. But before her hand made contact, he lifted his head, eyes wide open and alert.

"Are you okay, sweetie? You nodded off there for a second."

Jerome turned to look at her, his head swiveling slowly and deliberately. His face remained expressionless for a moment, but then his lips formed a smile.

"I'm fine." His smile grew wider. "Fine and fucking dandy."

Cheryl had never been to Bekka's place before, and as she pulled Mr Starkey's Lexus into the driveway, she had to admit she was disappointed. Bekka's house looked nothing like the place where a psychic lived and did business. To the right of the door a small sign was bolted to the brick: Spiritual Advisor, M-F 10-8, SAT 10-6, Closed Sundays. But otherwise there was nothing to mark Bekka's place as special. It was a two-story Cape Cod, with red brick, dark green shingles, and shutters to match. The yard was well kept—the grass neatly trimmed, flowerbeds with blooming tulips and daffodils well tended. It was almost stultifyingly normal.

Jerome opened the passenger door before Cheryl had put the Lexus in park. By the time she'd done so and shut off the engine, he was halfway up the small set of concrete steps that led to the porch.

As she got out of the car, she said, "Hey, wait up, Mr Impatient!" It was just a joke (mostly) but

Jerome froze on the second to last step and didn't turn around right away. Cheryl crossed the walkway and started up the stairs herself before he turned to face her. He smiled easily enough, but he stood stiffly, body tight with tension. And there was an intensity in his eyes, a cold scrutiny that made her almost take a step back.

"Sorry. Guess I'm just excited."

He said nothing more, but his eyes narrowed and Cheryl had the impression that he was waiting to see if she would accept his explanation.

He's been through a lot the last couple days, she told herself. And he didn't get any sleep last night. Add to that all the coffee he's been drinking to help him stay awake, and it's no wonder he's acting a little strange.

She returned his smile, took his hand and gave it a squeeze. He didn't respond to her touch; his hand was like a lifeless lump of flesh in hers. But she kept smiling and said, "C'mon, let's go."

Jerome hesitated a moment, then nodded, and together they stepped onto the porch and up to Bekka's front door. Cheryl expected Jerome to just open the door and walk in—it was his aunt's house, after all—but instead he opened the screen door and knocked. A moment later Bekka opened the door, and Cheryl nearly gasped in surprise. She'd last seen Bekka early this morning at the hospital, and she'd looked tired and stressed then. But, only a few hours later, she looked as if she'd aged ten years, if not more.

If Jerome was surprised by his aunt's appearance, he gave no sign.

Bekka smiled sadly. "I didn't mean to startle you. I should've warned you about my appearance when I called, but as fast as everything's been moving, it just didn't occur to me."

"That's all right," Jerome said. "No biggie."

Bekka frowned as she looked at her nephew, squinting her eyes almost as if she were trying to look inside him somehow. Jerome just stood expressionless as Bekka scrutinized him, and after a moment or two passed, she broke eye contact with Jerome and shook her head.

"Sorry. For a moment there I thought... well, it doesn't matter what I thought, does it? Come on in."

Bekka stepped back to make room for them to enter. Cheryl started forward without thinking, for normally Jerome, gentleman that he was, let her go first. But this time he brushed past her as if she wasn't there, and she had the feeling that if she'd been any closer to the doorway, he might've knocked her aside.

He's just nervous, she told herself. And who could blame him, considering everything that he'd been through? He was no doubt anxious to find out what Bekka had come up with to help protect him from Freddy Krueger. Still, the casual disregard for her feelings, for her, wasn't like Jerome. Wasn't like him at all. Cheryl tried not to worry about it as she entered Bekka's house. Jerome's aunt would help him and everything would be better. It had to be.

Bekka continued talking as she led Jerome and Cheryl through the foyer and into a room that, given the white cloth-covered table with a crystal ball resting on the surface, was obviously where Bekka conducted her business.

"My... efforts to help restore the dreamcatcher took more out of me than I thought they would." Her voice was soft and breathy, and the words seem to come to Bekka with more effort now. "But I suppose you already guessed that, eh?" She chuckled, but her laughter ended in a series of dry, rattling coughs. She stopped walking and started to sway, as if she were having a difficult time maintaining her balance. Cheryl expected Jerome to step forward and help steady his aunt, but when he didn't, Cheryl went to her side. She put an arm around Bekka's waist, which was tiny and felt fragile as an abandoned wasp's nest and helped the woman over to her chair at the table.

Bekka sat with an audible sigh and gave Cheryl a grateful look. "Thanks, hon."

Ten years, Cheryl thought? It's more like she's aged thirty or forty!

"Sit down," Bekka said, not quite an order but more than a request. Cheryl glanced at Jerome, but his face remained expressionless as he took one of the remaining chairs at the table. Sensing that something was wrong but unable to say what, Cheryl sat in the chair next to Jerome.

The crystal ball wasn't the only object resting on the table. In front of Bekka was a miniature version of the dreamcatcher that until the night before last had hung over Jerome's bed.

Bekka gestured at the object with a hand that trembled as if she had Parkinson's. "This is it, Jerome. I couldn't repair your dreamcatcher and I couldn't recreate it, not entirely. But with a..." another sad smile... "a little extra help, I was able to make this. It's a medallion. Not quite as powerful as your original dreamcatcher, I'm sorry to say, but it contains enough psychic energy to present a formidable defense against Krueger. If you start wearing it all the time, and you religiously practice certain meditative techniques I'll teach you before you go to sleep every night, you should be fine."

Jerome looked at the medallion, and though Cheryl saw something move behind his eyes, she couldn't tell what he was thinking. So she examined the dreamcatcher-medallion more closely to determine what, if anything, he might see in it.

"Nothing personal, Bekka, but I don't feel any 'power' radiating from it," Cheryl said. "Then again, I didn't feel any power when I was around Jerome's old dreamcatcher. Though sometimes I did get a kind of strange feeling from it. But maybe that was just my imagination."

She felt as if she were babbling, but she couldn't stop herself. Jerome's silence was beginning to make her nervous.

"As I said, the medallion's less powerful than the original dreamcatcher. I'm not surprised you don't sense anything from it." Bekka looked at the medallion and gently ran her forefinger around its circumference. "Truth to tell, I can't sense much about it, either. Creating the medallion tapped my deepest reserves of psychic energy, in effect making me psi-blind. Whether my abilities will ever return, I don't know. But even if they don't, their loss is a small price to pay for keeping Jerome safe from Krueger."

Cheryl had never had any doubt that Bekka loved Jerome, but now she truly understood the depth of that love. For Bekka, sacrificing her psychic power would be the equivalent of Cheryl giving up her eyesight or her hearing. Cheryl loved Jerome too, loved him more than anyone she'd ever known, her parents included. But even as much as she loved Jerome, could she make such a sacrifice for him?

She didn't have to think about it for long. Of course she could.

Bekka lifted the dreamcatcher-medallion by its leather strap and held it out to Jerome. "Here. Take it and put it on."

Jerome hesitated, but then he reached out and took hold of the medallion. Bekka withdrew her hand—almost reluctantly, Cheryl thought—and rose to her feet.

"I almost forgot. I have something else to give you. It's from your mother." She shuffled closer to Jerome, leaned down and kissed him on the cheek. But the moment her lips touched her nephew's flesh, Bekka's eyes flew wide, and she pulled her face away from his abruptly, as if she'd experienced an electric shock.

Jerome looked up at her, his lips forming a sly smile.

"Looks like you're not so psi-blind as you thought, huh?"

Jerome wrapped his fingers around the miniature re-creation of his old dreamcatcher and squeezed. The sound of snapping wood filled the room, the noise far louder than the destruction of such a small object could account for. Jerome opened his hand and dropped the broken pieces of the medallion onto the table.

Cheryl had trouble believing what she'd just witnessed. "Jerome, why..." She couldn't bring herself to complete the question, wasn't even exactly sure how to phrase it.

"It's because he's not our Jerome," Bekka said as she slowly backed away from the table. "It's Jerome's body, but the personality in control isn't his. It's the other Jerome, the one that Freddy created."

Jerome's lips drew back from his teeth in what Cheryl thought might be a grin but looked more like a snarl.

"That's right, you dried up old hag." He quickly rose to his feet, the abrupt motion knocking over his chair. "Your toy might've worked, too. If my soul brother hadn't been dumb enough to fall asleep and give me a chance to hop into the driver's seat for a while."

He glanced at the crystal ball, then at Bekka—who continued to slowly retreat—and a wicked gleam came into his eyes. Jerome placed his hands on either side of the crystal ball and lifted it off its base. "A tool of the trade, eh, Bekka? Well, you know what they say. She who lives by the ball, dies by the ball."

He lifted the crystalline sphere over his head and ran toward Bekka. Bekka raised her arms to protect herself, but she was too slow, too weak. Jerome—or rather, the evil thing in control of his body—brought the crystal ball down on Bekka's head. Cheryl watched in stunned horror as Bekka's skull exploded like a rotten melon, sending splatters of blood, chunks of brain and shards of bone flying everywhere. Bekka's body shuddered as if ten thousand volts of electricity coursed through it, and then her legs fell out from under her, and she began to go down. Her knees hit the floor with a pair of loud cracks, she remained motionless for a moment, mouth wide, eyes staring, and then she pitched forward and crashed face first to the floor.

Jerome regarded Bekka's corpse for a moment before turning his attention to the crystal ball. Its surface was slick with blood, and he gazed at it for a long moment, as if he were contemplating a work of art. Then he set the crystal ball back down on its base, speckling the white tablecloth with blood, and used his index finger to clean off two round spots and a half-circle. With a dizzying twist of nausea, Cheryl realized he'd drawn a smiley face in Bekka's blood.

Jerome smiled at her. "Have a nice day."

Cheryl wanted to scream, could feel a scream, wild and insane, deep down inside her, desperate to get out. But she couldn't give voice to it. She was too terrified of what Jerome, this Jerome, might do to her. So like a small, frightened woodland creature that has had the misfortune to suddenly find itself in the presence of a hungry predator, she remained very, very still and very, very quiet, and prayed to Christ that the beast that had hijacked her boyfriend's body would somehow overlook her. His face, hands and clothes were covered with blood spatter and globs of gray matter that slid off him and fell to the floor with meaty wet *plaps*.

"Sorry you had to see that, Cheryl. I'd have preferred to wait a while before revealing my true identity to you. At least until I'd banged you a few times." He laughed. "But I can't afford any loose ends, and neither can my... benefactor. So I'm afraid you're going to have to die, too. But not before I've had some fun with you. Think of it as the equivalent of a last meal for someone about to be executed, only in your case, it's a last fuck. I promise to do my best to make it a good one." He grinned. "Good for me, anyway." He started walking toward her.

Cheryl had remained seated during Jerome's attack on Bekka. But she rose from her chair and, just as Bekka had done only a few moments earlier, she backed slowly away from Jerome's advance.

"You may not be my Jerome, but I know he's still in there. He loves me, and he won't let you hurt me."

Jerome continued coming toward her, leaving a trail of bloody shoe prints behind him. "He loves Bekka, too, but you saw how much that helped her. Jerome's not in control anymore, and he's not going to be ever again. Meet the new boss, definitely not the same as the old boss."

Cheryl gazed into Jerome's eyes and tried to see beyond the lust and madness that currently filled them, tried to see past this thing that had stolen her boyfriend's body, and all the way to *her* Jerome, the real one. The one that loved her and would never ever do anything to hurt her, who'd give up his own life to save hers if he could.

"Jerome, honey, you saw what he did to Bekka. If you don't do something to stop him, he's going to do worse to me. A lot worse. Please, I love you so much. I... I don't mind dying if it's my time, but I can't stand the thought that it'll be your hands that take my life. Hands that I've held so many times... Hands that I've kissed... Your hands, Jerome. Not his!"

Jerome stopped advancing and then frowned as if suddenly confused. His facial muscles twitched and contorted, and his whole body began to shake as if he were having a seizure. No, Bekka thought. As if he were desperately trying to wake up from a dream. Jerome's spasms became more violent as the two personalities that inhabited his body battled for control. Cheryl knew that she should take advantage of the Jeromes' struggle for control, but she couldn't bring herself to abandon the man she loved, even if he did currently share his body with a homicidal maniac.

A few seconds later, she had cause to regret her choice to stay as Jerome lurched forward—facial muscles rippling as if they might tear themselves free of his skull any second—and then his fist came swinging toward her face in a vicious arc. A burst of white light exploded behind her eyes as the fist connected with her jaw, then the light faded, leaving only darkness behind.

Jerome stared at Cheryl's prone form lying on the floor in a pool of his aunt's blood. Bekka's body lay several feet away, and on the table, the bloody smiley face his other self had created gazed at Jerome with mindless joviality.

He'd killed Bekka! Killed Cheryl! No, not him, the *other* Jerome, the one infested with Freddy's evil—that fucker was responsible.

His other self had retreated, leaving Jerome in control once more, but Jerome sensed the other's presence lurking just beneath the surface of his consciousness, like a crocodile submerged in dank river water, only its eyes visible, waiting with inhuman patience for prey to draw near the water's edge.

We did it together, bro. Your body, my wicked, wicked mind.

His other self laughed inside Jerome's head, the sound harsh and guttural, just like Krueger.

Jerome wanted to jam his hands tight against his ears to shut out the foul laughter, but since it issued from within his own skull, he knew there was nothing he could do.

Cheryl stirred and groaned then, and the laughter cut off as if someone had pressed a psychic *MUTE* button in his mind. Jerome knelt next to Cheryl and fixed his gaze on her face, not allowing himself to believe she was alive, afraid that her movement had been only another of Krueger's cruel tricks. But after a moment, she groaned again and her eyes fluttered, though they didn't open. Thank Christ, she was alive! Her jaw was rapidly swelling and already starting to bruise, and Jerome feared it was broken. It was possible she had a concussion, too, or maybe a more serious head injury, but at least she was alive… for the moment. But she wouldn't remain that way, not if his other self assumed control again.

Though Jerome didn't want to leave her side, though it broke his heart to abandon her when she was hurt, by his own hand, if not his own will, he knew he couldn't stay. He couldn't risk his other self regaining control and attacking her. Jerome had failed to save Bekka, but he was determined not to lose Cheryl as well. And there was only one way he could think of to ensure her safety. He had to get away from her as fast as possible.

He reached out to touch her face one last time before he left, but when he saw his fingers were slick with Bekka's blood, he pulled his hand back. He stood, then turned and began heading for the front door, leaving behind the two women he cared for more than anyone else in the world. One dead, the other injured and perhaps in need of medical attention. He was determined to make their attacker pay, and pay dearly for what he'd done. And when Jerome was finished with the son of a bitch, he'd never hurt anyone ever again.

EIGHTEEN

Jerome stood looking down at the river rushing below. It had rained all last week, and the water was brown and sludgy, the level much higher than normal. It wasn't quite dark yet, but the sun had dipped past the trees that dotted the western horizon, leaving the bridge and the river it stretched across painted in shadow. If Jerome hadn't known the water below was brown, he might've thought he was looking at a torrent of flowing ink, or perhaps blood so dark it appeared black. Debris bobbed in the churning water—broken tree branches, plastic soda bottles and at one point what appeared to be the body of a dead dog. Jerome was grateful for last week's storms; the swollen river would make what he intended to do easier.

His dad's Lexus was parked at the northern end of the bridge, just off the side of the road, keys still in the ignition. Jerome wasn't going to be needing a ride home.

The bridge was located a couple miles outside Springwood, part of a country road that didn't see much traffic—something Jerome was counting on. He gripped the bridge's metal railing and hesitated only a moment before swinging his right leg up and over, followed by his left. He sat on the railing, hands still gripping tight for support, legs dangling out into space. If this had been an urban or even suburban area, the railing would have been built high enough to discourage people from attempting what Jerome was about to do. But this was a country bridge, at least twenty years old. It was the kind of place people drove across or fished from, not jumped off.

He gazed down at the water and listened to its sibilant whispering as it rushed by beneath him. He found the sound soothing, and he wished he could sit here and listen to it forever. But he couldn't; he had work to do.

He figured it was thirty, maybe forty feet down. Not so far that a drop would prove fatal in and of itself, but then he hadn't expected it to. He was counting on the river to take care of business. Now that he was there and about to go through with it, he was mildly surprised to discover that he wasn't afraid. If he had to die to stop his other self and prevent Krueger from gaining an agent in the real world, then so be it. He only wished that he'd found the courage to take his life earlier. If he had, Bekka would still be alive.

Once again he saw Bekka lying on the floor of her sitting room, head crushed, surrounded by a widening pool of blood.

He squeezed his eyes shut and tried to banish the image from his mind. He didn't want to go to his death with that picture in his head. Sorrow gripped him then, so overwhelming that it took all his strength not to break down sobbing. He couldn't afford any weakness, not now. Not until after he'd jumped and it was too late.

He loosened his grip on the railing but didn't let go, not yet.

He hoped Cheryl would understand and maybe even one day find it in her to forgive him. He wondered if El—after the pain of losing a friend had eased somewhat—would be able to make jokes about his high dive someday. Jerome hoped so; he wanted El to remember him with laughter. He regretted the pain his suicide would cause his family. Jerome was the last living link his dad had to Joanna Larkin. When Jerome was gone, Joanna would be, too, forever. Lynn wasn't his birthmother, but Jerome thought she'd feel sorrow at his loss, maybe even as much as she'd feel at losing one of her biological children. But of everyone he would be leaving behind, Jerome regretted the effect his death would have on his half… on his brother and sister. Brian and Mary were too young to have to experience such loss, and if there was any other way to put an end to Krueger's plan, Jerome would've done it. But he could see no other way, and the longer he hesitated, the greater the chance that his other self—who, since Jerome had left Bekka's, had been strangely silent—would attempt to reassert control. If Jerome was going to do this thing, he had to do it now.

He took a deep breath, removed his hands from the railing, and leaned forward.

The moment he began falling, he was seized by panic, and his arms and legs began flailing of their own accord, desperate to find any sort of purchase in the air. Though he was reconciled to dying, wanted death as much as he'd ever wanted anything in life, it seemed his body had its own ideas. His stomach leaped into his throat and he couldn't breathe. It felt as if his heart suddenly stopped beating in anticipation of a full body shutdown.

A shock of impact, accompanied by a sudden bone-numbing cold, and Jerome felt his descent abruptly slow. It took a second for him to realize that he'd hit the water, was in fact beneath it, and then he was tumbling as the river's current took hold of him. He began thrashing—or rather, his body did—in a desperate attempt to swim to the surface. But Jerome forced himself to go limp and let the river do with him as it would. To help things along, he opened his mouth and expelled the air his lungs had been hoarding in a gout of bubbles, then he took a deep breath in. Panic returned as thick, heavy liquid filled his lungs, and his hands clawed the water, trying to pull the rest of his body toward the surface and the sweet air beyond.

He took another breath, then another. With each there was less air in his lungs and more water, and he quickly lost buoyancy. He sank deeper, and while his hands continued to paw the water, their exertions were becoming increasingly feeble. A not altogether unpleasant numbness settled into his body, and a profound sense of peace came over him. He'd done it—he'd beaten Freddy Krueger! Just a few more moments, and it would all be over...

He felt his consciousness begin to slip into the darkness within his own mind, his interior world mirroring what was happening outside. His spirit, essence, whatever it was called, would be swallowed by darkness, leaving his body to the river's mercy. But just as the everlasting night was about to take him, Jerome had a realization: once his soul was gone, his body wouldn't be empty. Someone would be left behind, someone that would no longer have to worry about fighting another personality for control. Someone who'd be free to do whatever he pleased, to whomever he pleased.

Jerome knew then that he'd fallen right into Freddy's hands. The bastard had wanted him to commit suicide so his nightmarish offspring could take permanent control of Jerome's body. Even now, with his last remaining shreds of self-awareness, Jerome could sense his other self taking the reins of their body, could almost hear the mocking laughter as he gave voice to his triumph.

Jerome tried to resist the darkness pulling him downward, but it was too late. The eternal void claimed his spirit and he knew no more.

Jerome's body crawled onto the riverbank and got onto its hands and knees. With a series of heaving coughs, it expelled the water from its stomach and lungs. When the body could breathe freely once more, it flopped onto its back and lay there for a time, staring up at the darkening sky while waiting for its strength to return. Full night had fallen by the time the body rose unsteadily to its feet and began making its way up the riverbank. It was quite a way downstream from where Jerome had jumped, but that was all right. The personality that was the sole inhabitant of the body didn't mind. In fact, it was rather looking forward to the exercise. Plus, it would give his clothes the opportunity to dry some more. He didn't want to get the interior of the Lexus any more wet than he had to. It was a damn fine car, and it would be a shame to ruin the upholstery.

Jerome—the other Jerome, the only Jerome, the once and future Jerome—smiled. He couldn't wait to hop behind the Lexus's steering wheel and return to town. There were some people that he really wanted to see.

See dead, that is.

Jerome laughed as he continued making his way up the riverbank, his body growing stronger with every step.

* * *

Gary Houser sat on a metal folding chair, grading student homework to the soothing sound of working washing machines and dryers. Ever since his own student days, he'd needed white noise to concentrate, but only recently had he been coming to the laundromat to find it. Not that he came here by choice. Four months ago, his wife had decided that they'd "grown apart" and needed "time alone to find themselves," and then she'd kicked him out of the house and refused to answer the phone when he called. He'd found a cheap apartment downtown, but the building didn't have a laundry room, so once a week he shoved all his dirty clothes into a canvas bag and hauled them here, to the Tidy Rabbit. What the hell a rabbit had to do with a laundromat, he had no idea, but the place had been here for decades.

The sign outside depicted a smiling cartoon rabbit in a dress, cleaning clothes using an old-fashioned wooden bucket full of suds and a corrugated washing board. Though the name and mascot of the establishment made no sense to him, they did appeal to his biologist's sense of humor. How many rabbits had he dissected over the years? When he was finished with them, they weren't tidy rabbits anymore. No, they were quite messy ones.

He was sitting in front of a dryer, and he found himself looking up from his grading to watch through the round glass door as his clothes tumbled around and around. It was almost hypnotic, and far more interesting than reading another poorly written essay on mitosis. The gem of the batch so far had been a nearly unreadable epic consisting of a grand total of twenty-eight words attempting to define mitosis as a form of bad breath.

So when the dryer's time ran out, he noticed. He put the stack of papers on the floor, then stood and, with an almost pathetic eagerness to do something other than grade, he walked over to the dryer and began fishing in his pants pocket for change. He withdrew a quarter, examined the date it was minted to stall a couple more seconds (it was 1982), then inserted the coin into the appropriate slot and activated the dryer. He watched as his clothes began to tumble once more, knowing they might well be dry already, but not prepared to return to his small and quite lonely apartment just yet.

"Getting some religion, Mr Houser?"

Startled, Gary turned toward the voice and was surprised to see Jerome Starkey standing there.

"Pardon?"

Jerome was smiling, but there was something about the expression that unsettled Gary. The lips seemed stretched a bit too wide and pulled back from the teeth a bit too far.

"You know what they say: 'cleanliness is next to godliness'."

It took a second for Gary to get the joke. "Ah, yes! I see. Clever." Not that he thought it was especially, but he couldn't think of anything else to say.

Jerome didn't respond. He just stood there, smiling that strange smile of his.

Gary began to feel nervous and awkward, and not entirely due to Jerome's odd expression. Like many teachers, he disliked encountering his students outside of school. Not because he hated them—well, not all of them—but because he never had any idea what to say. It certainly didn't help that away from school, any authority he had as a teacher was meaningless. He was just some guy washing his clothes, and Jerome was a kid who no longer even had to pretend to respect him.

"We missed you in school today. I heard about the accident. Everyone did, of course. Ms LeClair made an announcement during home room period. I'm glad you weren't seriously injured. It's a shame what happened to Pat Cottril and the others, though."

"Yeah, a real shame."

Jerome's reply was toneless, and Gary couldn't tell what, if anything, he was feeling. Must be the shock of the experience, he decided. It had only been a day since the accident, after all. He pointed to Jerome's hand. "Looks like you got burned, huh?"

"It's not too bad. See?" Jerome held the hand up for Gary to inspect. The flesh was red and shiny-tight, but it didn't look like a recent burn. Rather, it appeared to be one that had undergone a significant amount of healing. Certainly it wasn't an injury from last night's accident. Gary had no idea why Jerome felt the need to lie about his burn, but he decided not to remark on it.

Gary caught a whiff of a musty-dank smell, and he noticed Jerome's clothes were damp and had splotches of mud stains here and there. "I can see why you came here," he said with a smile.

Jerome scowled, and for an instant his entire face darkened in a way that made the hairs on the back of Gary's neck stand up. But then Jerome looked down at himself and his scowl melted into an expression of understanding.

"Right." He chuckled, and for some reason, the sound made Gary's hackles rise even more. "I was messing around down by the river a while ago, just doing a little extra-curricular schoolwork, you know?"

"I'm surprised you felt up to going anywhere, let alone down to the river."

Jerome shrugged. "I started going stir crazy sitting around the house. I thought if I got out it might take my mind off things, you know?"

"So what are you doing here, Jerome? The laundromat seems like an odd place to visit just because you're bored."

"I came here looking for you, of course."

Gary couldn't have been more surprised if Jerome had told him he was here to give Gary a million dollars in cash. "I don't understand."

"Not to get too personal, but all the kids in school know that you and your wife have, ah, temporarily parted ways. Some of the kids have seen you in here doing laundry, so I took a chance you'd be here tonight. Looks like I lucked out, huh?"

Gary was still having difficulty wrapping his mind around the concept of a student willingly seeking him out, and after school, yet. "Sorry, Jerome, but I'm still not following you."

"I told you I was down by the river. While I was there, I found a really freaky frog. At least, I think it's a frog; I've never seen anything quite like it before. I managed to catch it, whatever it is, and I figured I'd show it to you and maybe you could tell me what it is."

"I'm surprised, Jerome. I didn't have you pegged as someone with that sort of scientific curiosity. But why go to all the trouble of tracking me down tonight? Why not just bring this mysterious creature of yours to school tomorrow?"

"That's the thing, see. I'm not exactly experienced at catching animals, and I didn't have a net or anything. I just grabbed it with my hands and... well, I'm afraid I must've squeezed it too tight to keep it from squirming out. I'm sure I hurt it, and I think it might be dying. I wanted you to see it before it croaks—no pun intended." Jerome looked at Gary expectantly after he finished.

Gary wasn't sure how to take the boy's story. It made sense on the surface, but it seemed out of character for Jerome Starkey. He was a good enough kid, despite yesterday morning's episode of weird behavior. Still, the thought of checking out a mysterious specimen—one that, for the moment at least, was alive—intrigued Gary.

Certainly it would be a hell of a lot more interesting than grading essays.

"Where is it? You're not carrying it around in your pocket, are you?"

"No. It's outside, in the trunk of my dad's car. You want to come out and take a look at it?"

Gary glanced at the dryer. His clothes still had plenty of time to go in this cycle. He turned to Jerome. "Sure, why not?"

Jerome smiled. "Great!" One corner of his mouth rose in a half-smile. "I think you're going to be very surprised."

"Wake up, Mr Houser."

He felt a hand patting his cheeks, right, then left. He tried to open his eyes, but his head hurt so much that all he wanted to do was go back to sleep until the pain was gone. The hand hit him harder this time, hard enough to jar his head and start it throbbing even worse. The pain was too much to ignore, and despite himself, Gary Houser opened his eyes.

He saw Jerome Starkey kneeling over him.

"Welcome back to the land of the living." Jerome smiled. "At least for a little while."

Gary wanted to ask what had happened, but the words came out as muffled mumbling, and he realized he'd been gagged. He tried to sit up then, but Jerome planted a hand on his chest and shoved him back down with surprising strength. Gary fell back to the ground, cracking the back of his head against hard asphalt. The pain in his head quadrupled and he almost passed out again, but Jerome gave him a hard pinch on the cheek.

"Stay with me now, Mr Houser. It took me long enough to wake you up the first time. Besides, you don't want to miss out on the fun, do you?"

Gary struggled to remember how he'd gotten there. He recalled grading essays in the laundromat, Jerome arriving and telling him about a strange sort of frog that he'd captured. He remembered following Jerome outside to a Lexus—he recalled that part very well, for he knew he'd never be able to afford a Lexus, pre-owned or otherwise, on his teacher's salary. He remembered Jerome popping the trunk open and gesturing for him to look inside. He'd leaned down into the trunk, looking to see whatever Jerome had in there, but as near as he'd been able to see, the trunk had been empty. He'd been about to ask Jerome if this were some sort of joke, when he sensed sudden movement from the boy, and then pain exploded in his skull, and he remembered nothing else until Jerome started slapping him.

He thought he understood what had happened, though. Jerome had slammed the trunk lid down hard on his head and knocked him out. He'd then gagged him and brought him here, wherever that was. He tried to turn his head to examine his surroundings, but even the slightest movement set off a fresh wave of agony in his skull, forcing him to lie still.

"Let me guess," Jerome said. "Trying to figure out where you are? I didn't take you too far. We're in the alley behind the laundromat. As you've no doubt figured out by now, there was no strange frog. That was a lie I used to get you outside so I could knock you out—just to make you temporarily more cooperative, you understand. We're about to embark on a little scientific experiment, you and I. Dissecting a frog in class is interesting and all, but I thought I might learn more by dissecting a… more complex organism. And a living one, at that." He frowned. "Though isn't it called vivisection when you cut up something that's alive? I guess it doesn't really matter. It's the cutting that's important, right?"

Jerome smiled and Gary felt cold terror take hold of him and wipe away the pain in his head. He started to sit up, but Jerome shoved him down again and placed his right foot on Gary's left wrist.

"Can't have you wriggling while I work, can we?" He reached down and picked up a metal spike and a hammer. "Brace yourself; this is going to hurt a bit. Aw, who am I kidding? This is going to hurt like a son of a bitch."

Gary tried to plead with Jerome not to do this, but the cloth gag in his mouth made his words unintelligible. Not that he thought Jerome would pay any attention to them anyway. Jerome kept his foot on Gary's wrist while he placed the spike point first on Gary's palm. He raised the hammer high, his gaze fixed on Gary's eyes, and then he brought it down in a single, swift stroke. The spike penetrated the flesh of Gary's hand and dug into the asphalt beneath, pinning him in place.

Gary shrieked through his gag as agony beyond anything he'd ever known exploded in his hand and raced through his central nervous system like rapidly spreading fire.

"One down," Jerome said, grinning. "Three to go."

Jerome continued driving spikes through Gary's flesh until both arms and both legs were nailed to the asphalt. Gary was sobbing, the pain so intense that he couldn't stand it, but so strong that it denied him the escape of unconsciousness. Gary turned his head—the pain in his skull nothing compared to that caused by the spikes—and saw an assortment of tools laid out on the ground next to him.

Jerome lay the hammer aside and picked up a pair of garden shears. "Not exactly the right equipment, I know, but then the hardware store I stopped at didn't have a biology supply section, so I had to improvise."

Jerome used the shears to cut Gary's shirt down the middle, then he pushed the flaps to either side, exposing the bare flesh of the teacher's chest and abdomen. Jerome put the shears down and thoughtfully examined the rest of his tools. "What to start with?" he wondered aloud. "Something sharp, of course, so it makes a clean first cut, but something that won't do too much damage right away."

Tears streamed down the sides of Gary's face and he whimpered behind the gag.

Jerome brightened. "I know! How about this?" He picked up an exacto knife, thumbed the switch, and a length of ultra-sharp razor blade *snicked* out of its plastic housing.

Gary's eyes widened as he stared at the blade. Jerome went to work then, and it was a long time before Gary's eyes closed for good, and before they did he learned more about human anatomy than he'd ever wanted to know.

NINETEEN

Cheryl awoke calling Jerome's name, though she wasn't sure why. She sat up and put a hand to her throbbing head as she struggled to orient herself. Once she saw the smiley face crystal ball, the blood all over the floor, and of course Bekka's dead body, it didn't take long for her to recall what had happened.

She rose to her feet and closed her eyes as a wave of dizziness hit her. She inhaled deeply, hoping it would help the dizziness pass, but she breathed in the stink of blood and death through her nostrils, and her stomach instantly revolted. She turned her face away from Bekka's corpse, not wishing to violate the poor woman's body any further, and vomited.

When she was finished, she staggered off in search of a phone.

* * *

El was scanning returned movies back into the computer system when the phone rang. He glanced away from the terminal he was working at and checked to see if either of his parents was going to answer it. Dad was out on the floor helping a customer find a movie, and mom was helping another customer check out. With a sigh, he reached past his mother and picked up the store phone's receiver.

"Showtime Video, where the stars shine day or night. How may I help you?"

There was no response at first, and El figured it was either a wrong number who hung up or an impatient customer who got tired of waiting. He was about to hang up himself, when he heard a soft snuffling on the other end of the line, and he realized that he was listening to someone cry.

"Hello? Who is this?"

A pause, and then so softly he almost couldn't hear it, a voice spoke.

"He killed her, El... Hit her on the head with her... with her..." The voice broke in choking sobs, but it didn't matter. He'd heard enough to recognize it.

Questions tumbled out of his mouth. "Cheryl, what's wrong? Where are you? Is Jerome with you? Are you both okay?"

"I'm at Bekka's house. You know, Jerome's aunt? He killed her, El. She's dead."

It felt like his heart was suddenly encased in a grip of ice. He'd always feared that Jerome's temper would get him in serious trouble one day.

In fact, he suspected it had somehow played a part in last night's car accident, though he hadn't told his parents that. They were upset enough as it was. But he'd never for a moment thought that Jerome could be capable of murder—and of one of his own relatives, yet.

"Is he... Are you in danger?"

"No, he was gone when I woke up."

"Woke up? Christ, what had happened over there? Listen, you hang up and call 911 right now, before he comes back."

"You don't understand. I can't call the police. Jerome didn't do it. Not our Jerome, anyway. Look, I can't explain over the phone. I need you to come pick me up. He took the car, and besides, I'm not in any shape to drive."

El glanced at his mother. She was busy with another customer now and wasn't paying any attention to his conversation with Cheryl.

"All right. I'll make up some kind of excuse and get out of here. I've got a pretty good idea where Bekka lives," make that lived, he added mentally, "but if you could be standing outside waiting for me, that'll help."

"Sure, no problem. It's not like I want to stay in here any longer than I have to."

In here. What she left unsaid was, with Bekka's body. El shuddered.

"One more thing. Once I pick you up, what are we going to do?"

There was no hesitation in Cheryl's voice. "We're going to find Jerome and we're going to save him."

El sighed. "I figured you were going to say something like that."

Jerome stared up at a star-filled sky. He was surprised to see that the afterlife appeared to have the same constellations as the world of the living. A breeze moved across him (there was wind in the afterlife?) making him shiver. As he shivered, he realized that his clothes were wet. Which was, of course, why the breeze made him feel cold. But if he had clothes and could still experience the sensation of cold that meant he still possessed a physical body. And if that was the case…

He sat up and looked around. It was too dark for him to make out his surroundings, but the sound of rushing water close by, not to mention the squishy mud beneath his hands, told him that he was sitting at the edge of the river, up on the bank. He wasn't dead! Somehow, he'd managed to reach shore before he passed out, and the other Jerome hadn't been able to take control of his body.

You blew it, you son of a bitch! he thought. I'm still in charge!

He expected his other self to come back with some manner of mocking taunt, but there was nothing but silence in Jerome's skull. Maybe his other self had been chastened by his setback, but somehow that didn't feel right to Jerome. While he'd tossed and turned in the river's wild current, he'd sensed his other personality lurking just below the threshold of consciousness. But now he sensed nothing at all of his other self. It was as if Jerome was once more alone inside his own head. Was it possible that somehow the dark aspect of his self had died instead of him? Jerome didn't see how that could be, though. He hadn't drowned; his body was still alive. And he—the original personality—was still present. So what could have possibly caused the death of the other Jerome? Presuming, of course, that he was dead and not just off sulking in some corner of his host's psyche.

Another breeze set him to shivering again, and he decided the matter of his other self could wait for the time being. All he wanted to do was get out of the wind and start drying off. He rose to his feet and started making his way up the riverbank, being careful not to trip in the dark. He was halfway up the bank when he realized he was no longer wearing a bandage on his left hand, and what was more, the hand didn't seem to hurt anymore, despite the severity of the burn he'd suffered. The bandage was no big mystery; he'd surely lost it in the river. But the loss of pain was less easily explained. Maybe it was numb from the cold and would start hurting once the hand warmed enough. Maybe, but the lack of pain still troubled him. It just didn't seem natural. He forced himself to put it out of his mind and keep climbing. He would worry about his hand when he was warm and dry again.

After several more minutes of effort, he reached a spot where the ground began to level off and the going became easier. He stopped and looked around, trying to get a bearing on his location. It was still too dark for him to make out more than the silhouettes of trees against the night sky, but he was fairly confident the bridge wasn't in the vicinity. Which only made sense, given how fast the water had been flowing. He'd probably been carried downstream quite a ways. But if he wanted to find the bridge, along with his dad's Lexus, it was simple enough. All he'd have to do was follow the river upstream, and sooner or later he'd return to the point where he'd jumped in. Then he could get into the Lexus, turn on the engine and crank the heater as high as it would go.

He started walking.

He had no idea how long he traveled, only that he was damn cold and beginning to wish his suicide attempt had succeeded after all by the time he reached the bridge. His discomfort was soon replaced with anger when he saw the Lexus was gone. Anger, but not raging fury. For the first time in his life, his anger didn't feel like a pressure cooker about to explode. The emotion was there, but it was less intense, more manageable. Maybe the awareness that his hair-trigger temper had been caused by his other self was enough to help him finally get control of his anger. Maybe. He shouldn't have left the keys in the ignition. Someone had driven by, probably with a passenger in the car, had seen the Lexus and stopped to check it out. When they saw it was abandoned, doors unlocked, keys dangling from the ignition, one of them had hopped behind the wheel and started the car up while the other returned to their original and, in all likelihood, much less nice vehicle. Then they'd driven away, unknowingly leaving Jerome to stand there in the middle of the bridge, freezing his ass off. He wondered how he was going to explain this to his dad.

I decided to go for a little swim and figured the car would be all right until I got back.

Somehow, he didn't think that was going to do the trick. He'd have plenty of time to think of a better explanation on the long hike back to town. The sooner he started walking, the sooner he'd get to someplace warm. He turned toward Springwood and started walking once more.

From somewhere off in the darkness, he heard the sound of a chattering nightbird. And if the call resembled the cold, cruel sound of a certain undead madman's laughter, Jerome told himself it was just his imagination, and kept on walking.

Assistant Principal Catherine LeClair sat behind her desk, going over paperwork despite the lateness of the hour. That was one of the downsides to having the word "assistant" in your job title. The principal got to be the "vision guy", as he so often put it, while she was relegated to handling discipline problems and completing forms. But when the principal retired, if all went well, she'd get his job, and then all these late nights would finally pay off and she could dump all this donkey work onto *her* assistant principal. Some days—far too many, it seemed—this thought was the only thing that kept her going.

She'd just finished approving a requisition for new gymnastics equipment for the PE department when she heard a sound in the outer office. At least, she thought she'd heard a sound, like a shoe scraping across the floor. But as she listened she heard nothing more, and she started reviewing the next form on her stack.

There came a soft tapping at her door, almost but not quite a knock, as if whoever was there wasn't sure he wanted to be heard.

Catherine set aside her form and in a clear, strong voice called out, "Who's there?"

Several minutes passed as she waited for a reply. Finally, a timid voice replied, "I was told to come see you, Ms LeClair."

"It's late. Come back tomorrow."

"I'm sorry it took me so long to get here, but it's really important I see you tonight, Vice Principal. I'll be in real trouble if I don't."

"Sure you will. That's what they all say."

The door opened and Sam Neilson stepped into her office, frowning.

"What do you mean, all?"

Catherine giggled. "All my many lovers, of course. They're usually lined up outside my office, down the hall and out the main entrance."

Sam's frown eased and he smiled. "No line out there tonight, Ms LeClair."

Catherine rose from behind her desk and came around to meet him. "Then I suppose I'll have to settle for you, then."

She put her hands on his broad shoulders (she loved those shoulders!) and he slipped his strong hands around her waist and held her gently. The feeling of him keeping his strength in check as he touched her always drove her crazy. They kissed, slow and loving at first, then with increasing urgency and building passion. Just as they were about to reach what Catherine thought of as the point of no return, she drew back from Sam, though she didn't break their embrace.

"What about Nina?" she asked.

"Don't worry about her. She's got 'garden club' tonight—which means she'll be out drinking with her friends until midnight at least. We've got plenty of time."

"Got any ideas how we might spend that time?"

Sam grinned. "One or two."

"You've got to be kidding."

"C'mon, Catherine. It'll be fun. Besides, it's how the ancient Greeks used to wrestle."

They stood in the gym, light set low so that most of the space in the auditorium was filled with shadow. Lying on the floor in front of them were several wrestling mats.

Catherine folded her arms across her chest and eyed the mats skeptically. "I don't mind indulging in occasional role-playing, but this is a bit much."

Sam came up behind her, slipped his arms around her middle and began nuzzling her neck. "I promise to take it easy on you," he whispered in her ear.

She turned around in his embrace until she was facing him. "You do, and I'll never forgive you."

They kissed once, twice, and were about to zoom right past the point of no return when laughter drifted out of the shadows.

Catherine froze in Sam's arms.

"Who's there?" Sam demanded, no longer the ardent lover but instead the tough as nails wrestling coach.

The only answer he received was more laughter. Given the darkness and the acoustics of the gym, it was impossible to determine precisely where the sound was coming from. It seemed to come from both everywhere and nowhere.

Catherine stepped out of Sam's embrace even though she didn't want to let go of him. The feel of his strong arms comforted her. But it would be devastating to both their careers if their affair was exposed—not to mention what it would do to Sam's marriage. Catherine wasn't married, but once it got out that she'd had a relationship with one of the teachers, she might well be fired, and even if she wasn't, she could forget about ever becoming principal.

"Maybe it's one of the custodians," she whispered to Sam.

"I don't give a goddamn who it is," he said, not bothering to lower his voice. "If he doesn't show himself right now, I'm going to go get him!"

"Try it, asshole. I'm waiting."

Catherine recognized the voice.

"It's Jerome Starkey," she said.

"So the bastard's looking for a little payback for the other day, huh?"

Catherine was afraid that their secret was going to be revealed, afraid of what Jerome—with his unpredictable temper—might do to them. But she was also disappointed. She'd hoped that Jerome might be helped somehow, that a way could be found to help him cope with his anger. But now it seemed he was beyond help.

"Jerome! Don't make this any worse on yourself!" she called out. "Just leave and we'll forget this ever happened, okay?" She didn't like hearing the pleading tone in her voice, but she couldn't help it.

"How about you two forget I'm here and get on with getting it on? I'd love to watch you wrestle—especially ancient Greek style." Then he laughed again.

"Fuck you, jack-off!" Sam snarled. Hands curled into fists, he started toward the darkness.

Catherine put a hand on his arm to stop him. "Shouldn't we turn the lights up all the way? Wouldn't it be safer?"

"Screw that. I've got nothing to be afraid of from Starkey." Sam shrugged off her hand and continued walking toward the shadows. He was quickly lost to her vision, but she could still hear the sounds of his footsteps echoing through the gym.

"C'mon, kid, what are you waiting for?" Sam taunted. "I'm right—" His voice suddenly cut off, then there was the sound of feet scuffling on the gym floor, followed by several dull meaty thuds. Then the gym was silent once more.

"Sam?" Catherine called. "Are you okay?"

Sam didn't respond, and she began to fear that perhaps he couldn't.

"Jerome, what did you do to him? If you hurt him, it'll go hard on you, I promise!" She fought to keep the rising panic she felt out of her voice, but it was no use. She sounded as hysterical as she felt.

A form emerged from the shadows, flying through the air and landing on the wrestling mat just in front of Catherine's feet. It was Sam. His eyes were closed and he wasn't moving.

"Omigod!" She knelt down and lay two fingers against his carotid artery. She detected a pulse and let out a breath, relieved her lover wasn't dead.

"He's just knocked out. For now."

Jerome walked out of the darkness, striding comfortably, as if he were in his natural environment.

Catherine continued kneeling next to Sam. She knew that she should stand and confront Jerome, use her authority and age to get him to back off, but she was too afraid. All she could do was tremble as she watched him approach.

"What... what are you going to do with me?" The question came out not in a vice principal's voice, but rather the voice of a terrified little girl.

Jerome stepped onto the wrestling mat and stood gazing down at her. It was difficult to tell in this dim light, but it looked as if his clothes were covered with dark splotches resembling mud, or something much worse.

"Like I said, I was hoping to watch you two wrestle. I've got a special move I want to show you. It's called the Gordian Knot."

Jerome reached for her and she screamed.

"You both thought you were playing it so cool, but everyone in the school, students and teachers alike, knew what you were up to. You can't keep a secret in a small town like Springwood."

Catherine didn't reply. She couldn't draw in enough breath to speak.

"Sorry I had to break some of your bones, but it was the only way I could get you two to fit together. Guess I broke a few too many on Mr Neilson, though. Looks like he's checked out on us."

Catherine—her broken limbs so intertwined with Sam's that she had no idea where he began and she ended—started to cry silently.

"I tied you together pretty tight," Jerome said. "I really don't know how long you'll be able to keep breathing. If you're lucky, you might make it to morning when someone will find the two of you like this—naked and combined into a position not covered in the Kama Sutra. If you're not lucky, well, someone will still find you; it'll just be too late to do you any good. Have a pleasant evening, Ms LeClair."

Unable to turn her head to watch him go, she could only listen as Jerome's footsteps grew quieter until they faded altogether. A moment later the gym lights, already dim, went out completely.

In the darkness, bound to the dead body of her lover, her own body in unimaginable agony from what Jerome had done to make it malleable enough to work with, Catherine concentrated on remaining calm and taking in slow, even breaths. It was a long way till morning.

Jerome wasn't sure how far he'd walked. It was difficult to judge distance at night, especially outside of Springwood, where so much of the countryside looked the same. What he did know was that he was still wet, still cold, and still in need of a place to get out of the chilly night air.

A few minutes later, he saw just what he'd been searching for: a house. It was set well back from the road, but then a lot of houses out here in the country were like that. All Jerome cared about was that this house had the porch light on. With any luck, someone was home who'd take pity on a wet young man and invite him in to get dry. He started jogging so he'd reach the house all the sooner.

He came to a battered mailbox on a worn wooden post set into the ground next to the end of a gravel driveway. There was no name on the side of the mailbox and no address, either. Out here, people didn't need to bother with such things, Jerome thought. The mail carrier probably knew who lived at what house. Besides, it wasn't like there were all that many houses out here. Jerome hadn't seen any other lights the entire time he'd been walking.

He started jogging down the driveway, gravel shifting and crunching beneath his shoes. It was too dark to make out many details of the yard, but he could see trees against the night sky, could hear crickets and nightbirds calling to one another. The more closely he listened to their calls, the more they sounded like whispering voices. He couldn't make out what words they might be saying, but they possessed a sinister undercurrent of menace, as if they were taunting him. Or maybe warning him. He shrugged the feeling off with a nervous laugh. It was just the night and his imagination playing tricks on him.

He kept his gaze fixed on the porch light's beacon as he ran, but the farther he went, the farther the light seemed to recede, as if the house was determined to maintain its distance from him. He increased his pace until he was running full out, but still the house remained as far away as ever. Jerome's lungs burned, his heart pounded, and sweat poured off him, mixing with the river water coating his skin and making him smell like old algae and rotted fish. Finally, he couldn't keep it up any longer, and he stumbled and fell forward onto the driveway. He hissed in pain as the small stones bit into his palms and knees. Then he rolled over onto his side and rested, gasping for air. When his breathing and pulse had returned to something approximating normal, he rose to his feet and brushed pieces of gravel off his clothes. He then looked to the house and saw it lay only a few yards away. Must've been some kind of optical illusion, he thought. The house hadn't been receding from him at all.

He started forward.

TWENTY

The wooden porch steps creaked ominously beneath Jerome's weight as he ascended them. He couldn't escape the feeling that there was something familiar about all this, almost as if he'd been here before. But the last time he'd visited a farm had been during a field trip in fourth grade, and that had been a modern hi-tech dairy farm. Nothing like this place. He decided not to worry about it; he'd remember when he was ready.

As he stepped onto the porch, he heard something skitter below the wooden planks. Just a rat or a cat, he told himself, maybe even a raccoon or a groundhog. Nothing to be concerned about, nothing dangerous. Still, he continued shivering as he stepped up to the rusty screen door. He gripped the cold metal handle and pulled the door open. Hinges that had likely never been oiled since their installation groaned in protest, but the door opened easily enough. Jerome held the screen open with his hip and rapped his knuckles on the surface of the weathered oak door of the house.

As he stood there, bathed in the sour yellow glow of the porch light, waiting for someone to answer, he caught a faint whiff of acidic chemicals, and he wrinkled his nose in disgust. The smell reminded him of the hospital he'd been in just that morning: the nauseating stink of medicine and disinfectant. Why would a farmhouse have a smell like that? Cows, pigs, horses, the rank stench of manure—those were the sort of odors a farm should have. Maybe he was smelling some kind of chemical fertilizer or something. Whatever it was, it was making him queasy, so he decided to breathe through his mouth for a while to avoid the stink.

Still no answer. He decided to knock again, only this time he made a fist and pounded the door hard, calling, "Hello? Is anyone home? I need help!" He pounded a couple more times, then waited, listening.

At first he didn't hear anything, and he feared the farm's occupants had gone out for the evening and left the porch light burning to serve as a beacon for their return. He was about to turn away and head back to the road, when he heard the sound of movement from behind the door. A slow, heavy, shuffling, as if someone large and overweight was drawing closer. Rather than being afraid, Jerome felt frustrated. All of this—the house, the porch, the heavy footsteps—was so familiar. If only he could—

Locks snicked as they were disengaged, and the front door swung open wide.

"Hey, Starkey. Good to see you."

It was Pat Cottril. Standing on his right was Brent Haney and on his left, Eddie Jackson. The three of them weren't exactly in peak condition, though. Pat and Brent were covered with burns, skin cracked and blistered, hair—what remained of it—nothing but scorched stubble. Eddie's face was swollen, bruised and crusted with dried blood. His hair was a matted tangle, and the top of his skull sat askew, as if it had been removed and then poorly replaced. The Three Pus-keteers stood almost cheek to cheek, and Jerome couldn't figure out why...

...until he lowered his gaze from their faces and to their body. Singular. The three shared one massive muscular body garbed in jeans and gray sweatshirt that said: FREDDY WENT TO HELL AND ALL I GOT WAS THIS LOUSY SHIRT... AND A COUPLE OF EXTRA HEADS.

Jerome took a step back, shaking his head. "This... this can't be real! You're dead—all three of you!"

With a surge of horror, Jerome then remembered why all of this seemed so familiar. He was living a scene right out of the schlock cult movie El had been playing on the monitors of the video store the other night. What was the title again?

Two Heads are Deadlier Than One. But in this version—written, directed and produced by Freddy Krueger, no doubt—the number of heads had been upped to three.

Jerome understood then that he hadn't woken up on the riverbank as he'd thought. He was asleep or unconscious. Maybe even dead. But whatever his specific condition, he no longer inhabited the physical world; he was trapped inside the Dreamscape, where as Freddy had told him, the bastard maniac was God.

Jerome turned to run, but the Incredible Three-Headed Pus-keteer reached out with one of its meaty, thick-fingered hands and grabbed hold of his shirt collar. Jerome struggled to pull away, but the creature yanked him backward and then wrapped its arms around Jerome's chest in a crushing embrace.

"Gee, guys..." Jerome said through gritted teeth. "I didn't... know... you cared."

"We don't," Eddie growled. "But Dr Krueger does."

The Three-Headed Pus-keteer dragged Jerome into the farmhouse and kicked the door shut behind them. Outside, dark laughter echoed on the night air.

Jameson Belasco, who never allowed anyone to refer to him as "Jim," not even his wife, was grinding his teeth. It was a bad habit, one that he was hardly aware he had. But whenever he was upset, which, given his tendency to be overly fussy, was more often than not, he ground his teeth. He just never realized when he was doing it, not unless someone told him.

Business was slow at the moment, so Jameson stood behind the front counter, reviewing customer accounts on the computer, flagging those with late fees so far in arrears that it was time to remand them to a collection agency. He felt fingers touch his jaw muscles on each side and begin to massage them. He instantly recognized the touch as his wife's and knew that she had caught him grinding his teeth again. He forced his jaw muscles to relax as Miriam worked on them, and he continued reviewing accounts for several moments until she removed her hands and stepped back.

"Better?" she asked.

Jameson turned away from the monitor screen and gave his wife a lopsided smile, the kind he always gave her when he was both embarrassed and grateful.

"Yes, thanks."

"Still thinking about the Eldorado?"

Jameson shook his head, though he had been, if only a little. "I'm thinking about Ellery."

Miriam sighed. "Me, too."

"Do you think it was a mistake to let him go pick up Cheryl?" Unspoken was this additional thought: And was it a mistake to lend him our car?

"Why would it be? Her car broke down and she couldn't get hold of her parents. He just went to give her a ride."

Miriam was nearly the polar opposite of Jameson. Where he was high-strung, she was laid-back. Where he overthought everything, she tended to go with the flow. For another couple, these differences might've been a source of great friction, but not them. They balanced each other out quite effectively, and it was one of the aspects they appreciated most about their marriage. Because while both of them would've had trouble articulating it, they knew they needed that balance in order to keep them grounded and help them navigate through their daily lives. Simply put, they were badly needed emotional compasses for each other.

Normally, Miriam's reassurance would've made Jameson feel better, but not tonight. "That's what Ellery told us. But that doesn't necessarily make it true."

Miriam's mouth gaped almost comically in surprise. "You're accusing our son of lying to us?" Miriam liked to believe the best of people, especially when it came to their son.

Jameson chuckled. "He's a teenager. Of course he lies to us. The only questions are about what and how often. When he asked permission to go help Cheryl, did he seem to you to be… I don't know. Worried? Upset? Preoccupied?"

"Not really. But you were the one he talked to. I was busy with a customer, remember? I believe you," she hastened to add. "But El's behavior doesn't necessarily mean that something's wrong. Maybe he just has a crush on Cheryl."

It was Jameson's turn to be surprised. "But Cheryl's Jerome's girl. Ellery would never come between them!"

"He might not want to, but he can't help how he feels."

"Did he tell you he… cares for her?"

Miriam shook her head. "Not in so many words. But a mother can sense these things."

Miriam's intuition was sharper than his, so he tended to give her the benefit of the doubt in situations like this. "If Ellery does have feelings for Cheryl, that makes me even more worried. Jerome's always struggled with his temper. Sure, he's a good kid overall, a hard-worker, and a loyal friend to Ellery…"

"But you're afraid that if Ellery ever expresses his feelings to Cheryl and Jerome finds out…"

Jameson nodded. "I don't mean to say that Jerome would purposefully hurt Ellery or anything, but after the last couple days…" There was the car accident last night, and while the police had filed no charges against Jerome, yet, when they'd spoken to Jameson and Miriam, the officers had hinted that the boys might have been racing. Perhaps Jerome's temper had gotten the better of him and goaded him into racing the other boys. And Ellery had told them about Jerome's trouble in detention earlier. Not for the first time, Jameson wondered if Jerome might not be the best friend for his son to have, and with Cheryl suddenly thrown into the mix, well, he wasn't sure what to think.

Miriam touched a hand to his cheek, and he realized he'd started grinding his teeth again.

"I wouldn't worry too much. Jerome might be going through a bad patch right now, but he'll come out of it okay, and hopefully be all the stronger for having made it."

The bell jingled as the front door opened, and Miriam quickly removed her hand from Jameson's face. Not because she was embarrassed, he knew. Hardly anything embarrassed her. But because it might look unprofessional to the customer. But the person who walked in wasn't a customer. It was Jerome.

Speak of the devil, Jameson thought, but when he saw the cold smile on the boy's face and the dead look in his eyes, he instantly regretted it.

Unlike both Jameson and Ellery, Jerome had never been overly concerned with looking his best, but his clothes were always clean, his hair washed, face shaved. But this time his clothing was covered with mud, along with darker, harder to identify stains. And a rank smell clung to the boy, like something long dead that had been washed up on the riverbank.

"Good evening, Mr and Mrs Belasco," Jerome said jovially. "Sorry I'm late for work."

Jameson saw that the boy hadn't come in empty-handed. In one hand he carried a large plastic grocery sack. A black handle stuck out of the opening, but otherwise Jameson couldn't tell what was inside.

"I... I thought you were going to rest at home tonight, dear," Miriam said, sounding both confused and concerned. "To tend to your burn."

Jerome held up his empty hand and turned it back and forth so they could see both sides. There was no bandage, and the flesh was smooth, pink, and healthy looking.

"I heal fast," Jerome said. Then he lowered his hand to his side. "Where's El?"

Jerome asked the question easily enough, but there was an undercurrent of urgency in his tone, as if he really wanted to know right now. Jameson started to answer, but Miriam cut him off.

"He's on his way to visit you," she said. "You two must've passed each other without knowing it."

Jerome gazed at her with those strange eyes of his for a moment as if trying to peer inside her mind and gauge her sincerity, before finally relaxing. "Maybe we'll run into each other later," he said. "But the people I've really come to see are you two."

"Oh?" Jameson didn't like the sound of that. Though he had no real reason to be suspicious of Jerome, he nevertheless edged closer to the portable phone on the shelf below the computer monitor, so he'd be able to reach it and dial for help if need be.

"That's right. I had an idea for a new promotional stunt. You know over by the Highland Apartments, how the management always has someone dress up like a Scotsman in a kilt and hold up a sign saying 'No Security Deposit and First Month's Rent is Free'?"

"Sure," Miriam said.

Jameson didn't respond. He was too busy slowly making progress toward the phone.

"I thought we can do something similar, only with movie characters." Jerome turned his back to them and reached into the grocery sack. With a rustle of plastic, he pulled something out and slipped it over his face. Then he gripped the black handle, shook whatever it was attached to, and the plastic bag slid off the object and onto the floor.

Jerome turned around and said, "Ta-dah!" his voice muffled by the white goalie mask he was wearing. In his hand, he gripped the handle of a large machete, its sharp steel blade shining silver as it reflected fluorescent light from the fixtures overhead.

"What do you think?" Jerome asked.

Jameson and Miriam exchanged glances.

"It's ah, quite eye-catching," Jameson said. "But that machete looks real. Wouldn't it be safer to use a plastic one, like the kind they sell at Halloween?" Keeping his gaze on Jerome the entire time, Jameson bent his knees and reached for the phone. He wasn't sure what this "promotional idea" was all about, but Jerome wasn't acting at all like himself, and Jameson's instincts told him something was very wrong here.

Jerome slashed the machete back and forth several times, the blade softly hissing as it cleaved the air. "Nothing to worry about. It only looks sharp." He angled the machete so the blade pointed straight up, then he pressed his thumb to the edge. "See?" He started to run his thumb along the blade, but then suddenly jerked it away. "Dammit!" Jerome swore. Blood welled forth from the fresh cut on his thumb.

"Just stand still, Jerome," Miriam said. She grabbed a box of tissues from beneath the counter and hurried out from behind it. She'd always been faster to react during a crisis than Jameson. He just stood there, phone in hand, and watched as she pressed a tissue to Jerome's wound.

Jerome laughed. "Psych!"

He swung the machete and struck Miriam at the juncture of her neck and shoulder. The blade bit deep and Miriam screamed as her blood sprayed the air. Jerome yanked the machete free and raised it for another strike. Though his face was concealed by the hockey mask, Jameson could see the insane glee shining in the boy's eyes.

Miriam stumbled backward and put up her hands to defend herself as blood continued to pump from the gash in her neck. Jerome took a step toward her and, without thinking, knowing only that his wife was in danger and needed him, Jameson hurled the phone at Jerome. The hand-unit flew through the air and smacked into the forehead of Jerome's mask. It bounced off and tumbled to the floor where the plastic casing broke apart to reveal the electronic components inside. Jerome, quite uninjured, turned to look at

Jameson, and despite the deadly seriousness of the situation, the man shrugged almost apologetically.

Jerome then returned his attention to Miriam and brought the machete down on her. She screamed once more but Jerome swung his blood coated blade two more times, and she fell silent. As Jameson looked at her body lying on the tiled floor in a pool of blood, he knew he'd never hear his wife's voice again.

Jerome, white hockey mask speckled with dots of crimson, turned to Jameson, and he heard the laughter in the boy's voice as he said, "Your turn."

TWENTY-ONE

Jerome struggled against the leather restraints that bound him to the table. He knew they weren't real, that none of this was real, but the knowledge didn't do him any good. The restraints held.

The basement, along with the makeshift laboratory it contained, wasn't real, either. But Jerome could see the bright fluorescence from the light fixture above him, could smell the dust and mildew, feel the cool, dank air on his skin, hear the electronic humming of various pieces of equipment warming up. For a dream illusion created from his memories of one of El's beloved schlock films, it was damn detailed.

"It's always satisfying when one's artistry is appreciated."

Jerome heard feet clomping down the wooden stairs that led to the basement. He strained to see who was coming—more than one person from the sound of it—but the position he was in made it impossible. But then he didn't need to see to know who it was. Who else could it be?

Krueger came around to the side of the table, the Three-Headed Pus-keteer right behind him. Jerome could see the ragged stitches where the Pus-keteer's three heads were attached to its body. The sewing was sloppy, with loose ends of threads sticking out, and Jerome doubted such poor stitching could hold two pieces of cloth together, let alone flesh and bone. But this wasn't the real world, and the rules of logic and cause and effect didn't apply here.

"How's our patient feeling this evening?" Krueger was dressed in a green operating gown and surgical mask, just like the mad doctor from *Two Heads are Deadlier Than One*. "Ready to make medical history?"

"Ready to tear your goddamned ugly head off!" Jerome struggled against the restraints again, but with no more success than before.

Freddy's eyes—the only part of his face visible—gleamed with dark amusement at Jerome's efforts. "Now, now, don't be like that. Having a positive attitude before surgery can make all the difference in one's post operative recovery. We wouldn't want you to experience more discomfort than necessary, would we?"

"Screw you and screw your games!" Jerome snapped. "If you're going to kill me, why don't you just do it and get it over with?"

Freddy raised his claw-glove, but there were no blades attached this time.

"Killing's the least of what I do, kid. Don't get me wrong: I love it and I'm damn good at it. But creating fear, causing suffering, devouring a soul piece by delicious piece... These are a few of my favorite things."

Krueger chuckled as he pulled a tray attached to a rolling stand toward him. The metal tray was covered with a filthy blood stained rag upon which rested a collection of rusted metal implements. Knives, corkscrews, hacksaw blades, drill bits; Freddy looked over the assortment for several moments before selecting four and attaching them to his glove. When he was finished, he turned and showed Jerome the tools he'd chosen.

"I must apologize for the quality of my instruments, but after all, this is a low budget movie, right?"

Drill bit, saw blade, corkscrew and knife—all four rusted, edges and points dull. Jerome didn't want to imagine what the tools would feel like as they worked to penetrate his flesh.

"And speaking of our budget, we can't afford anesthesia, so I had to come up with something else to distract you while I'm slicing and dicing." He nodded at the Pus-keteer, and the monstrous abomination lumbered off to one of the basement's shadowy corners. A moment later he it they returned, pushing an old-fashioned television set—the kind with a round screen that looked like a monitor from an alien spaceship—set atop a wheeled stand. Grinning with three separate mouths, the creature positioned the set near Jerome's head so he could see, then turned it on.

The screen flickered to black and white life, displaying an image of a man lying in an alley. Not just any man, Jerome realized. It was Mr Houser, his biology teacher. And he wasn't simply lying there—he'd been nailed to the ground with spikes through his hands and feet. He'd been cut open from chin to crotch, and his body cavity had been hollowed out. The man's organs were lying nearby, lined up against a wall in a neat row, and carefully labeled with index cards. Heart, lungs, stomach, liver, kidneys, spleen.

"Your other self does good work, eh, Jerome?" Freddy asked. "Very neat and precise. He has all the makings of a first-class surgeon—or serial killer."

Freddy laughed, and as if the sound were a cue, the TV changed to another channel. Now Jerome was looking at a picture of the school gym. Lying on a wrestling mat was a tangled mound of flesh and limbs. At first Jerome couldn't make out what he was seeing, and he thought maybe it was some sort of strange mutation, like the Three-Headed Pus-keteer. But as he peered closer he realized that he was looking at the naked bodies of two people that had been tied together into a sick pretzel of broken bones and twisted limbs. It was Mr Neilson and Vice Principal LeClair, and they were both quite dead.

Freddy twitched. "Poor thing. I didn't think she'd last long."

The channel changed again, and now Jerome saw the interior of Showtime Video. Mrs Belasco's mutilated body lay on the floor surrounded by a pool of blood. Mr Belasco lay behind the front counter, a figure wearing a white goalie mask crouching over him. The masked man wielded a bloody machete and he hacked away at Mr Belasco's dead body with a steady rhythm, as if he was a lumberjack cutting down a tree with an axe. *Chuk-chuk-chuk-chuk-chuk...*

Hockey Mask stopped for a moment, looked toward the camera, and waved. Then he returned to his grisly work.

Jerome didn't have to ask who was behind the mask, any more than he had to ask if the same person was responsible for the other murders he'd been shown.

"He's doing an even better job than I'd hoped," Freddy said. "He has a real... *enthusiasm* for the work. Once the bodies start piling up, the people of Springwood will start talking about the latest series of murders to plague their picture-perfect town. They'll wonder who's responsible, who could've done such a horrible thing. And then they'll start to whisper my name. Just a few of them at first, just those that remember. But word will spread fast, just like a fire, and before long everyone will be talking about Freddy Krueger again. Everyone will fear me again. And when that day comes, Springwood and all its children will be mine forever."

Jerome felt sick despair at the images he'd been shown, but he forced himself to keep his emotions in check. "Nice try, Krueger, but do you really expect me to believe any of that crap is real? This is the Dreamscape, a place of lies and illusions, and you're a master of deception. You're just making this shit up to torment me."

"You wound me, Jerome. While I admit that I'm not above indulging in a little creative license now and again, I assure you these images are indeed real. Your brother killed those people, and right now he's finishing up Mr Belasco while waiting for the arrival of his next two playmates."

The channel changed one more time. The TV displayed a shot of the inside of the car. El sat behind the wheel, Cheryl in the passenger seat next to him.

"I don't know what to do, El. If we call the police, Jerome—or at least his body—will end up in prison. And if he manages to get his body back, he'll have to serve time for a murder he didn't commit. Or at least that his personality didn't commit."

El shook his head. "This is getting to be too much for me. All I know is that Jerome's my friend, and I'll do whatever it takes to protect him. But with Bekka gone, I don't see who can help us fight Krueger and Jerome's evil psychic twin."

Cheryl shrugged. "I suppose we'll just have to do the best we can."

Jerome hated to hear the numb weariness of a trauma survivor in Cheryl's voice, but he was glad to see her alive and uninjured.

"The first thing we need to do is find him," Cheryl said.

"I beg to differ," El replied. "First we need to stop by my parents' store. We'll be safe there while we decide what to do next."

When El said that, Jerome thought he might have felt a surge of jealous anger toward his friend, but now he was merely grateful Cheryl and El had each other to lean on. Then he understood why he felt none of his usual rage: it had come from his other personality, and the two of them were separate. For the first time since his birth, Jerome's anger no longer controlled him. But that really didn't matter right now. If the images Krueger had shown him were real, and despite his earlier words to the contrary, Jerome had to assume they were, then Cheryl and El were heading straight into a trap. And as long as he was Freddy's captive, there was nothing he could do to help them.

Jerome forced himself to look away from the screen and toward "Doctor" Freddy. He had to think fast. "What are you going to do with me?"

Freddy flexed the surgical instruments attached to his glove. "I thought we'd start off with a little exploratory surgery, and then move on from there."

"And what about your three-headed assistant?" Jerome nodded toward the amalgamation standing next to Krueger.

Freddy scowled. "What do you mean?"

"Aren't you going to get them in on the fun? After all, I killed them. If anyone deserves revenge, it's them."

Three pairs of eyes looked at Krueger.

"The Pus-keteer is my creation, and it'll do exactly what I tell it to." Krueger leaned his scarred face closer to his "patient", and Jerome smelled the faint odor of smoke and seared meat. "You're my plaything, Jerome—and I don't share my toys with anybody."

Jerome glanced at the creature assembled from the remains of his three tormentors. He had no idea if they were truly the spirits of Pat Cottril, Brent Haney and Eddie Jackson, or if they were simply another one of Krueger's illusions. Either way, Jerome hoped they'd at least react like the real thing.

"Too bad. You have me strapped down to this table real good. They could do anything they wanted to me, and there's no way I could stop them."

The Pus-keteer's three heads exchanged glances, as if they were consulting with one another, though no words were spoken.

Freddy straightened and chuckled. "Think you're pretty smart, eh? Well, your little ploy isn't going to work, Jerome. Remember what I told you on the lake. This is my world, and here I'm gah—" The word was choked off as the Pus-keteer fastened its hands around Freddy's throat and squeezed.

"He's ours!" three mouths shouted in three separate voices. "He belongs to us!"

Freddy struggled to tear the Pus-keteer's hands from his throat, but its grip was too strong. Krueger then jammed his glove with the rusted surgical tools into the creature's gut. The Pus-keteer's mouths howled a chorus of pain as blood jetted forth to darken the front of Krueger's surgical gown.

Freddy yanked his claw-glove free of the gut wound he'd created, releasing a fresh gout of dark blood, and then he rammed the instruments into another section of the Pus-keteer's abdomen. The creature screamed in three-point agony, but didn't release its grip on Krueger's neck. With the strength of three men, the Pus-keteer lifted Krueger off his feet and hurled him toward a bank of electronic equipment on the other side of the basement. Freddy flew over Jerome's table and slammed into the machinery, and though it looked like nothing more than a cheap movie prop made of metal panels and flashing Christmas tree lights, the equipment exploded in a shower of sparks and a cloud of white smoke. Freddy cried out in pain as electricity coruscated across his gowned body for an instant, then he fell onto the floor, still quivering from the shock he'd received.

Sporting a trio of evil grins, the Pus-keteer lumbered toward its downed master.

Jerome was nowhere near the film buff El was, but he'd seen enough cheapo horror flicks, mostly thanks to his friend, to know that the hero always got some sort of chance to escape, usually when he least expected it and in some sort of convoluted fashion. So if this dream scenario followed those rules...

The Pus-keteer shoved Jerome's table aside so that it could get at Krueger more easily. The table slid into the tray of rusted operating tools, knocking it over. Metal implements coated with reddish-brown flakes flew into the air, and one, a scalpel whose edge wasn't quite as dull as the rest, tumbled down toward Jerome's left hand. It was too good to be true, of course, and in real life he'd never make the catch. But this wasn't real life. The scalpel landed neatly in Jerome's hand. His fingers closed around its handle, and then he carefully turned it over until the blade lay against the restraint binding his wrist. Then he began sawing.

The Pus-keteer straddled Freddy's chest and locked its hands around his neck once more. It slammed Krueger's head against the basement's concrete floor, once, twice, three times. Freddy roared with a combination of pain and fury, and he stuck his claw-glove against the neck of the Pus-keteer's left head, which happened to be Eddie's. Freddy began using a knife-claw to cut through the haphazard stitches that held Eddie's head to the Pus-keteer's body. Eddie's eyes went wide in alarm, and he managed to shout, "Wait a minute!" just before Krueger cut the last stitch around his throat. Blood gushed, Eddie's eyes rolled white in their sockets, and his head flopped backward, exposing raw muscles and severed neck bone. The head would've fallen all the way off, but the stitches around the back of the neck kept it hanging to the body, if only just.

The two remaining heads looked frightened as Freddy grinned.

"One down..."

Krueger jabbed his claw-glove at the head on the right, Brent's, and began swiftly cutting through its neck stitches.

Jerome kept an eye on Krueger's progress as he continued sawing away at his leather restraint. Almost there. With one last cut, the restraint came off. Jerome almost shouted in victory, but he kept quiet, not wishing to alert Freddy to what he was doing. With his left hand free, he was able to sit up partially and start sawing at the restraint encircling his right wrist. He had a better angle this time, and he was able to cut through this one quickly. He then sat all the way up and, since both hands were free, he set the scalpel down on the table and started to undo the buckles on the ankle restraints.

Brent's head flopped backward to join Eddie's, both of them staring sightlessly at Jerome as he struggled to escape.

"One to go," Freddy said.

Pat glanced at the bloodless neck stumps on either side of him, and the fear in his eyes transformed into fury.

"I already died once, damn you! I'm not gonna do it again!"

Whether this was Pat's real spirit or just a Dreamscape copy, it seemed he had the same temperament as the original. Pat, the sole operator of the Pus-keteer's body, clamped his hands tight around Krueger's throat and squeezed with all his might.

Jerome finished undoing the restraint on his left ankle and started on the right.

Freddy jabbed his surgically equipped claw-glove at Cottril's neck, but Pat ducked and dodged, and though Freddy managed to snip a couple threads, they weren't enough. The undead maniac's eyes began to bulge out of their sockets, swelling grotesquely until they looked like white balloons with pupils painted on them.

Jerome tried not to stare in horrified fascination at Freddy's bulging eyes and concentrated instead on undoing the last restraint holding him to the operating table. Just a bit more, the last restraint came unbuckled—he was free! Despite himself, he glanced toward Freddy and Cottril and was shocked to see that Krueger's eyes had swollen to the point where they obscured his entire face. Pat no longer looked furious but instead scared and sickened. But still he kept choking Freddy, straining so hard that the two heads dangling against his shoulders wobbled back and forth almost comically.

The white eyes bulged one last time, and then exploded in a flood of yellow gunk that looked more like pus than vitreous fluid. Pat was covered by the viscous shit, and several splatters hit

Jerome. Since the substance had issued from Krueger's body, Jerome had expected the crap to start eating through his clothes and skin like acid, but it did nothing of the sort. It just clung to his clothing in greasy globs, giving off a rank odor.

Pat cried out in alarm, and Jerome looked up to see Freddy looking at the last Pus-keteer with empty sockets where his eyes had been. No, Jerome realized, not empty. A slender tendril slithered forth from one socket, followed by another and another. Soon the tendrils were emerging from both sockets, perhaps two dozen of them in all. Each tendril had a small fleshy nub at the tip, the skin there puckered and striated like scar tissue. Then the nubs opened tiny bloodshot eyes and Jerome understood. The nubs were in fact miniature replicas of Freddy's head, complete with hate-filled eyes, hook noses, and mouths filled with tiny teeth. Very sharp tiny teeth.

Pat still gripped Krueger by the throat, but at the sight of the tendril heads, he let out a shriek and released his hold on Freddy. Pat tried to scrabble backward off Krueger's chest, but it was too late. Like writhing serpents, the tiny Freddy heads struck. They bit into the soft flesh of Cottril's face with their sharp, yellowed teeth and began tearing. Pat screamed in agony and clawed at the tendril heads as they ripped out one tiny chunk of flesh after another with lightning speed, but it was no use. There were too many and they were too fast. Within seconds, Cottril's exertions began to lessen until finally his hands slumped to his sides. He swayed as the Freddy-serpents continued to go about their work, and Jerome was sure the Pus-keteer's body would've slumped to the floor if the serpents themselves hadn't helped to hold it up.

A couple more moments, and it was done. The tendril heads had cleaned the flesh from Pat's skull as swiftly and efficiently as a school of piranha. The tiny heads drew back, and now the Pus-keteer's body leaned to the right, slipped off Krueger's chest, and smacked onto the floor. The impact was enough to break the last of the stitches holding Eddie's and Brent's heads to the body, and they bounced away across the floor like a pair of flesh bowling balls.

Jerome sat on the edge of the operating table and stared with disbelief at what was left of the Three Pus-keteers. And then Freddy turned to look at him, tendril heads swaying slowly back and forth.

"Smart move," Freddy said in a tone of grudging admiration. The tendril heads echoed his words in a chorus of hissing whispers.

"Smart move, smart move, smart move, smart move..."

Freddy got his feet beneath him and stood. "But you should've taken advantage of your opportunity to escape when you had the chance."

"Chance, chance, chance, chance, chance..."

Krueger raised his surgically equipped glove. The rusted tools were covered with bloody shreds of Pus-keteer flesh and bits of thread. There was a soft clicking sound, and the drill bit attached to the middle finger began spinning.

"There might have been a few complications, but as doctor to patient, I can assure you this operation is going to be a complete success."

"Success, success, success, success, success..."

Freddy started toward Jerome, brandishing his claw-glove with the whirring drill bit. Jerome snapped out of his paralysis and jumped off the operating table. Without looking, he turned to run and his right hand collided with the screen of the old-fashioned TV set the Pus-keteer had wheeled over. But instead of smacking against a glass screen and maybe knocking the set over, Jerome's hand passed through the screen, as if it wasn't there. His hand was instantly leeched of all color, but otherwise it didn't feel any different. Jerome withdrew his hand easily, then held it up to examine it. Its normal color had returned and—he wiggled the fingers experimentally—it seemed to be fine.

He glanced at the screen. His other self was standing over the bloody ragged ruin that held little resemblance to Mr Belasco. The other Jerome still wore the hockey mask and still had hold of his machete, but he stood unsteadily, teetering back and forth, as if on the verge of passing out. But then the other Jerome shrugged off whatever was bothering him and returned to violating what little remained of Mr Belasco's corpse.

A wave of electronic distortion passed across the screen then, and when it cleared, Jerome looked at the TV in wonder. No longer did it display an image of his other self savaging Mr Belasco's body. Now it showed Bekka's smiling face. She looked the way Jerome remembered her—not how he'd last seen her, after his other self had finished with her. She looked whole, healthy and happy. She met Jerome's gaze, and he had the sense that she was more than just an electronically created picture. She could actually see him.

She made a "come here" gesture but before Jerome could react, the picture dissolved into distortion, and when it cleared, the screen once again showed the interior of Showtime Video where the other Jerome continued hacking at Mr Belasco's body with his machete.

Jerome had no doubt that he'd just received a message from his aunt's spirit. He had felt her essence, felt her love for him emanating from the screen, and there was no way Krueger could've faked that. The bastard didn't have it in him. Bekka had obviously been trying to help him, but what did she want him to do?

Then all at once it came to him.

Jerome turned to Freddy. "That's my way back, isn't it? Like Alice through the looking glass. If I go through there, I end up back in my own head, back in control of my body again." He didn't wait for Freddy to confirm or deny it. Jerome turned, stretched out both arms before him, and dived for the TV screen. Behind him, he heard Krueger roar in frustration, and then the sound was cut off as dizzying darkness descended over his consciousness.

TWENTY-TWO

For an instant, it felt as if he was no one and nowhere, but then the sensation of vertigo passed and Jerome opened his eyes.

He was looking through the eyeholes of a mask, and he could feel plastic pressed tight against his sweaty face. He looked down and saw that his clothes were so covered with blood they appeared to have been dyed crimson. In his hand he gripped the handle of a blood-smeared machete, and he straddled a pile of blood, bone, flesh, and organs that had once been his best friend's father. Despite the horror of the scene he found himself in, Jerome felt a surge of triumph. He raised the machete over his head and shook it, sending bits of blood and meat flying.

"Fuck you, Krueger! I did it! I'm back where I belong!"

A bell tinkled as the front door opened.

"Oh my God. What have you done?"

Jerome whirled about to see El staring at his mother's body in horrified shock. At his side was Cheryl, but she wasn't looking at Mrs Belasco's corpse. She was looking straight at Jerome, the expression on her face unreadable, but the sorrow in her eyes clear enough.

Jerome didn't know how to begin explaining, or even if he could explain. He came out from behind the counter and dropped the machete to the floor with a metallic clatter. He then removed the hockey mask and tossed it aside. "El, I know what this looks like—"

"You son of a bitch! You killed my parents!"

Face a mask of loss and fury, El came running at him, teeth bared, hands outstretched, fingers hooked into claws, and all Jerome could do was stand and watch him come. Jerome was so surprised by his friend's unexpected ferocity that for a moment he only stood there. The last thing he wanted to do was fight, so he sidestepped as El grabbed for him. Unfortunately the tiled floor was slick with his mother's blood, and El's highly polished dress shoes weren't designed for traction. His feet slipped out from under him and he fell sprawling to the floor. He landed in blood and droplets splattered into the air.

"El, wait!" Jerome shouted. "It's me—Jerome! The real one!"

El slowly began rising to his feet, clothes soaked with his mother's blood.

Jerome hurriedly continued. "I managed to get control of my body back. I don't know where the other me has gone, but he's the one that killed your parents, not—"

He was forced to break off as El released a cry of rage and came lunging for him. He sidestepped again, but this time one of his feet came down in a puddle of blood and threatened to slide out from beneath him. He fought to maintain his balance and succeeded in not falling. Unfortunately his efforts gave El the time he needed. He slammed into Jerome's middle and wrapped his arms around his waist. Air whooshed out of Jerome's lungs as El's tackle knocked him backward, and the two of them fell to the floor in a tangle of arms and legs.

El pushed himself on top of Jerome and began hitting him with his fists. Tears streamed down El's face and he punctuated each stroke with a voice thick with grief.

"Damn you! Damn you! Damn you, straight to hell!"

Jerome knew he hadn't been the one who'd wielded the machete against El's folks, even though his hand had done the dark deed. Nevertheless, he couldn't help but feel that maybe he deserved El's wrath, that he deserved to be beaten to a pulp by his closest friend. If only Jerome had been stronger over the years, he might've been able to keep Krueger from accomplishing his goal of gaining an agent in the real world.

Suddenly Cheryl rushed over and grabbed hold of El's arm.

"Stop it, El! It's Jerome—our Jerome!"

Confusion passed across El's face, and he paused in his attack. Jerome watched the struggle on his friend's face as El tried to decide what to believe. Grief won out in the end, and El's features once more hardened into a mask of fury and he pulled his arm free from Cheryl's grip. But before he could strike again, Jerome shifted his weight to the side, throwing El off balance. El slipped off Jerome and fell onto the floor, once more splattering himself with blood.

Jerome got to his feet and turned toward Cheryl. "You're right, it is me! I was trapped in the Dreamscape while my other self had control of my body! But I've got control again now, and—"

Jerome didn't get to finish his sentence. He felt something slam into his side and he went down hard. His head cracked onto the tiled floor, and a dark wave washed over his consciousness and carried him away.

Cheryl watched El plow into Jerome and knock him down. He hit the floor and lay there, unmoving.

"What the hell did you do that for?" She ran to Jerome's side and knelt down. She was terrified that the impact had killed him, but a quick check revealed he was still breathing, though she had no idea how injured he might be.

El just stood, fists at his sides, breathing hard from the exertion of fighting Jerome. "C'mon,

Cheryl. It was a trick. He was lying to us. Our Jerome would never do..." He looked at the bodies of his parents—his mother nearby, his father behind the counter—and his face went pale. "Do this."

Cheryl took Jerome's hand and gave it a squeeze. It felt so limp and lifeless that she almost started crying. "But Jerome told me he'd just managed to get control of his body back!"

"At the exact moment before we came in? Right. You know what the odds against that are?" He turned and started walking toward the checkout counter.

"What are you doing?"

"Calling the police." El pointed to the broken portable phone lying on the floor. "That unit's been trashed, but there's a regular office phone behind the counter." He took a breath, and then added in a softer tone, "Provided I can make myself go back there."

"El, I can't pretend to imagine I know what you're feeling right now, but please, before you call, think for a minute. If Jerome's personality is in control of his body again, then the police will be arresting the wrong person for killing your parents!"

El didn't respond. He walked behind the counter, studiously avoiding looking at his father's mangled corpse. He reached for the office phone on the counter, picked up the receiver, and started to punch buttons.

Cheryl felt fingers close around her neck and cut off her air.

"I'd do what she says, old pal—unless you want to hear what a neck sounds like when it snaps."

Cheryl couldn't move her head to look at Jerome, but she didn't need to see him to know what had happened. The other Jerome was back.

El stared at Jerome for a moment before slowly returning the handset to its cradle. Without slackening his grip on Cheryl's neck, Jerome got up from where he lay and scooted behind her. Then he urged her to stand with him and, not having a great deal of choice in the matter, she did. Jerome's grip then loosened a fraction, just enough so that she could breathe, but that was all.

"You should've listened to her, El. My bro did manage to find a way to boot me out of the driver's seat. But when you knocked him out, I got a chance to return the favor." He reached up with his free hand and touched the side of his head. His fingers came away tacky with blood, none of it from El's parents. "Looks like I picked up some damage in the process, but that's all right. Thanks to Uncle Freddy, this body can heal minor injuries fast as long as I'm in control. I'll be a hundred percent again in no time." He smiled. "Which is more than I can say for you two."

El's expression was a mixture of fear and anger. "Let her go, whatever your name is, and just get out of here before the cops come."

"No need to hurry. You didn't complete your call, and unless an officer suddenly has the urge to rent a *Police Academy* DVD, I think I'm pretty safe for the time being. And as for my name... I admit, I've never had one of my own, and while I understand it's confusing to keep calling me Jerome, you might as well get used to it. This body, this identity, this life is going to be mine from now on. I am the only Jerome Starkey, the one who had a ball slaughtering your parents."

Cheryl wanted to warn El that the evil Jerome was just trying to bait him, but she couldn't draw in enough breath to speak. The ploy was working, though. Trembling with fury and sorrow, El slowly came out from behind the counter. He began walking toward Jerome and Cheryl, eyes blazing with a need for vengeance.

"The machete's a wonderful invention," Jerome said. "Nowhere near as versatile as Uncle Freddy's knives, of course, but it does have a certain crude effectiveness, don't you think?"

El's gaze fixed on the bloody weapon lying on the floor. Barely pausing in his advance, El picked up the machete. He gripped it so tight his knuckles turned white, and still he kept coming toward Cheryl and her captor.

"My bro never gave it much thought, but I figure you've got the hots for my attractive little hostage here. What do you say? Inquiring minds want to know!"

El's teeth drew back from his lips in a silent snarl. He was almost in striking range, but the evil Jerome showed no sign of nervousness. He held onto Cheryl's throat as tightly as ever, and she wondered if he were going to use her as a shield against El, maybe shove her forward and impale her on the machete. If she had to sacrifice her life to help stop the evil Jerome, then so be it. She wanted to close her eyes, but she resisted the urge. Whatever fate she was about to meet, she wanted to be able to look it square in the face as it came.

When El was close enough, he lifted the machete in preparation for a strike. "This is for my mom and dad, you son of a bitch!" El said, but before he could swing the blade, Jerome's foot swept out and knocked El's legs out from under him. El fell backward, losing his grip on the machete as he instinctively windmilled his arms to try and catch himself. The machete tumbled through the air, and swift as a striking cobra, Jerome's hand shot forth and snatched the weapon out of the air.

Jerome then released his grip on Cheryl's neck as he lunged forward, spinning the machete around in his hand until the blade was pointing downward. Then, just as El hit the floor, Jerome stabbed the blade into his chest. El's eyes flew wide and bloody froth bubbled past his lips. His body twitched as if he were experiencing a series of electrical shocks that diminished with each passing second. Blood spread out from beneath his back, giving him a pair of dark crimson wings as if he were some sort of death angel.

His gaze, already dulling, sought out Cheryl, but his eyes seemed to be having trouble focusing because they never fixed upon her. And then, just as she thought he was finally looking at her, his body stopped trembling and went slack, and the last remaining bit of life left his eyes. A final hissing breath escaped his lungs, and then he lay still, staring sightlessly at her, and Cheryl knew El was dead.

Evil Jerome regarded El's corpse for a moment before turning his attention to her.

"That was fun. What do you want to do now?"

Her throat finally free of his grip, Cheryl took a long, deep breath and then screamed as hard and loud as she could.

Jerome opened his eyes and winced as the light sent a wave of pain crashing through his skull. He groaned, as much from exasperation as from the throbbing in his head. He was really getting tired of being knocked unconscious. He opened his eyes once more, but this time kept them squinted against the light. He pushed himself to his hands and knees—moving carefully to avoid slipping on the blood-slick tile again—and rose unsteadily to his feet.

"Cheryl? El?"

"She's gone. I, unfortunately, am still very much present."

The voice came from behind Jerome. It belonged to El, but he spoke in a cold monotone with no trace of his usual humor. Unease fluttered in Jerome's gut, and he tried to make himself turn to look at his friend, but he couldn't do it.

"When you say Cheryl's gone, do you mean–"

"Don't worry. She's still alive. Which is more than some of us can say."

Jerome then heard a scratching scuffling sound that made him think of a crab clawing its way across rock. The sound was coming toward him, but he still couldn't force himself to look, nor could he make himself flee. He could only stand there and wait for whatever was going to happen next.

"It's too bad you didn't succeed in drowning yourself," El said.

A second scuttling sound, this one also nearby. "Yes, too bad." A woman's voice, one he recognized.

More sounds of movement, these from behind the front counter. "Would've shhpared us... shhuffering." A breathy gurgle barely recognizable as a human voice, a sound that might've come from a mangled throat and a mouth filled with broken teeth.

The scratching scuttling sounds came from three directions now, and they were all converging on him. Jerome, his back still to whomever, or whatever, made those sounds, imagined three human sized crabs moving toward him like a trio of armor covered spiders.

"I'm back in the Dreamscape again, aren't I?" he said.

The Belascos—mother, father and son—ignored his question as they continued crawling across the blood-covered floor toward him.

"I thought you were my friend," El said.

Jerome knew he wasn't hearing the voice of the real El, and that this was just another of Freddy's endless supply of torments. Nevertheless, he couldn't allow that statement to pass without comment. He turned to face the Belascos.

El and Mrs Belasco were the closest to him, both crawling on all fours, arms and legs outstretched and bent at unnatural angles, heads raised high, eyes that should've been dead instead horribly alive, moving rapidly back and forth, scanning their surroundings like foraging insects. Mr Belasco was just coming out from behind the check out counter, his body a broken, mutilated ruin of meat, bone and blood that held only the merest resemblance to human form. He was forced to move by pulling himself forward with his only good hand, sliding across the tiled floor, dragging viscera behind and leaving a bloody trail like some nightmarish species of snail.

Jerome knew they weren't real, prayed to Christ that they weren't, but he couldn't keep himself from responding as if they were real.

"I'm so sorry..." His voice was thick with grief and tears began streaming from his eyes. "I tried to kill myself, I really did, but it was the wrong thing to do. Freddy wanted me to attempt suicide so that my other self—"

The Belascos had continued scuttling and sliding toward him while he talked. El was the first to reach Jerome, and without hesitation he bared bloodstained teeth and bit down on

Jerome's left ankle. Jerome howled in pain and tried to shake El off, but his friend held on with the tenacity of a pit bull. If anything, his teeth sank even farther into Jerome's flesh, and he wondered how long it would be before he felt his best friend's teeth gnawing on the bone beneath.

A crazy thought flashed through his mind then. El—the real one—would've appreciated the irony of the situation: he'd become a monster starring in his very own schlock horror movie—Night of the Living Belascos.

Mrs Belasco was nearly upon him, and Jerome knew that if she got hold of him, it was all over. He had no idea what would happen to him if he died here in the Dreamscape, and he really didn't want to find out. Mrs Belasco lunged for his other ankle, mouth gaping impossibly wide, as if like a snake she'd unhinged her jaw to feed. But before she could sink her teeth into him, Jerome kicked out with his right foot and connected with her nose. Cartilage smashed, blood squirted, and Mrs Belasco's head snapped backward with a sickening crack. Jerome had broken her neck.

Her body slumped to the floor, and while her eyes didn't stop their hideous back and forth movement and her teeth didn't stop gnashing, the rest of her remained limp as a puppet tossed aside by its master. It was a horrible sight, but he didn't have time to react to what he'd done. El's mouth was clamped to his ankle, and like a vice, it seemed to tighten with the passage of each agonizing second.

"I hate to do this, El," Jerome said through pain-gritted teeth, "but it's you or me, pal." He lifted his right foot and brought it down swift and hard on El's neck. Another snap of bone, and El's teeth were torn from his leg by the impact. Jerome cried out in pain as El's body went limp as his mother's. But El's head still held on to its mockery of life, including the power of speech.

"You'll never get back to the real world," El said. "Your body is lost to you, along with your identity. You're not Jerome Starkey anymore. He is. And you..." El paused and then his lips formed a grin, stretching so wide that they split at the edges, sending fresh runnels of blood streaming down from his mouth. "You're nothing more than a dream."

El laughed then, as did his mother, their voices wild and mad, like the cries of hyenas in the night. Far worse was Mr Belasco. The bloody mound he'd become had almost managed to drag itself to the rest of them, and his laughter came as a horrid snuffling of air through a ravaged windpipe, crimson froth spraying the air like the spouting of a dying whale.

Unable to stand the hellish laughter, Jerome turned and limped toward the front door, ankle throbbing, left shoe full of blood and squishing with every step he took.

Outside it was night and a light rain was beginning to fall. There were no cars on the street and none of the businesses with the exception of Showtime Video had lights on. But otherwise there was nothing to mark the street as out of the ordinary, as something that existed only in Freddy Krueger's diseased imagination.

Jerome stood on the sidewalk and stared out into the darkness as rain pattered down on and around him. The drops felt cold on his skin, but they seemed like nothing more than ordinary rainwater. Jerome knew that this could change any second. At Freddy's whim, Jerome might find himself standing in a deluge of urine, or perhaps a shower of razor blades. The sidewalk might turn to hot tar and swallow him, or stone hands might form from the concrete, grab his legs, knock him down, and then begin tearing him apart. Krueger could do anything he wanted, anytime he wanted. And Jerome was powerless to stop him.

He sat down at the curb, crossed his arms over his knees, and lowered his head. His other self had his body, and far more importantly, had Cheryl, and there was nothing Jerome could do to save her.

He'd failed.

He heard a sound, a distant rumbling that sounded like thunder, except it didn't pass. It continued, growing louder, nearer. Light gleamed on the wet street, and Jerome looked up and turned toward its source. He saw a pair of headlights at the far end of the street, and he knew then that what he'd first taken to be thunder was instead the sound of a powerful engine. The vehicle rapidly drew near, and Jerome knew that he should get up, move, seek shelter. But he couldn't bring himself to care. If the car intended to hit him, then so be it. He was too full of despair, too weary, to do anything about it.

The car came roaring up and for an instant Jerome thought it really was going to swerve and strike him, but at the last moment the brakes engaged and the vehicle, which Jerome could now see as a red Firebird, fishtailed to a stop directly in front of him. The engine continued to rumble, the front of the car shaking as if it could barely contain the power surging underneath the hood. Wisps of what looked like steam curled from beneath the hood, filling the air with an acrid stench that smelled like burning hair and flesh. The driver's side window rolled down, and Jerome wasn't surprised in the least when Freddy Krueger's scarred visage leaned out.

"Lookin' for a ride? Gotta warn ya, though, kid: ass, gas, or grass—nobody rides for free!" Freddy brayed demented laughter.

"I'm not going to play anymore, Freddy," Jerome sad in a defeated voice. "Just do whatever you're going to do with me and get it over with."

Freddy's dark merriment instantly vanished, and he frowned. "What are you talking about? You'll play as long as I say you'll play." He patted the steering wheel and gave Jerome a sly smile. "Like my ride? It's the same one I used to run down your mother—and that I used to infect you with your dark brother."

As Krueger spoke, long needle-like spikes jutted forth from the Firebird's front bumper. Thick black fluid oozed from their tips, dark seed that instead of creating life was capable only of fostering death.

Jerome had a flash of memory: a patchwork of images, emotions and sensations that he could barely make sense of. He saw a long, sharp object coming slowly toward him, an alien presence invading the warm comforting darkness that was his entire world. As it pierced the flesh of his umbilicus, he felt terror and pain and above all an overwhelming sense of loss.

And then he was looking once more at Freddy Krueger's flame-scarred face.

Freddy sneered. "A real blast from the past."

"What do you expect me to do?" Jerome asked. "Wail in anguish for my dead mother? Curse you for violating me in the womb? I'm sorry to disappoint you, but I just don't give a damn anymore."

Freddy glared at Jerome for several long moments, his eyes blazing with internal fire. Finally, he said, "You're pathetic, kid. Most of my playmates at least have the cajones to go down fighting. I'd finish you off here and now, but you're not worth the effort."

Freddy threw the Firebird into gear and hit the gas. Tires squealed on wet asphalt, and flame jetted out of the exhaust pipe as the car roared off down the street, leaving Jerome sitting alone at the curb in the falling rain. He was beyond feeling despair, beyond feeling anything. And that's when he heard a soft, gentle voice whisper his name.

Jerome...

A woman's voice, one he knew well. It seemed to come from below him, so he looked down and saw that a puddle of rainwater had formed in the gutter. Light from the Showtime Video sign was reflected in the water, along with Bekka's face. Jerome quickly looked over his shoulder, expecting to see his aunt standing behind him, but aside from himself, the sidewalk was empty. He turned back to look to the puddle and saw that Bekka was now smiling at him.

"This is just another trick. You're not real."

Bekka replied, her voice faint as if she were speaking to him across a great distance. "Search your feelings, Jerome. You know it's not a trick."

For the first time since walking out of the video store, Jerome did feel something. He felt love. And hope. This was Bekka, all right.

"How?"

"We don't have much time. Freddy has momentarily drawn his awareness from you in disgust over your refusing to amuse him. That's given me a few precious moments to contact you without his knowing, but we have to be quick before he senses my intrusion into his realm. So just listen, hon, all right?"

Jerome nodded.

"There's still a chance for you to regain control of your body. Right now, this section of the Dreamscape mirrors the layout of the actual Springwood. If you can occupy the same space here as your other self does in the physical world, then you can attempt to force him out of your body and retake control, just as you did in the video store."

"But how do I know where he's at? I can't see into the real world from here, and I have no idea where he'd go."

"Don't you?" Bekka said with a tone of sadness. "He's killed everyone else you know or care for. Who's left?"

Jerome felt a cold twist of fear knot his gut. "My family." His dad, Lynn, Brian and Mary.

"Yes. Once you're close enough to him, you'll be able to sense his presence. But you'll have to act swiftly because he'll be able to sense you as well. I—" She paused and looked past Jerome, as if someone were approaching him from behind. She then looked back to Jerome. "He's found me. Good luck, sweetheart. Stay strong."

The puddle suddenly burst into flame. The fire flared bright then burned out quickly, leaving behind only wisps of steam. Freddy's distant laughter echoed on the night air.

Jerome got to his feet, mind racing. He had to get home, and he had to get there fast. He couldn't walk and he couldn't just wish himself there. This might be the Dreamscape, but he didn't have that sort of power here. Only Freddy did. Jerome would have to find a more mundane method of transportation.

Bekka had said the dream Springwood was a copy of the real one. If buildings and streets were duplicated, then maybe cars were, too. The Lexus wouldn't be here; his other self would've taken it in the real world, so the copy would be gone. But El had to have driven something to pick up Cheryl, probably his parents' car. They always parked behind the building, so El would have, too. The copy of the car should be there, just waiting for him. Once he retrieved the duplicate of the keys.

He turned toward the entrance to Showtime Video. He did not want to go back in there and face the broken yet still animated corpses of El and his parents, but that's where the keys would be, most likely in El's pants pocket. Jerome took a deep breath, then started toward the door.

TWENTY-THREE

"It'll be all right, sweetheart."

"He's been gone for hours, Don. He didn't take any supplies to change his bandage. Cheryl's parents don't know where he is—or where she is, for that matter—and no one answers the phone at the video store. Bekka doesn't pick up, either, and both Jerome's and Cheryl's cellphones are evidently turned off." Lynn knew she sounded on the verge of hysteria, but she was too worried about Jerome to care. She sat on the couch in the living room, turned sideways so she could look out the picture window. The curtains were drawn open, giving her an excellent view of a rainy night and an empty street. She didn't want to admit it, but after all the talk about Freddy Krueger last night, she was beginning to fear that something was seriously wrong.

Don sat in the easy chair next to the couch, legs crossed, cup of tea in hand, the bottom of the cup resting on his knee. He might make out that he was relaxed, but Lynn knew better. He'd brewed the tea an hour ago and hadn't so much as taken a sip of it.

"He's got the Lexus," Lynn said.

"So?"

"So aren't you upset that he's kept it out so long? He promised he'd only be gone a half hour or so. What's more, aren't you concerned that he might not be able to handle it in his..." She paused as she searched for just the right phrase. "Current state?"

Don shifted uncomfortably in his chair, sloshing tea onto his pants without seeming to notice. "What, you mean his burn? Even one handed, he's a good enough driver—"

"I mean after last night's accident." She turned away from the window to look at her husband. She loved Don Starkey, but sometimes she had the sense that he was purposefully being obtuse. "I'm not talking about his physical condition. I'm talking about his emotional condition. Maybe Bekka was wrong about Freddy Krueger being involved with Jerome's... difficulties."

"Difficulties?" Don nearly shouted the word. He uncrossed his legs, leaned forward, and set his tea down hard on the glass surface of the coffee table. The handle broke off the china cup, and it tipped onto its side, spilling tea all over the table.

"Goddamn it," Don said in a quieter voice. Tea began dripping over the table edge and down onto the cream colored carpet. "I'll go get a hand towel and mop this mess up."

He started to stand, but Lynn said, "Forget about it. We can clean it up later. Why don't you come sit next to me?"

Don hesitated a moment. "Maybe I should go check on Brian and Mary." They were in the den playing video games. At least, that's where they'd been the last time either adult had checked on them, and that had been over half an hour ago.

"They're fine," Lynn said. "It's Jerome I'm worried about right now."

Don gave her a small smile, nodded, then joined her on the couch. He sat sideways too, facing her, and they held hands as they looked out the window together.

After a few moments, Don said, "All right, I admit it. I'm worried, too."

Lynn squeezed his hand. "Of course you are." Now it was her turn to offer encouragement. "But like you said, he'll be okay." I hope, she added mentally. And if Jerome's problems really were emotional instead of supernatural, perhaps it would be best if he spent some time at Westin Hills. It would break Don's heart; he'd be convinced that he'd somehow failed his oldest son. But if she could just get him to see that not getting Jerome the help he needed would be the real failure, then maybe…

Outside, headlights approached. The car slowed as it neared their driveway, and Lynn saw that it was a Lexus. Jerome was home at last.

"What should we do?" Don asked. "Should we read him the riot act as soon as he walks in, or should we play it cool and wait to see what, if anything, he has to say for himself?"

"Let's start off playing it cool," Lynn said. "We can always yell at him later." She said this with a nervous smile. She was glad Jerome was home, but she was fearful, too. It was hard to guess how he would act and how they should in turn react to him.

"Should we move away from the window?" Don asked. "So we don't look like we're trying to spy on him?"

"Too late. He's bound to have seen us by now."

They watched as Jerome turned into the driveway too fast. The rear end of the Lexus went wide and the back tires churned up grass and soil before sliding onto the driveway. He accelerated as he came down the driveway, and Lynn's first thought was that Jerome must really be upset about something to drive this way. But he continued to accelerate and angled the front of the car toward the house. The Lexus leaped off the driveway and careened across the yard, tearing up grass as it went.

"What the fuck?" Don yelled, but it was a question Lynn didn't have the answer to. She didn't know why Jerome was doing it, but she knew what he was doing; he was aiming for the picture window—and them.

Still holding onto Don's hand, Lynn jumped off the couch and tried to pull her husband after her, but he sat frozen, staring out the rain-streaked window at his very own certified pre-owned Lexus coming straight toward him. The car's front wheels hit the edge of the porch and the front end bounced up. Headlight glare blazed through the windows, and for an instant it was as if night had suddenly transformed into day. Then the picture window exploded, and the deafening engine roar filled the room. Flying glass sliced into Lynn's face and neck, and she felt Don's hand torn from hers as the Lexus smashed into him and bore him backwards. Lynn was thrown to the side by the impact, and so was spared being crushed as the Lexus's front end shattered the glass coffee table before slamming into the living room floor. The car stalled out and sudden quiet descended, marred only by the ticking of the engine.

Lynn tried to stand, but when she put her hands down on the carpet to brace herself, she cried out in pain. Her palms were full of glass shards, and thick red blood welled from the wounds. She could feel more blood running down her cheeks and neck, could see drops from cuts on her forehead falling past her eyes, and she knew she must've resembled a human pincushion. But she didn't care about the pain, didn't care how seriously she was injured. All she could think about was the mangled bloody thing that had been crushed beneath the front of the Lexus as it came to a halt. She leaned forward and, using her elbows instead of her hands, crawled awkwardly over to what was left of her husband.

He'd been caught between the Lexus and the coffee table, and the impact had reduced most of his torso to crimson jelly. His remains were in two large chunks: head and shoulders, trunk and legs. His arms were still attached (mostly), but they were shattered, floppy things more suited to be the limbs of a rag doll than a human being. Tears mixed with blood as Lynn cried over Dan's wide-eyed, open mouthed face. Red-tinged tears splashed down onto his eyes, but he didn't blink.

The driver's side door of the Lexus opened, and someone got out, stepping first on the broken ruin of the couch, then to the floor. Lynn didn't look up to see who it was. What did it matter? Don was dead.

"I told Cheryl that we could make the jump through the window, but she didn't believe me."

The familiar voice tugged at Lynn's traumatized consciousness, and she slowly turned and looked upward at a young man wearing clothes soaked with blood. It looked like Jerome, but she knew it wasn't him.

"You're not my stepson." Her voice was flat, toneless. The voice of a woman who didn't care if she lived or died. "I can tell by your eyes. Who are you?"

Jerome, or rather the thing that had stolen his face, only grinned.

Lynn looked toward the Lexus. Given the angle the car now rested at, she could easily see through the windshield. She saw the airbags deflating, saw Cheryl, mouth and wrists bound by duct tape, slump against the glass. At first Lynn thought the girl was dead, but then she stirred, though she didn't open her eyes. She was alive then, though how badly she might have been hurt from the crash—or from what her captor might have done to her before the crash—was impossible to say.

"I've got to hand it to you, Lynn. You've got good reflexes. A lot faster than your better half down there." He nodded at Don's corpse. "Or maybe I should say better halves." He started to laugh, a horrible obscene sound that seemed to burrow into Lynn's ears like a parasite searching for something soft and sweet to feast on.

But his laughter ended abruptly when two children came walking slowly into the room, pale faced and trembling.

"What was that awful noise, Mommy?" Brian asked. "It sounded like..." His voice trailed off as he took in the scene of death and destruction before him.

"An explosion," he finished in a whisper.

Mary said nothing, but then she didn't have to. Her wide-eyed gaze of shocked disbelief said it all.

The monster impersonating her stepson looked upon Lynn's two youngest children with an expression she could only view as lust.

"You know, Lynn, I think I'll take a few minutes to bond with my siblings before I finish with you.

Don't go away now." He turned toward the children. "Want to play, kids? I've learned a lot of new games since I saw you last, all courtesy of our loving Uncle Freddy. And I'm just dying to show them to you."

He started toward Brian and Mary, chuckling softly.

Jerome could feel the presence of his other self as soon as he approached the house. The streets of Springwood had been deserted—at least here in the Dreamscape—so he'd driven the Belascos' Altima at top speed, ignoring stop signs and traffic signals. He whipped into the driveway and, sensing a need for urgency, he angled into the yard and drove right up to the door. He threw the car into park and hopped out with the engine still running. As he started toward the door, he experienced a disorienting moment of vertigo. He glanced at the picture window and saw the phantom image of the rear end of his dad's Lexus sticking out. He realized that he was catching a glimpse of the real world, and he understood why he felt such a sense of urgency to get inside. His other self was already here.

Jerome ran onto the porch and grabbed the doorknob, hoping it would be unlocked here in the Dreamscape. But when he gave it a turn, his hope was dashed. It had been a foolish hope; nothing could be that simple in the Dreamscape. He'd never tried to kick open a door before, but he'd seen it done plenty of times on TV, and he was extremely motivated. He centered his weight on his left leg—ignoring the pain from the still bleeding bite wound zombie El had given him—then raised his right foot. He kicked the door right next to the knob as hard as he could. The door shuddered, and he was rewarded with the sound of splintering wood as the jam cracked, but the lock still held. Jerome tried again, and then a third time, and finally the door crashed open, the bells hanging from the inside knob ringing wildly.

He rushed inside, hurried down the foyer, and found himself in the living room. Like the rest of the Springwood replica here in the Dreamscape, the living room was empty, the picture window unbroken. But he could feel the presence of others, could sense pain and fear and the dark anticipation of a hungry predator about to feed. Jerome ran toward the spot where he felt the darkness lay and soon overlapped it.

He experienced a fresh wave of vertigo, but this time it was accompanied by a sense of resistance, as if some force were fighting him, trying to push him away. Jerome concentrated all his will on pushing back and suddenly the dizziness passed and he found himself looking into the pale frightened faces of his brother and sister. He'd done it! He'd retaken control of his body once again! But he could feel the presence of his other self nearby, presumably inhabiting the Dreamscape at this moment, and he knew he wasn't going to be able to keep this body without a fight.

"It's okay, kids. It's me—your real brother. Where's—" He turned to look for his dad and Lynn, but he was shocked into silence by what he saw. The Lexus had crashed through the picture window, pinning down and killing his father. Lynn crouched next to him, looking at Jerome and crying, her face, neck and hands dotted with fragments of glass embedded in the flesh—no doubt a result of the car smashing through the window. He looked around the room, but he didn't see any sign of Cheryl at first, and then he glanced at the Lexus and saw her collapsed against the car's windshield, eyes closed and mouth covered by duct tape. He couldn't tell if she was alive or dead, and at this point, he couldn't have said which was preferable.

Forcing himself not to look at his dad's body and keeping the grief he felt at bay lest it overwhelm him, he turned to Lynn.

"Don't be afraid. I've got control back. For now, at least."

Lynn looked hard into his eyes for a moment before letting out a sob of relief. "It is you! Thank God! That… that thing that took over your body, killed your father, and he was about to… about to…"

Jerome didn't need Lynn to finish her sentence. He had a general idea of what his other self had been about to do to his stepsiblings. "Are you okay enough to walk?" he asked her.

"I think so, but I can't stand up. My hands…"

Jerome was too afraid to go help her up himself. He didn't want to get too close to anyone in case his other self chose that moment to attempt to regain control. He turned to his brother and sister. "You two go help mom up."

Mary looked confused, like she no longer understood English, but Brian nodded. He took Mary's hand and led her over to Lynn. Together, they managed to help her get to her feet. Once up, Lynn took a couple experimental steps, then nodded.

"Great. Take the kids somewhere, anywhere. Just so long as it's away from me—and pick someplace I'd never guess you'd go. If I can't find you, he won't be able to, either."

Jerome felt intense rage emanating from his other self like waves of heat radiating off a blazing fire.

"Hurry—I don't know how much longer I can hold him off."

"Jerome..." Lynn looked at him, so much in her gaze. So many emotions, so many things that she wanted to say, that he wanted to hear, but there was no time.

"I love you, Mom." Then he smiled at the kids. "And I love you two squirts. Now get going—and don't stop for anything."

Lynn hesitated one last moment before nodding. Since Brian and Mary couldn't hold her hands because of the glass shards in them, they held onto her wrists. Together, the three of them headed for the front door. It was too bad the Belascos' car only existed in the Dreamscape. If not, they could've used it to get away.

"One more thing," Jerome called after them.

Lynn paused and looked back over her shoulder.

"If you see me again… If I try to approach you… Run like hell."

Lynn nodded, eyes filled with sadness. Then she turned and led the children out of the living room. A moment later, Jerome heard the front door open, he'd kicked in the door of the Dreamscape house, not this one, but he didn't hear it close again. They'd made it outside. He was tempted to look out what remained of the picture window to make sure they got away safely, but he didn't want to know which direction they were heading. He couldn't afford to let his other self pick up on that knowledge.

You think you're so goddamned smart.

For the first time since his unsuccessful suicide attempt, Jerome heard his other self's voice in his head.

But tell me this, genius: why didn't you tell them to take your girlfriend with you? Did you forget about her? Or are you secretly hoping I'll take over our body again so you can watch me have some fun with her? Tell you what, bro—you let me back in and I won't kick you out. We can share our body… and then we can share hers.

The offer made Jerome feel sick, but he ignored it.

"They couldn't take Cheryl, not as long as she's unconscious. Lynn couldn't carry her, not with the way her hands are injured."

So what now, Mr. Hero?

"Now I call the cops. Once they have me in custody, even if you get control of my body back, it won't matter."

You'd go to jail for murders you didn't commit? You're an idiot!

"It's the only way to keep you from hurting anyone else—and to keep Freddy from succeeding in making people remember him again. Prison is a small price to pay for that."

Your plan might've worked before I offed Daddy-dearest, but his death put me over the top power-wise. You can't keep me out now.

The living room shimmered, and everything became wavy and disoriented, as if Jerome were viewing it through water. The room was now both real and unreal, of the waking world and of the Dreamscape. He could see the picture window, the couch, the coffee table, all unbroken and the room empty save for him. But he also could see the shattered window, the Lexus, the smashed couch, the broken coffee table, and his father's body, blood and chunks of organs strewn on the carpet around him. He could also see Cheryl in the front seat of the Lexus, pressed against the windshield due to the angle at which the car rested.

But in this view, Jerome wasn't alone.

"Hey, bro. Nice to finally meet face to face, huh?"

It was nearly like looking into a mirror. The other Jerome was the same height and weight as he, and was dressed in the same blood-covered clothes. They had the same hair, same eyes, nose, mouth, chin. But this second image of Jerome Starkey sported a grin that was more suited to Freddy Krueger: sly, cold and cruel.

Jerome didn't know how his other self had done it, but somehow he'd created an area where both the real and dream worlds overlapped. They stood neither in one nor the other but somehow in both.

Before Jerome could react, his other self slammed a fist into his gut, and Jerome doubled over in pain. Laughing, Jerome's doppelganger kicked him hard in his wounded ankle, and Jerome's leg folded beneath him. He fell to the carpet and lay on his side, clutching his abdomen and moaning. He turned his head and found himself staring into the face of his dead father.

"I didn't think you'd go down so easy, bro." The other Jerome sounded almost disappointed. "But I guess whatever stones you once had came from me, and since we've parted ways, metaphysically speaking, you no longer have the balls to take me."

While his double spoke, Jerome felt around the carpet until his fingers closed on a large jagged shard of glass that had once been part of the coffee table. He gripped it tight, feeling sharp pain as the edges cut into his flesh, but not caring, drawing strength from the pain, and then he rolled onto his feet and lunged toward his other self, aiming his improvised weapon directly at his double's unprotected throat.

His other self caught hold of Jerome's wrist and stopped the glass shard less than an inch from his carotid artery. Jerome tried to push the shard forward, and the glass sank even deeper into the meat of his hand until he thought he could feel it grind against bone. But his double was too strong and Jerome couldn't force the shard any further. Blood poured down Jerome's hand and spilled onto his double's. From there it dripped down to the carpet, causing a crimson stain that slowly grew wider with each new drop.

"Damn nice try, bro!" the double said appreciatively. "But you never had a chance. Like I said, I'm too strong now. It's over."

The double squeezed Jerome's wrist until the bones began to crack. With a cry of pain, Jerome released the bloody shard and it fell to the carpet. The double gave his wrist a last agonizing squeeze, then shoved Jerome backward. He stumbled but didn't fall. Cradling his injured hand to his chest, Jerome gazed at his darker side made flesh, eyes gleaming with hate.

"I'm going to kill you, you son of a bitch."

"Cut the bullshit, bro. You're going to stand there and watch as I pull your girlfriend out of the car, carry her outside, and then walk away. And you're not going to follow us. Do you know why?"

Jerome didn't answer.

"Because I may not know where Lynn's taken the kids right now, but they have to sleep sometime. And when they do, they won't have any magical dreamcatchers to protect them. Uncle Freddy will find them, and then he'll tell me where they are. And then I'll pay them a visit. But if you be a good boy and behave, I might—just might—forget about tracking them down. It's your call, bro. What'll it be?"

Jerome looked at Cheryl. She was still unconscious, but she was beginning to stir. It wouldn't be long before she came to. Once she was conscious, maybe together they could...

No, it was a stupid idea. His other self had grown too strong, and while Jerome knew the double couldn't be trusted, he couldn't risk Lynn and the kids' lives, not when he'd only just helped them escape.

He looked down at the carpet. It was all the answer his other self needed. Chuckling, the double started toward the Lexus.

TWENTY-FOUR

Cheryl became aware of cold first, followed by wet, then by the sensation of being carried. She opened her eyes and saw only darkness, and feared she was blind. She tried to cry out for someone, anyone, who might help her, but she couldn't open her lips and the sound came out muffled.

"You're awake. It's about damn time. I've been carrying you ever since we left my brother's house."

Jerome's voice, but not Jerome. Him.

The sensation of movement stopped and the world momentarily spun for Cheryl. Her feet came in contact with a hard surface, but something held her ankles together, and she couldn't spread her legs to get her balance. She started to fall, but strong hands caught her roughly by the upper arms and gave her a shake.

"Snap out of it already! You weren't hurt that bad in the crash!"

Crash? She had a memory flash of him turning the Lexus into Jerome's driveway, angling it into the yard, aiming for the house. She remembered the car hitting the porch and, because he hadn't buckled her in when he put her in the passenger seat, the impact caused her to fly forward. Her wrists—like her feet—were bound by duct tape so she wasn't able to brace herself. Her forehead slammed into the dashboard, and that's the last thing she recalled until now.

She became aware of a shadowy shape standing before her, and she realized that she wasn't blind. It was night, and her eyes were only now adjusting to the darkness. Though she still couldn't make out his features, she knew the person standing in front of her was him, the other personality that had taken control of her Jerome's body. As to where they were, they were outside, obviously, and had been for a while. It was raining and her hair and clothes were soaked. Though there were no lights around, she could feel concrete or asphalt beneath her feet, so she was standing on a sidewalk or maybe the surface of a parking lot. Her head ached, but the pain wasn't too bad. Hopefully he was right and she hadn't been hurt seriously in the crash.

What had happened after she'd blacked out? Had he done anything to Jerome's family? What about Mary and Brian? Had he hurt them? She started to ask, but then quit when she remembered that he'd covered her mouth with duct tape.

He gave her another shake, harder this time, and the ache in her head increased to a painful throb that brought tears to her eyes.

"Stay with me now. You don't want to miss what's next."

He turned her around to face a large dark shape that loomed against the night sky. A bolt of lightning streaked across the heavens, momentarily illuminating the dilapidated, abandoned house he had brought her to. Cheryl realized then that she was standing in the driveway of Freddy Krueger's house. She tried to scream, but all that came out through the tape was a terrified *mmm-mmm-mmm* sound.

The creature that wore Jerome's body laughed. "Stand still and I'll cut the tape around your ankles so you can walk. Don't try anything, though, or I'll just knock you out again. If I'm not careful, I might hit too hard and you'd never wake up again. And I don't much feel like being careful right now, got me?"

The lightning flash was long gone, but Cheryl still saw the purple afterimage of the Krueger house glowing on her retinas. She nodded, not knowing if he could see the gesture in the dark. He let go of her arms and she saw him pull an object out of his belt. He knelt down and sawed through the tape wrapped around her ankles. It parted, but he didn't bother removing the pieces of tape from her socks. He stood, then tucked the knife, which she presumed he'd taken from the Starkey household, back beneath his belt.

"Let's go. Uncle Freddy can't wait to meet you."

He took hold of her upper arm once more and escorted her to the front steps. The skin on the back of her neck began to crawl as they mounted the steps, and she suddenly found it more difficult to breathe, as if the air were somehow tainted and unclean. A fluttering panic began to rise in her chest, and if he hadn't been forcing her to continue, she'd have turned and fled, for all her instincts were screaming that this was a bad place, a wrong place, a place she shouldn't enter at any cost, because once she was inside she might well never get out again.

The feeling only got worse as they stepped onto the porch and walked up to the front door. As he gripped the knob and began to turn it, she couldn't help herself. Despite his threats, she couldn't go in there. She pulled out of his grip, turned, and started to flee. But he lashed out with a foot and knocked her own feet out from under her. She fell lopsided to the porch, cracking her right knee and elbow as she hit. She let out a cry of pain that was loud even with the tape covering her mouth. Her knee hurt like hell, but her elbow felt as if it were on fucking fire. She was sure she'd broken it.

"Dumbass," he muttered. He grabbed her by her injured arm, and she cried out behind the tape.

"Save your screams for Freddy." He pulled her back to the door, opened it, and shoved her over the threshold. She stumbled, but she fought to maintain her balance, not wishing to fall on her broken elbow again. Sharp pain shot through her injured knee, but it continued to support her weight, and she managed to remain on her feet.

He stepped inside the house and closed the door behind him. He didn't slam the door, and it didn't shut with an ominous sound like booming thunder. The door made almost no sound as it closed, as if the air inside the house was too stale and dead to carry sound very far. Cheryl took a breath through her nostrils and almost gagged. A greasy foulness hung in the air, like the lingering scent of a long desiccated corpse. She couldn't help feeling that the air was tainted somehow, maybe even poisonous. She felt panic rising, along with her gorge, and she experienced an overwhelming need to vomit, as if her body were desperate to purge itself of whatever toxins it had just taken into its system. But she fought against the urge. If she threw up with her mouth covered by duct tape, there was a good chance she'd choke to death on her own vomit, and she didn't want to give Jerome's other self—or Freddy Krueger—the satisfaction of seeing her die in such a humiliating fashion. So she choked back hot bile and held her breath until the need to regurgitate had passed.

There were no lights in the house. She knew from years of driving past the Krueger house that there were no curtains and what could be seen of the boarded-up windows was dirty and smeared, as if the foulness of the interior atmosphere had left a nasty residue on the glass. After she was actually inside, the filthy windows admitted no light whatsoever—not that there was much outside this rainy night—and the place was dark as a cavern carved deep in the earth. Cold, too. Cheryl shivered, though she doubted the chill she experienced had anything to do with the temperature in here.

"Uncle Freddy!" called the thing that possessed Jerome's body. "I'm home! And I've brought a friend with me!"

Nothing happened at first, but then a crimson glow filled the house, making it look like a photographer's dark room. She could determine no source for the reddish illumination; it appeared to just be, as if it came from everywhere all at once.

"Well, what do you think? I admit it's a fixer-upper, but with a little work, it'll make a wonderful home."

The wooden floor of the foyer was scratched and worn, and the wallpaper was stained and peeling in numerous places. From where they stood, she could see into the front room: chairs with ripped upholstery and stuffing poking out, a couch with a faded floral pattern, cushions missing and springs protruding from the bottom, chunks of plaster missing from the walls, floorboards warped, twisted and broken. As she watched, wisps of steam curled up through cracks in the floor, and the air suddenly began to grow hotter, humid and more oppressive. She remembered something about Freddy then. He'd taken his young victims to a boiler room where he *played* with them before slaughtering them. He'd then disposed of their bodies in the boiler's flames.

She turned to her captor and gave him a questioning look. In response he reached out, took hold of the edge of the tape over her mouth, and yanked it off her with a single, swift stroke. Cheryl gasped as much in relief as in pain from the tape's less than gentle removal. In a rough, hoarse voice, she managed to croak out, "Home?"

"Of course! I've got to have somewhere to hang my hat while I go about my work. What better place than this? If anyone hears sounds from the old Krueger place, sees strange lights through the dirty windows, so much the better. After all, getting people to remember Uncle Freddy—making him strong again—is what it's all about."

The creature that inhabited Jerome's body got down on one knee then and took both of her hands in his.

"I'd be honored if you'd share my new home with me, Cheryl. I mean, take a look at this dump—it sure could use a woman's touch!" He laughed then, and the sound seemed to echo all around them, as if the house itself were laughing too.

Cheryl just stared at him, too afraid to think of a reply.

"No answer?" He released her hands and rose to his feet. "I understand. You need some time to think it over."

He grabbed hold of her broken arm and she shrieked as white-hot pain shot from shoulder to fingertips. He pulled her toward the couch, then hurled her onto it. Without any cushions to soften her landing, she hit hard, but the sensation was nothing compared to the agony in her arm. She turned around to face him, tears of pain running down her face. But before she could say or do anything more, the springs sticking out of the couch extended outward and wrapped around her like coiled metallic serpents, entwining and interlocking until she was held tight to the couch.

"Comfy?" Jerome's darker self asked. "Meeting your boyfriend's relatives is stressful enough, so I want you to be completely at ease."

The wooden floor rippled, changing, shifting, until it resembled a surface composed of cracked, scarred flesh. A large blister formed in the center of the flesh-floor, swelling quickly as it filled with discolored serum.

The thing chuckled with Jerome's mouth. "Welcome to the family, Cheryl."

The blister exploded in a shower of black fluid, and a grinning form rose upward from beneath the floor. It was Freddy Krueger.

After the duct tape had been removed, Cheryl was able to scream long and loud.

Jerome watched the Krueger house from across the street, crouched behind an oak tree in the yard. He'd left the Belascos' car parked at the other end of Elm. He had no idea whether his other self would be able to sense the car in the Dreamscape, but he didn't want to take any chances.

After his "brother" had left the Starkey residence carrying Cheryl slung over his shoulder, the real world and the Dreamscape had become completely separate again. When Jerome had looked out the front door, he saw no sign of them. What he had seen was the Belascos' car, keys still in the ignition, engine still running. At first he'd been surprised that his other self hadn't taken the car, but then he remembered. This was the Dreamscape, and this version of the Belascos' car existed only here. "Bro" hadn't taken it because it didn't exist in the real world. Which meant Jerome could beat his other self to the Krueger house and be waiting for him when he arrived.

Jerome had no doubt his dark half would take Cheryl to Krueger's place. He'd sensed it when the two of them had been briefly merged again. Besides, where else would he go?

Jerome had hurried to the car, holding his cut hand against his stomach to slow the bleeding. He'd slammed the driver's door shut, put it in gear, and roared across the lawn onto the street, steering with his good hand. He'd driven in the opposite direction of Elm at first, not wishing to get too close to the Dreamscape location parallel to where his other self was walking, lest he sense what Jerome was up to. Jerome had been forced to take a circuitous route to Elm, but without any traffic to slow him down, he was able to haul serious ass, and he arrived well before his other self and Cheryl. He'd parked and taken up his position behind the tree across the street and waited, cradling his wounded hand and wishing Dreamscape rain didn't feel as cold and wet as the real thing.

He watched his other self's arrival and witnessed Cheryl's return to consciousness. He was near enough to perceive them, but only as faint, ghostly images. He assumed he'd appear the same to them and was glad to be well hidden. It was all he could do to restrain himself from running across the street to help her, especially when the son of a bitch knocked her down and she got hurt. But he knew he was only going to get one shot at the bastard who'd stolen his body, and he couldn't afford to waste it. He'd lost his mother to Freddy Krueger before he was born; he wasn't going to lose Cheryl too.

So he waited until they went inside and a baleful crimson light glowed through the few clean spots on the windows. A tornado had come through Springwood when Jerome was a child, and he still remembered how the air had gone suddenly dead—no sound, no movement—and the light took on an eerie dark purplish cast. He experienced a similar sensation now, as if a force of vast power was swiftly approaching, and Jerome knew that Freddy Krueger was manifesting within his house—the center of his power in both the physical and dream realms.

This was what Jerome had been waiting for. He hoped that Freddy's overwhelming aura of evil would cloak his own presence from the perceptions of his other self, at least long enough for him to do what needed to be done. He left his hiding place behind the oak tree and started running toward Krueger's house.

The ankle where zombie El had bitten him throbbed as he put his weight on it, and, as if in sympathy, his wounded hand began to hurt afresh. Jerome stopped running and reached down with his good hand to massage his injured ankle. Damn it, he couldn't afford this, not now! He needed to be able to move swiftly if he hoped to...

And just like that, the pain in his ankle vanished, as did the pain in his hand.

Jerome looked at the palm of his hand. There was still blood on the skin, but the palm itself was smooth and unbroken, without so much as a scar to show where the jagged shard of glass had sliced into it. He assumed his ankle was also healed. A thought came to Jerome then, and he smiled grimly. It seemed he had more power here in the Dreamscape than he'd realized.

He continued toward Krueger's house, running easily and without pain, ready to confront whatever fate awaited him inside.

And that's when Cheryl screamed.

TWENTY-FIVE

"Well, well, well... Aren't you a pretty one?"

Krueger's scarred skin seemed to radiate the same crimson as the light that filled the house, and as he spoke steam wafted from his mouth. He wore his legendary claw-glove on his right hand, but the blades were coated with flickering flame. The floor still resembled his scarred flesh, and he stood in the remains of the burst blister, his boots covered by black gunk, and globs of the foul substance clung to his hat, sweater, and pants.

"I'd hoped you'd approve, Uncle," Dark Jerome said.

"Oh, I do. It's been far too long since I had anyone this tasty come visit me. An old boogeyman like me gets lonely, you know." He roared mocking laughter. Curls of flame licked past his teeth, and a red-orange glow was visible at the back of his throat, as if he contained a furnace—or perhaps a boiler—inside himself.

"This can't be happening!" Cheryl said. "I'm not asleep!"

"Ordinarily, you'd be right," Freddy said. "But here in my house—and with this fine upstanding young man to create a bridge between worlds for me—it can be happening. And it is!"

Krueger stepped toward Cheryl, his boots tracking black glop across the scarred flesh-floor. Freddy rose and fell slightly as he walked, and Cheryl realized the floor was actually breathing. She struggled against the springs that bound her to the couch, but it was no use; they were too tight.

"Careful, girl," Freddy growled softly. "You wouldn't want to hurt yourself."

A shimmering ripple passed over the springs and they became razor wire. Cheryl gasped as sharp blades cut into her skin, and she tried very, very hard not to move. Freddy walked up to the couch while Jerome's other self stood by, watching and grinning. Of everything that had happened to her, that was the worst, seeing the image of the man she loved looking on in amusement as she was being tormented by Krueger.

Freddy leaned his face down close to hers, and she could feel the heat radiating from his ruined flesh. His breath reeked like the foulest sewer in the bottommost pit of Hell, and his eyes gleamed with the fire of madness.

"You have such a lovely complexion, my dear," Freddy said, almost purring. He brought one of his fire-coated claws close to her left cheek and held the tip only an inch from her flesh. "It would be such a shame to ruin it."

She couldn't stop herself from trembling. She hissed in pain as razors bit into her flesh and blood began to trickle from her new wounds. Freddy closed his eyes and inhaled, a rapturous expression on his hideous face as if he were a wine connoisseur smelling the bouquet of a particularly fine vintage.

"Mmmmm... delicious."

His tongue extended, stretching like a long pink snake, and began lapping up her blood, darting between the coils of razor wire without cutting itself. Cheryl bit her lip to keep from screaming again, afraid that she'd only injure herself further by moving. She turned to look at the other Jerome, hoping to draw at least a bit of comfort from seeing his body, if not his soul.

But something strange was happening. The other Jerome's eyes went wide and his entire body stiffened. His arms and legs began to jerk as if his nervous system was short-circuiting. His facial features contorted and for a brief instant his face actually seemed to go blank, nothing but smooth, featureless skin, and when it returned to normal, she knew the being looking out from behind those eyes was her Jerome.

"Hey, Freddy!" Jerome called out.

Krueger's tongue flew back into his mouth and he turned to scowl at Jerome. "What do you want, kid? Don't you know it's not good manners to bother your Uncle Freddy when he's busy?"

"I thought you might like to play a quick game of tag," Jerome said. "You're it!" The carving knife his other self had taken from the Starkey home was still sheathed beneath his belt. Jerome drew the knife and started running toward Freddy, blade raised high, ready to strike.

But just as Jerome reached the undead madman, Freddy lunged forward and buried his flaming claws in Jerome's abdomen. Jerome cried out in pain and dropped the knife. Blood bubbled past his lips, and he looked at Freddy, a lost, confused expression on his face.

"F-Father?" he whispered.

Freddy stared at the young man he'd just skewered, and a look of horrified realization came into his eyes.

"Noooooo!" he shouted.

Jerome's body slid off the claw-knives and slumped to the flesh-floor. It lay there, eyes wide and unblinking, arms and legs still. Krueger's blades no longer burned; their flames had been snuffed out in Jerome's gut.

"Guess who jumped out at the last second?"

Cheryl knew that voice. She looked toward it, and at first she didn't see anything, but slowly Jerome's form appeared, standing only a few feet away from Krueger. His clothes were no longer bloody from his other self's rampage of terror, and he showed no sign of having been injured by Freddy's claws.

"You fool!" Freddy snarled. "You just sacrificed your own body to stop me!"

Jerome smiled. "What can I say? It seemed like a good idea at the time."

"DAMN YOU!" Freddy roared, and the entire house shook as if in the throes of a violent earthquake. "I'll torture your spirit until the end of fucking time for this! I'll do things to you that Satan himself couldn't stand to watch!" He paused and then turned to look at Cheryl, and his cracked, scarred lips stretched into a sly smile. "And as an appetizer, how about we start off with a little sliced hottie?"

Krueger gestured with his claws, and Cheryl screamed as the razor wire that held her began to slowly tighten.

Jerome ran forward and grabbed Krueger's claw-hand by the wrist. He forced it upward, and the razor wire stopped contracting. With his other hand, Jerome grabbed Krueger by the throat and squeezed as hard as he could. Soft, wet choking sounds came out of Krueger's mouth, and his eyes were wide with fear.

"I've discovered something since the last time we saw each other. You did too good a job when you injected some of your darkness into me." Maintaining his grip on Krueger's throat, Jerome began to slowly force him backward, step by step. "You not only passed some of your evil on to me—evil that became a second personality—you also gave me power over the Dreamscape. I can sense what that black shit is where you came out of the floor. Bekka told us about it. It's all the negative energy that dreamers purge during nightmares, isn't it? Fear, hatred, despair, loneliness, envy, selfishness and all the other dark emotions—all gathered beneath your house like a basement where a septic tank's backed up."

Jerome was forcing Krueger toward the broken blister, where a pool of viscous ebon filth bubbled and oozed. Cheryl thought she could feel what Jerome was talking about, sense the accumulated awfulness of all those negative emotions like psychic toxic waste lying beneath this house.

Jerome continued. "It's the source of your power, Bekka said. But power is just a tool. It can be used by anyone—as long as they know how."

Jerome had pushed Krueger to the edge of the blister-pool, and the black gunk bubbled upward, becoming thicker, more solid, lengthening until it had formed a large ebon tentacle. The black limb wrapped around Freddy's midsection just as Jerome released his hold on the undead maniac. The tentacle pulled Krueger down into the black pool, and he frantically slashed at it with his claws, but the gunk just oozed back together after every cut. As Freddy continued to sink, he stopped fighting and fixed Jerome with an angry glare.

"This isn't going to stop me, you know. I'll be back. I always come back!"

Krueger laughed as the black goo rose past his neck, up and over his chin, finally covering his mouth and silencing him. His eyes continued to blaze with fury until they too sank below the ebon surface, and Freddy Krueger was gone.

Jerome stared at the bubbling black pool for a few moments, as if waiting for Krueger to suddenly reappear and attack, but the pool—as well as the scar tissue floor—began to fade, becoming once more only cracked and warped wood. It was over: if not for good, at least for the meantime.

Jerome turned to Cheryl and gestured. The razor wire became simple springs again, and they fell away from her and retracted into the couch. She was bleeding from dozens of cuts, but she didn't think any of them were serious. She stood, ignoring the pain in her broken arm and sprained knee, and went to Jerome as quickly as she could manage.

He held up his hands to stop her before she got too close.

"You can't touch me." He nodded toward his body, lying motionless on the floor several feet away. "That's all that remains of my physical form. I'm... just a dream now." He smiled sadly. "And a fading dream at that."

Tears rolled down Cheryl's cheeks, but these weren't tears of pain or terror; these were tears of love and sorrow.

"I just wish..."

"I know. Me, too. I'd heal you if I could, but you're real and the two worlds are drifting apart. I'm afraid you'll just have to get better the old-fashioned way."

She smiled. "I'll manage." She was beginning to have difficulty seeing him. The crimson glow that lit the Krueger house was growing dim, and Jerome's form was becoming blurry and indistinct, as if her eyes could no longer keep him in focus. She understood that he belonged to the Dreamscape now, and as the two realms pulled apart, so were the two of them being separated.

"Will I... will we ever see each other again?" she asked, afraid of what his answer would be.

Jerome smiled and shrugged. "Anything's possible in dreams. I love you."

"I love you, too."

And then he was gone, and darkness filled the Krueger house once more. All was silent, save for the sound of a young woman crying softly.

TWENTY-SIX

It continued raining for almost a week after that night, but on the morning of Jerome's funeral, the clouds finally retreated and the sun returned. There had been a lot of funerals in Springwood recently—the Three Pus-keteers, Mr Houser, Mr Neilson, Ms LeClair, Mr and Mrs Belasco, El, Mr Starkey and Bekka—and so Lynn had held off on Jerome's for several days longer than she might've otherwise. Out of respect for the other families, if nothing else.

Cheryl appreciated the extra time. Her broken elbow had required orthopedic surgery, and she was only now feeling up to the ceremony. Her elbow had pins and wires inside holding the shattered bones together, and she wore both a cast and a sling. At least her knee hadn't needed surgery, and none of her cuts needed more than a few stitches here and there. She'd gotten off lucky, a lot luckier than so many others, Jerome included.

The only ones present at the graveside that morning were Lynn, Brian, Mary, Cheryl and a rent-a-minister Lynn had been forced to bring in from the nearby town of Ash Creek. All of Springwood's clergy, sympathetic toward Lynn's situation as they might be, had refused to conduct her stepson's funeral service. Jerome's coffin was already in the ground—there'd been no viewing at the funeral parlor—and the rent-a-minister mumbled a few insincere words over Jerome's grave, then, check already in pocket, he got the hell out of there as fast as he could.

The four mourners stood silently for a time, looking at the mound of earth beneath which Jerome was buried. There was no headstone yet. All the better, Cheryl thought, as it would make locating Jerome's resting place more difficult for both vandals and the morbidly curious.

After a time, Lynn said, "Thanks for coming, Cheryl."

"My parents didn't want me to. I told them if they ever wanted me to speak to them again, they should shut the hell up and get out of my way."

Lynn smiled. "Guess they did, huh?"

"Yep."

They fell silent again for several moments. A gentle breeze blew through the cemetery, setting the trees to rustling. Birds sang, oblivious to the grief of four humans standing beside a mound of dirt.

"It's pretty here, Mommy," Marie said. "I think Jerome would like it."

Lynn smiled down at her daughter and lay a hand on her head. "I'm sure he does, honey."

Mary moved closer to Lynn and hugged her waist. On the other side of their mother, Brian edged closer as well, and Lynn put a hand on his shoulder.

"It's not fair," he said. "Everybody thinks Jerome killed all those people... That he killed daddy. But it's not true!"

Lynn gave her son's shoulder a reassuring squeeze. "You're right. It isn't fair. Jerome saved the four of us, and he'd have saved the others if he could have. He gave his life to stop the bad man who really was responsible for all those deaths. No matter what anyone else says or thinks, your brother was a hero. Don't ever forget that."

Brian didn't reply, and Cheryl wondered if the boy would ever fully understand what had happened. Hell, she wondered if she ever would. The official version of events was that Jerome—a teenage boy with a known history of "anger management issues", as the media put it—had snapped and gone on a murderous rampage. A rampage that ended, gruesomely enough, in the house of a dead serial killer, when his girlfriend was forced to stab him to death to save her own life. This despite the fact that the knife she'd supposedly used to kill him had neither her fingerprints nor his blood on it.

Lynn and Cheryl had told the truth to the police, and Cheryl was certain the cops believed them. After all, this was Springwood. But she also knew they couldn't afford to allow any talk of Freddy Krueger to start up again, and so they'd fed the media a story that was safer, even if it wasn't true.

"What now?" Lynn asked her. Cheryl didn't need the woman to clarify. She knew she meant: How are you going to go on from here?

"I'll graduate soon, and then I'll go away to college somewhere far, far away and never come back. What about you?"

"I have a cousin in Maryland who's divorced and doesn't have any kids. She's invited us to come live with her for a while. I... don't think we'll be coming back to Springwood either."

Cheryl didn't blame Lynn. The memories the town would hold for her kids and herself would be bad enough, but as long as they stayed in Springwood, Brian and Mary would always be the siblings of the crazy kid who'd murdered eleven people. That was no way for children who'd already experienced so much trauma in their young lives to have to grow up.

"Would you write me when you get settled in Maryland?" Cheryl asked. "Just to let me know how you're doing?"

"Of course, dear."

But Cheryl could tell by the look in Lynn's eyes that she didn't really mean it. Lynn gave her a hug then, careful of Cheryl's arm. After she pulled away, Lynn looked at Jerome's grave one last time.

"I really did love him, and I tried my best to be a good mother to him. In the end, I hope he knew that."

"I'm sure he did, Mrs Starkey." And she was.

Lynn gave her a grateful smile, and then she led the kids away from their brother's grave. Cheryl watched them walk between the gravestones—there were so many here in Springwood—and up a gently sloping hill to their car. Lynn got the kids in, then gave Cheryl a last wave before climbing behind the wheel and driving off.

Cheryl turned back to Jerome's grave. She knelt and pressed the tips of her fingers into the freshly turned earth, as if by doing so she might somehow connect to Jerome's spirit.

"I miss you," she said softly. She didn't expect a reply, of course, but she paused a moment anyway. Just in case. "It's been pretty crazy since you, since you left. Reporters from all over the country in town... Hourly updates on all the news shows... TV producers calling me for interviews... One guy even wanted to pay me for the rights to make a movie of my 'harrowing tale of survival', as he put it." She laughed and shook her head. "It's nuts."

She grew more serious then. "They're talking about him again. Krueger, I mean. Every reporter is rehashing the story of the Springwood Slasher and all the children he killed, and how he was finally burned to death by the vengeful parents of his victims. As I walked out of my house to come here today, I saw a couple neighbor girls jumping rope on the sidewalk. They were chanting a nursery rhyme, and even though I hadn't heard it since I was a little kid, I'd forgotten all about it, actually, I remembered every word as soon as I heard those girls chanting. One, two, Freddy's comin' for you..."

She took in a deep breath and let it out as a long sigh.

"He won, didn't he?"

The only answer she received was a sudden gust of wind that blew through the cemetery, carrying with it the sound of dark laughter.

ABOUT THE AUTHOR

Tim Waggoner is the author of ten novels: *Like Death* (Leisure Books), *A Shadow Over Heaven's Eye* and *Dark Ages: Gangrel* (both White Wolf), *Temple of the Dragonslayer, Return of the Sorceress* (both Wizards of the Coast), *Necropolis* (Five Star), *Defender: Hyperswarm* (I-Books), *The Harmony Society* (Prime Books) and *Dying for It* (Foggy Windows). He is also the author of the short story collection *All Too Surreal* (Prime Books). He's published over seventy short stories in the fantasy and horror genres, and his articles on writing have appeared in *Writer's Digest, Writers' Journal, New Writer's Magazine, Ohio Writer, Speculations* and *Teaching English in the Two-Year College.* He teaches creative writing at Sinclair Community College in Dayton, Ohio. His home page is located at *www.timwaggoner.com*